THE ELEVENTH HOUR SERIES

TAKE  ROOT

BRIT KS

Take Root is an imprint of Romance Ain't Dead

Copyright 2025 by Brit K.S. Romance Ain't Dead

PO Box #5382 Atlanta, Ga 30307

Printed in the United States of America

ISBN: 979-8-9882277-4-8 & 979-8-9882277-5-5

Cover Art by Warickaart

Interior Formatting by Quirky Circe

Interior art by _spotlessmind_

Developmental Editing by Golden May Editing

Line Editing/Proofreading by Early Editing LLC, Kaila Desjardins Editing

Map by Andrés Aguirre Jurado (aaguirreart)

"The world seems full of good men—
even if there are monsters in it."
— Bram Stoker, *Dracula*

This book is for all the fighters, the believers, and the dreamers who refuse to let their inner critics have the last word.

CONTENTS

TRIGGER WARNINGS

Dear Reader,

Take Root contains themes and content that may be sensitive for some readers. I advise caution and provide this list of specific themes for your awareness:

- **Loss of a loved one:** The story deals with themes of grief and bereavement.
- **Mention of substance abuse:** References to a past addiction.
- **Murder referenced:** Indirect references to past events.
- **Violence:** Includes scenes of physical and verbal confrontations and knife and gun violence.
- **Adult language:** Use of strong, often vulgar language throughout the book.
- **Sexually explicit scenes:** Contains sexually explicit scenes, including detailed descriptions of intimate encounters. Please be advised that there is a sex scene set in a cemetery, although no grave desecration occurs. Due to the mature sexual content, this book is intended for adult readers only.
- **Demons (daemons):** Demonic characters/practices are present.
- **War:** Depictions and references of wartime scenarios.
- **Bullying:** on a page and past references to bullying.
- **Political upheaval:** This book depicts a society with a strict social hierarchy. Due to their lower social status, certain characters are treated as second-class citizens, leading to unequal treatment and limited opportunities.
- **Depiction of blood consumption and blood-related violence:** This book contains scenes involving vampires drinking blood, sharing blood, and engaging in blood-related violent acts.

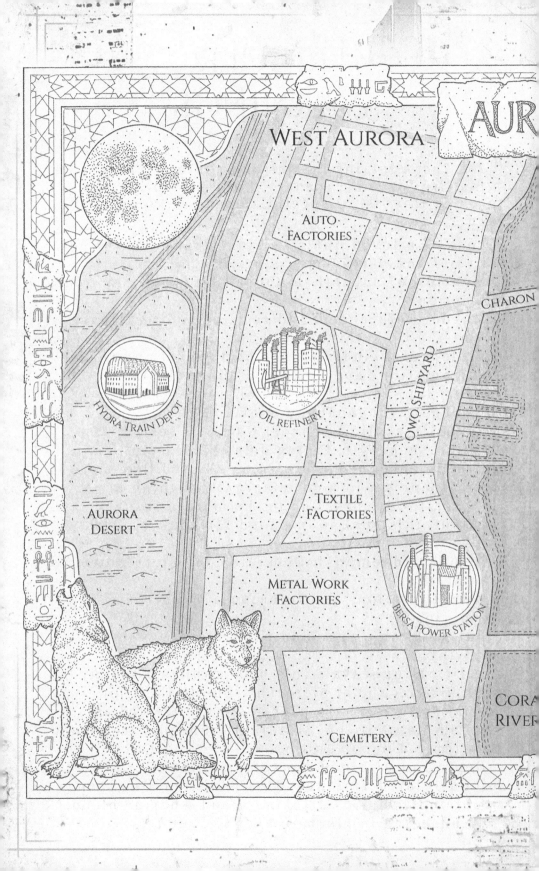

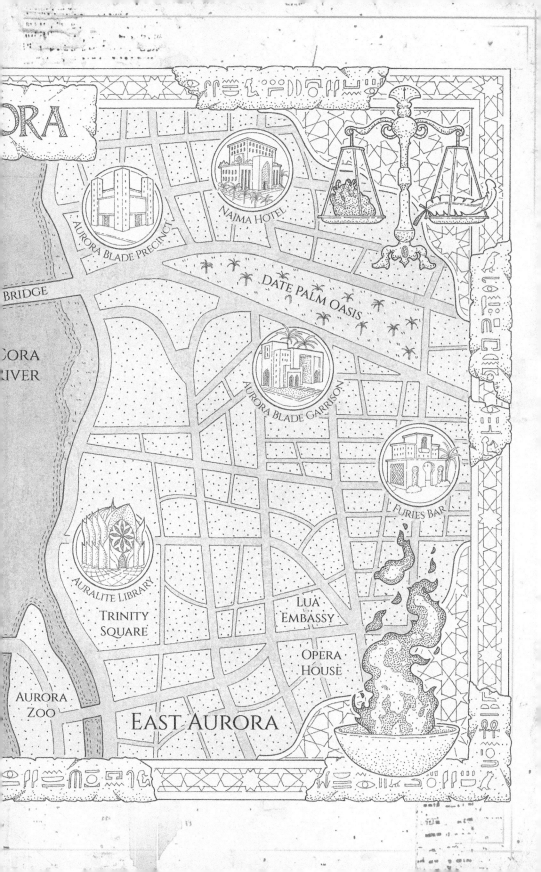

ORA

AURORA BLADE PRECINCT

NAJMA HOTEL

BRIDGE

CORA
RIVER

DATE PALM OASIS

AURORA BLADE GARRISON

FURIES BAR

AURALITE LIBRARY

TRINITY
SQUARE

LUA'
EMBASSY

OPERA
HOUSE

AURORA
ZOO

EAST AURORA

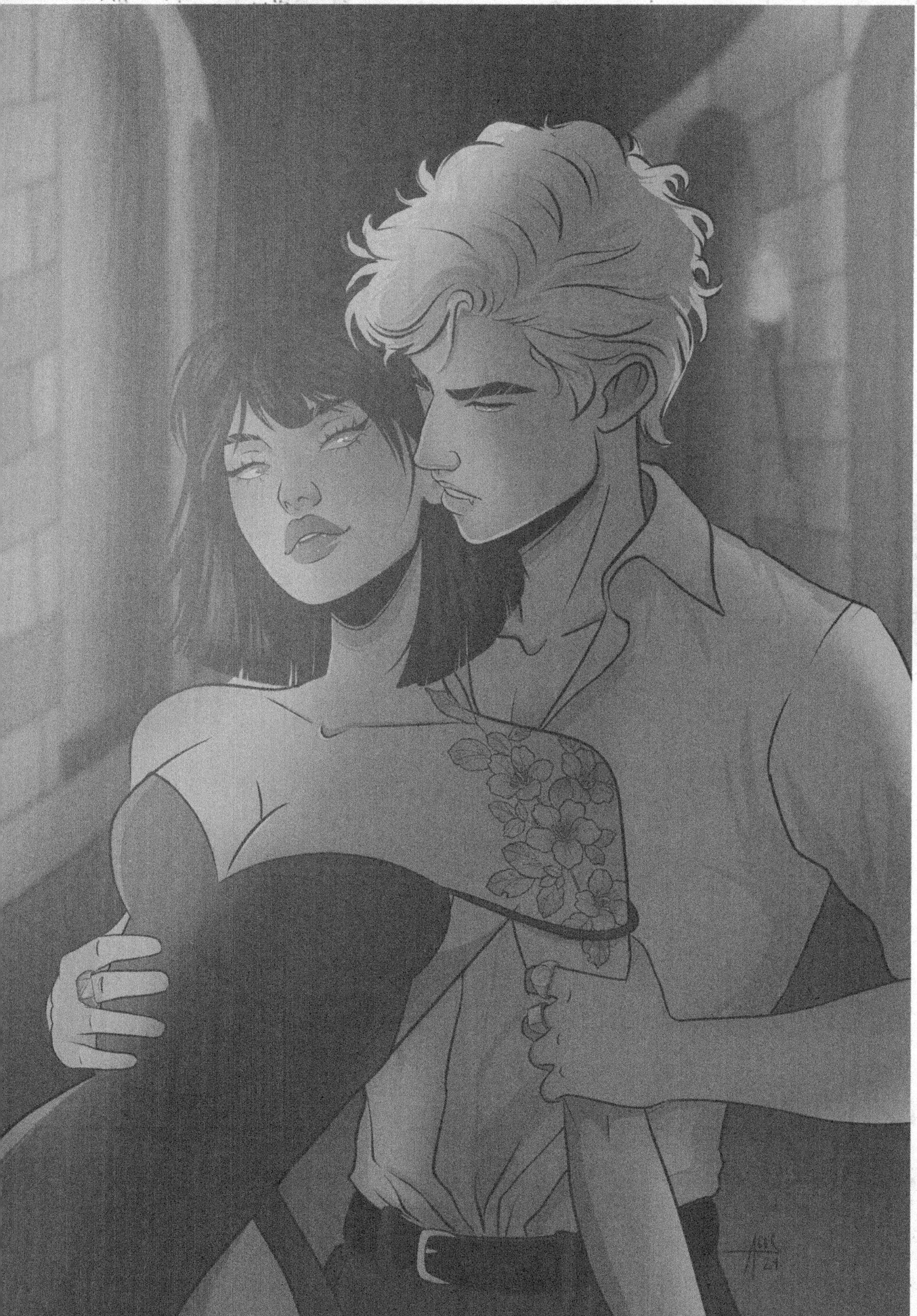

THE ELEMENTAL WITCHES

A GUIDE

In this world, the arcane and the tangible intertwine, where magic is as real as the air we breathe. This guide introduces the five elemental witches, each embodying a unique aspect of the natural world and wielding abilities that define their connection to these elements.

LUNAR WITCH

Abilities: Masters of the unseen, communicate with spirits, traverse astral planes, enter dreams, control shadows, and sense spiritual life and death.

SOLAR WITCH

Abilities: Their power mirrors the sun's intensity, summoning fierce flames, controlling their own body heat, and infusing firearms with solar energy.

SEA WITCH

Abilities: They command the waters, manipulate tides, foresee through scrying, empathize deeply, and transform water into ice.

GREEN WITCH

Abilities: Connected deeply with nature, they possess healing powers, an understanding of herbology, and a unique bond with the Earth's flora.

COSMIC WITCH

Abilities: Masters of the air, manipulate winds, harness electricity, and skillfully bend light to their will.

PRONUNCIATION GUIDE

Alec Erinye *AL-ek · eh-RIN-ee-eh*

Alden Lupas *AWL-den · LOO-pahs*

Amro *ah-mro*

Anselm Raymor *an-sel-m · RAY-more*

Aradia Graves *ah-RAH-dee-ah · GRAYVES*

Aurora *aw-ROHR-ah*

Balam *bah-LAHM*

Borealis *bor-ee-AL-is*

Brigid Eddo *BRIJ-id · ED-oh*

Charon *keh-ruhn*

Chiron Lyra *KAI-ron · LY-rah*

Chiara Dunn *kee-AH-rah · DONE*

Desiree Dunn *dez-ih-RAY · DONE*

Domna *DOHM-nah*

Gianna "Gi" di Siena *jee-ah-nuh · "GI" · dee · see-EH-nah*

Glaucus *GLAW-kus*

Gwyn Raelyn *GWIN · RAY-lin*

Harborym *HAHR-boh-rim*

Icarus *i-kr-uhs*

Isolde Faez *ih-ZOLD · fah-EHZ*

Ivah Graves *EE-vah · GRAYVES*

Janus Dyer *JAN-us · DY-er*

Jorina Graves Raelyn *joh-REE-nah · GRAYVES ·
RAY-lin*

Leigh Raelyn *LEE · RAY-lin*

Megaera "Meg" Erinye *muh-geh-ruh · "MEG" ·
eh-RIN-ee-eh*

Nereus *neh-roos*

Orion "Ry" Niemon *oh-RY-on · "RY" · NEE-mon*

Pallas Lyra *pal-uhs · LY-rah*

Ravi Deyanira *RAH-vee · dey-ah-NEE-rah*

Sama Deyanira *SAH-mah · dey-ah-NEE-rah*

Soter Telfour *SOH-ter · tel-FOOR*

Stellan Navis *STEH-lahn · NAH-vis*

Vane Bathory *VAYN · BAH-thoh-ree*

Vyvyan Bathory *VIV-ee-ahn · BAH-thoh-ree*

Wilder Dunn *WYL-der · DONE*

Zeus Lupas *ZOOS · LOO-pahs*

PLAYLIST

Evermore	*hackedepicciotto*
How Villains Are Made	*Madalen Duke*
Me and the Devil	*Soap&Skin*
Deathbeds	*Bring Me The Horizon*
Seven Nights	*DEADSIREN,Majin Boo*
Diosa	*Mareux*
Labyrinths	*The KVB*
Keep Your Eyes Peeled	*ULTRA SUNN*
Lucid Dreaming	*Forever Grey*
Fantasmas	*Twin Tribes*
Open - Sword II Version	*Water From Your Eyes, Sword II*
Howl	*Florence + The Machine*
NO ESCAPE	*HEALTH,The Neighbourhood*
Lovesong - 2010 Remaster	*The Cure*
Spectral Tease	*Mareux*
The Apparition	*Sleep Token*
Wicked Game	*Madelyn Darling*
more than friends	*Isabel LaRosa*
HAUNT ME	*Johnny Goth*
Prayer from Nowhere	*Cold Cave*
Ache In My Heart	*Palaye Royale*
Off To The Races	*Lana Del Rey*
Used to the Darkness	*Des Rocs*
Burn	*The Cure*
DARK	*WesGhost*
Dammit (After Dark)	*Dead On A Sunday*
skins	*The Haunting*
Little Lies	*Mareux*
Psychic Sobriety	*Foie Gras*
The Down That Creeps	*R. Missing*
Placeholder for the Night	*R. Missing*

Fire Breather	*LAUREL*
Bad Dream	*Ruelle*
Polycephaly	*Doon Kanda*
Witches Tale	*Jah PHNX*
Howl	*Alexandra Savior*
Taste	*Ari Abdul*
suicide	*moonvampire*
Vicious Pastimes	*House of Harm*
Phantom	*Vestron Vulture*
Somebody's Watching Me	*Madelyn Darling*
Fangs	*Dionnysuss*
Daydreams	*Tempers*
Darkness, I'll Always Be Your Girl	*R. Missing*
Werewolf Heart	*Dead Man's Bones*
How Did It End?	*Taylor Swift*
The Ghost	*Trevor Something*
Magazine (Club Mix Instrumental)	*Chromatics*
The Perfect Girl	*Mareux*
Nervous	*The Neighbourhood*
Love	*Lana Del Rey*
Plainsong - 2010 Remaster	*The Cure*

The Tower

TOXIC

BOREALIS ELITE'S SCANDALS THREATEN COUNTRY STABILITY

By Stellan Navis

IN a startling new development amidst the chaos unfolding in Corona, former Councilman Evander Bishop was seen grave-robbing at Tsilah Cemetery. The once-respected Bishop family, along with the influential Evans family, has recently been expelled from the Corona Council due to their connections with Eos, a notorious Epsilon supremacist organization. This past autumn, Eos' leader, the enigmatic "Magician," was revealed to be none other than Queen Jorina's son, Don Raelyn, who now faces life behind bars for the murders of Prince Gwyn Raelyn and Prince Fynn Raelyn.

As the royal family grapples with this tragedy, Queen Leigh is reshuffling her cabinet, sending tremors throughout the nation. The War Letters—a series of explosive documents—have exposed the Epsilon class as the true instigators of the First War, overturning centuries of belief that the war was instigated by the Nebula. This revelation has rendered the Labor Laws—which have unfairly oppressed the Nebula people since the First War—obsolete, and yet, they have

Tribune

TRUTHS

not been officially repealed. Tensions are boiling over as Nebula individuals across the country stage mass protests, demanding fair wages and equal treatment from their Epsilon employers. The queen's appointment of three Nebula councilors is a significant step toward equality. However, many question whether this represents a steadfast commitment to change or merely a symbolic gesture.

As Corona holds its breath, all eyes turn to President Janus Dyer and her upcoming audience with Queen Leigh. The revelation that the queen poisoned Janus at the Daughters of the Witches You Could Not Burn (DWYCNB) gala, hosted at former President Elio di Siena's manor, has cast a pall over their meeting. The nation wonders whether these two formidable leaders can set aside their differences to work together to steer Corona through these turbulent times or if their animosity will deepen the nation's vast divides. Thanks to my well-placed source within the Council, I will continue to uncover the secrets of the Borealis Elite in the coming weeks. The truth—no matter how unsettling—will be brought to light. Stay tuned as the drama unfolds and the government's true motives are revealed . . .

CHAPTER ONE
LEIGH

PRESIDENT JANUS DYER SMILES, sharp and calculated, and I know I am in trouble.

"Your Majesty," she purrs, her voice as smooth as silk. She leans in to kiss my cheeks, her oleander perfume intoxicatingly sweet. "I look forward to hearing your proposals."

I suppress the shiver threatening to race down my spine as I return her smile, my lips twisting with their own thorns.

It is evident in her tense shoulders and guarded caramel eyes that Janus is wary of me, and for good reason. I am the reason she spent several agonizing days at Hebe Hospital in October, her veins burning with the white-hot agony of daemon venom. In a misguided attempt to save my country from war last autumn, I made a deal with the Magician—the leader of Eos—to raise a daemon and harvest its venom in exchange for the War Letters, which I thought contained harmful information regarding my family. I had no idea the Magician, a.k.a. Uncle Don, planned to use the venom on Janus. I didn't intend for her to get hurt. A fact I had explained extensively during my tell-all with the *Imperial Inquirer* before my coronation. It doesn't appear she accepted my public apology, but hopefully, when she hears my proposals today, she'll realize I've only ever put my country first, and I intend to continue doing so.

"Please take a seat. I've ordered tea," I say steadily, despite the butterflies in my stomach. I settle into the plush armchair next to my grandmother, holding the thick envelope containing the proposal plans I've been working on for weeks. These proposals aim to make our country more equitable. They will address the wrongs of my ancestors, who created the Labor Laws that unjustly punished the Nebula and forced the vampires underground. Additionally, these changes will ensure a safer environment for Lunar Witches by closing the asylums.

I was crowned three weeks ago, and since then, the ethereal spirits of my ancestor Aradia and my father have been guiding me for this pivotal first meeting with Janus. From this point onward, I will meet with Janus weekly to discuss kingdom affairs and any changes I wish to propose for our governing policies before presenting them to the Council for a vote. I intend to continue attending these meetings with Janus and presenting a united front.

The door swings open, and a palace attendant carries a rattling silver tea tray. She sets it before me with a soft clink, quickly preparing my tea just as I like it—with one lump of sugar and no cream—before tending to my grandmother's.

The room is heavy with tension and the overpowering scent of our perfumes. Ornate furniture and luxurious draperies envelop us, reminding me of the wealth and power I embody and the past wrongs I must correct.

"Let's begin with the vampires, shall we?" I say. "Doctor Chiara Dunn has requested financial support from the Council to research a cure for vampirism. I want to invest in her research, but I want to make sure you do as well."

Janus's eyes search mine. "Done," she says. I press my lips together to suppress a triumphant smile until she adds, "On one condition. We've only begun mending relations with Queen Vyvyan's court. The reaction to a cure is unknown and, therefore, a risk I'd rather not take unless we're sure that Doctor Dunn's research is successful."

I reflect on Janus's request. I had promised myself that during my reign, I would no longer keep secrets from my subjects, including the vampires, but I see a risk in raising people's hopes if we fail to deliver.

"Fine, but since Queen Vyvyan and Prince Vane will attend the Council meeting tomorrow, it may be difficult to keep the hunt for the cure a secret."

Janus nods. "It's easily handled. We'll use approved funds and reallocate them for Doctor Dunn's research, so it doesn't need to be mentioned again."

"Smart thinking, Madam President," my grandmother says, making Janus beam with smug satisfaction. Her rich brown skin glows in the soft, watery sunlight that peeks through the heavy gray clouds for the first time in days. February in Borealis is always dreary, and this winter is no exception. We've experienced record snowfall, but nothing like what they've faced in Glaucus. The roads there have iced over more than once, and the Solar Witches have had to work overtime to keep the treacherous northern streets safe.

"Leigh," my grandmother says, turning her attention to me. "Doesn't that sound reasonable?"

"Oh, yes, very reasonable," I say through gritted teeth. I hate that it feels like we are betraying the fragile trust of the vampires, though I understand both sides.

"Good, what else?" Janus prompts.

I clear my throat. "I propose we close all Lunar Witch asylums immediately and transform them into reentry facilities."

Janus stares at me. We need to change society's perception of Lunar Witches. We are not dangerous; Aradia told us this much when I summoned her before the crowd at the capitol. We are historians—vessels who pass down knowledge from our ancestors, not heathens. Lunar Witches are not born evil but are made evil, so we must help them after centuries of abuse.

"Lunar Witches deserve freedom, but we must assist them in their transition. The reentry facilities will offer medical care and safe housing, but—"

"No," Janus says.

I blink, stunned. "I beg your pardon?"

"I understand this is deeply personal for you, Leigh, but that's just it—it's personal."

I cross my arms, heat simmering beneath my skin. Of course, it is personal. I condemned Lunar Witches, buying into the stigma against them even after I Emerged as one of them. Rewriting the narrative is important to me. I was part of the problem.

"The Lunar Witches are currently safe within the asylums. They have food and a place to sleep, but it is still unsafe for them outside those walls," Janus says.

"You would leave innocent witches falsely imprisoned in cages disguised as hospitals?" My voice rises an octave. My grandmother shifts beside me.

"Of course not, but there are more urgent issues at the moment."

I wait three agonizing seconds before responding, hoping my heavy silence conveys the depths of my disgust. "If helping wrongfully persecuted witches isn't worth our time, then what is?"

Janus's piercing gaze drifts toward my grandmother, which only fuels my ire. My grandmother isn't the queen; I am. Her presence at this meeting is entirely ceremonial.

"*What?*" I snap.

My grandmother breaks the loaded silence. "Leigh, helping the Lunar Witches is important, but so is stabilizing the country. The Nebula people refuse to adhere to the Labor Laws. Riots erupt nightly in most cities where the Epsilon refuse to raise people's pay, and the skyrocketing popularity of *The Tower Tribune* has only made matters worse. This is especially concerning because we know someone on the Council is aiding Stellan Navis's crusade to reveal salacious gossip masquerading as truth, fueling the hatred between the factions and causing people to doubt the government, particularly in Aurora."

We can't force people to follow the Labor Laws. They were implemented when people believed the worst about the Nebula class following the First War. I want to remove them entirely. It is here in the envelope that I am white-knuckling. We will eliminate the Labor Laws, giving the Nebula a choice for the first time in their lives about how they envision their futures. At least, that is my desire. "Stellan is a problem, but is he dangerous?"

Stellan is a reporter who previously worked in the mayor's office in Aurora. He concentrates on covering the political climate there. Recently, he has broadened his scope by criticizing the Council and me. He raises a valid point: We must do more for the Nebula people. Giving them representation on the Council is a positive step, but it's insufficient. A civil war is not out of the question if the current situation persists, which terrifies me.

Take a deep breath, Aradia's ghost whispers. I don't understand how she can be so calm. Closing those asylums means as much to her as it does to me.

"Leigh, you know the pen is always mightier than the sword. Identify the mole among your ranks and focus on what is the bigger threat. Like our borders," my grandmother replies, and Janus nods as if they've already discussed this at length. I glare at them both. Maybe they have. "King Simon Lupas of Lua and his sons declined their invitation to your coronation. But that doesn't mean they haven't been watching you closely."

"The werewolves share a border with us. It makes sense that they would keep tabs on me, but wouldn't that take time if they plan to invade? It shouldn't be at the forefront of your mind, Grandmother," I say, ignoring the quiver in my stomach. Corona and Lua have been at odds for centuries, ever since the wolves' failed invasion to obtain our oil resources during my great-great-grandfather's reign. King Simon declined my invitation for health reasons. His sons, Zeus and Alden, chose to stay behind and care for him. Yet, my grandmother has me questioning if something more nefarious is afoot.

"Paw prints were seen leading from Canis Pass into our territory," my grandmother says, and I tense. Why is this the first time I'm hearing this? "The wolves should be your primary focus, Leigh. Invasion could be imminent."

Janus slips her trembling hands into her pockets. "If that's true, I'll be ready for them. As president, I—"

My grandmother shakes her head. "A divided Corona is a vulnerable Corona. You must unite to get through this transitional period intact."

Janus's gaze meets mine, but her attention quickly shifts away from me to focus on my grandmother. "What do you suggest then, Your Majesty?"

My patience snaps. "Well, for starters, we tell people the full truth about the wolves. Perhaps the fear of an invasion will inspire them to get along."

Janus blanches. "That's an awful idea."

"Well, I don't see you offering any better ones. We need to regain people's trust."

"Scaring them into submission isn't how we do that."

"That isn't what I—"

"If I may," my grandmother says, "you both need to focus on mending your relationships, both with each other and within the Council. Stellan's articles have you cornered. Uncover who is collaborating with him and why. The wolves and Stellan pose real threats. We must demonstrate our unity. Deny Stellan any material to write about, and he will lose interest. If we show the wolves that we are united and stronger, they will think twice before attacking."

I peer at Janus. We're not at odds. I have no problems with her.

"How about this . . ." my grandmother continues. "Should one of you take the train to Glaucus to assess the borders? Meet with the Blade Commander there and devise a plan to rectify the situation while the other works with the Council to stop Stellan."

I shake my head. My reign has just begun. I must stay to prove to my people that I am trustworthy and involved. Janus's presidency is temporary; she is only here until the next election. She needs to campaign if she wants to keep her position. I can tell by the way she's eyeing me that she'd sooner chew off her foot than leave me unsupervised. I must admit, I feel the same.

"Fine." My grandmother sighs. "I will go to Glaucus. Heaven knows I need a break from Borealis."

Relief washes over me. My grandmother will handle the border, and I will have one less thing to worry about. Don's trial recently concluded, and the backstabbing bastard was found guilty on multiple counts, including capital murder, for orchestrating the attack that killed my father and brother. My grandmother hasn't stopped beating herself up for not seeing through his duplicity sooner or for not trusting me when I came to her about the letters. A trip to Glaucus is a chance for her to recharge and make amends for her mistakes. It will also allow me to stretch my legs as queen without everyone deferring to her, as if the crown doesn't rest upon my head.

"I'll arrange your travel," I say to her. She nods in agreement. With that, I turn to Janus. "Now, regarding tomorrow's meeting."

"It appears our time is up. My next appointment is across town," Janus announces abruptly.

I suck in a sharp breath. "But we haven't covered everything."

Leigh, Father's ghost admonishes, *remember what I told you. Stay in control.*

I take a deep breath, filling my lungs with the sweet scent of fresh flowers from the tall arrangement to my right. My father has supported me in my mother's absence over the past weeks. He claims that helping me adjust to my new role is part of his unfinished business.

Janus shrugs. "Until you revise your proposals, I've heard enough."

I rest the folder on my lap. I need her approval before proceeding with my proposed policy changes, but if she's not willing to listen, I won't submit.

"Travel safely, Madam President. I look forward to seeing you at tomorrow's Council meeting," I say, reaching for my still-hot tea.

Janus bows. "Your Majesties."

As she exits, her back straight and confident, I accept that I underestimated her as an opponent.

My grandmother turns to me. "Leigh, for the sake of the realm, you and Janus must learn to get along."

"Janus had no intention of hearing me out or agreeing to any of my changes unless they were trivial," I seethe. She means to control me, just like my uncle did.

I refuse to stay quiet when I know something isn't right in my heart.

"Excuse me," I say tightly. "I have calls to make." I stride out, a plan already forming. If Janus thinks she can outmaneuver me, she's sorely mistaken. I'll find a way to push my reforms through, with or without her approval. The future of Corona depends on it.

CHAPTER TWO
WILDER

A FLASH of movement catches my eye, but it's gone before I can focus. My racing heart slows as I scan the abandoned di Siena property grounds, snow crunching beneath my boots.

"Marlowe?" I whisper, my breath creating fleeting clouds.

Delicate snow flurries swirl in the ash-gray sky. I suppress a shiver. This better not be another dead end. It's been three weeks since President Janus Dyer named me Borealis Blade Commander, and the replica of Dad's old pin feels heavy on my jacket. The real pin vanished nearly fifteen weeks ago with my predecessor, Marlowe Wilkes. Now, fleeting sightings of Marlowe have led me to this desolate place where the scent of decaying leaves mingles with the snow.

The empty house looms like a gothic monolith perched on the cliff's edge. Waves crash against the jagged rocks below as I scan the house's vacant windows. It's the ancestral home of Elio di Siena, our former president, who was recently exposed for killing vampires and harvesting their tears to create magic-enhancing drugs. Convicting him would have been my first move as Blade Commander, but I allowed the vampires to get to him first.

Marlowe is who I want, anyway. She was the *one* person I thought I could trust before she began manipulating me like a puppet on a string. Marlowe cheered me on to enter and win the trials for promotion to Domna, the Blades' second-in-command—*Marlowe's* second-in-command. But she didn't support me out of belief in my abilities. No, she and Chiron had their own agenda. Their encouragement disguised how they were using me as a pawn in Nyx's vengeful schemes against the

Council and all the Epsilon for their treatment of the Nebula. If I had emerged victorious as Domna, Marlowe would have exploited my position, using me to turn the Blades against the Council in a violent coup.

I wipe my hand down my face, scanning for any sign of movement, though I know I won't see anything. My vision is blurry from exhaustion. I have a thousand other duties in addition to searching for Marlowe. But I need to find her; I need it to make sense. I just can't reconcile the Marlowe I knew—the one who would leave casseroles in our fridge when our parents worked late shifts, who helped me with calculus homework, and listened to my sister Desi's teenage drama—with the one who chose such violence. How can they be the same person? I need to look her in the eyes and understand why. Why did she abandon everything after preaching about making change through patience and persistence? Until I confront her—until I know the truth—I'll never be free of this betrayal eating away at my core.

A car engine rumbles in the distance. Soter. My Domna, arriving late as usual. I melt into the shadows as he pulls up the long driveway, unaware of my presence. He steps out of the car, and the wind tousles his two-toned hair. I can't help but notice what an easy target he'd make.

Adjusting my jacket, I creep toward him. With his back to me, Soter places a cigarette between his lips. He casually snaps one of his jewel-encrusted fingers, and a flame materializes. The rich scent of tobacco wafts through the crisp winter air.

"Bang," I say, pressing my gun-shaped fingers against Soter's shoulders.

He stiffens, preparing for the inevitable. But the shot never comes.

I laugh. "If I were Marlowe, you would be dead."

Soter exhales with a shaky, sharp laugh. "I knew it was you, Wilder."

I roll my eyes. Soter's excuses are as predictable as the sunrise. "You're late."

Soter shrugs, inhaling the nicotine from his cigarette. "I got held up. Another fight broke out between a Nebula and an Epsilon in Asterhead."

I clench my jaw. Damn. Is he serious? That's the third fight this week, and it's only Wednesday. With their entitled swagger, the Epsilon can't handle that their pet Nebula aren't submitting anymore. And the Nebula? Years of being treated like second-class citizens have left them craving payback. They're done being nice. I'm running myself ragged, trying to maintain the peace, but for every fire I extinguish, two more flare up. There aren't enough hours in the day to deal with this chaos. "What happened?"

Soter takes another long drag. "If you're so concerned, maybe you should have been there, boss."

I scowl at him. He didn't use my title as an endearment. But I am determined to get along, so I swallow the insults on my tongue.

As students at the Blade Academy, we pushed each other through countless skirmishes and competitions, always striving to gain the upper hand. Soter even pursued my girlfriend, Isolde, behind my back. He flaunted his half-Epsilon status while I had none. However, competing in the Blade's Domna Trials this autumn changed everything. Our masks crumbled, revealing that we are two sides of the same coin. Both of us were motivated by a hunger for a promotion that would grant us the power to right the wrongs that haunt our pasts.

I see Soter now. His Epsilon father is a cruel tyrant, and his half-brother Keris, a Council member, has always looked down upon him for the crime of being born a Nebula. Keris has since come out as pro-Nebula since the revelation of the War Letters.

My rivalry with Soter blinded me to Marlowe's manipulation. I ignored his warnings about her connection to Nyx, too proud to admit he might be right. That mistake allowed her to slip through our fingers. Now that I've earned this interim commander title—ironically, by finally putting aside that petty competition—I won't fail again. My title might be temporary, but while I have it, I'm determined to keep the Nebula and Epsilon from tearing each other apart, starting with Soter and me.

"Do you think we've finally found her?" Soter asks, referring to Marlowe.

We've been searching for months. My instincts suggest that my old mentor has fled the country, yet we occasionally receive tips about sightings in the city. I never ignore a possible sighting.

"No, I don't," I reply.

Soter flicks his cigarette to the ground and crushes it beneath his foot. "You can't know that for certain." He exhales smoke from the corner of his mouth.

Soter's right, but I know Marlowe better than anyone. She wasn't just my boss—she was my mom's best friend, my dad's Domna, and a constant in my life since before I could walk. I know she wouldn't risk returning to Corona unless something big was at stake. Something worth gambling everything for. And that's exactly what worries me.

As we step inside the manor, the large door creaks. Every piece of furniture lies under untouched white sheets.

I peer around the spacious room, showcasing a wealth I could never dream of having. But unlike the row house I grew up in, this palace offers no warmth, as if a family never lived here. Like a ship at the bottom of the sea, this place is a crypt of terrible memories.

We check the downstairs and the cleared-out wine cellar before heading upstairs to the bedrooms. Elio's office is empty, but Soter pauses to stare at a pompous painting of the former president.

"Something is missing," he muses before approaching Elio's desk to search for a black permanent marker. He tugs the wooden coffee table against the wall with a screech, stands up, and draws horns, a mustache, and a tail on the artwork.

I struggle not to smile. "Come on, quit fucking around."

Soter hops off the table to admire his work. "I should have been an artist."

"You are many things, but artistic isn't one of them. Let's go."

The bedrooms are empty, and the beds remain untouched. If Marlowe were staying here, there's no way she would sleep on the floor. She always complained about an old injury that flared up during stakeouts with Dad. Though I knew she wouldn't be here, my heart sinks a little.

"When you find Marlowe," Soter asks as we wander through an empty bedroom, "what do you intend to do?"

I close the drapes covering the double doors that lead to the deck. "What kind of dumb question is that? I'd arrest her."

A moment of silence passes before Soter asks, "Would you?"

I groan. Soter always knows how to push my buttons. "I'm the commander, and she is a wanted criminal."

"But she is also your friend."

My hands tighten into fists at my side. The Marlowe I trusted implicitly feels like a distant memory now. Once, she had been more than just a mentor to me; she had been a confidante, a second mother figure who always had my back. She penned a glowing letter of recommendation when I applied to work as a Blade at Dad's precinct. And in my darkest hour, when I thought I had lost everything after Desi died, she welcomed me home with open arms. A bitter poison flows through my veins, settling in my chest.

"Don't insert yourself into a situation you know nothing about," I tell him.

Soter stares at me intently. "I'm observant. Marlowe favored you above all of us. You are a skilled Blade, but it was more than that. She trusted you to have her back and to stand by Nyx's side."

My posture stiffens like steel. There are no *sides* left after the revelation of the War Letters. If Nebula and Epsilon can't learn to work together, we lose the opportunity the letters provide us to find peace and finally build an equitable society. Nyx failed to realize this months ago and, as a result, squandered their chance for justice in their thirst for revenge. I refuse to watch history repeat itself.

"Marlowe chose violence," I say. "Of course, I didn't agree with her. I still don't."

Soter nods. "Revenge and retribution are often confused. You're chasing ghosts while there are bigger issues at hand. Let me handle finding Marlowe. You're too close to this."

I glower. "Marlowe attempted to kill Leigh, and for that alone, I want her to suffer."

Soter grins.

Dammit. He's right. I am too close to this case.

"Go, busy yourself with the many other projects piling up on your desk, and trust that I can manage Marlowe. You're stretched too thin."

"You can't handle her alone."

Soter shrugs. "Then send Isolde to help me."

My eyes narrow. Soter would love to work with the woman he stole from me. But Isolde would rather submit to water torture.

My phone vibrates.

JAXSON

You're needed in Bardhyl. A group of kids just tried to rob a bank.

"I have to go." Soter nods and then looks away, but not before I catch his triumphant smile. He knows he's won. When push comes to shove, Marlowe needs to answer for her crimes. Except I can't be trusted to handle her trial without bias. "Check the neighboring houses and the Kelpie Racetrack. If Marlowe was here, she didn't get far."

I call Jaxson to get up to speed so I can decide how to reprimand a group of misguided kids.

"What exactly happened?" I ask instead of greeting Jax, closing the door behind me.

As I descend the stairs, my mind races with conflicting priorities. I know that the decisions I make in the coming days will shape not only my future but also the future of us all.

CHAPTER THREE
DESIREE

"FUCK, FUCK, *FUCK!*"

I fumble with my phone, catching the contraband device in my sudsy, gloved fingers right before it lands in the toilet bowl at Little Death. A pungent cocktail of bleach, ammonia, and leather burns my nostrils.

We don't open for another hour, but the bass pulses through the walls, echoing my frantic heartbeat. Queen Vyvyan has had me on cleaning duty ever since I snuck out of the Nest to warn my brother and Jaxson about Nyx's attack a few months ago. Wilder had been in trouble, and I might have gotten away with helping him if I hadn't asked Prince Vane for assistance.

My hands are raw, and my pride is bruised, but I don't dare complain. Not when Vyvyan can turn my life into a living hell. I enjoy living here—more than anywhere else I've ever lived.

"What happened now?" Misty asks from the adjacent stall. She isn't on cleaning duty with me, but as my best friend, she stays with me for company.

"I almost flushed my phone," I reply.

Misty's laughter is like wind chimes. "You're brave to keep that phone," she observes as she exits her stall. She's right; if Vyvyan knew Wilder had given me a way to contact him and Mom, her rage would be apocalyptic. Vampires aren't allowed to own phones. Period. I need to get rid of it. Soon.

I can't risk losing my place here, and I fear what might happen if I continue to break the rules. Shuffling out of the stall and toward the fancy sink, I read the text that made my heart jolt. Misty rests her chin on my tattooed shoulder, a feat that would be impossible without her platform boots.

"What did he say this time?" she asks.

I bite my lip as I peel off my gloves. Jaxson and I have been exchanging flirty texts non-stop since Leigh's coronation. Before I was Turned, Jax was my boyfriend. When he's being cute and kind, it's a bit too easy to forget how he left me.

JAX

> Can we talk on the phone tonight? It's hard not hearing your voice.

My smile reaches my ears. Jaxson has always made me feel special. He embraced my jagged edges as if they were soft curves. At least, he did until the day he chose Wilder over me. I had faced rejection before, but never such overwhelming desolation. Jax was more than my boyfriend; he had been my best friend. With Wilder in Aurora and Jax ignoring my calls, in a way, I lost both of them all those months ago.

I felt lost and aimless until a woman whispered the password to Little Death, and I found myself in this bar. Even though I had to wear a mask, I had never felt so seen.

Misty squeals. "How cute! How will you respond?"

I shake my head, yet my grin remains steady. "We spoke last night."

"So? You're hot; he's hot. Forget the call. Video chat. Naked."

"Your persistence says more about your sex life than mine."

"I'm a desert, and if I want to have sex, I have to do it vicariously through you. Write back that you want to video chat," Misty encourages. Her wide smile is as red as her cherry-colored hair. "I'll scream 'fire' to clear the dorm."

I look at her with wide eyes. Clearing our shared room of hundreds of vampires is impossible. Only Queen Vyvyan and Prince Vane have private quarters. But for those she loves, Misty would move mountains. It's the same for the people she hates; they better watch their backs because Misty would have no trouble stabbing them.

"I don't know." I chew my thumb. "I don't want him to get the wrong idea," I admit, tucking my phone into my corset. "I haven't decided if I want to date him again."

I am unsure if that's what Jaxson wants. If it is, he is certainly taking his time.

"Why not?" Misty furrows her brow. "If Vane wanted me the way Jaxson wants you, I'd jump at the chance. You just need to put yourself out there, Desi. Anyone would be lucky to have you."

I turn away, concealing my unease. Misty doesn't know that Prince Vane, Vyvyan's heir, is my sire. She never will. A part of my agreement with Vyvyan, when she permitted me to stay at the Nest after I became a vampire, was that I would keep my sire's identity a secret. Instead of becoming Desiree Bathory, I remained Desiree Dunn. I had a place to stay as long as I kept my mouth shut. So far, I haven't had any issues keeping my most embarrassing secret to myself, and I intend to keep it that way. My friendship depends on it. Thoughts of Vane ignite old anger, flaring red at the edges of my vision, but I shove them aside. I asked him to Turn me, but what happened afterward was utterly humiliating.

"Desiree, are you okay?" Misty asks as I wipe down the counter. "Did I overstep? I thought you seemed interested given how much you've been texting."

I pause. I hate lying to her, but I don't have a choice. "No. It's fine," I say, shoving the anger aside. "You did nothing wrong. It's just that—"

The bathroom door bangs open, revealing a vampire dressed in a skin-tight latex skirt. "Desiree, darling, the queen is asking for you in her private chambers," she announces.

"Why?" I blurt out, struggling to keep my voice steady.

Queen Vyvyan never invites us to her quarters. Everyone in the Nest has designated roles, with Vyvyan and Vane leading the way. If we get into trouble, she publicly exemplifies us in the throne room. This is how she has maintained order for centuries. Having the Eurynomos daemon judge guilt and administer punishment keeps her hands clean.

The vampire glances up. Her eyes are so heavily made up that I'm surprised she can even open them. "You know better than to question

Vyvyan. Now, unless you want a spanking, I'd suggest you traipse that cute butt of yours downstairs. You know how impatient she is."

I force a smile, telling myself not to panic. Am I about to get into trouble? I wring my hands together and reach for my cleaning supplies.

"Leave it," the vampire says. "I'll take care of it."

"I'll save you a seat for breakfast, Desi," Misty offers.

The other vampire looks at her. "Vyvyan said you were supposed to go with her."

Misty and I exchange furrowed looks. Why would Vyvyan want to see us both? A chill settles deep in my bones as Misty mouths, "Phone," to me, her eyes darting to where I've hidden the device. I cover the spot between my breasts.

If Vyvyan knows about the phone, I must protect Misty. She shouldn't suffer because of my mistake. I'll say and do whatever it takes to take the blame.

As I navigate the candlelit corridors beneath Little Death with Misty, I try to compose myself through steady breaths. The path leads to a heavy door flanked by several imposing vampires.

I squeeze Misty's hand. "Whatever happens," I whisper, "I've got your back."

She nods, but confusion and fear battle in her red eyes. I swallow hard.

Queen Vyvyan's chambers are carved into the bedrock deep beneath the Iron Parthenon, imbuing the space with an ancient gothic splendor. Burgundy silks drape luxuriously over a four-poster bed, while centuries-old antiques whisper tales of Vyvyan's long life. Vyvyan rests daintily on a silk settee at the center of the room.

"Your Majesty," Misty and I say in unison as we curtsy.

Vyvyan's piercing gaze is fixed on us.

"Desiree Dunn and Misty Vosa," she says, placing her wineglass of blood on a glass table. "How kind of you to join me."

This summons was far from optional, but I nod stiffly. Angering Vyvyan would mean angering the entire coven.

"Is everything—" The door behind us swings open, and my words fade away.

The air shifts, and every nerve in my body ignites. Vane. I don't need to turn to know it's him; my traitorous body recognizes his presence instantly. Goose bumps cover my exposed arms and legs from his weighted gaze. Vane lingers behind me. His silence is likely because of me. We do our best to avoid each other.

"What are you waiting for, an invitation?" Vyvyan barks.

Vane strolls past me.

With a deep breath, I look up. The last time we were in this room together, he confessed to Vyvyan that he regretted Turning me, shattering my heart with casual cruelty. Vyvyan sat in the same place she occupies now, shaking her head.

"Where have you been?" Vyvyan snaps.

"I went out for a walk," Vane replies, pouring himself a glass of blood. His shoulders are tense in his crisp black dress shirt.

Vyvyan hisses at him, flashing her fangs. Misty gasps, but I remain still, knowing better than to get between Vane and Vyvyan.

"You expect me to believe that?" Vyvyan's voice drips with venom. "You've been gone for hours, and the sun just set."

"I'm back, aren't I?" Vane's calm response only seems to infuriate her further. He turns to us. "And just in time, for what, I wonder?"

My chest rises and falls in unsteady breaths.

The night Vane turned me, we were in my room at my mom's place. I'd officially ended things permanently with Jaxson after he tried one last time to get back together but still wouldn't tell Wilder about us. I considered it because of our history and wasn't sure if I had a future with Vane. He was a vampire prince, after all. Vane wanted to see the childhood I had assured him was anything but glamorous before I moved into my own place. As a girl, I spent most nights alone, blasting angry music and pouring my pain into my journal. Seeing Vane—his otherworldly looks and designer clothes—surrounded by band posters and my old tie-dye bedspread made me laugh hysterically. I wasn't the same Desiree who Jaxson had dumped. I was dating a vampire and hiding the War Letters. I had finally taken control of my life.

I asked him then and there to Turn me. At first, he was reluctant, but after I dropped to my knees to beg, he agreed. He laid me down on my bed with the utmost gentleness, undressed me with reverent hands, and made love to me to mask the pain of his fangs tearing into my neck.

As I lay dying, Vane whispered apologies into my ear, his words a haunting lullaby. I'd thought the pain in his voice was genuine, but now I know all of it was all for show.

When I woke up, I was a vampire. And Vane discarded me like a forgotten toy.

He stood beside Vyvyan as she gazed down at me with pity, telling me I wasn't the first to fall for Vane's schemes and wouldn't be the last.

I had been naive enough to believe he loved me.

Aside from Vyvyan, Vane only loves himself.

He smirks as his gaze roams over me, and heat surges through my veins. He enjoys making those he loathes squirm. He revels in asserting dominance over me. Once upon a time, I enjoyed it, too, until I learned better. It takes every ounce of self-control not to run from the room. I hate him that much.

"Why are we here?" I interject.

Vyvyan's attention snaps back to me. "So impatient, Desiree. Is there someplace else you'd rather be?"

Yes. "No, your Majesty."

"Are you sure?" Her voice gains a taunting edge. "Perhaps you are eager to return to the hospital?"

I blink. Was someone hurt? Is my mom okay?

"I don't understand," I say.

"Rumor has it that Chiara Dunn has requested funding to develop a cure."

"A cure . . ." My question trails off.

"For vampirism."

The words hit me like a physical blow. A cure for vampirism? That's impossible.

"That seems like a waste of time," Misty pipes up, a slight tremor in her voice.

Vyvyan's smile shows all her teeth. "That's what I thought as well,

Misty. That's why I want to hear from Desiree. Well, Desi? Why is your mom researching an impossible cure? Is it because you asked her to? After all I've done for you, are you unhappy here?"

I open and close my mouth. No, I didn't ask Mom to find a cure. I have no desire to be a witch again. My time as a human is over, filled with memories so painful that I never want to relive them. "No, I am very happy here."

Vyvyan's smile wavers. She must not trust me.

I steal a glance at Misty. A growing dread threatens to swallow me whole. This meeting involves far more serious accusations than my secret cell phone. Vyvyan believes I betrayed her. She thinks I asked Mom for a cure. She thinks I don't want to be here.

"Prove it," Vyvyan demands.

I wince. How am I supposed to do that? Vyvyan has never liked me. From day one, she has seen me as a threat to her relationship with Vane. But she has nothing to worry about. She can have him; Vane means nothing to me. He made it clear that I'm nothing to him.

"I—I—" Why can't I speak? I should say that the Nest is my home, and the vampire coven is my only family, but I can't. Wilder, Mom, Dad, and Jaxson are out there, and while they are alive, I also want to be close to them. But not at the cost of losing what I've gained here.

I peer at Misty. She's the only true friend I've ever had.

"You wound me, Desiree," Vyvyan says. "After all I've done for you—taking you in, ensuring you have a roof over your head, money in your pocket, and blood in your belly—this is how you repay my kindness?"

I close my eyes. Her kindness? Vyvyan is more like a dictator than a queen.

"Whoever told you about the cure got their wires crossed," I say quickly, my voice steady despite the fear swelling inside me like a balloon. I glare at Vane. Did he use his gift to uncover Mom's plans and tell Vyvyan to fuck with me? "My mom might be researching the cure, but it's not for me." When no one responds, I add, "Honestly."

The silence in the room is deafening, disrupted only by the gentle crackle of flames.

"I wouldn't take it, even if she succeeded," I insist. "This is where I want to be, and I can prove it to you. I'll go to Hebe right now. My mom's working tonight; I'll ask her to stop."

Queen Vyvan examines me. "It's amusing how you believe I'll allow you to leave after what happened last time."

"Vyv, I thought we had moved past that." Vane sighs. "I helped her to help Leigh."

I chew the inside of my cheek, the taste of copper flooding my mouth. Why is he pretending to help me? Probably because it'll make Vyvyan less likely to . . . Fucking sadist.

"You would believe her, Vane." Vyvyan laughs. "The girl's your little pet, after all."

My nostrils flare. Misty glances at me, but I focus on the spatting royals. If Vyvyan spills my secret to Misty, life here will be unbearable. Misty is in love with Vane. She has been since she first saw him. She wanted him to Turn her, but he refused. Vane doesn't Turn other vampires, so I don't know why he Turned me. Maybe because he enjoys lording over me.

"Vyvyan." Vane utters her name as a warning. "Don't."

Vyvyan grins wickedly. "Don't tell Misty how you broke your vow never to sire other vampires when you Turned Desiree?"

Misty gasps.

Air rushes from my lungs. *Shit.*

"Is that true?" Misty asks me. Vyvyan doesn't hide her smile. "Vane sired you?"

Yes, Vane sired me, but it's not what she thinks. Vane used me. He toyed with my heart and lured me into his bed so he and Vyvyan could laugh at my expense. Vane messed with the Blade Commander's daughter. I was merely a joke to him, that's all.

A joke that went too far.

I face Misty, reaching for her hand, needing her to understand I didn't lie to hurt her, but she rips her hand from mine. Neon tears mist her eyes. "How could you?"

"You don't understand—"

"You lied. After I shared my past with you. My . . ." A sob escapes her.

Misty confided in me that, when she was still a witch, her fiancé had cheated on her with her cousin, whom she regarded as a sister. To make matters worse, they approached her on her *wedding day* to inform her that they were running away together. Misty opened her heart to me, but I couldn't reciprocate because of Vyvyan's orders.

I look from Vyvyan to Vane, silently pleading with her to set the record straight and admit that they *ordered* me to lie.

Neither vampire says a word.

"You made everyone think you couldn't recall your sire," Misty says.

I gag at the bitter taste in my mouth. "What can I do to fix this?"

"Nothing."

The walls close in. I couldn't have told her. Vyvyan forbade me to. Even now, Vyvyan waits for me to slip up and reveal the truth to Misty. Any sign of disobedience would allow her to kick me out.

"Oh no, Desiree, how could you betray your friend like that?" Vyvyan mocks.

Vane glares at her. "Shut up, Vyvyan. You're being nasty."

I can't focus on why he is defending me. My heart breaks as Misty steps back from me.

"Misty, please!"

My friend faces Vyvyan. "May I be excused? My shift is about to start."

Vyvyan nods, then Misty dashes from the room. I rush after her, my hand outstretched, eager to explain.

"Desiree, stop," Vyvyan calls, and I freeze. No matter how nasty Vyvyan is to me, she's still my queen. If I want to live here, I must obey her. "I'm sorry, but you had to be punished."

My hands bunch at my sides. "For what? I already told you I didn't ask for the cure!"

"The deal for you to live here was that you couldn't tell anyone who sired you."

"I didn't tell a soul."

"But that's not true, is it?" Vyvyan taunts, rising on her stiletto heels to refill her glass. "You told your brother and his friend."

I gasp. Vane must have told her I revealed he was my sire to Wilder and Jaxson. I had no choice; after faking my death and returning as a vampire, they deserved answers.

"They wouldn't have told anyone," I insist. "You didn't need to tell Misty. Bring her back in here and tell her the truth—"

"It's done," Vyvyan declares, adjusting her flawless appearance in the full-length mirror. "But I've decided how you'll make it up to me."

"How?"

"Go to Hebe as you mentioned. Stop Chiara's research. Show that you are loyal to me."

Vane turns away, breathing hard. I avoid looking at him. He did this.

"When?" No one leaves the Nest without Queen Vyvan's permission. She aims to protect us, especially after Elio di Siena killed many vampires last year to procure our tears for his drug trade. It was a joyous day when the Eurynomos found him guilty. The celebration that followed as we danced upon his grave lasted three days and three nights.

"Tomorrow evening, we meet with the Council," Vyvyan says. "You may speak with your mother while we're at the meeting. Use that time to persuade her to abandon her research. But understand this—if you're even a second late to meet us afterward, you'll be locked out of the Nest forever. Got it?"

"Got it." I'll make it back before she does. Mom and I are on good terms now; she will listen to me.

"Good," Vyvyan says, waving her hand. "Now, go."

I turn to leave. How could Mom not tell me about her research? Unless it's a secret.

I'm several paces away from Vyvyan's door when I hear, "Desiree!"

My muscles tense as I walk faster. Someone grabs me, and I spin around, glaring at Vane. We are alone in a dark tunnel. "Come to gloat?" I growl. "Misty hates me because of you."

Vane scowls. "Forget about Misty. You need to allow your mother to continue her research. It's bigger than you."

My jaw drops. Why would he care about my mom's research? He wouldn't. Does he *want* me to fail? It's the only explanation that makes sense. He's setting me up so Vyvyan will punish me. After all, when has Vane ever put anyone's needs before his own?

"You're just saying that because you don't want me here, you—"

"Why do you care about what I want?" he challenges.

My chest rises and falls faster. "I don't."

"You shouldn't."

I grimace. "Did you come after me to intimidate me? Because you don't scare me. You're pathetic."

Vane shakes his head and smiles. He has a perfect smile with gorgeous straight teeth, minus his fangs. Fangs so sharp I remember them piercing my flesh the night he killed me. I turn to leave.

"I know better than to intimidate you, Desiree," he says, stopping me. "We both know how much you enjoy being scared." Rage and something darker coil in my stomach. Damn him. He moves closer, his lips brushing my ear. I hate how my skin prickles with awareness. When he pulls me against his solid chest, my traitorous body remembers every sinful moment we shared.

"You made these delicious sounds that drove me mad," he murmurs, and I can't stop the gasp that escapes me. "Like that," he purrs.

His answering groan reverberates through my back, turning my knees to jelly even as fury ignites within my chest. My head tilts back against his chest. I loathe how my body melts at his voice, how my eyes flutter shut.

"What are you doing, Desiree?" he whispers.

But the question sounds more like, *What are you doing to me, Desiree?*

My eyes snap open, and I jerk away from him. "Stay the hell away from me," I pant.

"I'm trying," he says. As he walks away, his laughter echoes in the hall.

I lean against the cold stone wall. The ache between my legs is maddening. Vane's lingering touch sears like a brand on my skin.

"Fuck," I snarl, dragging my hands down my face. What kind of masochist am I to let him get that close again?

CHAPTER FOUR
WILDER

MY FEET DRAG as I enter Leigh's bedroom after my shift, bone-weary from the day's events. Three Epsilon Solar Witch teens held up a bank teller at gunpoint today—desperate kids claiming they needed money to secure their formerly bright futures. The arrest was a complete mess, serving as another glimpse of the fear taking root in our country. The terror in their eyes haunts me, and all I want is to lose myself in Leigh's embrace.

But the room is empty. Water gurgles from the adjacent bathroom, and my attention drifts to her pristinely made bed—specifically to the pile of unopened letters on it. One return address makes my blood run cold: Kratos Prison. The urge to tear open whatever her wretched Uncle Don wrote burns like acid, but I resist. Trust between us remains fragile, and I can't afford to burn that bridge.

With a gentle knock, I enter the bathroom. The fragrance of violets swirls with the ethereal glow of candlelight. Leigh stands before her marble vanity, a vision of royal beauty as she removes her gold jewelry. The soft clink of metal against stone rings in the steam-filled room.

Leigh catches my gaze in the mirror, her smile—rare and precious these days—illuminating her face. "Took you long enough," she says.

"How did you know it was me and not an intruder?" I ask, leaning against the doorframe.

"The ghosts."

"Do you hear them now?" I ask, and she nods. We've had many discussions about her magic, and while I try to be understanding, a sense of unease sometimes grips me, like it does now, as a chill runs down my spine. "I thought they were quiet around me."

"Only sometimes."

I tilt my head. "Sometimes?"

"They aren't scared of you anymore."

I laugh. Leigh mentioned they were quiet around me because I'd somehow been touched by death when Desiree died. Since we were twins, we shared a bond, proving a piece of me perished with her, yet I was still alive. To the ghosts, I am an anomaly. "Pity."

I drink in the sight of the witch before me. Even Aurora's expansive desert night skies pale in comparison to her.

"Unzip me?" Leigh requests, gathering her long hair over one shoulder.

As I comply, her breath catches. The sound draws me closer. My finger traces the exposed skin of her back, feeling goose bumps rise under my touch. She clutches the fabric to her chest, spinning to face me with those mesmerizing gray eyes.

"I've been waiting for someone to unzip me for hours," she mutters, her tone a mix of teasing and accusation. "I almost asked one of the guards."

Frowning, I pull her closer. The tension in my body melts as she wraps her arms around my waist. "In case you forgot, Your Majesty, you have a country to run, and I have a city to keep safe," I tease back, trying to lighten the mood, but it's hard when everything—apart from us—seems to be falling apart.

"Ugh, don't remind me."

My body begs for rest, but something in her tone stops me cold. I'd shoulder any burden for her, no matter how weary I am. "Did something happen? Want to talk about it?"

Leigh sighs, pulling away from me to rest against the counter. "I think Janus hates me."

I laugh, but her scowl tells me she's serious. "Why do you think that?"

Leigh's eyes dart sideways, but I grip her chin gently. "Tell me," I press. I fight the urge to kiss her as she licks her lips. Her mouth has captivated me from the moment we met—beautiful in its duality, capable of both cutting words and tender whispers. And other, more sinful things I try not to dwell on.

"I told her my proposals, starting with the Lunar Witches, and she didn't even let me finish before she shut me down." Anger seeps into Leigh's tone. "Why would she do that? It felt like an attack."

Janus knows Leigh is the reason she was poisoned last October. If she harbors resentment, the two of them need to resolve it. It will be messy initially, but it will ultimately benefit the country's stability.

"What exactly did Janus say?"

"She said it was personal for me, and then my grandmother told me that we need to worry about external threats."

My Blade instincts perk up. "Such as?"

"Stellan's articles, the Labor Laws, Lua." She lists each on her fingers. "My grandmother is afraid the wolves will plan something now that there's new leadership. Paw prints were spotted in our territory."

I tense, racing through potential scenarios and security protocols. "How many?"

Leigh shakes her head. "Unsure. My grandmother is going to Glaucus tomorrow. Official business, she says—checking for threats." A pause. "But really, she just wants to escape."

The vulnerability in her voice cuts deep. Her grandmother running to Glaucus, her mother gone silent, and those haunting letters from her uncle in prison. She's being abandoned, piece by piece.

I came here craving her comfort, but seeing her like this—so close to shattering—I know she needs mine more.

"I'll contact the Glaucus Blade Commander at the precinct tomorrow. We've had a few conversations. If Lua is threatening our borders, she'll tell me."

Her soft eyes meet mine. "Thank you," Leigh whispers, leaning into my touch.

I smile. "Always." Then, to lighten the mood, I add, "Now, tell me more about this proposal of yours. What exactly did you say to ruffle Janus's feathers so much?"

As Leigh recounts her meeting, frustration and hurt radiate from her in waves. The strain between her and Janus, the pressure from her grandmother, the looming threat from Lua—it's all piling up, threatening to crush her.

"But the Lunar Witches," she insists, shoving at my chest when I suggest she listen to Jorina and Janus and focus on stabilizing her Council first. Janus isn't dismissing her proposal to help the Lunar Witches, just tabling it. If Leigh could see what I see as a Blade—the raw hatred that's surfaced since those letters leaked, the daily violence—she'd understand why Janus believes the asylums, for now, are safer than the streets. But that's not what she wants to hear.

"Sometimes we have to work with people we don't like, and meeting Janus halfway on this doesn't mean your fight to liberate the Lunar Witches has to end," I tell her.

Leigh laughs. The sound is tinged with frustration. "So, you are on her side?"

"Leigh, you taught me that sometimes peace requires chaos. If anything, I am following your example."

"If that's true, then you'd come with me right now and free all the Lunar Witches."

I fold my arms. "I'd follow you anywhere, but are you sure that's a good idea? It's snowing and you look more ready for bed than a massive prison break."

Leigh pouts. I smile, and she rolls her eyes. Yeah, that's what I thought.

"Don't look so smug," Leigh says.

"How should I look?" I ask.

"Like you want to kiss me."

The energy in the room shifts as our eyes lock. I lean in, capturing her lips in a kiss that steals my breath and stirs my element to life. The outside world disappears.

"Like this?" I whisper against her lips.

Leigh pulls away, and I watch as she slides the loosened straps of her dress down her arms to reveal her round breasts and toned midriff. The dress falls to the floor, leaving Leigh clad only in her lacy panties. She's a vision of beauty I'll never tire of witnessing.

The words "I love you" hover on my tongue, but Leigh presses her finger to my lips before I can utter them.

"Shh . . . no more talking."

I nod, even as the organ in my chest aches to express the depth of my feelings.

I respond to her next kiss with equal hunger, the raw intensity of our connection burning between us. With each brush of our lips, I savor her taste and the soft feel of her skin.

Leigh winds her arms around my neck, and I lift her to the counter, hands curved beneath her. She tangles her fingers in my hair, pressing her hips against mine until I'm aching, my whole body burning with need. Every brush of her fingers sends sparks racing beneath my skin. Our kisses grow heated, messy with need as she strips away my defenses—jacket and shirt falling to the warm tiles below. Her mouth maps the tattoos across my chest. I shudder, and my muscles tense as her tongue traces each line. When she blazes a path up my throat, my pulse hammers beneath her lips, and I forget how to breathe.

Fuck. Leigh drives me crazy in ways I never thought possible.

Before her, I used to calculate every move. My every action served as a careful step toward my next goal. But since meeting her, I've learned to surrender to the moment. It goes against everything I am and yet pleasing her comes as naturally as breathing.

A soft whimper escapes her lips as I end our kiss, lowering myself to kneel at her altar. I take her panties with me, reverent in my worship. Her head tips back as I spread her thighs, and the sight of her steals my breath. Her arousal overwhelms my senses until I have to close my eyes, groaning with barely contained need.

Fucking perfect, and so fucking *mine.*

As I ease my fingers inside Leigh, she rewards me with a breathless curse. I capture her clit between my lips, and her moan of ecstasy sends a jolt straight to my groin. No longer able to hold back, I let myself devour her.

"You taste so good," I murmur against her sensitive flesh. "Such a good girl. So soft."

"Oh, fuck!" she gasps as she rides my tongue.

"I want to memorize every sound you make," I say, flicking her swollen nub repeatedly.

Leigh shatters for me, my name falling from her lips between desperate pants. Her fingers clutch my hair as steam dances around us, clouding the mirror. As her breathing steadies, I slide my fingers free and raise them to her mouth. When she takes them between her lips, sucking them clean with wicked intent, a primal groan rips through me. I've had plenty of sex before, but with Leigh, it's different. She matches my need for need, and the knowledge that I'm the only one who gets to see her like this —wild and wanting—sets my blood singing.

I want her so badly that sometimes it's all I can think about.

She's my curse and my salvation. My *everything*.

"Please," she begs. The corner of my mouth lifts. "I can't wait any longer."

I loosen my belt. The sound of leather sliding through fabric loops seems unnaturally loud. Leigh's hands replace mine, making quick work of my remaining clothes. When she wraps her fingers around my length, I curse under my breath. The sight of my dick, hard and heavy in her delicate palm, sends heat rushing through my veins.

Leigh's eyes darken, and her tongue darts out to wet her full lips.

Her hand strokes me deliberately, each pump making my breath catch. She scoots to the edge of the sink, spreading her thighs wide, and the sight of her glistening center makes my mouth water.

"I'm still throbbing from your mouth," she pants, "but I need more. Need all of you."

A low growl escapes my throat as I dive to capture her lips with mine, claiming her with a bruising kiss. "Hold on to me," I command, my voice rough. I align myself with her slick entrance, the heat of her already threatening my control. Leigh's fingers dig into my shoulders, and when our eyes lock, I see that familiar wild gleam in hers. But as I press forward, stretching her slowly, that gleam transforms into something more desperate, her eyes widening with pleasure. "Don't. Let. Go." Each word punctuates a gentle thrust, watching as she takes me inch by inch.

"Never," she says in a throaty whisper.

A cry tears from Leigh's throat as I sink all the way inside her. Her long legs squeeze my hips, intensifying the pressure. My eyes roll back as I curse. "Gods, Leigh." I pull out, just to thrust back in harder and faster than before. Her moans bleed through the walls, a sound that often replays in my dreams.

"You are amazing," she pants, sounding desperate as she watches me enter her repeatedly. "Like you were made for me."

"You fit me like a glove, so tight and perfect."

My heart races as I dive into her with a measured force. Her nails leave crescents on my shoulders as I go in for another charged kiss, all passion and untamed need. We aren't being quiet, but I can't care. Lately, our time together has been stolen moments wherever and whenever we can find them. But right now, I want to savor every second, every sensation.

"Holy fuck!" she gasps, body arching. "Don't stop. Please . . . don't stop."

She looks intoxicating like this, but I can't stop imagining turning her to face that mirror. Having her watch as I take her from behind, her breasts bouncing with each thrust, her lipstick smeared from our kisses.

"Turn around," I command, my voice barely recognizable to my ears.

Leigh's laugh is pure sin. It's dark and promising as she slides off the counter. My breath catches as she turns, presenting herself with a deliberate slowness that makes my mouth go dry. Those perfect curves, the elegant arch of her spine as she leans forward . . . The sight of her offering herself like this shorts out my brain. My hand connects with her flesh before I can stop myself, the sharp crack of the slap echoing off the bathroom walls. Her surprised gasp is music to my ears, but it's nothing compared to the desperate moan that follows as I drop to my knees. I press my lips to the reddened skin, soothing the sting with my tongue, tasting her skin.

"Stop torturing me," she groans, undulating her hips.

"How can I? Your body is a feast."

"*Please.*"

The sound of her begging is my undoing.

I grip her hips hard enough to brand her with my fingerprints, claiming her as I sheathe myself inside her. Leigh's hands fly up to brace against the steam-clouded mirror.

"Yes," Leigh pants. Her palms slide across the slick surface, leaving streaky handprints in their wake. She struggles to find purchase, her fingers scrabbling against the slick glass with each thrust. Each exhale fogs the glass further, but I can still see the way her mouth falls open, the way her eyes flutter shut as I fuck her.

"There! Oh, shit. Right there!"

"You're everything to me," I growl. "Say you are mine."

"I'm yours," Leigh gasps, her inner walls fluttering around me. "Oh, gods, I'm *yours.*"

Her thighs shake and her muscles quiver. I'm determined to send her over the edge. I reach one hand between her trembling thighs to rub tight circles on her clit, already sensitive from earlier.

Her climax hits like a thunderstorm. The way she cries out my name, raw and desperate, triggers my own release. I press my face into the curve of her neck, breathing in her intoxicating scent as pleasure crashes through us both. Her pulse races against my lips as we shudder together.

Carefully, I withdraw from her. We both wince slightly at the loss of connection.

Leigh breathes heavily, bent over the vanity as I mutter, "Fuck. I could spend forever with you like that. You are perfect. You know that?"

"I can't feel my legs." Leigh laughs, the sound all tired and cute.

After checking the temperature, I help Leigh settle into the bath. Leigh sighs as I locate my pants. The last thing I want is to leave after what we just did, but my stomach rumbles. I haven't had dinner, and though I could feast on Leigh, I need sustenance to keep up with her.

"I like having you here," she tells me before I walk out the door.

I shoot her a cocky grin. "Yeah, I know."

She shakes her head, smiling. "I mean, I like how we no longer have to sneak around."

Same here. Now that I am no longer her guard, I come and go as I please. We've spent these last few weeks after her coronation learning what makes each other tick. Like how I love black licorice, but Leigh finds it disgusting despite having no problem eating spicy pickles with cheese, which isn't as nasty as it sounds.

"Hurry back."

With a sigh, I exit her room, and navigate the never-ending twists and turns of Rowan Palace. Just as I reach the kitchen on the first floor, I collide with Gianna, who's holding a box of mint chocolate cookies—my favorite. She doesn't offer me one. I take one anyway.

"It's hard to get any sleep around here," Gianna remarks, and I choke on my cookie. "Even with the storm sounds I conjure, I can still hear you going at it."

I smile at the disgust in her voice. "Maybe invest in some earplugs." Or maybe her mother shouldn't have moved back in with her parents before Gianna checked out of rehab.

I was in her childhood home earlier. The place was a fucking tomb. All that was missing was Elio's disgruntled ghost haunting the halls. It's understandable why she'd rather be here.

Gianna had been drugged and treated like a doll her entire life. She'd been born a Nebula, but instead of admitting Maria had an affair, Elio and his wife chose to hide it. Maria di Siena gained a conscience that night at the capitol, when Elio had used his magic to cut Gianna's air supply to keep her from spilling his secrets. He had squandered the family fortune, regained most of what they lost by selling VT on the black market, and forced Gianna to marry a wealthy Epsilon husband. She was proposed to twice but has yet to walk down the aisle.

"I'm not going to stop sleeping with my girlfriend," I assert.

Gianna raises an eyebrow. "And I'm not leaving until I find my birth father, so I guess we're at an impasse."

"Your birth father?" I inquire, and she nods.

"I'm not a di Siena, and I refuse to take my mother's name after she abandoned me," Gianna explains. I munch on another cookie. "So, I'm on the hunt for my father, though he probably doesn't even know I exist."

I grab another cookie. "Have you asked Maria?"

"Yes, Mama said I ask too many questions and am ungrateful."

"You're not one to give up easily, Gianna." I pluck the sleeve of the cookies from her. "Goodnight."

"Keep it down!" Gianna calls after me.

"Not a chance," I mutter, a smile playing on my lips.

When I slip back into the bathroom, I find Leigh lounging in the tub with her eyes open and wearing a troubled expression. Seeing her unease, my brows dip. Not again. I quietly undress and slide into the warm water behind her. I wrap my arms around her waist to help ease her burdens.

"Hey," she murmurs.

I kiss her temple. "I brought cookies."

Leigh chuckles softly. "I'm not hungry."

"Fine, more for me."

As we sit in the warm water, surrounded by bubbles, I'm struck by how perfect this moment is. Despite the challenges we face and the threats looming on the horizon, right here, right now, we have this.

And I'll do whatever it takes to protect it.

"Leigh," I whisper, my lips close to her ear.

"Hmm?"

"I love you."

For a moment, she's silent. Did I overstep? I couldn't keep it bottled up. I love her. I am in love with her. It's scary as hell, but what's more frightening is when she turns around and kisses me, she doesn't say it back.

CHAPTER FIVE
LEIGH

THE FOLLOWING EVENING, surrounded by Council ministerial aides, I stand in the glass-encased elevator as it ascends through the heart of the capitol building. As we breach the cloud layer, I press my hands against the cold, tempered glass, my stomach fluttering with anticipation. The nearest aide murmurs, "This way, Your Majesty."

We glide down the polished hallway, my reflection shimmering on its topaz surface. The massive crystalline doors open to reveal a soundproof room suspended in the heavens. Windows on all sides of the Council chamber offer a breathtaking vista of swirling mist and inky darkness. To accommodate Vyvyan and Vane's aversion to the sun, the meeting has been moved to nighttime, and artificial light illuminates the chamber. With its ring of sixteen cushioned chairs, the sterile space feels more diminutive than I had imagined. As I enter, the ghosts whisper in my ears, telling me where to sit, how to behave, and when to smile. But I ignore their chatter.

I deliberately arrived at the Council chamber early with a calculated purpose: winning over key councilors before the session begins. My proposals are controversial, starting with the closure of asylums and the dismantling of the outdated Labor Laws, but I know which Council members might be persuaded. Last night, Wilder advised me to maintain peace with Janus, but I won't let her resistance delay these reforms while more witches suffer. I can secure their support before the formal vote by sharing these plans with the more progressive councilors. Even if Janus maintains her opposition, I'll have built a coalition strong enough to push through these essential changes. Let her and her conservative faction object. I only need enough votes to pass these reforms, not universal approval.

More Council members file in, including Keris Telfour, who is on my list to talk to, but Bennett approaches first. His navy suit makes his blond hair gleam like spun gold, and his expression barely conceals a sense of urgency when he speaks. "Leigh," he says. "We need to talk about Stellan."

"Can it wait?" I ask as Keris crosses the room to the water station in the back.

"Did you read the latest article in *The Tower Tribune*?" Bennett asks.

A pit forms inside me. "I did."

Bennett's pain is written across his face. Stellan's article exposed Hammond's father's crimes, and the Bishop family's hasty departure from town only twists the knife deeper. While I feel for him, my window of opportunity is shrinking. I need to reach Keris before the meeting starts in ten minutes.

"I'm sorry you're going through this," I offer quickly. "Hammond was . . . complicated. And I know the Bishops were your friends." I shift my weight, torn between showing proper sympathy and pursuing my goal. The reforms can't wait, but neither can I completely ignore Bennett's obvious distress.

"Huh? I am not talking about Hammond," Bennett says. "I am worried that Stellan might be taking things too far. The photos he posted should never have seen the light of day." Bennett's phone then chirps incessantly.

I pause, not recalling any photos accompanying Evander Bishop's grave robbing article. "What photos?"

"The ones of an inebriated Keris at the Little Death with a curvy brunette," Bennett whispers.

"Keris Telfour?" I ask. His phone dings again. "Someone's trying to reach you."

Bennett shrugs. "It's my grandmother."

He turns the phone over, presumably to silence it, but not before I glimpse the screen. The name that flashes isn't *Grandmother*, as he claims. It's Corvina. My eyes narrow. The only Corvina I know is my brother's ex, Corvina Miller. She's a Nebula Cosmic Witch and has been out of the picture since their breakup two years ago. Fynn dumped her for Gianna, and she didn't take it well.

I squint at Bennett, recalling how we had moved past the lies after he went public about his time with Eos. He had given a story to the newspapers, claiming that his grandmother, Edith, a former councilwoman, had dementia and was unfit for office. This was done to take her spot on the Council, which Eos orchestrated to ensure Bennett's vote for Elio in the upcoming election. Even though Edith and the public had forgiven him for his crimes, I couldn't shake the feeling that old habits die hard. Even if he committed such crimes to help me.

"Oh, how is Edith?" I ask, giving him a chance to come clean.

"Fine," Bennett answers, his eyes not quite meeting mine behind his glasses. "It's the anniversary of my parents' death."

My heart constricts, both from sympathy and annoyance. Why is Bennett lying?

Before I can press further, Keris takes his seat closest to mine, his azure eyes swirling with caution as he surveys the room. Now is the time to talk to him. He is a minnow in a room full of piranhas. He could use an ally like me after Stellan's article.

I squeeze Bennett's shoulder. The gesture feels hollow. "Don't worry about Stellan. I'm sure the scandal will blow over soon."

I leave Bennett, who looks torn between chasing after me and throwing his phone at my head.

"Good evening, Keris," I say, settling into my chair.

Keris Telfour dips his chin. "Your Majesty."

"I heard about the article." He flinches at my words. "I am sorry someone leaked photos of you and your date. I've been in a similar position countless times before."

"I don't understand why someone would take those photos in the first place or how Stellan spun a story using them to claim I am unfit for office because of my leisurely activities." Keris sighs. "You see, we were in one of the private rooms at Little Death. Someone must have followed us there to capture those photos."

I blink, remembering that Little Death has numerous private rooms.

During my first visit, Vane and I conversed in one of them to gather information about the letters. There, I discovered his gifts don't work on Lunar Witches, revealing that he had guessed my secret but chose not to say anything. This proved his trustworthiness and good nature.

I glance toward the door. There is no sign of Vane or Vyvyan. Have I miscalculated in my efforts to bring them to the table? I meet Bennett's questioning gaze beside me. "Where is everyone?"

As seconds turn into minutes, with no sign of Janus or the vampires, my attention drifts around the room. The tension is palpable, with each Council member eyeing the others with suspicion they barely conceal. Stellan's articles have sown seeds of distrust, which now bear bitter fruit.

"Keris, I hoped to have your support today—"

"I just heard from the president," a councilor interrupts. "She isn't coming."

I sit straighter. "Did she say why?"

"No, ma'am," the councilor replies as he slips his phone into his pocket.

My eyes narrow. Is she unwell? Janus seemed healthy in our audience yesterday.

"No matter, we can still present without her."

Bennett shakes his head. "Protocol states that without the president present to call the vote, we can't make any presentations."

"Are you kidding?" I demand.

"Sorry, those are the rules, Leigh." Bennett sounds anything but sorry.

My hands tremble as nervous conversation fills the chamber. The president's unexplained absence leaves me no choice but to act now. These changes can't wait. Within ninety days, we could transform the asylums from prisons into sanctuaries. By abolishing the Labor Laws, we could ease the suffocating tension gripping our nation. I had planned to speak with Keris and others first, but another week of delay means another week of the witches suffering. I won't let that happen.

I stand. "Although the president is missing"—all eyes drift toward me; a few narrow their eyes— "I would still like to propose my changes to you all."

A few members whisper to each other. I strain to hear what they say, but I can't, as Keris asks, "You want to breach protocol?"

"What I've been working on could change things for the better," I begin, but someone interjects.

"You're new here, Your Majesty, but we have rules for a reason. We need order now more than ever, which is why I must insist we wait for Janus," a female Epsilon councilor with gray hair and green eyes says.

My stomach turns as another councilor, a Nebula, exhales before saying, "Our focus shouldn't be on governing policies. Not when Stellan Navis is attacking the Council. He knows things about us, and I fear none of us is safe from his pen. How do we expect the nation to listen to us when they are busy listening to him?"

"I agree," someone else says, a man from one of the oldest Epsilon families in Corona. "Stellan means to take us down. The information he shares is unsettling. It's dividing the populace. Those for and against us."

"How did Stellan even get those photos, Keris?" someone else asks, and Keris shakes his head.

"Who else here was at Little Death last night?" someone asks.

No one says anything, and Keris scoffs. "We can subpoena the video footage from the vampires. You can't hide. You might as well speak up."

"I was there," someone says, and Keris's gaze turns murderous. "But I didn't see you."

"Neither did I," another says.

My breath catches. Anyone could have sent those photos, but Stellan bragged about his source being on the Council. My gaze falls on one person after another. They could all be lying.

"We are losing focus," I say, but no one listens.

"What if you sent Stellan those photos to draw the blame away from yourself that you are working with Stellan, Keris?" another councilor asks. "Your brother is Nebula. Perhaps you are trying to avenge him after what the letters revealed."

Keris balks. "I wouldn't send photos of myself having sexual intercourse, you moron."

The room erupts into chaos, accusations flying.

I wish I could reassure them, but I can't. Someone is using the War Letters to justify helping Stellan, turning the country's leaders against each other. We won't see eye to eye until we find the mole . . . who could be sitting in this room or working with someone connected to Stellan.

As the shouting continues, the overhead lights flicker. A breath later, the room plunges into darkness.

Confused murmurs reach my ears as I blink, trying to adjust to the sudden darkness. As the councilors realize that the power has gone out, I go to the window and squint through the glass. I witness the lights across the city extinguish, block by block. My hands are clammy. Is this some kind of protest?

It's happening, the ghosts whisper in my ears.

"What's the meaning of this?" a panicked voice calls out.

"It must be an attack!" another shouts.

"Are we being invaded?" Bennett asks.

I clutch my chest above my ricocheting heart. The memory of the paw prints in Glaucus surfaces. Could this be it? Have the wolves finally arrived? Grandmother left for the north this morning, and although she called to confirm her arrival, a chilling thought grips me. What if she was too late?

As if on cue, guards shuffle into the room, their faces grim in the emergency lighting. My adrenaline spikes. One announces, "Your Majesty, Council members, the entire city has lost power. We need to get the queen to safety immediately."

As the guards usher me out, I glance back at the chamber one last time. The dim light reveals the panic etched on every face, perfectly reflecting my rising terror. Everyone fears the worst, whatever may be happening out there. I have a strong urge to invite them all home and offer them safety and protection, but the knowledge of a traitor in our midst stops me.

Navigating through the shadowy corridors, an unsettling sensation grips me, whispering that this blackout is merely the prelude to something far more sinister. A gnawing terror of the unknown has replaced my once-unshakable certainty and I am woefully unprepared for what lies ahead.

CHAPTER SIX
DESIREE

HEBE HOSPITAL LOOMS like a beacon of hope over the whispering pines beside Tsilah Cemetery. The hospital's polished stone façade and gleaming windows paint a picture of serenity, but my vampire senses pick up the frantic heartbeats and raised voices within.

I step inside, and the world shifts. Fluorescent lights flicker, casting an eerie glow on the faces of harried staff and frightened patients. A backup generator hums a low, persistent drone that sets my teeth on edge. The hallways twist and turn like a giant maze, flooded with bodies desperately seeking care.

The call to heal pulses within me—a forgotten melody awakening after months of silence. But I'm not here to save lives. I'm here for answers. My plan is simple: find Mom, convince her to stop her research, and return to Vyvyan before she goes back to the Nest. But the citywide blackout has thrown everything into chaos. The blackout delayed my arrival, so I have no time to waste. Not if I don't want to get locked out of the Nest.

A team of healers rushes past, pushing a gurney. The man on it is a mess of blood and broken bones. His life essence spurts from a gash in his neck. The scent hits me like a physical blow, and I grip the wall to steady myself. The lead healer's voice cuts through the din.

"Male, late thirties, motorcycle crash, with neck hemorrhage, multiple lacerations, and right femoral fracture. Needs airway management, hemorrhage control, and a femur X-ray—prep for neck exploration and possible femur stabilization. Order four units of blood and start antibiotics. Ortho, be ready for OR. Someone page Doctor Chiara Dunn!"

"She's finishing with our VIP patient," is a surgical resident's reply.

"Tell her to hurry."

As they wheel the patient around the corner, I follow, planning to catch Mom before she disappears into sterilization. The familiar routine of the trauma team brings a pang of nostalgia. Once, I was one of them. I had interned under Mom's watchful eye for years. After Wilder left for Aurora, I threw myself into healing, channeling all my loneliness and anger into saving lives. Still, no matter how much time and effort I put in, it wasn't enough.

I still wasn't enough.

The double doors to the operating room swing shut in my face. The air carries the metallic tang of death. I scan the packed hallway—worry lines are painted on passing faces, the trembling hands of a nurse clutching a clipboard. And then I see her.

Mom appears in her mint-green scrubs, her dark brown hair—like mine before I started dying it—pulled back in a tight bun beneath her surgical cap. She doesn't notice me until I'm right in front of her.

"Desiree?" she breathes, her gaze darting to the operating room doors. The urgency to be inside, to save a life, overshadows any desire to engage with me. "Is everything okay? Wilder, is he—"

"He's fine, but I'm not," I say, blocking her path.

She exhales. "Are you sick?" I shake my head. "Then can it wait? I'm about to head into surgery. Let's catch up later."

"I only need a second of your time."

"Desiree, I have a patient. Whatever this is, it can wait."

"Your patient is stable." My enhanced hearing picks up the steady beep of monitors and the calm voices of the team inside. They won't let him die. "Please, give me two seconds."

Mom frowns as the OR doors swing open behind me. "Doctor Dunn, we're ready for you," a familiar voice calls out, sending heat down my neck.

"Thank you, Juliette. I'll be right in," Mom replies.

My body tenses, but I step closer to Mom. "Please, I heard about what you're working—"

"Desiree, heavens, is that you?" Juliette's saccharine voice grates my nerves. My childhood nemesis is now a colleague of my mom's. The irony is not lost on me.

"Doctor Dunn, hurry," another healer calls out, and just like that, Mom is leaving.

Over her shoulder, she calls, "Come by the house this weekend, Desi," then she disappears through the operating room doors, leaving me alone with a smirking Juliette.

"Well, don't I get a hug?" Juliette insists, arms outstretched.

Juliette envelops me in an embrace that feels more like a trap. My body goes rigid, every instinct screaming to push her away. Suddenly, I'm back in high school, hearing whispers and giggles related to Juliette's latest rumor about me. I'm shivering in Equinox Park, rope biting into my wrists as I pray someone will find me before dawn. I'm in the hospital, discovering my charts have been tampered with, knowing it was her but unable to prove it.

The fear and anger I had growing up comes rushing back, amplified by my vampire senses. I can hear Juliette's heartbeat and smell the rush of blood coursing through her veins. Does she know how close I am to losing control? Does she have any idea of the damage she's done?

To stop myself from going for her throat, I take a steadying breath. She's not worth it. I'll be locked out of the Nest forever if I do not meet Queen Vyvyan by her deadline.

Who knows what else Vyvyan will do if I don't get Mom to promise to end her research?

"Wow, you look hot," Juliette remarks as she pulls away, her gaze sliding over my revealing vampire-style outfit like oil. I suppress a shudder.

"I need to talk to my mom," I say, stepping toward the double doors.

Juliette slides in front of me. Her smile is as condescending as it was when she started dating Wilder all those years ago, acting as if our toxic past was water under the bridge. As if she hadn't spent years making me feel worthless, invisible, unwanted. "It'll be a while before she's free."

My sigh conveys the pressure I'm under. Vyvyan will be furious, but surely, she'll understand the blackout derailed our plans and let me try again. Won't she?

"You know, Desi, I'm happy I ran into you," Juliette continues, using the nickname that only friends and family have earned the right to use. Each word is like a needle under my skin.

I glare at her while years of pent-up anger bubble to the surface. "Why? You hate me."

"I don't hate you."

I can't help but laugh bitterly. "Every bad memory from my childhood connects to you." The isolation, the constant fear—it all leads back to her. "You know what? I don't have time for this. I have somewhere I need to be."

I turn to leave, and Juliette grabs my arm. The touch awakens something primal within me. I hiss, fangs bared, my vision tinting red at the edges. Juliette recoils, the color draining from her face. For a moment, there's genuine fear in her blue eyes, and part of me revels in it.

"What the hell, Desiree? I try to have a cordial conversation with you, and you try to eat me." Juliette glances sideways. I notice a few staff members watching our exchange.

The fight leaves me. Their faces are a cocktail of fear and contempt. I shake my head; the truth hitting me anew: I never belonged here and never will. Juliette made sure of that long ago.

"Excuse me." I head for the exit.

"You're still the same, Desiree," Juliette calls after me. "Better clothes. Still lost and alone!"

The brisk night air hits my face when I burst through the hospital doors. The city stretches before me, a patchwork of darkness and emergency lights. In the distance, Equinox Park beckons, a slice of nature in the urban landscape. I take a deep breath, then set off to find Vyvyan.

CHAPTER SEVEN
DESIREE

MY FEET barely touch the ground as I race toward our rendezvous spot, pushing my vampire speed to its limits. The wind whips through my short hair as I run through the blackout-stricken city. Vyvyan's impatience is legendary. If I am a second late, I will find myself locked out of the Nest forever, cast adrift in this cold, dark metropolis.

As I pass a group of teenage male witches tagging a department store window, the streets pulse with sinister energy. Veering off the main roads to avoid potential threats, I plunge into the relative safety of Equinox Park. The sudden absence of urban noise is jarring, replaced by the soft crunch of snow and grass beneath my feet. Patches of white glisten beneath an impossibly bright moon.

I approach the designated meeting spot outside the Iron Parthenon, and the air thickens. The wooded area surrounding the Parthenon reeks of death—a sickly sour odor—and my senses scream. A chill that has nothing to do with the temperature crawls over my body. Every instinct urges me to flee, but I force myself forward.

"Vyvyan? Vane?" I call out, my voice sounding fragile in the vast darkness. The silence that greets me is absolute, swallowing my words whole. I'm about to call again when a feeble cry for help pierces the stillness, sending my feet charging through a thicket of oak trees.

"Vyvya—" The name catches in my throat as I freeze at the sight before me.

The fierce and indomitable Vyvyan lies crumpled on the ground; her usual regality reduced to something fragile and broken. Vane cradles her in his arms. Tears mingle with the blood on his cheeks, the crimson streaks glistening.

A sizable wooden stake protrudes from Vyvyan's chest.

"Holy shit." I drop to my knees in the damp grass beside them. "What happened?"

"Desiree, finally!" Vane gasps. "I need your help."

How long have they been like this?

Vyvyan gasps, the sound wet and painful. My attention snaps to her wound. The stake narrowly missed her heart—there's a chance, slim as it may be, to save her. And I'm damn well going to take it.

"We need to move fast." My voice is steady. "Hebe isn't too far from here. My mom is there. She can help."

Vane shifts as if to follow, but Vyvyan's hand shoots out, gripping his bicep with surprising strength. "N-no," she wheezes. "You'll k-kill me if you move me."

I groan. Even facing death, Vyvyan clings to control. "You'll die if you stay here. You need blood. Lots of it, if you're going to heal."

"I'll die anyway," she rasps, her red eyes flickering with a chilling resignation.

No, I think. She can't die. If she does, I'll never forgive myself. As a healer, I took an oath.

"She needs blood," I repeat.

Vane's brow furrows. "You said that. But in case you haven't noticed, there's no one ar—"

Before Vane can finish, I tear into the flesh of my wrist with my fangs. The pain is sharp, but I barely register it. Vane gasps in horror as my blood, so dark it looks almost black in the moonlight, wells up, and begins to drip onto the dirt.

I shift toward Vyvyan, but Vane twists to shield her. "What the fuck are you doing? You aren't giving your blood to her."

"Do you have another suggestion?" I snap, meeting his gaze defiantly.

Vampires do not share blood outside of mating purposes. A blood bond links a pair together empathically. However, there's also a risk that a bonded pair could become addicted to each other's blood or have one swap a mate for a master.

Vane hesitates, then rolls up his sleeves. "Let me do it. She's already my sire." He doesn't sound excited.

For a moment, I'm tempted to accept his offer. It would certainly make things less complicated between Vyvyan and me. I know she hates me and having her feel how uneasy she makes me on a visceral level for all eternity sounds terrible. But another part of me—the part that still resents Vane for his rejection, for the pain he's caused, for how close he and Vyvyan are —decides for me.

"No," I say firmly. "I'm the one with medical training. If this doesn't work, you need to be at full strength to address the vampires in her place. We can't have both of you weakened."

Vane's jaw hardens, but he nods reluctantly.

"I promise you," I say, my voice softening, "I'd much rather be doing this with a potential mate if I had one, but I know how much Vyvyan means to you and the other vampires."

Something flickers in Vane's eyes. "You want to find a mate?" he asks, surprise coloring his tone.

I shift uncomfortably. It was mostly a joke, but suddenly, I feel exposed. Yes, deep down, I hope that someone—someday—will love me enough to choose me over everything and everyone else. That being with me is worth the potential consequences the blood bond creates.

I push past the moment of vulnerability. "Am I doing this or not?"

Vane holds my gaze for a long moment before nodding. "Do it."

I press my bleeding wrist against Vyvyan's lips, urging her to drink. Despite her weakened state, her survival instincts kick in. She latches onto my wrist, her fangs sinking into my flesh with a greedy swallow. I gnash my teeth against the initial pain.

As Vyvyan drinks, an unexpected sensation washes over me. With each gulp of my blood, a fraction of my vitality drains away. But it's replaced by building pressure, an intoxicating euphoria that starts low in my core and radiates outward. A soft moan escapes my lips before I can stop it, and my eyes lock with Vane's.

A jolt of electricity sparks through my body. His pupils are dilated, nostrils flared, and I can see the rapid pulse in his neck. I realize with a start that he's affected by this, too. The air between us feels impossibly charged.

Vyvyan's lips are scorching, and my breathing quickens. I find myself imagining Vane's lips on my body, his fangs in my flesh instead of hers. The fantasy is so vivid I can almost feel his hands on me, his body pressed against mine—wetness pools between my clenched thighs. My free hand claws the dry grass, seeking an anchor as the sensations threaten to overwhelm me.

"What do you feel?" Vane asks. His low voice sends warmth across my skin.

"*Everything*," I breathe, unable to look away from him.

A small, knowing smile tugs at the corners of his mouth. In the euphoria of the blood exchange, the hatred and resentment I've harbored toward him seems to melt away, replaced by a primal, urgent need.

He leans closer. "Desiree—"

Whatever Vane is going to say dies on his tongue as Vyvyan's wounds gradually heal. Her color returns to normal as her body expels the stake. It rolls into the grass, her skin knitting itself together. But I barely notice, lost in the anguish of Vane's gaze. I want him to touch me, to taste me like Vyvyan is. The desire is so strong it's almost overwhelming.

"That's enough, Desiree," Vane commands suddenly, his tone sharp.

I shake my head, not wanting this feeling to end. It is the first time I've felt happy since he and Vyvyan outed me in front of Misty. Vane cups my cheek. The contact sends my body into a spiral. I rub my cheek into his palm.

"I said, that's enough," he repeats softly, his thumb caressing my lower lip. My tongue darts out to taste him. Just as I remember, he tastes sinful, like pomegranates and red wine. "Don't let her take anymore from you. Leave some for yourself."

The intimate gesture, combined with the authoritative tone of his voice, sends another rush of heat through me until Vyvyan stops feeding from me. Emptiness caves through me like a void. The world spins slightly off-kilter as I sit back, lightheaded from blood loss and arousal. I blink to steady my attention as Vane fixes his gaze on Vyvyan, cradling her with so much reverence I want to scratch his eyes out for looking at anyone other than me with such adoration.

I want to . . . Shit. What have I done? I hate Vane, yet here I am, acting like he belongs to me.

"It wasn't you. It was the blood," Vane tells me.

I nod, unable to meet his gaze. The chasm within me threatens to swallow me whole. "I know," I lie.

Vane stares at Vyvyan. Already, she looks stronger. Her chest rises and falls with vitality, and the blood on her clothes is the only sign there'd been a struggle. In awe of Vyvyan's transformation, Vane's expression shifts from concern to profound gratitude. With Vyvyan stabilized, I pick up the stake, rising to my feet to throw it further into the trees. Anything to get away from the intimacy passing between them.

"Who attacked you?" I ask.

"Balam," Vane mutters.

"Balam? As in the daemon?" Surprise heightens my pitch.

"Yes. Caught us by surprise."

The pieces fall into place—the claw marks on Vane's body, the overwhelming sense of wrongness I felt upon arriving. Balam, a daemon with the strength of ten men whose curse is to obey its summoner, is not a force to be trifled with. The fact he was here, in our world, means someone summoned him. The question is, who? And why?

I push to my feet, swaying as I scan our wooded surroundings.

"What are you doing?" Vane asks, lips pursed.

"Daemons always leave behind some sort of signature related to their summoner," I explain while I search the ground. At first, I see nothing, but then—*there*. Faint impressions in the mud and leftover snow catch my eye.

"What is it?" Vane calls.

"Tracks." I crouch to examine them more closely. "Like from a dog, but bigger."

"How big?" The urgency in Vane's tone makes me look up.

I place my hand beside one of the prints. "Big."

Vane curses. "Not dogs. Wolves."

"Wolves as in—"

"Werewolves," Vane confirms.

An owl hoots, causing me to flinch. Wolves haven't set foot in Corona for hundreds of years, but their hatred for vampires is no secret. Our kind's history is fraught with betrayal and bloodshed, stemming from the time when rogue vampires fled to Lua, leaving destruction in their wake. Vyvyan's refusal to call them back, branding them traitors and deserters, deepened the rift.

Still, a werewolf attack is not a laughing matter. The other vampires may be at risk. "Who else knew you were meeting me here?" I ask, folding my arms.

Vane's silence speaks volumes.

"Who?" I press, watching him wince.

"No one," he insists, but there's a flicker of uncertainty in his eyes.

"What aren't you saying?"

Vane's gaze grows distant before he nods. "Well, we sent word to the Council that we were on our way, but no one answered."

I open my mouth to say more, but Vyvyan stirs more insistently in Vane's arms. We need to get her inside where it is safe.

"I think she's going to be okay," I say, bowing my head.

Vane nods, his gaze holding mine. "Thank you."

The heat that pulsed between us earlier returns, a tangible thing in the cool night air. I look away. Vane lied to me. He manipulated me into thinking he cared about me. Vane is the reason Misty is angry with me. Whatever I feel when I am around him is left over from before. He's grateful I helped Vyvyan, nothing more.

"If you were a minute later, Desiree," Vane continues, "I'm afraid of what might've happened. If the Balam came back, or—"

"We can't stay here," I interject, turning on my heel.

"But Vyvyan—"

"Is healing." I've never known Vyvyan to have a lover. I'm uncertain if she and Vane were ever together. He never shared intimate details about his past. Still, I hate seeing them together. "Until she stands and speaks coherent sentences on her own, we're not out of the woods. She'll need monitoring for any side effects, though."

"You were amazing tonight," Vane says, a shy smile playing at the corners of his mouth. "Vyvyan owes you her life."

"Let's hope she sees it that way when she wakes up." Vyvyan is going to kill me. I don't feel much of a pull toward her. That would change if she gave me her blood in return, but when she wakes up, she'll have a front-row seat to my life that resembles a melodrama.

"Let's go home," I say.

Vane adjusts Vyvyan in his arms. We move swiftly through the darkened park, neither of us speaking. As we reach the entrance to Little Death, I gather myself, and face Vane one last time. I wait for him to say something—anything. The silence becomes uncomfortable.

"Keep an eye on her, and I'll check on you both tomorrow," I tell him in a rush, then hurry down the stone steps into the club before Vane can respond.

As I lock myself in my coffin, I shut my eyes, and offer a silent prayer to whatever gods are listening. Vyvyan is going to be okay. She has to be. Because if she's not, I won't be either. The weight of what I've done—the blood bond I've created, linking myself to her, the lines I've crossed—settles over me like a shroud. I may never truly be free of tonight's consequences.

CHAPTER EIGHT
WILDER

"LEIGH!"

I tear through Rowan Palace, my shout echoing off the walls. Darkness engulfs me, thick and oppressive, broken only by the occasional flicker of the flames I've conjured to light my way. The silence is deafening compared to the palace's usual bustle. My heart booms in my ears—each beat a reminder of the precious seconds ticking by. She must be here.

The scent of burning plastic and chemicals drifts in through an open window, serving as a grim reminder of the pandemonium outside. Adrenaline surges through my veins, causing my vision to blur. I blink rapidly to clear it. Leigh hasn't been answering my calls. Was the blackout a distraction to get to her? Fear threatens to crush me.

"Leigh!" I holler again. The silence that follows is like a closed book.

I check my phone for the hundredth time. The screen's harsh glow reveals three missed calls from Soter, two messages from Jaxson, and one voicemail from Isolde. The city I've sworn to protect is falling apart, and I can't stop it. I think of my mom at the hospital, of Desiree in the Nest—are they safe? My dad's voice echoes in my head, disapproving and cold: *"If I were in your position, I would never have allowed this to happen."*

I grit my teeth.

I channel the lessons I learned from Commander Eddo during my year in Aurora. "Don't panic," I mutter, forcing deep breaths into my lungs. "Assess the direst situation first, then start from there." Leigh is the queen. Finding her is the priority. Though I admit she would be my priority even if she *weren't* queen.

I redial Leigh's number, but the call goes straight to voicemail. Cursing, I dial Gianna's number but get the same result.

"Where the hell is everyone?" I yell into the darkness.

Distant sirens pierce the night, accompanied by breaking glass and angry shouts. Uncertainty gnaws at me, threatening to unravel my fragile composure.

I stare at Leigh's last text. She'd sent it hours ago, before her Council meeting. My heart constricts painfully. If anything happened to her . . .

"Wilder, are you okay?" Leigh's voice cuts through the silence like a blade. Relief showers me so intensely that I must clutch the railing to keep from falling. I am so dizzy.

She appears at the top of the grand staircase. I take the stairs two at a time, scanning her for any sign of injury. I can't speak—can't move. The fear and panic of the past hour crashes over me, leaving me breathless.

"Say something; you're scaring me," she mutters. Leigh tucks a strand of hair behind her ear—a nervous gesture I've learned.

And suddenly, I'm laughing. It bubbles up from deep in my chest, bordering on hysterical. Leigh takes a step back.

"I'm scaring *you*?" I manage between gasps of laughter.

"Yes." She stares at me as if I've lost my mind. And maybe I have.

As quickly as it came, my laughter dies. I close the distance between us with three quick strides, my earlier fear morphing into something darker —more primal. Leigh swallows hard, and I watch the delicate movement of her throat. It would be so easy for someone to hurt her.

"When you didn't answer your phone, I panicked," I tell her.

Leigh blinks. "I—I'm sorry. I left my phone in the car. But I've been here. I'm trying to pinpoint who could be feeding Stellan his information. Who has the motive?"

I shake my head, crowding her until her back hits the wall. One of her ancestor's portraits glares down at me disapprovingly, but I couldn't care less. This is between us.

"You lost your phone in the middle of an emergency?"

"Y-yes." Her breath hitches.

I shake my head. "Leigh, what am I supposed to do with you?"

She holds up her hands in surrender. "I'm sorry."

"I was worried out of my skull," I admit, a bit harsher than intended. How could she be so careless?

"Awe, poor baby," she coos, gliding her hands up my chest. The touch sends sparks through my body, and I curse her hold on me. My life would be much easier if she weren't such a distraction. "What if your enemies find out the Blade Commander scares so easily?"

I groan, pressing my forehead to hers. The contact grounds me. Inhaling, I let Leigh's familiar violet scent wash over me. "I don't give a shit what anyone else thinks. You are what matters, which is why I am here when I should be out there—"

Leigh kisses me, soft and sweet, but pulls away before I can react.

Gods. I want her. All the fucking time.

"I'm sorry," she whispers again. "Thank you for checking on me, but I am fine and safe. I sent some of my guards to get Gianna, and the others are inspecting the perimeter."

"You drive me so goddamn crazy," I murmur. Leigh's eyes widen slightly, and a mix of emotions flashes across her face.

Say it, I urge her. I want to hear her say it.

I'm not going anywhere. She can rely on me if she can't rely on anyone else.

"I'm sorry." This time, there's a hint of a smile playing on her face. "I'll try to be more careful."

I sigh, tearing a hand through my hair. "You better."

She nods, her expression softening. "I promise."

Good.

"How bad is it out there?" Leigh asks, worry creasing her brow.

"Bad," I admit. The streets remind me of a dystopian novel. People are fighting, looting, and scared for their lives.

Leigh rolls her bottom lip between her teeth. "What caused the blackout?"

"I don't know yet, but I have Soter looking into it."

"Well, while he's at it, he should look for Janus Dyer."

"What do you mean? Where is the president?" I ask.

Leigh snorts. "Your guess is as good as mine. She no-showed to our Council meeting." Her gaze darkens. "She did it on purpose."

"Woah." I steady her with my hands on her shoulders. "Slow down. What do you mean?"

"I can't present changes—"

"No, sorry, what do you mean she no-showed?"

"She called and said she wasn't coming, and then the power outage happened."

My attention drifts out the window facing the city, and unease tightens my shoulders. If Janus is out there and in trouble, we need to find her.

Without another word, I release Leigh and take out my phone, bringing it to my ear.

"Who are you calling?" Leigh asks, touching her face.

"Soter."

"Why?"

"To tell him about Janus."

Leigh's brow wrinkles. "Do you think she's in trouble?"

"It's possible." Considering how I overreacted about Leigh, I don't want to jump to any conclusions about Janus. But we can't be too careful until we know what's going on.

"Oh, gods." Leigh starts to pace. "What if something happened to her?"

"It's going to be—Soter!"

"It's about fucking time," Soter replies. "Did you find her?"

"Yes," I grumble.

Soter laughs, but there's no humor in it. "I told you so."

"When you are done preening, we have a new situation on our hands."

Soter stops laughing. "What sort of situation?"

"Janus Dyer called out of the Council meeting before the blackout. I want to know why," I explain, and Soter curses under his breath. "Find her and ensure her safety. But don't alert the media. We don't need the whole city searching for her in this circus."

"What do you want me to do?" he asks. "Go to her house?"

"Where are you now?"

"Poseidon's Wharf," Soter replies, and I scratch my head. He's too far. Janus and her wife live in Broomwood. Leigh watches me with vast, worried eyes.

"Jaxson's closer," I reply. "I'll have him go."

Leigh says something.

I cover my phone's mouthpiece and lower it. "What?"

"The vampires," Leigh says, her hands clench at her sides. "They didn't show up either."

That's suspicious. Dread settles over me like an icy cloak.

"WILDER!" Soter screams into my phone.

I cringe and raise it. "What?" I snap.

"I know what caused the blackout," Soter says darkly.

"What is it now?" Leigh's eyes search mine.

I put my phone on speaker. "Soter, you're on speakerphone with Leigh."

"Hi, Leigh," Soter purrs, but there's an edge to his voice.

"What's going on?" Leigh asks, all business. Gone is my girlfriend, and in her place is my queen, her spine straight, her gaze fierce.

Soter clears his throat. "Wilder, check your messages. I just sent you Stellan Navis's latest article. You will want to read this."

Leigh peers at my phone as I open the attachment.

The Tower Tribune

CHAOS REIGNS

The Queen's Failures Laid Bare

By Stellan Navis

AS darkness engulfs half the nation due to the Bersa Power Station workers' strike, demanding higher wages from Epsilon Plant owner Michael Bersa, who refused to increase pay following the War Letters revelation, one thing is crystal clear: Queen Leigh's leadership is severely lacking.

Plant workers left their posts this afternoon, leaving the plant undermanned. This caused a fire, which darkened parts of Aurora and several other cities, including the capital. These cities share the Bersa Station grid. Countless citizens are left without power, and lives are in disarray.

Where is our queen during this crisis? Instead of demanding a solution or retribution for the Nebula people, she spent the evening swapping stories with the Council. She is too self-absorbed to realize that the Nebula people her ancestors betrayed are crying out for her. She has tunnel vision, prioritizing her pet projects over the needs of the masses.

We need better leadership.

I plan to provide that leadership. Consider this article my official bid for Mayor of Aurora. I am kicking off my campaign now and will see that Aurora and the Nebula people are cared for. We will no longer be ignored or left in the dark. It's time for a change, and I am ready to lead us into a brighter —

"That bastard," Leigh screeches. "I was going to propose dismantling the Labor Laws as well as the Lunar Witch centers, but his articles riled up the damn Council too much for them to listen to me!"

I stop reading. My fist clenches around my phone. Leigh is seething, her face flushed.

"Soter, I am going to have to call you back," I say.

"Someone on the Council is Stellan's source." Leigh's voice shakes with rage.

I glance between my phone and Leigh. "That's what he claims, but you can't know for su—"

"No. I believe it. Most of what he says is too personal." Leigh paces before me again, her footsteps heavy on the floor.

"What about your grandmother?" I ask, and Leigh shoots me a death glare. But then she pauses. I can practically see the wheels turning in her head. Don betrayed her, so why wouldn't Jorina?

"Hmm," Leigh muses, her brow furrowed. "My grandmother knows about my intentions with the Lunar Witches. But why betray me? She has nothing to gain." She goes silent. But then adds, "Janus wasn't at the meeting tonight . . ."

The hair on the back of my neck lifts. "Leigh, you should talk to Jorina and Janus before you drive yourself mad with conspiracy theories," I say. "They might've advised you to pause on your Lunar Witch endeavors, but assisting Stellan seems brash."

"True, but what should I think, given the circumstances? Someone is betraying me and the Council, and until we learn who, the Council will be at odds. It's what Stellan wants."

I pinch the bridge of my nose. "Leigh."

"The president is purposely being vague, Borealis is in shambles, and Stellan Navis, who is intent on sowing division, has declared that he's running for mayor. What am I supposed to do, Wilder? I can't deal with everything happening here and what's happening there. But someone has to stop him. Another article, and I am afraid he'll push us all over the edge."

I nod. Leigh's right. Someone needs to deal with Stellan and see to the power outage issues, but she can't be in two places at once. I don't want to go, but Leigh needs someone she trusts to align Aurora with Borealis. I fear that if Stellan continues to post his rhetoric, he may achieve the support of all Nebula there and here, at the cost of angering a lot of influential Epsilon. They won't stay quiet for long. And when they retaliate, it won't be pretty.

"I'll do it." Leigh's eyes widen at my words. "I'll go to Aurora, tend to the power outages, and find Stellan."

"And get him to shut down his paper?" she asks, a hopeful note in her voice.

"Technically, he hasn't done anything wrong," I tell her.

Leigh groans, rubbing her temples. "Stellan is turning all the Nebula people against me." My heart aches for her. "He is running for mayor, building his platform by taking me down."

"Let me talk to him. I used to live in Aurora. I have friends there. They will help me find him, and when I do, I can convince him that if he keeps publishing those articles, he will have a civil war on his hands."

Leigh isn't looking at me anymore. Her equerry is walking up the stairs.

"Yes?" she asks the tall, decorated woman, her voice hard.

"There's someone here to see you," the equerry says. Leigh and I exchange wary glances.

"Now?" My hand instinctively reaches for my weapon.

Leigh notices and rolls her eyes. "Who?"

"A representative from Lua."

My eyes narrow at the equerry's reply.

"Lua? The wolves?" Leigh purses her lips.

"But why now?" I ask. Of course, they show up when the city is at its most vulnerable. They could mean her harm, but Leigh is already heading down the stairs.

"Leigh! Wait," I protest, but my phone rings. It's Soter. Goddammit. It could be about Janus. "Fuck." I point at the equerry. "Alert the guards if you haven't already. Stay with her."

"It's my job to keep her safe. I suggest you do yours," the equerry says, then she hastens after Leigh.

With Janus missing in action, Stellan's rising influence, and now the wolves at our door, I fear we're in for a rough ride and not the enjoyable kind.

CHAPTER NINE
LEIGH

AS I MAKE my way toward the throne room, shadows press in. With each step, my mind races.

Lua is already at my doorstep, and the fact I had no idea they were even in my country has me jumping at every little sound. It isn't as if I'm alone—there are always numerous attendants inside the palace. My equerry traipses behind me. Her breathing is loud in the heavy silence. I wrap my arms around myself, trying to ward off the cold that emanates from within, but it is useless. My world is crumbling.

I nod to my equerry, then step inside the throne room to meet Lua's representative.

The large gold-painted walls gleam before me. Sizable chandeliers hang from the sloped ceilings, and crystal sconces catch the moonlight. Mirrored walls scatter its brilliance in dazzling patterns. During the day, they reflect sunshine pouring in from outside, filling the room with otherworldly light. My breath catches in my throat.

A stranger sits upon my throne.

His posture is relaxed and confident, as if he belongs there. He is a reed-like man, perhaps in his late twenties, with thick, short, coal-black hair, and golden-brown skin. His heavy threaded clothes, more suitable for the northern climate, are out of place here, but they mold to his body like a second skin. He appears to be talking to himself, yet that's not the strangest thing about him.

He's not a werewolf. He's a witch.

He doesn't have elongated canines or pointed ears.

"Comfortable, isn't it?" My voice rings through the space. He jolts when my voice echoes off the walls.

The Lua representative shoots to his feet. "Your Majesty," he says with an accent can't quite place. "Forgive me. My curiosity got the better of me. I never should have—"

"Who are you?" I interrupt, folding my arms across my chest. The witch opens and closes his mouth. I forge ahead. "Well? Who the hell are you? Are you really from Lua, or was that a lie to get my attention?"

The stranger steps toward me. "Your Majesty, please, I mean you no harm. I am a friend—more than that. I am *family.* My name is Ravi Deyanira. I am distantly related to Ivah, Aradia's sister. I guess you could say we are cousins. Like you, I am a Lunar Witch."

My glare could melt tungsten. In the television broadcast I made before my coronation, I mentioned hoping to find my lost family members. It seems too much of a coincidence that one has found me now, dressed in wolves' clothing, in the middle of a disaster when my kingdom is most vulnerable.

"Fuck you," I say, my voice cold.

"What?"

"Do you want money? Is that it?" Ravi blinks at the bite of my words. "Are you here to exploit me?"

Ravi shakes his head. "No. I am here to help you."

"Liar," I spit.

He doesn't know me. No one is that selfless.

"Why would I lie? I don't need money."

My laugh is bitter. "Who do you work for?"

He hesitates, and I see red. I don't get the chance to continue before he says, "Prince Alden Lupas."

King Simon's second son. "A witch working with wolves? Forgive me if I call your bluff."

Ravi exhales. "Are you always this suspicious?"

I'm a product of my circumstances, so yes.

"I bet you aren't even a Lunar Witch. You probably—"

Ravi closes his eyes, and his body slumps back onto the throne. I gasp as his astral form rises from his body, shimmering but not translucent. He stands before me with a smug smile on his face. His eyes glow with an otherworldly horror.

"Do you believe me now?" he asks, his voice ringing strangely.

I can only nod, too stunned to speak, as Aradia's voice whispers, *He can teach you magic, Leigh.*

I shake my head. I have more pressing matters than learning magic from this trickster. And just because he is a Lunar Witch doesn't mean we are related, or that he knows Prince Alden. The proof is in the details.

Ravi does have Ivah's bone structure, Aradia says.

I close my eyes, praying for strength.

Ravi's astral form sinks back into his body. He opens his eyes, meeting my gaze.

"What do you want?" I ask.

Ravi presses his lips into a thin line. "Officially, I'm here on behalf of Prince Alden Lupas of Lua. He requests a visit to discuss the possibility of an alliance between your people. The sooner, the better. He is at your disposal." Ravi retrieves a missive from his pocket with a wolf insignia in a teal seal. He holds it out to me.

I snatch it.

Inside, the script signed by Alden claims the wolves want to open negotiations for continued peace and need Corona's resources. Oil reserves are running low in the north, and they want access to our oil fields in Aurora. Alden hopes to come to a solution that will benefit our countries and wishes to visit in two days' time.

I frown. Corona and Lua have been enemies for a long time, fighting over resources—mainly oil—and territory. If the wolves wanted peace, they would have accepted my coronation invite. Prince Zeus is Simon's heir, the golden boy of Lua. Alden Lupas is the Lua enforcer, the cutthroat leading the king's armies.

"If Lua wants peace, why not send Zeus to discuss terms?" I ask.

Ravi lowers his outstretched hand. "Zeus won't leave his father's ailing side. Alden is acting on their behalf." Or Alden wants to suss out the competition, so he knows what size army to use when he tries to invade us.

I peer at Ravi. Why would Alden Lupas send this witch to talk to me instead of coming himself? To seem like less of a threat. Does he know Ravi is claiming to be my ancestor?

"You said you are here *officially* to deliver the missive," I point out. Ravi shifts. "What about unofficially?"

Ravi's expression darkens. "Unofficially, I'm here to warn you. You must refuse the invitation. Don't let Alden come. He—"

"*What?*" I snap. Is he serious? "You want me to guarantee war by dishonoring Alden's request for peace? I'm sorry, but are you high?"

"No. But—"

"So, you have a death wish? Because if I do that, I'll be digging both our graves." My voice rises with every word. Who the fuck is this guy? Is he trying to goad me into disrespecting Lua, so Alden has an excuse to attack? It's the only explanation that makes sense.

Ravi steps forward. "The wolves can't be trusted. If—"

"Obviously!" I snap. Ravi gapes at me. "But if I reject Alden, he will have every excuse to invade."

"You're making a mistake," Ravi quietly replies.

I scoff. "If Alden thought sending you to pretend to be my family would convince me to give him an excuse to go to war, he seriously underestimates me. We are not family—but even if we were, that doesn't mean anything." Not anymore. Don ensured that.

Something dark slots into place over Ravi's eyes, erasing his wide-eyed mask. Is this his true face?

"Tell Alden I will have a room made up for him," I say. "We look forward to his arrival." We better have power by then. Ravi bows and then leaves, his footsteps thundering in the empty throne room. I'm brimming with dread. My hands won't stop shaking. I just invited the wolves into my country.

That took an unexpected turn. Didn't it, Dynamite? my father's ghost says.

"It did," I reply. "Now what?"

Invite him back, and tell him you are sorry, Aradia suggests.

Hell will freeze over before that happens. "Anything else?"

Talk to your mother. You need people you can rely on right now, Father's ghost says.

Father's right, but not about Mother. Her withdrawal has proved that I cannot count on her. Someone on my Council is betraying secrets to Stellan. The wolves are coming, and Janus is still missing. Somehow, I need to find Stellan's mole while convincing Alden that Corona is intact, powerful, and not to be trifled with—even when we're on the brink of collapse. Wolves are predators. If they smell blood, they will attack.

As I leave the throne room, Aradia says, *I know what you're thinking, and I don't know if I like it.*

If I am going to emerge from Alden's visit unscathed, I need advice from someone who has mastered the art of deception. "I want to see if Gianna is home yet."

CHAPTER TEN
WILDER

AS WE TRUDGE BACK into the Blade Precinct, the sun is just beginning to peek over the horizon. Our bodies are heavy with exhaustion. I've been breaking up fights, putting out fires, and ensuring the blackout didn't cause any irreparable damage. Most places have backup generators, but areas like the Burned-Over District remain shrouded in darkness. Smoke clings to our clothes, and the gritty feeling of tiredness burns in our eyes. But I still need to tell my team I am going to Aurora. We need to come up with a plan for while I am gone.

I collapse into a chair at the large, oval table in the debriefing room. Scattered pens and notepads litter the surface. Soter sits across from me while Isolde leans against the wall, her arms crossed tightly, as she stays as far away from Soter as possible. The whiteboard behind us is a blank canvas, wiped clean of the chaotic scribbles and diagrams that once mapped out our latest case.

"I go to Aurora in two days," I announce, and Soter narrows his eyes.

"You can't fucking leave," Isolde says.

"It's already been decided," I say. Leigh sent me a message about her time spent with the Lua representative, who happened not to be a wolf but a witch. She mentioned that the witch, Ravi, said he was her distant cousin, but she didn't believe him, given his ties to Alden. It seems too quick to dismiss his claims, but I understand her hesitancy. Trust doesn't come easily to her. But when I pressed her for details, her texts stopped. She probably fell asleep. At least, I hope that's the case. I wanted to stay with her during the visit, but a prison breach required my attention. The power outage had left jail cells unlocked, with prisoners wandering the halls—we nearly had a full mutiny on our hands.

"You are needed here," Soter says.

I blink between them. There was a chance they would gripe about my departure, but I didn't think they would outright refute it. "Soter, you're in charge," I announce.

Isolde balks. "Are you kidding?"

I groan. "Soter is Domna."

She shakes her head, her blue hair catching in the morning sun. "I refuse to answer to *him*."

"Excuse you, I have a name!" Soter yells.

Isolde laughs. "Yeah, *Satan*."

"Is that so?" Soter grins. "Well, honey, if this is Hell, I am dragging you down with me."

I trail a hand down my face. Neither of them has that little voice inside their head—the one that keeps people from saying things they shouldn't. I'm too tired for them both to have a tantrum.

"I learned my lesson the first time. I'm not going anywhere with you, ever," Isolde growls.

Soter rises to his feet, fingers clawing at the table. "I happen to remember it being more than onc—"

"Shut up! Both of you! You are Blades. Start acting like professionals, or get the fuck out of my precinct," I yell. They both fall silent, gaping at me.

Isolde yanks out a chair to sit. "We're up to our necks in shit here, and you're just going to take off?"

"Look, I know the timing sucks, but I volunteered to go. We need the power back online, and someone needs to talk to Stellan. I know Aurora. My friends are there, and I know the power station's owner. I can make a difference and help ease the situation."

Soter raises an eyebrow. "Friends? Wilder, when did you last speak to anyone in Aurora?"

I brush off his question. It's been months since I responded to texts and emails, but they know I am overworked. They'll understand. "Soter, I need you to contact Commander Eddo to arrange my arrival with the Aurora precinct."

Soter nods, his jaw tight. "I'll take care of it. But, Wilder, are you sure—"

The door to the debrief room bursts open, and Jaxson stumbles in with an exhausted expression.

"Janus is safe," he shares before collapsing into the chair beside me. "But she's not talking. She says she can't tell anyone where she's been. Has anyone made coffee?"

A knot tightens in my gut. "Janus is the president, Jaxson. She can't just disappear and then refuse to explain herself."

"Coffee's brewing, but you can have this." Isolde slides a power bar toward Jax.

Jaxson tears the wrapper, saying, "I tried to get her to talk. But she says it's classified. I can't exactly force her."

I sink my teeth into my bottom lip. Leigh is going to think the worst about Janus. Fucking perfect.

Jax clears his throat. When I turn to him, his expression is uneasy. "There's something else, Wilder. Pallas and I spoke on my way here. He mentioned that Prince Alden Lupas is visiting Leigh the day you leave for Aurora. Leigh invited him to stay at the palace."

During Nyx's trial, Pallas has been bunking with me at Desiree's old loft. He testified last week, ensuring Chiron remains a permanent resident in his little cell beneath the sea. The trial has been hard on him, but now that it's over, I guess I have my answer to what he will do to keep busy.

"I know that Alden is coming to discuss an alliance with Leigh, but how the hell does Pallas know that?" Alden coming to stay with Leigh while I am away doesn't sit well with me. I trust her, but his reputation precedes him. He's about as moral as an alley cat.

I hold up a hand when Jaxson opens his mouth. "Don't tell me because then I will have to do something about it."

"Wilder, I think you should reconsider Aurora. With Alden visiting and Janus going silent, Leigh needs trustworthy people. She needs you," Isolde says.

"And what about Marlowe?" Soter asks.

A chill spreads over me at the thought of leaving when issues keep piling up. But at the same time, I know I can't turn my back on Aurora; everything happening there affects us here.

"I hear you both." I sigh. "But, Soter, I trust you'll keep an eye out for Marlowe and run the show." My attention moves to Isolde. "You're right. Leigh needs trustworthy people around her, so I'm sending you to the palace to keep an eye on her."

Isolde fists her hands atop the table. "You want me to play chaperone for your girlfriend?"

"Is there a problem?"

Sol clenches her jaw but doesn't fight back.

Soter takes a breath. "So, Isolde gets to play princess while I have to do all the work?"

"Soter, you have a team of Blades at your disposal, which includes Jaxson." Jaxson's smile fades at this. "He's to be your second-in-command while I'm gone. He can search for Marlowe while you run things."

"My week just got a lot worse," Jax grumbles with a look at Soter. Soter glares back.

I swallow to force down my annoyance. Jax never wants to take on more responsibility. He had the chance to compete in the upcoming Domna Trials in Glaucus, but he refused to put himself out there, content to coast instead. I thought that with me as commander, he would take more initiative, but I was wrong. I still trust him more than anyone and need him at the center of things while I'm gone.

I roll back my chair to stand. "I need to go to the palace. Jaxson, you're with me. Isolde, go pack, and meet us there when you are done. Soter, do something productive. And please, try not to burn the place down while I'm away."

Soter folds his arms. "Why does Jaxson get to go with you? I'm your Domna."

I frown. "Because he told me about Janus."

"Idiot," Isolde mumbles.

As Jaxson and I leave the precinct, an overwhelming weight tugs at my heart, pulling me in a thousand different directions. Leaving Borealis and Leigh is a painful separation, the hardest thing I have ever faced. Yet, the chance to create a real difference in Aurora sparks a determination within me. I know I must embrace this opportunity, even if it requires temporarily sacrificing my happiness.

I just hope that when I come back, there will still be a city left to protect and a woman waiting for me.

CHAPTER ELEVEN
DESIREE

IT'S LATE. After what happened with Vyvyan and the Balam, sleep evades me. I toss and turn in my coffin, the velvet lining clinging to my sweat-dampened skin as thoughts of Vane plague my mind. Heat crawls down my neck as I relive my body's reaction while Vyvyan drank my blood. I wanted Vane so badly—craved his touch—and was ready to say, "*Fuck it*," letting him take me right there in the dirt, with Vyvyan dying beside us.

It wasn't me. Whatever I am still feeling is the result of the blood-sharing. I don't want Vane—not after how he treats me. How could I when he's the reason I lost Misty? Vyvyan doesn't want me either, but she is stuck with me. My blood binds me to her. When she heals, she will sense every emotion I express. If I had her blood, I'd feel just how much she hates me—viscerally, not mentally.

With a groan, I push the lid of my coffin open. It squeals on ancient hinges. Beside me, Misty's coffin lies empty, and so do dozens of others. She and many other vampires are not back from the club yet. Misty and I haven't talked since everything went down in Vyvyan's room. I was giving her space, but now it gapes like a trench.

I pull a sweatshirt over my tiny tank and sleep shorts before creeping into the hall to catch her on her way back. It's barely past sunrise, but we close the club at dawn.

I wait in the hallway, my gaze shifting each time someone walks past me. A restless energy has me pacing back and forth. After what feels like an eternity, Misty's familiar laughter bounces off the walls. She appears around the corner, walking with her sire, Zev. They speak in hushed tones. Whatever he's saying is meant only for her ears—a private bond between sire and progeny that twists my stomach with envy. I'll never experience that kind of connection.

"Misty," I call, my voice small with uncertainty. The laughter leaves her eyes. "Can we talk?"

Misty folds her arms across her chest. Her brocade corset, pleated leather skirt, and boots give off a sinful schoolgirl look that probably had the Little Death clientele pining for her attention. "I'm talking to Zev."

I offer Zev an apologetic look. "It's important."

Misty scoffs, but Zev steps in to say, "It's okay, Misty. I'm tired anyway." My heart swells with gratitude toward him, even though he's probably just helping me because he owes my brother for helping him stay in contact with his wife. He must know I lied about Vane siring me. Misty told *everyone*.

As soon as he's gone, I say, "Vane means nothing to me," but the words taste like ash.

Misty tucks a scarlet ringlet behind her ear. She is hopeless with an iron, which means she asked someone other than me to help her get ready last night. "Well, that makes sense since you have Jaxson."

Even though Jaxson and I are in limbo, I nod. He's had ample opportunity to ask me out since learning I faked my death, but he hasn't, and I don't know what that means. I'm not even sure how I feel about it. Should vampires and witches even date? "You're right. I have Jaxson," I say anyway.

"You're a terrible friend and a worse liar," Misty snaps. "You never wanted me to be with Vane. Is that why Jaxson dumped you? Because you're a lying, cheating whore?"

I back up a step, blood singing in my veins. "Cheating? I never cheated on Jaxson."

"How am I supposed to know that?" she asks with a bite to her words. Misty is projecting what happened to her onto me. "You've been lying to me since we met."

"But not about that."

Misty laughs, the sound harsh and grating. "Too late. You've squandered my trust."

"No, you don't understand. Vyvyan ord—"

"Is everything okay here, Misty?" A group of vampires returning from Little Death slide accusing gazes over me like slippery serpents.

"We are fine," I choke out, but Misty approaches them.

"No, Desiree and I are finished."

My heart shatters into a thousand tiny shards.

Her words have a subtext, a finality that goes beyond this moment. She means in more ways than one, and how the others gaze upon me with disgust, they are done with me, too. I am cast out like last year's style.

"Come on, let's go," Misty says.

They leave me in the hall with my jaw on the floor.

I consider charging after them to plead my case, but they won't listen to me. They will, however, listen to Vyvyan. Turning on my heel, I charge down the hallway, my bare feet slapping against stone.

Fingering the tiny scars on my neck, I knock on Queen Vyvyan's door, the sound too loud in the morning stillness. She doesn't answer, and I am positive she is asleep, but I advised Vane to watch over her and told him I would check on her.

"Open the fucking door, Vane. It's Desiree, and you have three seconds—"

The door flies open, revealing a disgruntled Vane. His usually artfully tousled white-blond hair is a mess, and his perfect clothes from Equinox Park are still bloody and muddy.

"Desiree, now isn't a good time," he murmurs. But I am finished with him and Vyvyan dictating my life.

"We need to talk. Misty and the others—"

"Is that her?" Vyvyan calls, her voice weak and thready. Vane stiffens.

"Vyvyan, it's Desiree. We need to talk!"

"Let her in, Vane."

When Vane clenches his jaw, a muscle ticks in his cheek. "Don't say I didn't warn you, Desiree."

I push past him, muttering to myself that he is a controlling bastard, then stop dead in my tracks.

Vyvyan's room looks like a hurricane tore through it. All her luxurious belongings are strewn about. The plush carpet and silk sheets are a ripped casualty of the chaos. Blood seeps into the ancient rug from the shattered bar cart and decanter, the coppery scent filling the air. But that's not the worst of it. Not by a long shot. Vyvyan stands across the room in her silk sleep dress with one strap falling off her sculpted shoulder while she uses her other arm to clutch a bedpost for dear life. Sweat dampens her dark skin.

"Come to finish the job?" Vyvyan taunts. Her brown—not red—eyes narrow.

"Y-you're human?"

"No shit. You made me this way."

The world tilts on its axis, threatening to send me spiraling into an abyss.

"Is this your idea of a joke?" I ask, my legs giving out like a newborn fawn's.

Vane catches me, but his hold feels like a noose. I push at him to release me.

"How is she human?" I gasp, my voice barely above a whisper as my vision blurs.

Vyvyan glares at me. "You tell me!"

"M-me?" I shake my head. There's no way. Vampires share blood during consort ceremonies all the time. It tethers two vampires together and symbolizes marriage. I've never heard of anyone turning their mate human.

"Your blood cursed me," Vyvyan snarls.

I squeeze Vane's arm. "I don't understand. How? What is wrong with me?"

Vane shushes me, but I barely notice. My blood turned Vyvyan human. It's unthinkable. I'm an abomination—a vampire with the power to unmake vampires. I almost laugh. My mom is searching for a cure, and I *am* one.

"Turn her back," I say to Vane, my voice shaking.

"We already tried," he says at the same time Vyvyan orders, "Kill her."

"What? Why?" I cry out.

Vane's stare darkens with emotions I can't quite decipher.

"Your blood is a blight against our kind. We need to get rid of you before the witches find out what you can do," Vyvyan says. "They will use you against us. The ultimate weapon."

I jerk out of Vane's hold, stumbling into the overturned settee. My heart beats so hard I might pass out. I'm going to die, my life snuffed out by the very people I thought were my family.

"Please, you're not thinking clearly," I beg, but Vyvyan silences me with a sharp look. A sob escapes my throat. There must be an explanation. "I couldn't have done this. I'm a vampire. I have no magic."

"You must've maintained the ability to heal, Desi," Vane comments, merely watching as tears slide down my cheeks.

Most vampires don't maintain any magical abilities after they turn, but somehow, like Vane, I did. I don't have covetable powers like him, and my abilities will alienate me.

"Give it time," I whisper. "My blood must be working through your system. You won't turn back until you've digested it."

Vyvyan and Vane exchange guarded glances. "How long?" Vane questions.

"It depends on how fast she metabolizes it."

"Give me a number!" Vyvyan roars.

I flinch. "It takes thirty-six hours for food to pass through the body. But since it's magic, let's make it a week, at least."

I'm buying time, and they know it.

Vyvyan turns away, jaw clenched tight. "I still think you should die."

Vane shrugs, and nausea threatens to overwhelm me.

"What if we banish her instead?" Vane asks.

Banishment. A fate worse than death. Vampires need companionship to survive. The Nest is the first place I've felt accepted. If I leave, I may never find that again.

"There's a chance she'll tell," Vyvyan says.

"Let me help you," I blurt out. "I'll find out who sent the Balam while you heal. Vane will lead in your stead. During that time, I'll monitor your progress, and if nothing changes in a week, you can decide if I am still a liability."

Vyvyan considers me. "Witches are practiced liars. No one will admit they summoned Balam to kill me. It is obvious they mean to destroy our alliance."

My head falls sideways. I'm not convinced the witches sent the Balam. The paw print signature points to the wolves. But I'm not about to freak Vyvyan out. If wolves are in Corona, I will find them.

"I'm friends with witches. You said it yourself. I am connected to them, whether you like it or not." My heart is lodged in my throat. "I will find out who did this."

"She can help, Vyv," Vane admits.

I balk. I expected him to insist Vyvyan banish me. Now that everyone knows he is my sire, I am sure he isn't pleased about the unwanted attention.

Vyvyan hesitates, then nods. "Fine. But not a word of this investigation to anyone, or there will be hell to pay. If the witches sent Balam to kill me, they'll only try again while I am in this weakened state."

Vane nods. "Desiree is good at keeping quiet."

"She's good at causing a ruckus," Vyvyan states. She reaches for Vane. "Now, help me to bed. I am tired."

As Vane helps Vyvyan to bed, suspicion gnaws at me. With Vyvyan gone, Vane stands to gain the vampire kingdom, yet he's never shown an interest in the throne. Then again, he never told me much about his aspirations or past. Could his devotion to Vyvyan have all be an act, just like it was with me?

CHAPTER TWELVE
LEIGH

THE SIZZLING of eggs and the aroma of breakfast fill the palace's poorly lit kitchen, though the comforting scents do nothing to quell my troubled thoughts. With the spatula poised in my hand, I replay last night's Council meeting, grappling with the unsettling absence of Janus. Gianna slumps at the bar, her head cradled in her hands, topaz eyes glued to me, radiating concern and curiosity.

Exhaustion crushes me as I replay Janus's last-minute cancelation—which happened just moments before everything plunged into darkness. It was too perfect, too convenient. As president, she controls every shred of classified information, and the thought of her feeding it to our enemies, particularly Stellan, tightens my throat. Could Janus betray me after what transpired against us? I never intended to poison her. But the pieces align too neatly—she could easily exploit this chaos to turn the people against me while projecting the composed, trustworthy leader they crave. Gods, I loathe how paranoid I sound, but in the treacherous game of politics, coincidences rarely exist.

The palace generator hums in the background, bleakly reminding me that while we have backup power, most of the city remains engulfed in darkness. Due to the blackout, I gave most of the staff the day off to tend to their families, leaving me alone to tackle breakfast. It's a task I am woefully unqualified for.

"Are you sure you don't want some help?" Gianna asks.

I face her, the apron secured around my waist flowing around my legs. "I told you; I am cooking your breakfast."

"It looks like you're making enough to feed an army," Gi remarks while surveying the spread of eggs, toast, sausages, and hash browns.

"I might have invited a few friends," I admit, prodding the eggs with the spatula. "Does this look done to you?"

My father's ghost sighs in exasperation. *I've failed you*, he jokes.

One of Gi's sculpted eyebrows shoots up. "Who did you invite?"

Before I can answer, a voice cuts through the kitchen. "Is something burning?"

I turn to meet Bennett's puzzled stare, and my eyes widen. "Shit! The toast!"

I rush to the sizable multi-slice toaster. Smoke billows from its slots. I choke on the scent of charred bread. With wooden tongs, I remove a piece as black as graphite.

"I am not eating that," Gianna says.

"I thought charcoal was good for you?" I tease just as the eggs begin to furiously sizzle on the stove.

Bennett reaches the pan before I do, taking the eggs off the burner before they become inedible. He empties the pan onto a plate, cracking pepper over the eggs, and then turns his focus on the sausages and hash browns. His every movement is flawless with expertise.

I watch him, my mouth nearly agape. "I didn't know you could cook."

During our relationship, Bennett never offered to cook for me, but it makes sense, given that we both have staff available.

"My parents loved to cook," Bennett explains as he plates the hash browns.

I nod, a twinge of guilt aching in my chest. "I didn't know that."

"Yeah, my mother refused to let anyone in her kitchen, though she usually burned everything, like you." Bennett laughs, his eyes distant with memory.

Bennett's wistful tone tugs at my heartstrings, tempting me to abandon my original plan. I had asked him to breakfast to get him to tell me about his connection to Corvina, but now I hesitate. Are they simply friends, or is there something more between them?

Bennett's lie about Corvina haunts me, but I need him. He's my link to Janus—the only Council member who can confirm if she's feeding information to Stellan. Confronting him now would risk putting us at odds. I can't afford that with the stakes this high. So, I swallow my questions, lock away my doubts, and focus on what matters: Keeping the Council united and the country stable. The truth about Corvina can wait.

"You need an extra plate," I say. Bennett pauses, glancing over his shoulder at Gianna, who shrugs. He obliges.

We arrange four plates of food, and by the time I am gathering silverware, our fourth guest arrives. Pallas slinks into the kitchen, bypassing Gianna, and heads straight for the plate with his name on it. He snags it from Bennett, who hesitates, confusion wrinkling his brow.

"Why is he here?" Bennett asks as Pallas takes his first bite. His amethyst-colored hair is windswept, as if he walked or jogged here.

I untie my apron.

"I've asked you all here to help me spy on Janus," I say. Gianna chokes on her eggs.

Bennett gapes at me while Pallas continues to eat.

"Look," I go on, "without evidence, I am not accusing Janus of anything, but with Alden's upcoming visit, presenting a united front that the country is not in shambles is important. Finding Stellan's mole ensures Corona remains safe from invasion."

"You think Janus is his source?" Bennett asks, his face pale.

"That's what I want your help figuring out."

Bennett laughs, and the sound grates on my nerves. "Leigh, that's preposterous."

"Someone on the Council is working with Stellan," I insist, and Bennett's laughter dies, his face growing serious. "Unless you know who it is, my suspicion lies with Janus. We rule her out first before we focus on someone else."

Bennett stares at his untouched plate, guilt and uncertainty etched in the tight line of his mouth. I understand his reluctance. He's hardly regained any standing among the other Councilors since admitting he worked with Eos. But with the wolves coming, we can't risk having Janus anywhere near Alden if she's plotting with Stellan. One leaked detail to the wrong person could destroy everything we've built.

If Bennett uncovers Janus's deceit, he'll be helping me immensely. His actions could expose a dangerous threat and prevent further damage to our nation's peace. It's a chance for him to redeem himself and prove his trustworthiness.

I lean forward, my voice low and earnest. "Bennett, I wouldn't ask this of you if I didn't believe it was necessary. We need to know the truth about Janus's whereabouts last night, and you're the only one I know who can get close to her without raising suspicion."

"How can I help?" Pallas asks while Bennett stares into his food.

I smile, glad at least he is on board.

"I need you to track Janus's communications—find out who she's been in contact with. Watch her movements, see who she meets in private. We need to know if there's a pattern."

Pallas nods, his expression stern with determination.

"What about Gianna?" Bennett asks. "What's her role in this?"

Gianna's stare meets mine, our late-night discussion about Alden and Ravi heavy between us. A simple business deal wouldn't require the prince to journey hundreds of miles when a phone call would suffice. No, I suspect his true purpose is to evaluate Corona's defenses, to determine whether it's ripe for taking.

Gi gave me tips on keeping him entertained during his visit. By presenting strength and stability, I can ensure Corona appears formidable. When Alden leaves, he must believe any attempt to challenge my rule would be futile.

"Gianna already played her part," I hedge.

Bennett's brows lift. "That's reassuring."

"Are you going to help us, Bennett?" I ask.

Bennett's penetrating gaze bounces among us until his ocean eyes land on mine. "I'll try."

Fantastic. "Janus is planning a luncheon tomorrow for the prince. Use that time to get closer to her. Now eat—"

"I hope there's enough food for all of us," Wilder says, and I turn to find him and Jaxson filling the doorway, their disheveled uniforms and tired eyes a direct result of their long night.

"What brings you two here?" I ask, startled by the Blades' presence during my espionage meeting. Jaxson breezes past, ruffling my hair before he steals a sausage from the pan. His casual theft does nothing to mask the tension they bring. Wilder wants Janus and me to get along. This violates that desire in more ways than one.

Wilder's kiss is warm and familiar. From the corner of my eye, I catch Bennett's rigid posture as he sits next to Gianna, who watches with narrowed eyes and barely concealed impatience, eager for this display to end.

"I brought you a present," Wilder says. His voice is steady, but his smile falters.

A knock disrupts the room, and we all turn to see Isolde, a thin yet curvaceous blue-haired Blade who happens to be Wilder's ex. A bag hangs over her shoulder, but her focus is on Wilder from the doorway.

"Everyone, this is Isolde," he says, as if she needs an introduction. We all briefly met following the events at the capitol last autumn. "She will be staying at the palace while I am gone."

I choke out a laugh. "Um, what?"

Isolde meets my stare, and I can tell she loathes being here. This wasn't her idea; it was Wilder's.

I scowl at my boyfriend, but he says, "Isolde is your new guard."

"I have guards."

"Guards who leave you alone during a blackout," he says, his tone hard.

My breath quickens, chest tight with anger. I knew he'd use last night against me.

Investigating whether Janus is Stellan's mole with Wilder's pet sniffing around and reporting my movements. Dismissing her would only raise his suspicions. Better to see this through—either prove Janus's guilt or clear her name. At least I have the others to help.

"Welcome, Isolde. You can set up in one of the officers' quarters.

Wilder can show you the way," I say, my voice saccharine sweet. Wilder balks, his eyes narrowing at the dismissal.

He didn't warn me about Isolde, nor was he invited to breakfast.

Isolde shrugs, unfazed. "Cool."

She turns on her heel, ready to leave, but Wilder halts me with his intense gaze. "We will talk later?"

He means we should discuss Alden and Ravi further, but I have it covered.

"I'll check my calendar. I can squeeze you in somewhere," I reply, keeping my tone light despite the adrenaline coursing through me.

"Leigh." Heat pools in my belly at the bold challenge in how he says my name, that familiar tension crackling between us.

"Wilder." I hold his gaze. Two can play at this game.

"I am going to my room. Whatever sexually charged moment you two are having, I don't want to be part of it." Gianna leaves, bypassing Isolde with an assessing look, but Isolde doesn't wither under her stare. The Blade stands taller, her chin lifted in defiance.

"Shall we?" Isolde asks, clearly unsure where to go, leaving Wilder no choice but to follow her. I give him a four-finger wave, smirking.

His glare promises retribution, and my toes curl.

With Wilder out of earshot, I grab Jaxon's sleeve. "I need your help."

"Go on," Jaxon muses, excitement brightening his worn-out gaze.

"Can you go to Little Death and check on the vampires? I want to ensure they are okay."

Jaxon grins. His enthusiasm reveals that his eagerness is more about seeing Desiree than helping me.

"Go at dusk, ask to speak to Vane directly, but be mindful of his gift. Anything you'd rather the prince not know, lock it up tight and throw away the key," I warn him.

"Please, I am not scared of Vane."

I sense a challenge in his words, a hint of bravado that prompts my frown. "Just be careful," I say.

"I got your back, L-Rae."

Jaxson leaves, and Bennett invents an excuse to go, but before Pallas can run off, I call out, "Got a sec?"

He pauses, meeting my gaze with his expressive eyes and smooth complexion. "What's up?"

"Keep an eye on Bennett for me."

"Why?"

"He's keeping something from me," I say.

Pallas laughs. "You want me to spy on your spy?"

I hold his eyes as I reply, "Yes."

CHAPTER THIRTEEN
WILDER

I CAN'T SHAKE the sense of urgency as Leigh and I stand under an awning at Mensa Station, the nerve center of the country's rail network. Our timing is tight—Prince Alden's train will arrive just after mine departs. With the city still reeling from the blackout and my efforts to prepare Soter for my absence, we haven't had enough time to discuss Alden or Ravi.

Leigh's recent behavior troubles me. Finding her in the kitchen with Pallas, Bennett, and Gianna left me uneasy. She claimed they were just having breakfast, but I could sense she wasn't telling the truth. Leigh is hiding things from me. I worry that if she doesn't learn to set aside her differences and collaborate, friction will plague her reign. Without trust, we're left with doubt and division, and that's a dangerous path for both of us.

"Hey," I start, gently pushing a strand of golden hair behind Leigh's ear. "Will you do something for me while I'm gone?"

She smiles playfully. "Nope, not sending you any nudes."

I laugh. "I wasn't going to ask for that, but now that you mention it, why not?"

Leigh laughs, and I smile, the pressure lifting from my chest.

"Because I'm the queen," she says, rolling her eyes like it's obvious. "How do I know you won't sell them to fund some old flame in Aurora?"

I shake my head, playing along, but my mind drifts to Brigid, Commander Eddo's daughter. We were friends who fell into bed, nothing more. I ended things last year before I returned to Borealis, so resuming our friendship should be easy enough. Leigh has nothing to fear. Still, I like seeing her jealous; it's a fun reminder that I'm hers.

"You got me. I plan to use your photos to support my secret family in Aurora. My ex is expecting—not my child, of course—but I've got to look out for her, right?"

Leigh is not amused. She rears her fist back, ready to strike, but I grab her wrist with a laugh. She sucks in an angry breath.

"As your queen, I demand you release me!" She tries to wrench free.

I drop the teasing. "I'm kidding," I say seriously. "There's nobody in Aurora for me. Nobody that matters, anyway." I need her to understand—there's only her, and there will only ever be her. "Tell me you trust me."

Leigh struggles harder, but I hold firm, my eyes pleading with her, pouring out my love. We've moved beyond titles and hierarchy—this is about us as equals, as partners. She can't pull rank to get her way. Not anymore.

"Leigh, do you trust me?"

She peers up at me with those big gray eyes, and I fold like a deck of cards. "What did you want me to do while you're gone?" she asks, and just like that, I'm powerless.

I swallow. She's evading me, but our time together is running out.

"It's about Ravi," I start, noting her darkening expression. She needs to hear this. "While I am gone, try to get to know him. If you two are related, how co—"

"He is a liar."

"That's not fair. You don't know him," I say, frowning, but my words die in my throat as Leigh's attention shifts away. I follow her gaze, my own concerns instantly forgotten.

Prince Alden Lupas strides toward us with his entourage, and my muscles tense. He's got a battle-scarred appearance: Light brown hair closely shorn, scars crisscrossing his face, one bisecting his left eyebrow and a more prominent one on his chin. Behind him is a witch who can only be Ravi. He may look nothing like Leigh, but his guarded gaze reminds me of her.

Alden is earlier than expected, and his intense focus on Leigh as he approaches with a hunter's confidence makes my jaw clench. I fight the urge to step between them. Leigh wouldn't appreciate it, but everything in me screams to shield her from his predatory attention.

"Your Majesty," he greets with a voice that's more rumble than words. Leigh extends her hand, but instead of shaking it, Alden yanks her close. His surprising action culminates in a bold, territorial lick up the side of her face.

My fists clench at my sides. If His Royal Scarface weren't royalty, he might find himself uncomfortably close to the train tracks.

"Prince Alden, a handshake would have been less invasive." Leigh's fingers brush the drying saliva on her cheek. Her eyes briefly meet mine, and I don a neutral mask despite the rage simmering in my chest. My magic demands retribution yet burning him would thwart peace. Still, does he have to be so fucking disgusting?

"But that is so impersonal," Alden replies.

The impulse to rearrange the Wolf Prince's face intensifies as he smirks at her. His unnatural canines gleaming like weapons. Leigh's guards tighten their formation, hands twitching toward their weapons as they eye Alden warily. I hold them back with a subtle gesture. Alden won't hurt Leigh. Not here, not now, with so many witnesses.

"Sorry about the licking," Alden says, and Leigh forces a smile. "It's a custom back in Lua. I can't say I regret it. You taste like honey and smell like flowers."

I frown, my stomach churning at the thought of his tongue on her skin, marking her as his territory. Alden may be a prince, but he's being rude when I thought he was here to foster an alliance.

Ravi, to Alden's left, rolls his eyes—a gesture so Leigh it's uncanny. She ignores him completely. I get where her perspective, but snubbing him, or the fact that he might be her family, won't make him go away. She'll need to face him eventually. I'd planned to talk to suggest she give him a chance, but Alden's little display killed that conversation. Maybe I'll bring it up during our next call.

Leigh regains her composure. "Welcome to Borealis, Your Highness. I want to introduce you to Wilder Dunn, the Borealis Blade Commander and my *boyfriend*."

I extend my hand, letting a smirk play across my lips. "She's the only one allowed to lick me," I quip, my tone carrying enough heat to make my meaning clear.

Leigh is mine.

Alden's smile thins to a razor's edge, the kind of expression worn by someone who views "no" as a temporary inconvenience. When he grips my hand, there's an unmistakable intent to dominate in the squeeze, but I stand steadfastly. His fingers might as well be trying to crush titanium.

"Wilder, care to join us for lunch at the palace?" he inquires, voice honey-smooth steel.

"Wilder is on the next train out," Leigh says. Her gaze darts between us.

The train's whistle pierces my ears as if on cue.

Alden's façade of disappointment barely conceals his delight. "What a pity. But rest assured, I'll look after Princess Leigh while you are away. As if she were mine."

But she's not yours. The words are on the tip of my tongue. I force them back with a smile.

"Queen," Ravi corrects. "She is the *queen,* Your Highness." Leigh's attention snaps to him, but he remains emotionless and professional. Is he seeking her approval or putting Alden in his place? Either way, he's just drawn a clear line about Leigh's status.

Though I'm leaving, Leigh can handle herself.

Alden laughs as Leigh purses her lips. "Ravi, you're invaluable."

The train whistles again.

"Wilder and I need a moment." Leigh grabs my forearm, hauling me away.

Though my luggage is already aboard, a part of me hesitates to embark.

"I don't like him," I confess to Leigh.

She laughs, and I glare at her until she sighs. "Neither do I."

Good. Then he can go the fuck home.

"But," Leigh adds, "it probably wouldn't bode well to send him home without settling the score between our nations."

"We could take them," I offer, though we both know I'm lying. She's right. She needs to see if there's an opportunity to make peace, even if I don't like how Alden's watching her as if she's a pawn to be possessed. "Make sure Janus is there during your negotiations with Alden. I don't want you alone with him."

"Are you jealous?" Leigh teases.

My brows lift. I'm jealous, and I'm not stupid. Falling for a queen means others will want her too. I can't make it easy for them. "He shouldn't have touched you."

Leigh sighs wistfully as if my protectiveness amuses her. The final horn whistles.

"You better hurry, or you'll miss—"

I take her face in my hands and kiss her deeply, knowing she'll feel it between her trembling legs.

I step back, and Leigh touches her swollen lips. "Play nice while I'm gone." I sling my backpack over my shoulder, salute a glaring Alden, and head onto the train.

I navigate to my compartment in the first-class cabin. It's over the top and unnecessary, but the train ride is nearly six hours, and the rumor is they have better food in first class. Plus, it is a luxury afforded by my status as commander.

As soon as I slide the door open, I freeze. "What the hell are you doing here?"

Gianna barely glances up from her phone. "Heading to Aurora. Isn't it obvious? Why else would I be sitting in a tiny compartment that stinks of stale cheese?"

I hadn't the faintest idea she'd be here. "Did Leigh send you to keep an eye on me?" I wonder aloud. Is this some form of payback for Isolde? I peer out the window. Leigh stands where I left her, shading her eyes from the bright sun as Alden waves to me condescendingly.

Asshole.

Gianna sighs. "If you want to know, I'm following a lead on my birth father."

"In Aurora?" I sit on the upholstered bench across from her. "How did you even—"

"Mama says Stellan Navis knew him. That they worked together."

"You actually took my advice and called Maria?" I ask as the train lurches into motion.

"Wilder, your ideas aren't gospel." Gi reaches into her bag for headphones. She slips them over her head without disturbing her jelled ponytail. "Wake me when we get there."

"Oh, come on, if we are going to be stuck together, you might as well talk to me."

Gianna closes her eyes. "Shh."

I scowl at the shapely raven-haired woman. She's already a thorn in my side, and we haven't left the city.

Settling into my seat with my book on my lap, I watch Borealis fade, replaced by lush farmland. Each second brings me closer to Aurora, and a shower of unexpected dread washes over me. I took the job there after graduation, believing it would be my forever home. Now, returning as the Borealis Blade Commander, I bet nothing has changed—but I know I have. Will it still feel like home?

CHAPTER FOURTEEN
LEIGH

WILDER'S TRAIN pulls away with a metallic screech, and I stand on the platform alongside Alden, Ravi, their entourage, and my guards, watching it fade into the distance. A sigh escapes my lips. He'll fix things, restore the power, and stop Stellan. Wilder doesn't know how to let me down.

I face my royal companion with crossed arms. I can't risk taking Alden to the palace for lunch with Janus and the Council—it would jeopardize the illusion of unity and strength. Instead, I'll discuss our borders with him elsewhere, away from Janus's influence. If Janus is colluding with Stellan, I don't want her anywhere near Alden until he's agreed to a peace treaty. First, I need to know his terms. Why is he here? Why are his wolves encroaching on our territory if peace is his goal?

"So, what do you want, Alden?" I ask. "Peace talks could happen over the phone. Why travel hundreds of miles in your brother's place? You could have stayed with your father. Why didn't King Simon send Zeus?"

Alden grins, towering over my five-foot-eight frame. His scars tell the story of countless battles. Being a Wolf Prince means earning respect through combat—his title alone isn't enough. His rugged handsomeness is undeniable, but not enough to sway me.

"You'd prefer Zeus's company over mine?" he asks, feigning indignation.

"I was not born yesterday. You declined my invitation for my coronation. If you needed our resources, you could have asked then. Yet here you are, weeks later. So, why now?"

Alden steps closer. "You know, your picture doesn't capture your true beauty. The glowing skin, those soulful eyes that could bring any man to his knees, and a figure that begs for—"

"That's enough. Flirting will get you nowhere with me."

"Then why are you blushing?"

"Don't mistake my annoyance for interest," I state.

Alden's laugh is deep and rumbling. "Fiery little thing."

I force a smile. "Seeing as you lack a filter—no doubt something all the half-wit girls back home enjoy—there will be rules while you stay under my roof. We aren't going to hook up. We aren't going to be friends. Together, we are establishing an alliance. Do I make myself clear?"

Alden inhales deeply, his nostrils flaring. I stiffen. "What are you doing?" I ask, but he gives nothing away.

"Your scent. Anger can be intoxicating," Alden grumbles. "I can tell a lot about someone's smell: Age, rank, and breeding condition." He takes another sniff, pupils widening. "You enjoy sex. A lot. So, who will scratch that itch while your boyfriend's away?"

"Not you," I say through gritted teeth.

"It's okay, Leigh. I enjoy playing with toys that aren't mine."

I step back to create distance. "Unless you want to keep making an ass of yourself, tell your people to grab your things. We have places to be."

"I am excited to see how Rowan Palace compares to Nocturn Castle," Alden says casually as we leave the train platform.

"We aren't going to the palace."

Alden stops mid-stride. "Was the luncheon with the Council canceled?"

The luncheon is still on. Bennett will question Janus about the blackout. My absence will anger the president, but she shouldn't have vanished two nights ago with no explanation if she didn't want scrutiny.

"I thought you might like to see the city first."

"Are you keeping me from your Council, Leigh?" Alden sniffs my hair. "Do I smell trouble?"

I smile, though my insides turn watery. "The only trouble I have is with you and the company you surround yourself with." My scowl lands on Ravi, who blinks.

Alden laughs. "Ravi means you no harm, Leigh. He is here to help with your untrained abilities as a thank you for your hospitality."

"What?" I ask.

"He's a Lunar Witch—a talented one who happens to be your relative."

"So he claims."

Ravi must have shared the same story with Alden about his supposed ancestry to gain favor with the wolf royals. If he thinks Alden has a chance to seize my throne, he could plot against him, manipulating both sides to ensure his own success, no matter the outcome.

"Remember my keen sense of smell? Trust me, Ravi is your cousin." My breathing quickens. "But don't worry, he isn't here to challenge your throne. I just want us all to be friends."

"But why?" I ask, my voice hard.

"You have something I want."

"Oil?" I ask.

Alden grins from ear to ear. "That and other things. But we can hash those details out later."

I wish I had Alden's keen sense of smell to tell whether he is lying, but considering I invited him here to broker peace between us, rejecting his "gift" seems like a terrible way to start.

"Fine," I grumble. "I accept your gift."

Ravi glares at the concrete, his brows furrowed.

His presence offers a chance to investigate his relationship with Alden.

"Excellent," Alden says, and I lean away from his touch. I can't wait to shower.

"Now, may I make one request for our outing?" I nod, my stomach hardening in anticipation. "I'd like to end the day at that vampire bar, the famous one."

I falter. "Little Death?"

"Yes, I've been dying to go. Pun absolutely intended."

That's the last thing I thought he'd say. Werewolves and vampires don't get along. What is Alden's angle here?

My hands find my hips. "The vampires are Corona's friends now. If you mess with them, you mess with me."

Alden's eyes darken at my tone, and his jaw tightens. I straighten. Shit, did I declare war without even trying? But then his expression shifts, and he laughs it off like I'm some amusing child who doesn't know any better.

"I have nothing against the vampires," he says, his tone breezy. Too breezy?

"Okay," I say, unconvinced.

"I want to have a good time."

If Alden's at Little Death, he'll be drinking. "I'll make the call."

"Excellent." Alden strides toward the lower platform escalator, then suddenly stops, patting his pockets.

"My moonstone!" he barks, dashing toward his train at a speed that could shame Borealis' best athletes. His guards quickly follow.

"Leave it!" I shout, but he's already too far away. We have metaphysical stores littered throughout the city.

"It belongs to Tanith," Ravi murmurs behind me.

I whirl to face him. "Tanith?"

His expression clouds over. "Alden's mate."

"Alden has a mate?" I scoff. "You expect me to believe that?"

Ravi glares at me. "I've done nothing to warrant your distrust."

I snort. Right. Other than sitting on my damn throne. Just then, Alden reappears. Ravi and I step apart.

"I have the perfect afternoon planned," I say cheerfully to the prince. "You're not afraid of heights, are you?"

CHAPTER FIFTEEN
DESIREE

CURSING UNDER MY BREATH, I cut my twentieth lemon into wedges and toss them in the plastic garnish container behind the bar. Being assigned menial tasks like this is exhausting. If I want to uncover who summoned the Balam, I need to focus on productive activities—like revisiting the attack site for additional clues. Spending my time on bar prep does nothing to help improve Queen Vyvyan's situation or bring us closer to finding the person behind the summoning. How does she not see that?

"I feel bad for Vane," one of my colleagues whispers to another further down the bar.

"Me too," another replies, a hint of malice in her tone.

"Why doesn't she just leave? He doesn't want her, and neither do we."

"Yeah, not after what she did to Misty."

"Misty's so much sweeter, and he chose her?"

"Everyone is saying he regrets it . . ."

I lower my gaze, focusing on the cool water flowing between my sticky fingers. If only I could scrub away my past as easily as this lemon juice.

I hate him.

If I had been honest with Misty, none of this would have happened.

But that's Vane's fault, too. He made me lie.

The citrus scent washes over me as I scrub my hands. Suddenly, I'm transported elsewhere—tangled in cotton sheets, safe in strong arms that hold me like I'm precious. The memory is so vivid I can almost *feel* the warmth of his skin and hear the steady rhythm of his heartbeat against my ear. I blink, forcing myself back to reality, but the ghost of that embrace lingers.

"Hey, sunshine."

I lift my gaze, my heart leaping. Jaxson flashes a smile that could liven a morgue, and for a moment, I forget everything—until the weight of watchful eyes returns. I shut off the water and grab a rag, hands trembling as I dry them. Each step around the bar echoes with whispers from the vampires tracking my movement. Their judgment crawls across my skin. With forced casualness, feeling like there's glass in my throat, I tug Jaxson out of earshot.

"What the hell are you doing here?" I hiss.

If Vyvyan finds out he was here, there'll be hell to pay. Witches aren't allowed inside the club during off hours.

If she found out he came to see me, she'd make an example of us both.

Jaxson simply laughs, warm and nostalgic, melting some of my anger. But coming here is reckless. "Good to see you, too, Desi," he replies. "Even if you aren't answering my calls."

My lips purse. I don't have time for Jaxson's antics tonight. I've been ignoring his calls since I got called into Vyvyan's room about Mom's cure —not out of disinterest, but to keep him safe and my place here secure. He deserves an explanation, but not here.

"Do you have a death wish?" I ask, and Jax raises an inquiring brow. My stomach does a low flip as I take him in. By the stars, he's so attractive. Gone are his boyish good looks, and in their place are masculine features that seem chiseled from stone. He's a dangerous distraction from my promise to Vyvyan. "You need to leave. I'll call you—"

"Desi, I'm not here to see you."

I blink, finally noticing his uniform. Jax smiles again, and my heart pounds—betraying me, considering how easily he cast me aside for Wilder last year. The familiar ache of abandonment twists in my chest, as sharp as a scalpel, while heat floods my cheeks. That smile used to make me do unlawful things to him back when I thought I meant more to him.

"Then why are you here?" I ask.

Jax peers over my shoulder into the empty club. Soon, the dance floor will pulsate with energy, and the bar will bustle with patrons. "Is Vane around?"

My body goes rigid, my teeth set on edge. Jaxson knows Vane is my sire, but he doesn't know what happened between us. I never plan to tell him. It's none of his business.

"Vane isn't here."

"Then where is he?"

I scoff. "Do I look like his keeper?"

"If you are, you are doing a terrible job," a sultry voice says. My blood runs cold.

Vane commands the room like a king holding court when he walks in. His red eyes gleam as he adjusts the sleeve of his custom-tailored suit. Tonight's ensemble is a striking teal, accentuating his white-blond hair, which seems to glow under the club lights.

I want to squeeze lemon juice into my eyes.

"Jaxson." Vane extends a firm handshake toward the Blade. The air thickens as the two pivotal figures in my life, the only men I've ever loved, engage in a silent exchange that momentarily eclipses my presence. An urge to retreat behind the bar tugs at me, but curiosity pins me in place.

"Are you here to take in the sights?" Vane's gaze lands on me, and I roll my eyes.

Asswipe.

"I'm here on an errand for the queen," Jaxson says.

I bite the inside of my cheek. What's so important Leigh sent Jaxson to ask in person?

"If Leigh has questions, then ask them," Vane replies.

"Leigh wants to ensure you and Queen Vyvyan are safe after the blackout," Jax asks.

I scoff. Both men look at me.

Of course, they aren't fucking okay. Someone attacked Vyvyan and Vane, and that person wants her dead. There could be wolves in Corona, and here we are chatting in this club as if there isn't a killer on the loose.

Vane wears a mask of composure. "I told her we were fine. Something had come up."

I frown. It's so easy for him to lie.

"Perhaps I could see Vyvyan to confirm that's true?" Jaxson asks, and I tense. Ice floods my veins, memories of Vyvyan's lifeless body flashing through my mind. Jax frowns. He reads me like a book, sensing something is wrong. I'm losing control. If the Blades steal my case, there goes my bargaining chip, and I'll end up on the streets.

"Vyvyan's not taking visitors," I say.

Jaxson's stare intensifies. "Why?"

Vane scowls at me. "Desiree, don't you need to get back to work? We will open soon. Jaxson, we will need to reschedule this conversation. I'm busy."

Jaxson straightens. His posture brims with authority. "There's one more thing. Leigh requests permission to visit Little Death tonight with some of her people."

"Who?" I ask before Vane can shoo me away.

"A few members of the Council as well as Alden Lupas," Jaxson says in a low voice.

Confusion wrinkles my brow. "Who is that?"

"The Wolf Prince of Lua?" Vane answers.

My skin crawls at the recollection of Balam's signature. Paw prints.

"He's here?" Could the tracks at the attack site link to Alden? If so, I might have found my first suspect.

Jaxson nods. "It's a long story, but essentially, Alden is here to negotiate peace with Leigh. He requested to visit Little Death."

"Why does Alden want to come here?" I won't deny his being here will make questioning him easier. "Wolves hate vampires."

"Alden insists that isn't true," Jax says. Vane is rigid, and his calculating gaze seems far away.

"Tell Leigh she is always welcome," I say.

Vane blinks back to the present. "Excuse me?" he hisses.

I force a smile at Jax. "Give us a minute."

I pull Vane aside, leaving Jax with his arms crossed, staring at us like he has X-ray vision. Turning my back to him, I address Vane. "Let them come. They can use room two; it's the largest. I'll work the party to gather information. Those were wolf prints I found the other day, and I could use this opportunity to talk to Alden and see if he slips up."

Vane chuckles, the sound devoid of humor. "Oh, darling, I love watching you scheme. But Alden isn't going to tell you shit."

I bristle at the term of endearment. "Is that a challenge?"

He shrugs. "Why not? I always enjoy winning." His familiar cocky smile spreads across his face, and something inside me snaps. The casual confidence—the belief that everything is just a game he can master—is so perfectly infuriating I want to scream.

Vane leaves me frowning. "If that's all, officer, you may tell Leigh that Little Death will host her and her company tonight." Jaxson, however, lingers, his reddish-brown eyes fixed on mine. A muscle in Vane's jaw feathers. "Is there something else?"

Jax clears his throat. "I wanted to ask if you'd have dinner with me. To apologize."

My jaw drops. Jax can't be serious. The audacity of asking me out with Vane right there makes my pulse race. He's either clueless about vampire politics or foolishly brave. I glance at the century-old vampire, my stomach knotting as I gauge his reaction. Vane's face is an expressionless mask, cold and unyielding, reveling nothing about how he feels. That's what terrifies me most. I've been around vampires long enough to know that their stillness is often deadliest right before they strike. Jax has no idea he's painting a target on his chest with every word.

"Vyvyan will never let me," I say.

Challenge sparks in Jax's eyes. "Do you always do what Vyvyan tells you?"

I open my mouth to answer with a firm yes. But Vane answers, "I'll deal with Vyvyan." I blink until he adds for my ears only, "I'll tell her you're going out with Jaxson to glean information on the Council."

My jaw slackens. For Vyvyan, he'd do anything.

"Fine," I consent, and Jaxson sports a movie star smile. "We can go out. As *friends*."

Jaxson's grin wavers. But that's how it has to be until I regain Vyvyan's favor. Until then, I'm on thin ice.

"Tomorrow, Blue Sparrow, nine o'clock?" Jaxson asks.

I nod, but my inner conflict grows at the thought of going out with Jaxson. Given our shared history, I'm worried about what topics or unresolved issues might surface when we're alone. He said he wanted to apologize. Confronting our past and navigating the complexities of our relationship face-to-face fills me with apprehension as if I were preparing for a complicated surgery.

"So, nine?" Jaxson prompts once more, his eyes searching mine.

Vane inserts himself. "She'll be there."

I shoot Vane a glare. "I can speak for myself."

"Since you're here, Officer Foster-Reid, I have a message to pass to Leigh." Vane lowers his voice. Jax steps closer. "The night before the blackout, we had a visitor. Beatrix Marks."

Jaxson's takes an involuntary step back. "The anti-monarchist? Doesn't she live in Icarus? Why was she in town?"

Vane shrugs. "Visiting old friends."

"Interesting," Jax muses pensively. "I'll see you both later."

"Back to work, Desiree." I flip Vane off as he turns away. "I saw that."

"Good!"

CHAPTER SIXTEEN
WILDER

GIANNA and I wheel our bags across the scorching pavement outside the bustling Aurora train station, where people and stray cats vie for attention. Cats sprawl across sidewalks, empty seats, and street corners. The heat radiates through the soles of my shoes as I guide Gianna toward the cab station. With the ongoing blackout, few trains are running, and the precinct is overwhelmed. The Blades are all too busy to give us a ride.

"How far is the garrison?" Gianna huffs, shielding her face from the unrelenting sun.

"Not too far," I lie. The garrison is over the Charon Bridge, then another five miles north.

Leigh secured Gianna's rooms at the Blade garrison without telling me why. She'd be far more comfortable at the Najma Hotel, the favored haunt of celebrities and politicians in Aurora. I suspect Leigh wants Gianna to keep an eye on me, which is fine. She'll only see she can trust me. I doubt Gianna will appreciate sharing a coed bathroom with me and the rest of the Blades. Something tells me she's never had to share anything in her life. But we'll cross that bridge when we get there.

Refineries and the imposing Bersa Power Station, Corona's largest power plant, frame the cab stand. This side of town—West Aurora—is a far cry from East Aurora with its rich history, diverse culture, and unique architecture. To truly experience the city, one must explore the east, where most residents live in towering sandstone apartment buildings. The outskirts feature a few sprawling estates, mostly owned by affluent Epsilon oil magnates.

I set down my duffel and peel off my sweat-soaked long-sleeve shirt.

Crouching, I retrieve a fresh shirt from my bag and my water bottle. After taking a sip of the lukewarm liquid, I offer it to Gi, who turns up her nose.

"Can you hurry up?" Gianna groans, as if my shirtless state offends her. I deliberately slow my movements.

"What's the rush, country club?" I drawl, relishing her discomfort.

Gianna flashes her perfectly bleached teeth. "People are staring."

I pull the dry shirt over my head, rolling my eyes. "Believe me, they're not staring at me."

Dressed as if she just stepped off a runway—designer everything, perfect hair, long polished nails that have never seen a day's work—Gianna is counting every stare behind those oversized sunglasses. Sure, people are watching her. She's a Nebula clinging to her Epsilon roots. Sooner or later, she'll realize she's better off being herself.

"Whatever. When you are finished putting on a show, I'll be waiting in the cab." Gianna stalks to the cab stand, commanding the entire sidewalk, forcing pedestrians to bypass her.

I stand there, stunned, as a passerby chuckles. "Your girlfriend's quite something," he comments.

"She's not my girlfriend," I gripe, picking up the bags.

By the time I catch up, Gianna has already secured us a ride. The driver —a man with a silver front tooth and wandering eye—helps me load our things into the trunk. Gianna sits in the back, texting furiously. I'm sure she's complaining to Leigh about my insufferable behavior.

With a heavy sigh, I tell the cabbie, "We're going to the Aurora Blade Garrison."

The ride is uncomfortable, to say the least. The driver leers at Gianna through the rearview mirror, his eyes roving over her body to the point where Gianna ends up calling him out for being a pervert. Then, our luggage is unceremoniously dumped in front of the garrison, and some of Gianna's nice things blow in the dusty wind.

"Fuck . . . that . . . guy," she growls, tearing off a boot, and throwing it at the retreating vehicle.

I pick up her shoe. "Put that on. There are scorpions here."

Gianna grabs the boot. "Is this the place?"

I follow her gaze and smile.

The desert has forged the Aurora Blade Garrison into a resilient relic. This two-story fortress, with its number of rooms wrapping around an open-air courtyard, features columns that stand sentinel beneath the harsh sun. Except today, an unsettling silence reigns. No Blades train, and even the doorkeeper's post is empty.

"Come on, everyone must be inside."

As we step inside the garrison, Gianna lets out a soft gasp. The interior is a masterpiece—exquisite patterns adorn carpets, metalwork, and vibrant stained glass that filters light into a rainbow of colors, casting a magical glow on everything it touches. The scent of leather and polished wood fills the air.

"Wow, color me impressed." Gianna spins to take it all in. "It is stunning here."

"Wilder?" Commander Eddo's familiar voice interrupts the moment. Compact and muscular, with jet-black hair peppered with gray at the temples and a neatly trimmed goatee, Eddo has always been more than a commander to me during my tenure here—he's been a mentor, a friend, and at times, a father figure.

But, right now, he's approaching me as if I were a cobra poised to strike.

"It's good to see you," he says, pulling me into a stiff hug devoid of the genuine affection I remember. Eddo saw right through my anger when I first arrived—all that resentment I'd built up against my dad. He didn't just train me to fight; he taught me how to let go of that chip on my shoulder. *"You want to belong here?"* he'd say. *"Then you need to drop the attitude. We're your team, not your personal punching bag."*

"I apologize for not meeting you at the station," he says now. "Aurora has been a hive of activity since the blackout. Lately, it's impossible to be everywhere at once."

"Where is everyone?" I ask.

"Either out on their beats or at Furies. It's trivia night."

Furies is a local bar run by three Nebula Sea Witch sisters, a staple in Eddo's daughter Brigid's social circle. It is a popular spot for Blades to unwind. Eddo's gaze shifts from me to Gianna. She pushes her sunglasses to rest atop her head, and his strained smile slips entirely.

"Hello," Gianna greets.

"Miss di Siena, I heard you were coming." His clipped words are as frigid as a winter's night.

"Please, just Gianna or Gi. Can you point me to my room? I'd love to freshen up before dinner."

Eddo's eyes glint like shards of obsidian. "Your room isn't ready, and we have already eaten."

Gianna stiffens, and I fight a wince. I've never heard Eddo be so standoffish.

"Gi, you can use my room," I say. Eddo exhales a hot breath through his nose. "Unless my room isn't ready either?"

"Your room is exactly how you left it."

I nod, facing Gianna. "Upstairs, first door on the left, overlooking the street."

Gi hikes one of her bags over her shoulder, staring between Eddo and me.

"Thank you," she says to me. To Eddo, she adds, "It's nice to meet you." Grabbing only one of her many suitcases, Gianna leaves the room. The wheels rattle as she glances back once before disappearing up the stairs.

When she's out of earshot, I turn on Eddo. "Was that necessary?"

Eddo shrugs. "That girl doesn't belong here."

I blink. I had the same judgmental thoughts outside the train station, but hearing Eddo say it out loud reveals how wrong I was. "Why do I get the sense that neither do I?"

Eddo looks at me, no longer like a son, but an enemy. "Look, Wilder, it's good to see you, but considering the circumstances, it's probably best you return to the city. Aurora isn't safe for Epsilon right now."

What the actual fuck?

"Gianna isn't an Epsilon, and neither am I."

"I'm not trying to cause trouble," Eddo replies.

I can't help but laugh. "You could have fooled me."

"Wilder, we haven't talked in nearly five months. You left here a wreck, and now you return a bloody commander, dating the queen, and mingling with Elio di Siena's daughter. Have you forgotten he was one of the Council members who sentenced your dad to life in prison?"

The person across from me is a stranger wearing Eddo's face. "Eddo, my dad killed someone. Even if he thought it was for the right reasons, he still committed a crime."

Eddo's upper lip curls. "Sounds like you've seen him."

"You have no clue what my life has been like since I left."

"I could say the same thing, especially about you acting as if you own the place."

I scowl, and Eddo has the decency to look nervous.

"Eddo, respectfully, fuck off. I am here to help, not take your job."

"Excuse me?"

"You heard me. I'm here to assist, and that girl upstairs is searching for her family—her *Nebula* family."

"I don't need your help. I have everything under control," he says in a low, dangerous voice.

I raise my eyebrows. "Is that so?"

"Yes."

"What about Stellan, the riots, and the fire at the power plant?" There's more happening here than what meets the eye, which is why I am here instead of Borealis. Unless he doesn't want me here because he's part of the problem?

"Since I have you here," I say, "I need you to set up a meeting with Michael Bersa tomorrow at the plant. It's urgent we get the power up and running." I listen for the hum of the backup generator.

Eddo grumbles under his breath about me being an insolent little shit, and the words sting more than they should. With every cutting remark, he reminds me less of the man I admired and more of my dad. That comparison hurts worse than any insult.

"Michael Bersa hasn't left his mansion since the fire," Eddo says.

"Does that mean you won't make the call?" I keep my voice level, diplomatic. "He'd likely listen to you, a local authority, over a visiting one. Especially given our history."

Eddo offers a smile that doesn't quite reach his eyes. My impatience nearly bubbles over. Stellan Navis's advocacy for Nebula rights has garnered respect from all corners of Aurora, including those who enforce its laws. Eddo clearly sides with Stellan, assuming I am Team Epsilon just because I'm Team Leigh. How loyal Eddo is to Stellan is to be seen.

"The plant lies in Brigid's territory, and as you can see, she isn't here to help," Eddo says. "And I am far too busy for pesky calls."

I study my former boss. "That's all right, Ed. Never mind." Eddo smiles as if he's won. But if he isn't going to play fair, neither am I. "Is Brigid at Furies?"

Eddo glares at me. "You leave my daughter out of your scheme, Wilder."

The corners of my mouth lift in a humorless smile. "Last I checked, Brigid was the schemer."

"Brigid has enough on her plate. And you know her history with the Bersa family. I want to keep her away from them."

I sigh. I'm not here to corrupt his daughter or endanger her. Brigid only needs to talk to her dad. Eddo can connect me with Michael Bersa. She's his little princess, after all. One word from her, and Eddo will roll out the red carpet for me.

"Eddo, believe it or not, I'm not your enemy. I'm here to restore power and find Stellan Navis. Your help would make it easier, but I don't need it. Now, excuse me, but I've had a long day." I give Eddo one last disappointed look before gathering my duffel and as much of Gianna's things I can carry upstairs. "Let me know when Gianna's room is ready."

"And if I don't?" Eddo threatens.

"Then she'll stay with me."

I march off, leaving Eddo fuming in the foyer.

I stumble up the stairs with full arms. When I reach my room, I kick the door with my boot to alert Gianna who takes her sweet time answering. Finally, she appears in a loose-fitting dress better suited for the climate, the fabric flowing around her like water.

She gazes up at me with a mournful expression that tugs at my heart, reminding me of Desiree coming home from school upset about the other kids. Like then, I want to fight all of Gianna's battles.

"I can find a hotel," she says, her voice small with uncertainty.

I barrel into the room with our things. "Don't be ridiculous, you're staying here." After Eddo's reaction, I'm afraid of what might happen if I let her out of my sight. Gianna may have Nebula ancestry, but everyone still sees her as an Epsilon. Elio had more enemies than friends, and Gianna feels the brunt of that now. She needs to be careful, even if she isn't his biological daughter.

I collapse on my bed, gazing around my old room; its familiarity tightens my chest. It looks the same as I left it. The drawings of Brigid, the Erinye sisters, and Orion—Ry for short—still decorate the walls, their charcoal lines as vivid as the day I drew them. The books I left line the top of the desk, their spines worn and well-loved. But the room isn't dusty, the air smells fresh. Someone's been keeping it tidy, as if they expected me to return soon. My lungs seize. I need some air.

"Are you thirsty?" I ask Gianna. "There's this bar I'd like to go to. You'd like it. There's trivia."

She folds her arms. "Why would I like that?"

"Because you can show off that Sussex prep education; you might even win a prize."

She shakes her head, a small smile forming "Has anyone ever told you that you're mean?"

"Ah, you wound me," I reply, rising to my feet.

CHAPTER SEVENTEEN
WILDER

FIVE MONTHS HAVEN'T DULLED Furies's charm. The same fabric-covered barstools line the antique wooden counter, with brass footrails gleaming. Servers in white shirts and black shorts deftly navigate the crowded space, delivering magically chilled beer bottles to patrons. Despite the ongoing blackout, the place is brightly lit. In the distance, a backup generator rumbles while candles adorn the tables.

Even with the trivia night pandemonium, we get lucky and snag a recently vacated table in the back. Gianna wipes away the previous occupants' water rings with spare napkins before propping her elbows on the table.

"This is Furies?" she questions.

The competitive buzz of trivia night greets my ears, punctuated by cheers and groans with each new question. "Yeah, the Erinye sisters run it," I yell over the noise. "It was inherited from their dad, a Sea Witch. They've kept his tradition alive, occasionally tweaking a recipe."

Gianna scans the sticky bar menu. "Pomegranate infusion. Sounds yummy."

"Want one?" I offer. It's one of the mocktail options. I've noticed Gianna abstaining from alcohol since returning from treatment. Though she went to rehab for drugs, not drinking makes sense. It lowers inhibitions, and our brain's reward system doesn't discriminate. One substance can easily trigger cravings for another.

Her look turns contemplative. "What are we doing here, though? Aren't you supposed to be at the power station? And what about Stellan?"

I lean in. "That's exactly why we're here. My friends are around somewhere, and with some luck, they'll help." Brigid can assist me in convincing Eddo, and he likely knows where to find Stellan—who's been hard to track since he no longer works as a journalist for mayor's office and his paper only uses a PO Box.

Gianna hums. "I guess that's a good idea."

"It is."

She points at the menu. "I'll take one of these." It's a soda.

"Coming right up," I say, then head for the bar.

Squeezing between patrons, I try to catch the bartender's attention. He's a young guy with frosted tips and a face I don't recognize. Suddenly, an earth-shattering screech tears through the bar, causing him to fumble, and drop his shaker. Both of us look toward the source of the commotion, and I break into a smile.

"Hey, Alec," I yell over whirring blenders.

Alec Erinye, one of the trio who own the place, finishes setting a vat of freshly cleaned glasses on the bar, rounds the corner, and throws herself into my arms. Despite her towering platform boots, she's tiny, not even hitting the five-foot mark. For fun, I spin her around, almost bumping into a group waiting on their drinks from the fresh-faced bartender.

After setting Alec down, she playfully slaps my arm. "When the hell did you get back?"

"Today. I just ran into Eddo. He mentioned trivia night was still on."

She puts a hand on her hip. "Hell yeah, it is. The blackout couldn't stop us. Are you back for good?"

Before I can reply, Megaera or Meg, Alec's sister, strolls toward us with a guarded expression. Towering at almost six feet tall, she's almost always in sneakers, regardless of her outfit. The Erinye sisters share striking black hair, tanned skin, and deep, dark eyes. Meg is the eldest, Alec falls somewhere in the middle, and Phe, currently unaccounted for, is the baby.

"Hey, Meg, it's good to se—"

Meg's punch lands squarely on my jaw.

"What the fuck, Meg?" Alec screeches.

I rub my face, reeling from shock more than pain. Meg points an accusing finger at me. "That's for breaking Brigid's heart."

I roll my eyes. Brigid and I were never an official item; it was always casual. After her failed relationships, she wanted to keep things noncommittal. I wanted to forget about Isolde. We were friends, finding solace in each other as we nursed our broken hearts.

When I ended things before returning to Borealis at the end of last summer, she agreed it was for the best—at least, that's how I remember it. But Meg's cold shoulder and Eddo's biting comments suggest a different story. Could I have misread the situation? Brigid always had a knack for making others see her version of events, and if she convinced everyone I broke her heart . . . I push away the unease settling in my stomach. My time in Aurora might be more complicated than I thought.

"Brigid is fine, I promise," Alec tries to reassure me, but Meg's worry is written across her lowered brow.

"Where is she?" I ask.

Then Gianna appears, drawing the attention of half the bar.

"I'm thirsty," she declares, clearly frustrated. "Did you forget my drink?" Alec and Meg fall silent, sizing Gianna up and down.

"Hello, I'm Gianna."

Alec whistles. "Yeah, we know who you are." She gives me a questioning look that asks, *Why didn't you tell us she was here?*

Gianna laughs; it is an uncomfortable sound. A nearby table of refinery workers is watching her and whispering. "I wish people would stop staring at me."

Meg blurts out, "But you're beautiful." Immediately, her face colors. Usually, she is far more reserved.

Alec swoops in and links arms with Gianna, turning her toward the bar. "Are you here with Wilder?"

"We came together, if that's what you mean. Wilder's with my best friend."

"The queen?" Gianna confirms with a nod. "What's she like?"

"I . . ." Gianna glances back at me, and I shrug. "I don't know, she's Leigh. She's a combination of confident and suspicious."

Alec's eyes glimmer. "She's so pretty. Like a model." Gianna offers a noncommittal noise, and Alec slaps the bar to get the bartender's attention. "Yo, get my new friend Gianna whatever she wants. On the house."

"Where's Phe?" I ask Meg.

"With her husband."

I quirk a brow. "She's married?" Before I left, Phe hadn't had a boyfriend.

"Whirlwind romance," Meg answers. "She's a romantic."

I nod but notice how Meg keeps watching Gianna. It's hard to hear them over the commotion. Gi smiles at Alec while Meg plays with her hair. If Gi can get along with my friends, having her around will be easier. After Elio's arrest and subsequent death, followed by her mom's swift departure, Gianna has only Leigh. If she could make more friends, maybe she'd realize she's not so alone in this world. Plus, if she can talk to Stellan and learn more about her biological dad, she might lose some of that attitude.

"Is Brigid here?" I ask Meg.

"No," she says with a scowl. "But she's on the way. So is Ry."

Good. I'd like to see them both.

The bartender offers an awkward smile to Gianna, who finally orders for the both of us.

Drinks in hand, we head back to our table with promises from Meg and Alec that they will join us soon. However, it's their bartender's first week, so they can't leave him alone behind the bar for long, especially while it's busy. Due to the blackout, many patrons are out of work, causing the bar to be more packed than usual.

I sip my drink as the person on the microphone asks, "What's the rarest gemstone?"

The table next to us debates if it is a diamond or an emerald, and Gianna rolls her eyes with a mumbled, "Painite."

"Huh?" I ask.

"The answer," Gianna says a little louder, drawing attention from the party beside us. "It's painite. Only one thousand have ever been found. Mama has one."

I laugh. Of course she does. "You should sign up to play. You'd be an asset to any team."

Gianna sips her soda through a straw. "I find that hard to believe."

I open my mouth to ask her how she feels about uncovering her past. However, before I can voice my thoughts, Gianna voices hers. "What was it like living. . ." Her question hangs unfinished as two hands suddenly cover my eyes from behind.

I tense up.

A girl's voice teases, "Guess who?"

"Ugh, Brigid?"

"Yes!" Brigid squeals in delight, and drops into my lap, disregarding the empty chair beside me. "I knew you'd be back! I missed you so much. Did you miss me?"

Gianna's expression darkens at the sight of Brigid clinging to me, though Brigid seems oblivious to the tension her closeness creates. She flings her coarse, waist-length brown-black hair, which she usually has up in a topknot, over her shoulder. I resist the urge to drop her onto the dirty floor.

"I just ran into Papa, he said you were back. I checked your old room, and when I didn't find you there, I knew you'd be here."

"You went into my room?" I shift uncomfortably, aware of Gianna clenching her glass tight enough to suggest she's fantasizing about dousing Brigid with its contents.

"Is that a problem? It never was before." Brigid feigns innocence, but her gaze suggests something more sinister. She runs her fingers through my hair. "It's getting longer."

"I thought I made it clear before I left that we needed boundaries, Brigid?" I ask. When I ended things, she agreed wholeheartedly, saying I was a nice distraction but not the settling down type. After sleeping with her for months, I expected her words to sting, but I felt nothing but indifference.

"Relax, babe, I didn't touch anything. I'll wait until you ask me to." Brigid winks.

"Ugh, could you . . . move?" I ask, giving her a nudge for some personal space.

Brigid's always been flirty, but I'm not here to rekindle anything. I need her help with Eddo. That's it.

Brigid blinks, momentarily taken aback, but then hops off me gracefully. Her eyes lock with Gianna's, and the air crackles with an unspoken challenge.

"Who are you?" Brigid asks.

Gianna's response is cool; her smirk sharp. "I'm Wilder's *girlfriend's* best friend. Perhaps you've heard of her? Leigh Raelyn, your *queen*."

Shit. Angering Brigid before I could win her to my side wasn't the plan.

Brigid laughs. "I'm aware of who she is. Not that she'll be my queen for much longer."

I stiffen. "What's that supposed to mean?"

Brigid cups my cheek. Her thumb is dangerously close to my mouth. "Oh, baby, there's so much you don't know. How about we catch up tomorrow? Coffee before work?"

I peel Brigid's hand off my face. "I was hoping to talk tonight."

"About?"

"I need to check out the damage at the power station. Speak to Michael, but Eddo is being difficult. I hoped you could speak to your dad to set up the meeting."

Brigid cringes. When I first moved to Aurora, she had just broken up with Bryant Bersa—son of Michael Bersa, the power plant owner. Now, Bryant is serving time for trying to frame Brigid for a crime she didn't commit. Solving that case and proving her innocence was our first collaboration, and it cemented our friendship. I hate reminding her of that dark time when her freedom was on the line, but it's not as if I asked her to accompany me to the station. I can handle with Michael alone.

"I might be able to do that," she says. "If you agree to have breakfast."

"I thought Blades were against extortion?" Gianna mumbles.

Brigid glowers at her. "Seeing as you are Elio's daughter, you'd know all about that."

Gianna gapes at Brigid. So do I. "I thought you didn't know who I am?" Gi asks.

"Babes, I know all about you. Which is why—I hate to ask—but should you even be drinking?" Brigid's gaze lands pointedly on Gianna's drink. "Didn't you just get out of rehab?"

I suck in a breath. "Brigid, what the fuck? Not cool."

"Not that I need to explain myself, but it's non-alcoholic," Gianna retorts.

"Congratulations," Brigid says with zero enthusiasm. "Daddy must be proud you're sticking to the program."

Gianna's hands make fists, but Brigid smiles, eager for a fight.

"You should go, Brigid," I encourage. Her eyes widen, as if she's hurt I'm choosing Gianna over her. I'm trying to avoid turning Furies into a boxing ring. "I'll see you in the morning."

With a triumphant smile, Brigid stands. "Looking forward to it." Then she joins a nearby table of Blades I recognize.

Gianna speaks first. "I'm guessing you two had a thing, and I don't need to guess that she still isn't over it. I suggest you nip that in the bud before Leigh finds out." I open my mouth to explain, but she's already moving on. "Where's the fucking bathroom in this place?"

Once I'm alone, I bury my face in my hands. What the hell just happened? Angering Brigid couldn't have come at a worse time. I need her help. At the same time, upsetting Gianna, who I still suspect is here as some sort of spy for Leigh, is also not a good idea. By the end of this trip, these girls will tear me in half.

CHAPTER EIGHTEEN
LEIGH

THE PULSATING BEAT of Little Death thrums through my body as I take a sip of my lukewarm cocktail. Around the expansive private room, Council members—including the new Nebula representatives and Keris—indulge in the night's revelry. The pungent scent of alcohol and raucous laughter permeates the air. I'm surprised Keris accepted my invitation, given Stellan's scathing article about his last visit here.

Even more surprising is Alden. Instead of joining his rowdy companions, he's chosen to sit beside me on the stiff sofa. His piercing gaze holds a mix of mischief and something more profound that I can't quite read.

"Not having fun?" Alden asks, his attention drifting to my barely touched drink.

I've been nursing the same cocktail since we arrived an hour ago. The last thing I need is to let my guard down in this den of debauchery. I want to keep my mind clear while Alden becomes more befuddled with every beverage he consumes. By staying sober while he becomes increasingly intoxicated, I hope to catch him off guard and make him reveal something truthful.

My gaze drifts past Alden and settles on the door. Bennett should be here by now. The luncheon ended hours ago. I want to know what information he extracted from Janus. If she's Stellan's source, are her actions driven by retribution for the Harborym, or is there something darker at play?

Alden inches closer. "If you're not having fun, we could always go back to the palace. Just the two of us."

I wrinkle my nose. "Pass."

Alden laughs. "I keep trying to be your friend, and your rejection hurts."

"My friend?" I retort. "Friends don't proposition each other."

Alden sighs. "Who says I am pretending? Negotiations between us would go much smoother if we were horizontal."

"Does Tanith care that you're talking to me like this?"

Alden narrows his eyes. "Who told you about Tanith?"

A winning smile plays on my lips as his gaze darts across the room to Ravi, who is conversing with the striking redheaded vampire server. Alden's glare goes unnoticed by his friend.

I purse my lips in contemplation. If Ravi and Alden are conspiring against me, why is Alden so surprised that Ravi mentioned Tanith? Unless I'm right, and Ravi is working against Alden. He did warn me not to invite him here. Or maybe Ravi is on my side? I frown. The likelihood of Ravi being an ally feels farfetched. It's more likely they are both playing me.

"Trust me, Leigh. Tanith doesn't care what I do."

"Oh, and why's that? Did she dump you?" I chide.

"No, she's dead."

All air leaves my lungs. I fumble for words. "I—I'm so sorry. That was—"

"Don't worry about it." Alden's attention shifts to Vane as he enters the room behind Desiree, who balances a tray of shots with practiced ease. I have no clue how she can walk, let alone work in the dress she has on. It is so tight.

I sit up straighter, beckoning Desiree over, desperate for a distraction from the awkward tension my insensitive prodding has created. Desi's dazzling smile captivates the room, drawing in the attention of everyone present. Well, almost everyone. The redheaded vampire conversing with Ravi seems to be the only one immune to Desi's charm, ignoring her.

Alden's focus shifts to Desi, and the sadness in his gaze transforms into keen interest as he unabashedly appraises her. His eyes roam over her body like he is surveying a masterpiece, lingering on her breasts. I find myself chewing the inside of my cheek, understanding that Alden's flirtatious behavior might be nothing more than a carefully crafted façade to mask his underlying grief. This revelation leaves a sour taste in my mouth, and I can't help but question his sincerity.

Vane takes the seat to my left as Desiree hands one of the overflowing shots to Alden, who downs it in one go.

"And what's your name, gorgeous?" Alden asks my boyfriend's sister.

I catch Vane's eye roll as Desiree replies, "Desiree."

"Desiree, you've been working your ass off," Alden points out. Desiree blinks in surprise. "Why don't you take a seat?" He pats his lap.

Desiree laughs off the offer with grace. "If I stop working, who will refill your drinks when you get thirsty?" she counters, her voice like velvet.

Alden's smile turns predatory. "I am thirsty."

Desiree shakes her head, her short, glossy black hair swishing with the movement. "I'm flattered, but I need to get back to work. These drinks won't serve themselves."

Alden catches her hand, and Vane tenses on the other side of me. His muscles coil like a spring, ready to snap. I glance back at Desiree, who pointedly avoids Vane's gaze while Alden leers at him from the corner of his eye. Is he deliberately trying to provoke Vane by using Desiree as a pawn? It's a dangerous game, one that could easily escalate.

"When can I see you again?" Alden asks.

"That's funny. I was going to ask you the same question," Desiree says mischievously.

"Well, I just got here. We have a few days to get to know each other before Leigh kicks me out. Maybe I can crash with you? Do you live here?"

Desiree toys with her dress's plunging neckline. "I do. And you say you just got here, but I thought I saw some paw prints earlier this week in the park. Were they from you?"

Alden shakes his head. "Can't say that they were, gorgeous."

Desiree's smile falters, hinting at more to her questioning than mere curiosity.

"Desiree, people are waiting for their orders," the redheaded server calls out.

"That's my cue," Desiree announces to Alden.

"I wish you would stay."

Alden's appreciative gaze lingers on Desiree's retreating form as she saunters off. I tighten my grip on my drink, wishing I could drown him in it. A glance at Vane reveals he's doing the same, his glass of blood in danger of shattering under the pressure of his grip.

Something is going on between him and Desiree.

"She's a pretty girl," Alden says to Vane once he notices the tension. "Is she yours?"

"Desiree belongs to no one but herself," Vane replies.

"How chivalrous. If a girl who looks like that worked for me, I'd lock her up and throw away the key."

"Is that what you do to women back in Lua—lock them in cages?" I quip, unable to hide my disdain.

"Only if they ask nicely."

I roll my eyes. "Brute."

With a laugh, Alden rises from his seat. He walks over to Desiree and laughs at something Keris says. My people are winning him over. Alden slips his arm around Desiree's tiny waist, pulling her close to whisper something in her ear. She responds by biting her lip.

"I'm glad Jaxson isn't here to see this," I mutter under my breath as I wave enthusiastically at another of my councilors walking through the door wearing the signature Little Death red mask before taking it off.

"Did he pass along my message?" Vane asks. He speaks to me, but his eyes watch Alden possessively squeeze Desiree's hip. She doesn't swat him away.

"About Beatrix Marks? I have Pallas looking into her," I say in a low voice, sipping my watered-down drink. While I showed Alden around the city, Jaxson informed me about the visiting anti-monarchist. The news took me by surprise; I'd heard her name before. She opposes the monarchy and all inherited leadership positions. While she and others like her haven't posed a threat, I dislike having her in the city while Alden is here. "Is she here to jumpstart some sort of protest in light of the blackout?"

"She's here to meet with someone," Vane shares while glaring at

Desiree. With each touch and smile she offers Alden and the others, Vane bares his teeth a little more.

"Who?" I urge. Vane finally tears himself away from Desiree to meet my gaze.

He sighs. "I didn't get a name. But I suggest watching your back."

I frown. I'd need eyes in the back of my head to do that.

Desiree slips free from the conversation and leaves the room. Vane stands abruptly.

"It was good seeing you, sweetness." Vane hurries after Desiree then. He doesn't notice the redheaded vampire's piercing stare as the door closes behind them, sealing them off from her view.

The tension in the room hangs thicker than blood, and I can't shake the sense that there's more to this situation than meets the eye. With Beatrix Marks in the city and the enigmatic figures she's here to meet, I know I must stay vigilant. The blackout, Ravi, Alden's presence, already have me biting my nails. What other surprises await me in the shadows?

CHAPTER NINETEEN
DESIREE

I MANEUVER my way toward the bar, empty tray in hand, as my mind churns with suspicions about Alden's claim of not being in Borealis during the blackout. His statement doesn't sit right with me, and I contemplate coaxing a confession or more information out of him if I can get him alone. Alden seems to have taken a liking to me, which I could use to my advantage. By maintaining the pretense of flirting, I can lower his guard and extract the answers I seek.

Alden might not have directly ordered the Balam attack, but he might hold crucial information about who did. Maybe he is here to finish what someone else started? The thought raises the hair on my arms, but it also fuels my determination to uncover the truth.

"Desiree, a word," Vane says behind me.

My jaw tightens. "No time. I am working."

"Working or flirting? Because that sorry display of exerting sex appeal to get Alden to confess to a crime he didn't commit was pathetic."

I leave my tray on the bar and face him. "Excuse me?"

"Let's talk in private."

"Whatever you have to say, you can say it right here," I assert firmly, planting my feet, refusing to follow Vane into a dark corner. I see right through his ploy—he's trying to distract me, to throw me off my game so that I'll fail in my mission. If I slip up, he'll have the perfect excuse to convince Vyvyan to kick me out, I refuse to let that happen.

Vane shakes his head, his light hair falling across his brow, and stalks off, knowing I'll follow. He is still my boss, in addition to being my prince. I march after him, my blood boiling.

"If you have a problem with the way I am handling my investigation, then I hate to break it to you, but I don't give a flying fuck about what you think," I say as we slip into a quiet corner hidden behind heavy velvet drapes. The fabric brushes against my skin like a lover's caress, and I freeze. This is where we met. Almost a year ago, before I was a vampire, I came here hoping to get over Jaxson and find a semblance of belonging again. Instead, I found Vane.

Vane's eyes spark with barely contained rage. My heart pounds as I consider retreating toward the crowded room behind me, but then I think better of it. I'm not doing anything wrong. My conscience is clear. I step closer.

"What's your problem?" I ask. "Afraid I'm about to solve this case?"

"You won't solve anything by sleeping with the enemy. Alden isn't your guy," Vane snarls.

"How the hell do you know that? Let me guess, you had a premonition."

Vane frowns. "No, I didn't, but I know when people have something to hide. My magic may not work on wolves the same way it does with witches, but I can see through Alden's intentions. He's only entertaining you because he wants something. Open your eyes, Desiree. He's using you."

I place my hands on my hips. My fingers dig into the smooth fabric of my dress. "Are you sure you are talking about Alden? Because it sounds like you are describing yourself."

Vane lowers his brows. "Careful, Desiree, you are toeing a fine line."

I step closer to him, my eyes narrowed. "And what exactly are you going to do about it, Vane? Banish me? Oh, wait, you already tried that, didn't you? Last I checked, you're not the king. So why don't you just suck it up and accept the fact that I'm not going anywhere, whether you like it or not."

"You don't belong here, Desiree."

I flinch, and he smiles. "Screw you, Vane."

"Is that an invitation? I thought you wanted to fuck Alden tonight?" Vane pinches a strand of my hair between his fingers.

I swat him away. "Don't touch me."

"I may not be king, but I don't take orders from you."

"Why do you even care about what I do, Vane? If sleeping with Alden and his entire pack is what it takes to get the answers we need to help Vyvyan, then you shouldn't have a problem with it. Unless there's a reason you don't want me to unmask the killer."

I pause, a chilling thought paralyzing me. "Maybe the wolves have nothing to do with Vyvyan's attack. Maybe, just maybe, it was you all along." My voice drops to an accusatory whisper. "With Vyvyan out of the way, you'd be king, wouldn't you? It's the perfect motive."

Vane's expression shutters. In a blur, he spins me around and slams me against the wall. The impact isn't hard enough to hurt, but it's enough to send a jolt through me.

"I would never harm Vyvyan," he growls, his face mere inches from mine. "Don't ever accuse me of that again."

But even as his words register, I find myself distracted by the weight of his body against mine. His muscles are tense under his shirt. I let my fingers trail lightly down his chest, touching his smooth skin. My breath quickens, rising and falling with each heavy inhale. Vane's eyes darken as I whisper, "You're intense when you're angry."

I should focus on the case and finding Vyvyan's attacker, but now I can only think about him. His scent fills my nostrils and makes my head hurt.

"Desiree. . .don't play with fire." His grip on me tightens.

I lick my lips, my mouth suddenly dry. "Vane . . ."

Vane's gaze locks with mine, and for a moment, I swear I see a flicker of something raw and unguarded in his eyes as he leans in. But just as quickly, it's replaced by the cold, hard mask I've learned so well.

"Get back to work, Desiree," he says, his voice low and controlled. He releases me before turning on his heel and stomping away.

I laugh, bitterness coating my tongue like coriander or mint.

My date with Jax couldn't come soon enough.

CHAPTER TWENTY
LEIGH

FROM ACROSS THE ROOM, Ravi fixes me with an unwavering, deliberate gaze. Seeing I'm alone, he approaches. I watch him through slitted lids. He told me about Tanith yet conveniently left out the fact that she was dead. It's almost as if he's deliberately trying to stir up trouble, but to what end? Is it to give Alden and me a reason to fight, creating an opportunity for the wolves to invade, or are his motives far more selfish and personal?

Just as Ravi is about to reach me, Bennett appears, his face paling as he takes in the drunken revelry surrounding us. Alden's entourage howls with delight, laughter bouncing off the walls as they recklessly dance on tables. It's not just Alden's crew acting foolishly. The few Council members I invited are falling prey to the intoxicating atmosphere. For some, it's the first time here, and it shows. They succumb to the Allure just as I did back in October.

The Allure ambushed me like a thief, immediately stealing my inhibitions when I stepped through the club's giant steel door. My plans to find Vane and discuss the letters evaporated instantly, replaced by the carnal hunger burning inside me. All I wanted was to shed my clothes, and Wilder's as well.

"Fucking finally," I say when Bennett sits beside me, the cushions barely sinking under his weight. Ravi's expression tightens suddenly, and he retreats to his corner. "How was the luncheon? Did you speak to Janus?"

"She was pissed you weren't there," he says, loosening his tie.

"That doesn't surprise me. What else did she say?"

"Nothing." He watches the redheaded server saunter over.

I frown. "Did you not ask her about the black—"

"Hi, handsome," the redhead vampire working alongside Desiree purrs in a voice resembling a lullaby. Bennett's pupils dilate. "Can I get you anything to drink?"

"Bennett," he answers with a slight slur.

The pretty redhead laughs. "I'm sorry?"

He shakes his head, as if trying to clear the fog from his mind. "My name is Bennett."

Oh, no.

"Misty." The vampire places a hand on her chest. "Now, do you want anything?"

He nods. "You."

Misty cackles. "I'm not on the menu."

I roll my eyes, leaning into Bennett. "Tone it down. Don't you have a girlfriend?"

Bennett's gaze meets mine. His eyes are unfocused. "N-no?"

"No?" I ask, thinking of Corvina. If they aren't dating, why are they texting?

He blinks again.

"Well?" Misty flips her hair. The cherry strands tumble like yards of silk.

"It's the Allure," I say, grabbing Bennett's arm. His pupils are already twice their normal size. "The vampires are seducing you with it, but if you focus, you can snap out of it. Breathe through your nose."

Bennett leans closer, his lips parting slightly. "Like this?"

I nod, even as I scoot back. The faux leather of the couch creaks. Bennett has not made any advances toward me since I turned down his proposal, but he isn't himself, so I had better make this fast.

"What did Janus say when you asked about the blackout?" I ask.

"Other than how terrible it is? Nothing," Bennett says. To Misty, he says, "I'll have a glass of whatever this is." Bennett moves to pour himself a drink, but Misty playfully slaps his hand away.

"Allow me." The vampire winks. Bennett smiles, his eyes following her every move.

The vampire maintains heavy eye contact with Bennett as she pours him a fresh glass of sparkling wine. The bubbles fizz and pop between them. Their fingers brush when she hands it to him. Bennett shivers from the contact, a bead of sweat trickling down his temple.

"You have a beautiful smile," he tells her.

I groan. Can he stop thinking with his dick and remember he has a brain? I'm dealing with espionage, and he's flirting.

"Misty, will you give us a minute?" I ask. Annoyance drips from my tone.

Misty cowers before slinking off. Then Desiree returns to the room, a scowl on her face. Bennett pouts, his lower lip jutting out. I roll my eyes, my fingers drumming against my thigh.

"I liked her. She was nice and pretty, and—"

"Did you ask Janus about Stellan Navis or his articles?" I ask.

Bennett sinks into the cushions, rolling up his sleeves as he bobs his head to the beat, ignoring me. His lashes cast shadows on his cheeks. I sit up straighter. Is he for real?

As the seconds tick by and Bennett continues to avoid my gaze, my patience wears thin. With a sharp snap of my fingers inches from his face, I finally break through his dream-like haze. His eyes flutter open, a flicker of annoyance dancing in their depths.

"Well?" I prompt.

"Janus said she was dealing with a personal matter during the blackout when Stellan's latest story broke," Bennett says with a sigh.

"Did you ask her what *kind* of personal matter?" I ask through gritted teeth.

What's more important than your city and most of your country experiencing a blackout? Parts of Corona are still without power, and the darkness lingers like a suffocating mask.

Bennett peers over the back of the couch. Misty waves at him, her fingers wiggling in a coy gesture. "When something is personal, usually that person doesn't want to talk about it, but if you must know, she mentioned something about Hebe."

I frown. Why did Janus bring up the hospital? "Is she sick?"

"She seemed well enough to me," Bennett replies, still gazing at Misty.

"Did Janus seem surprised about Stellan running for mayor?"

Bennett's head lulls to the side, his glasses slipping down his nose. "No."

I jostle Bennett's shoulder. No, because she already knew what Stellan wrote because they are working together, or no because of some other reason? "Bennett—"

"Excuse me." Bennett leaves me gaping after him as he stumbles over to Misty.

I want to scream.

"Leigh, can we talk?" Ravi appears like some apparition, and I nearly jump out of my skin.

My patience snaps. "Now?"

"I need to speak to you."

I rise to my feet. Ravi's intentions are unclear, and now isn't the time to clear the air.

"Not now," I say firmly, meeting his gaze head-on.

I leave, fishing for my phone from my tiny purse, to call Pallas to check-in. My fingers shake slightly as I dial, and I pray he has news that will help me decide who to trust and who not to trust among my Council.

Pallas answers as I lock myself inside the black-and-red-veined marble bathroom attached to our private room, the door clicking shut behind me.

"Funny, I was just about to message you," Pallas says. "How's Little Death?"

"A total snoozefest," I say, my fingers absentmindedly running along my sleek, smooth ponytail. It felt strange getting all dolled up for tonight's outing, especially with the chaos and uncertainty plaguing my kingdom. But in these turbulent times, my appearance is one of the few things I can still control.

As I stare at my reflection in the mirror, I barely recognize the hardened woman staring back at me. My gaze is sharper than a blade, cold and unyielding as stone. The distrust radiating from my eyes serves as a silent warning to anyone who dares to cross me.

I cut straight to the point. "What did you find out?"

There's shuffling on the other line, a dinging like he's inside a car, with the engine rumbling in the background. Then he says, "I sat outside Janus's house all day and didn't see anything suspicious. Unless you count the insane number of shopping bags Daphne Dyer had on her when she came home this afternoon suspicious."

I tap my nails on the countertop. "So, there's nothing to link Janus to Stellan?"

"Not yet, but I did find something that links her to Beatrix Marx."

My heart skips a beat. "Janus and Beatrix know each other? That seems highly questionable, given Janus's position as the president and Beatrix's anti-monarchist stance. Is Beatrix here for Janus?"

"She and Janus were friends in Icarus before Janus's parents died, and she moved here, eventually inheriting her uncle's Council seat. But until I hear the president speak to Beatrix directly, I can't say exactly what Beatrix's intentions are and if they have something to do with Janus."

"The timing of her arrival is suspicious."

Pallas sighs, the sound crackling through the speaker. "It is, but she's the only member of her group here, which rules out a political protest."

"Do you think Janus invited Beatrix here?"

"For what purpose?"

"Maybe they are more than old friends. Maybe Janus believes in her cause?"

"Now, before you jump to conclusions," Pallas starts, "let's wait to see if Janus calls Beatrix back. As I said, there's no call history showing that Janus reached out to Beatrix first."

My teeth clench as a thought crosses my mind. "Could she have used Daphne's phone? Keep looking into it."

"Leigh," Pallas says. "Perhaps you should just talk to Janus. Clear the air."

"That's like inviting the devil to tea," I reply. Pallas laughs, but I am not being funny. "Keep an eye on them. Let me know the second Janus makes contact."

"On it."

I frown. If Janus, the leader of our democratic nation, is conspiring with known anti-monarchists, where does that leave us? Where does it leave me?

"Oh, and Pallas," I say. "Maybe see if Beatrix and Stellan are friends."

"Sure."

"Be discreet."

I hear the smile in his voice as he says, "I always am."

"What have you uncovered about Bennett?" I ask, my mind drifting to his cold and detached person in the other room.

We were once close, so close that I trusted him with my life. But now? I barely recognize the man he's become.

Pallas's voice pulls me back to the present. "Nothing much, but I honestly haven't had a lot of time to conduct a thorough search. Janus has been taking up most of my time."

"I appreciate all your help, Pallas."

"I like being useful. It keeps me from dwelling on thoughts of Dad and the others."

His words have the effect of being hit with several rounds of artillery. Pallas's confession played a crucial role in the Council's success in putting away most of the members of Nyx. But Nyx was his home, where he grew up, and now he's left with no one. His loneliness resonates with me, as familiar as the sound of my own voice. Pallas, Wilder, and I share a common bond—we all have family in Kratos.

Once I leave the bathroom, the door hasn't even swung shut behind me before I run into Bennett. He looks left and right, his head swiveling on his neck as if it isn't attached to his body.

"Have you seen Alden?" he asks.

I shake my head. "No."

"He's missing."

My attention darts around the room, searching for any sign of Desiree, but she's nowhere to be found. A sinking feeling settles in the pit of my stomach. What if Alden went after her? He claims to want friendship with the vampires, but his actions speak louder than his words. How he used Desiree to provoke Vane tells a different story. Alden's true motives remain in mystery, and I can't shake the nagging suspicion that his pursuit of Desiree is just another move in his twisted game.

"Fuck. If Alden does something to upset the vampires and ruin our progress with them, I'll neuter him."

"Where are we going?" Bennett asks.

"To find—"

"Does this belong to you?" Vane barrels into the room. He has a snarling Alden by the scruff.

"Let me go! I was only trying to find the bathroom," Alden shouts.

"Where did you find him?" I ask Vane.

Vane releases Alden, causing the wolf to stumble into Bennett. It's the most off-kilter I've seen him since his arrival. Despite his unsteady footing, his eyes remain sharp and focused, revealing that he isn't drunk. Vane's actions have clearly rattled him.

Vane's lip curls. "In one of the tunnels leading to the Nest. I smelled his canine stench and dragged him back here."

My gaze narrows. Why was Alden in the tunnels?

"Like I said," Alden spits, "I was looking for the bathroom. Ours was occupied."

Vane snarls, his teeth bared, but I step between the towering royals, my hands raised in a placating gesture. I'm not interested in having either cause irreparable damage to my realm by going to blows.

"Look, I'm sorry about the misunderstanding. Thank you for your hospitality," I say to Vane before glaring at Alden. "Let's go. We've overstayed our welcome."

"See that this one goes straight home," Vane commands when Desi peeks at Alden from behind Vane.

"I will," I mutter, wishing I could send Alden packing.

Alden claims to seek an alliance, but the wolf is more trouble than he's worth. While there's a slim chance he's telling the truth about getting lost on his way to the bathroom, it seems like a hastily crafted excuse.

My gaze shifts to Ravi, and a thought takes shape in my mind. I could turn the tables on him and use his own tactics against him to extract information about Alden. I can uncover the truth beneath the surface by pretending to be his friend.

CHAPTER TWENTY-ONE
LEIGH

EXHAUSTED from the day's events, I crave the escape of sleep, wishing I could slumber into the next century. As I slip between the cool sheets, the smooth fabric against my skin strangely reminds me of Alden's slippery, eel-like nature—nothing romantic about it. I believe I've demonstrated that my Council and I remain strong, despite the blackout and Stellan's articles, but have I convinced him? Tomorrow, I hope to discuss plans for securing peace while determining a date for his departure.

Alden could have made a mess for me tonight with the vampires. He claims the wolves want peace, and while his actions seem to support this, something still makes me doubt his sincerity.

With a pained groan, I grab my phone to text Wilder.

LEIGH

> Miss you. Talk tomorrow?

My phone vibrates a second later with a response. I sit up to read his reply.

WILDER

> How did things go with Janus at the luncheon?

I tighten my grip on my phone at Janus's mention. Her ambiguous connection to Beatrix Marks is deeply unsettling, and every scenario I imagine paints a grim picture. Janus, my supposed confidante, has eroded my trust with her recent actions.

If Janus is working with Stellan, perhaps Beatrix is involved, too. Stellan wants to turn the Nebula against me, and he could use Beatrix to sway public opinion and undermine my authority. I must act quickly to unravel the truth before it's too late.

Janus and I are still working things out.

I hit send, then reread my text. It's not an outright lie, but it isn't the truth.

WILDER

Good. Proud of you.

I release a heavy sigh. Wilder's unwavering belief in unity is admirable. He truly thinks everyone can put aside their differences and work together for the country's betterment. But he's not here. He didn't witness Alden's behavior tonight—the way he acted, the tension he created. And he certainly didn't see the cold, distant way Bennett treated me—the frigid reception that left me shivering.

Setting my phone aside, my thoughts switch to Bennett. He spoke to Janus about missing the Council meeting, yet his demeanor at Little Death was so aloof, so detached. The Allure played a role, but I wish I knew the words, the magic phrase that would make him open up to me.

I fluff my pillow and shut my eyes. But the second I do, I'm jerked awake—not in the familiar comfort of my room at the palace but somewhere outdoors, surrounded by grassy, rolling hills and leafless trees.

How did I end up outside?

I'm still in my pajamas, with no shoes on. The grass underfoot is soft, tickling my toes as dawn begins to paint the hills. Far off, a grand building looms.

"Ah, there you are," a familiar female voice says. I whirl to see Janus's long, dark hair whipping in the wind. "We can't stay here."

A squall of unease hardens my stomach as I hug myself to ward off the early morning chill. The cold penetrates deep, making me shiver in my exposed state. Janus seems oblivious or indifferent to the fact that I'm in a barely there nightgown, her attire in stark contrast with a professional jacket and trousers, as though she's just stepped out of a work meeting.

"Janus," I manage to say as she moves past me, heading for the building perched on the hill. "What place is this? How did I even get here?"

My last clear memory is falling asleep after I left the club. I'd stopped messaging Wilder, turned over, and then nothing. But now, here I am, outside, and not by myself. My heart races. Is this a dream? But everything feels so real. Could someone have slipped something into my drink?

"Almost there, Leigh. Keep pace," Janus says over her shoulder.

I hurry to catch up with her. Why isn't she bothered by my confusion? Unless she's who brought me here? Above us, birds circle—a murder of crows, identifiable by their dark plumage and raucous cries. The sight of them scouting for food, with just Janus and me in this vast field, spurs me to quicken my steps.

"Janus," I pant. "What's all this about?"

"Something we've been planning for a long while."

I blink. Frustrated with the vague responses, I grasp her shoulder, but the moment I touch her, a startling vision overwhelms me: a colossal black snake lunges at me, its fangs bared menacingly, yet its caramel eyes are unmistakably Janus's. The vision vanishes as soon as I let go, and I'm left gasping.

What the hell was that?

"We're here," Janus says, pulling me back to the present. I look around, eyes wide, to find we're standing at the entrance of the imposing, windowless building that seemed so distant a moment ago. She knocks thrice on the door, then faces me, her smile chilling, almost serpent-like. I step back. "What is this place?"

"Your new home."

The door swings open, revealing a blank-faced Bennett in somber black attire. He's the picture of an executioner in a hooded cloak as he reaches to pull me inside.

"I was starting to get worried," he remarks.

I dig my heels into the ground. "Can somebody please explain what's happening?"

Bennett and Janus exchange a creased look of weariness before Janus seizes my other arm. They drag me inside the mysterious building. As the door shuts with a thud, I find myself in a poorly lit, empty room.

My body screams for me to move, but I'm immobilized. Leather bindings secure my arms and legs to a chair. I struggle to free myself. It's pointless.

"Why are you doing this?" I demand in a gasp. The restraints are painfully tight, reminiscent of the vines Chiron once used to bind me before locking me inside a bank vault months ago. I release a worried cry. "What is this? Is anyone there?"

The silence is as final as a judge's gavel until the creak of another door heralds the entrance of Janus, Bennett, Wilder, and Doctor Chiara Dunn. A rush of relief washes over me at the sight of Wilder—surely, he will explain everything. He will unbind me. "Thank the stars. You're—" My relief is cut short at the sight of the ominous metal tool in Doctor Dunn's hand.

A leucotome—a chilling symbol of lobotomy.

I clench and unclench my bound fists. "What are you doing with that?" Desperation creeps into my voice. I look past Doctor Dunn, seeking Wilder's intervention, but he stands aside, arms crossed, unresponsive. "Someone answer me!"

"President Dyer has expressed concern about your well-being," Doctor Dunn says.

"What about it? I'm fine."

Janus answers with a weary sigh. "Let's not pretend."

"You've been running on empty, Leigh," Wilder adds.

I gape at him. Every part of me is indeed exhausted, but with good reason. I'm at the helm of a nation now, fully embroiled in turmoil, each day presenting its own set of fires to put out. And it's hardly helped by the layers of secrecy maintained by those I'm supposed to trust the most.

"Why am I here?" I snap, glaring among them all. "What is this, an intervention?"

Janus sweeps my hair back from my face, which I bet she meant as a soothing gesture, but it only fuels my anger. I lash against my restraints.

"Can't you see?" she croons. "You're here to rest."

"Rest is the last thing I need. Are you plotting against me?"

Janus just laughs, a sound everyone else in the room echoes. Their laughter swells, filling the space in a way that scratches my mind, propelling me into madness.

"Guard!" I cry out. Isolde, or someone else, might hear me.

"Leigh, no one's coming for you," Janus says, her tone bordering on sympathetic. However, it sounds more like a sneer. "Everyone's fed up with you. Every disaster that's befallen this country, it traces back to you. A Lunar Witch was never meant to rule, so we've brought you here—to one of those institutions you've been so intent on dismantling—to demonstrate just how futile your endeavors are."

Her words hit me like a splash of cold water. Am I in an asylum? I scan the room, which resembles a dungeon from ancient times more than any medical facility.

Tears sting my eyes, and my voice cracks as I ask. "W-why are you doing this to me?"

"Because," Bennett says, "Don was correct. A Lunar Witch will only doom us all. It's safer for everyone if you stay here, confined with others of your kind, while we rectify your havoc. Rest assured; I'll keep the nation secure."

"What havoc?" Janus's lips tighten at my question. "All I've done is attempt to mend this country. I've—"

In an oddly calm voice, Wilder advises, "It's best for everyone if you just go along with it."

I struggle to look at him, and his presence hurts worst of all. He said he loved me, but was that a lie? Was everything?

I need to get out of here. "Guard!"

I writhe against my bindings. This must be a nightmare. Yet, the vividness of my senses argues otherwise—the chill of the leather chair beneath me, the trace of salt in the air, the warmth of Janus's breath as she soothingly brushes my hair away from my face. Tears carve paths down my cheeks, one for every person in this room. Each of them watches, waits, complicit in whatever comes next.

"Stop," I plead between the tastes of salt and despair. "P-please."

Janus exhales. "Ever since your Emergence, things have spiraled from bad to worse. First, your father and brother die. Then, your uncle turns out to be the Magician. But was Don that out of line? Revealing those letters hurt us all."

"And what is your plan when I am gone?"

"We plan to consolidate the presidency with your royal title, assuming complete governance over Corona, and agree to an alliance with Lua." Her response is more horrifying than the leucotome in Doctor Dunn's grip. "Unifying leadership under one ruler is the only viable solution to combat the looming threat of war between the factions."

I laugh, which makes Janus step back. So, Janus consorting with anti-monarchists like Beatrix and Stellan has been to orchestrate my downfall.

"You don't want to help people. You want power all to yourself!"

"Enough," Janus barks. Bennett flinches. "Doctor, you may begin the procedure. It's time to relieve Leigh of all her burdens."

I scream, writhe, and scream again, yet it does nothing to deter Chiara's advance. I find myself unable to meet her severe green gaze, not just because of the resolve in them but because their color, so reminiscent of her son's, brings a different pain.

Wilder stands off to the side, unmoving. With no ally in sight and no rescue on the way, my resistance dwindles to resignation. My glare at Janus hardens. Defiance is my last stand.

I gasp out, "You'll lead us to ruin," as Chiara positions the leucotome against my retina.

With a start, I sit up. I'm in my bedroom.

Shaking my wrists out, I find them astonishingly free of any bindings.

A hand touches my shoulder. I let out a sharp scream, expecting to see Chiara or Janus, but it's a woman with striking cobalt hair and stars inked into her skin—Isolde.

"You were dreaming," she says.

I take a deep, shaky breath to dispel the lingering tendrils of the nightmare and clear my hazy mind. Sitting up, I push the blankets aside with trembling hands.

"It was all a dream?" I whisper, my voice hoarse and uncertain. I struggle to reconcile the vividness of the experience with reality.

I swing my legs over the edge of the bed, planting my feet on the cool floor to ground myself. After taking a moment to compose my breathing, my heart still racing, I stand. Each step toward the bathroom is unsteady, and I am desperate to outrun the haunting images that cling to me.

"Are you okay?" Isolde's concern-laced voice breaks through my turmoil.

"I'm—" I start to assure her, but the words falter on my lips. Glancing down, I notice the state of my feet—grass-stained and dirty, bizarrely mirroring the dream's outdoor landscape. I choke on a breath.

"Your Majesty?"

I muster a shaky smile. She can't know what happened to me, not when I grapple with the uncertainty. "Isolde, I'm fine. It was just a dream, like you said. You can go. Thanks for checking on me."

Isolde frowns, perhaps hoping for a more profound confession, a glimpse into the depths of my nightmare. But I'm not ready to share, not when the echoes of that dream stir real fears about my sanity. The suspicions about Janus's intentions and the unsettling reality of my dirt-caked feet will remain my burden.

Once alone, I call out, "Aradia?" Desperate for answers and some explanation of my bizarre experience.

But I'm met with a chilling silence that only amplifies my unease. With no response from Aradia, I think of Ravi, hoping he can shed light on the truth. Yet, a nagging doubt lingers in my mind. Will he manipulate the facts to serve his agenda?

CHAPTER TWENTY-TWO⊕
WILDER

THE POWER STATION control room lies in ruins after the fire. Smoke and charred electronics permeate the air while blackened control panels stand like grotesque sculptures, their components fused together. Cracked monitors and occasional sparks from severed wires complete the chilling scene.

I look up at the soot-stained ceiling, which is marred by gaping holes that expose the skeletal framework beneath. The silence is unnerving, broken only by the occasional creak of settling metal and the distant drip from the failed sprinkler system.

Brigid places a hand on my shoulder. "It's haunting, isn't it?"

I nod but turn to face Dimitri, the plant manager, a Cosmic Witch engineer. He holds a clipboard while glaring at me beneath his hard hat. Dimitri isn't the person I wanted to meet; I asked Brigid to ask Eddo to arrange a meeting with Michael Bersa, the plant owner. However, Eddo insisted Dimitri be present, considering he represents the Nebula plant workers whose strike led to the blaze.

During breakfast this morning, Brigid and Eddo announced that Brigid would accompany me to the station to oversee the conversation about plant repairs. Brigid claims to know Dimitri and his crew because they are regulars at Furies and ardent supporters of Stellan's cause.

But I think Eddo just wants Brigid to babysit me. He probably thinks I'm here to strike a deal with Michael Bersa, given my supposed obsession with Epsilons. But that's not why I'm here.

Dimitri and his Nebula friends—inspired by Stellan's rhetoric—want higher pay and respect from their Epsilon employers. I understand this;

they *deserve* better wages. But their strike tactics, meant to challenge the establishment, have created an ongoing blackout that hurts their own families most. Both Epsilon *and* Nebula businesses are losing money daily, but while wealthy Epsilon citizens have backup generators, it's the Nebula who suffer most from this outage. Power restoration shouldn't be political, yet here we are.

"Is Michael on his way?" I ask Dimitri.

The stout engineer shrugs. "The Bersas answer to no one but themselves."

"Michael likes to make an entrance. Or have you forgotten?" Brigid's gaze lingers, and I return to assessing the charred mess.

I had the dubious honor of encountering the Bersa family on my first day in Aurora last year when Eddo assigned Brigid and me to investigate a robbery of priceless heirlooms at their manor. The case twisted when Brigid became the prime suspect due to her relationship with their son, Bryant. While Brigid's taste in men was questionable, she was no thief. As Blades, we adhere to a code of honor. I proved her innocence by exposing how Bryant had framed her to cover up his gambling debts, believing no one would question his word over a Nebula's. His arrogance was his undoing.

Michael's likely late today because he recognized mine and Brigid's name and is trying to put us in our places. If that's the case, I'd rather deal with this situation by the time he arrives. All Michael needs to do is sign the check.

I lock eyes with Dimitri. "If you started repairs today, how quickly could you finish them?"

He chews on the eraser of his pencil. "I could have them done by next week if I had the funds and my crew."

"That's promising."

Dimitri frowns. "But Bersa needs to agree to our stipulations before we return to work. He may shovel money into this place, but we are the backbone of this business. He must pay us what we are worth and then some, or this place will never run properly again."

I slip my hands into the pocket of my fatigues and study Dimitri carefully. He'd let people suffer without power to prove a point. I've seen where he comes from, but extorting Michael isn't the answer. "How long have you worked here, Dimitri?"

"Fifteen years," he replies, raising his chin in pride.

I nod. That's dedication. "I'd say you know this place like the back of your hand."

"That's right."

"I assume you aren't receiving a paycheck if you aren't working. And how do you expect to feed your family if you aren't getting paid?" I glance pointedly at the ring on his finger.

Dimitri clenches his hand around his clipboard. "My wife has a job."

"That's excellent. So her job provides enough for your family?" I raise an eyebrow.

Dimitri's eyes narrow. "Are you saying I don't contribute?"

"On the contrary, I am trying to reason with you. Demand better pay from Bersa, but also understand that until this plant is up and running, the money you and your wife rely on to live won't be coming in. And Bersa? It might not matter to him if you refuse to return to work. Once the outage goes on long enough, he will find other Cosmic Witches more desperate than you, willing to come in, and get this place working for half the price."

Dimitri scowls, his face reddening. "That won't happen."

I tilt my head. "You sound so sure. Yet, I thought only Sea Witches had powers of premonition?"

"Stellan will be mayor long before Bersa can reliably replace me. He will force Bersa to meet our criteria or leave this city, which means this place could be mine."

I take a deep breath. Dimitri's belief in Stellan goes deeper than I expected. Does he really think Stellan will wave a magic wand and all the issues the Nebula face will disappear? Things will worsen before that day, and Aurora may not be unscathed. If the Epsilon choose to fight back, Dimitri and his wife may not survive what's coming. He has delusions of grandeur. I need him to stop relying on Stellan for all the answers and take matters into his own hands. That means working with, rather than against, Michael Bersa. No matter how self-inflated Bersa is. It also means

I need to talk to Stellan sooner rather than later. If I can reason with him, I can reason with his supporters. But he is more elusive than smoke.

"Are you close with Stellan Navis, Dimitri?" I ask.

"I don't know him well, but I admire him. He will make a great leader."

"Yet you are sure that if Stellan becomes mayor, he will give you this business, no strings attached?"

"Wilder, stop antagonizing him," Brigid mutters. I bristle. If she is okay with prolonging this blackout, then she isn't the girl I remember. She fought for the people in this city, yet by not pushing Dimitri to compromise, she's letting them suffer.

"I'm not," I shoot back. "We are having a friendly conversation before Michael arrives, trying to figure out how to work together to get this place running again."

Brigid narrows her eyes, and I glare back at her. She can go. I don't need two people undermining me when I only want to restore balance between the factions. We are the same, yet she lets Dimitri treat me like an outsider.

Dimitri shakes his head. "We aren't friends. Nor do we want the same things, so nothing you can say will get me to listen to you."

The hair on the back of my neck rises. "Why is that?"

He smiles, revealing coffee-stained teeth. "You call yourself a Nebula, yet you turned your back on our kind. The queen's ancestors persecuted us, but that doesn't matter so long as she warms your bed." Dimitri gestures to Brigid, whose eyes widen with indignation. "You could be with a perfectly good Nebula woman, like Brigid here, someone who understands you, yet you'd rather continue to let the Epsilon control you."

My anger boils over. Now I understand. Dimitri's hatred for me stems from my relationship with Leigh, which means he blindly believes Stellan's writings. People suffer from this power outage, just as we suffered because of the War Letters. We have a chance to fix both issues, but not when people like Dimitri think vengeance is the answer.

"My personal life has nothing to do with the power," I snap. "I know what I am and where I came from. Being with Leigh doesn't change that."

Brigid winces.

Dimitri scoffs. "Oh? Could have fooled me, given you are here at the queen's behest. If she and the Council want power back in Borealis, have your queen endorse Stellan's campaign. It will make people like her more."

I step forward, my hands flexing at my sides. "Stellan doesn't know the first thing about ruling a nation. There will be pandemonium in the streets."

"That's to be determined," Dimitri responds breezily. "Stellan has friends in high places."

"Who?"

"I am sure he'd tell you if he didn't think you were a traitor."

Brigid tenses. So do I. This term has followed me since Dad's arrest, and I thought we were past it.

Polished shoes slap the scorched concrete. We all turn to Michael Bersa, who grins in his fancy suit with his combed hair. "Ah, Wilder, I hope you haven't been waiting long," he says, as if we didn't part on bad terms.

Perfect. Fucking perfect. I'd made zero headway with Dimitri, and now Michael swoops in mid-failure. Between Dimitri's stubbornness and Michael's inevitable criticism, I'm about to get caught in a crossfire of Alpha personalities. This day just keeps getting better.

Michael steps past Brigid as if she were a ghost. She glares at him.

"Mr. Bersa, I'm glad you could finally join us," I say, polite but firm.

Michael's gaze darts between Dimitri and me, taking in our stiff postures. A smile spreads across his face—Dimitri's upper lip curls in response.

I sigh. I'm never going to find a middle ground.

"Please, call me Michael," he says, still in that eerily friendly voice. "You are here to get my business up and running, which means we are friends, not strangers."

Brigid and Dimitri exchange a loaded glance, and my stomach turns. They think this proves something.

"Mr. Bersa," I say evenly, emphasizing Michael's surname, "I'm here for one reason only—to restore power to Corona's citizens. Nothing more." I meet Dimitri's glare. "And nothing less."

"Exactly." Michael's smile doesn't reach his eyes as he steps closer.

"The Council sends you here to help me get my lazy crew back to work so I don't continue to lose money each day the power remains off." He places a proprietary hand on my shoulder, and I fight the urge to shrug it off. "The queen wants the power restored. So do I. As her representative, we are on the same side."

The calculated way Michael emphasizes "queen" and "representative" might as well be a match to gasoline. Dimitri's face contorts. He glances at Brigid, and they share another knowing look, this one screaming "traitor" so loud I can almost hear it.

I grit my teeth. Michael is reworking the narrative.

"Look, Mr. Bersa." I keep my voice measured, diplomatic. "The queen understands that a stable power grid and fair wages go hand in hand. Your profit margins matter"—I nod at Michael, whose frown deepens—"but so does ensuring the workers who maintain those profits are compensated fairly." I turn to Dimitri. "The queen wants power restored as soon as possible, which means we need both sides working together. Sign off on the equipment orders and wage adjustments, and everyone gets what they need—including Corona's citizens, who are counting on all of us."

Michael brushes away some ash that has fallen on his shirt. "Let me give you some advice, Wilder. Since you are new to having power, if you want to keep it, you must learn that people will walk all over you if you give them so much as an inch. Power stems from control." He glares at Dimitri. "If you and your crew want to keep your jobs, you will show up to work tomorrow, get this place cleaned up, and you'll be lucky if I don't use your wages to pay for the damage you and your strike caused me."

"The fire was deemed an accident," Brigid inserts, arms crossed.

"Let me make something clear," I say, my voice cutting. "The order to restore power comes directly from the queen and Council. If you don't want to explain why you're obstructing their directive, you'll stop pointing fingers and authorize Dimitri to order the parts his team needs."

I let that sink in for a moment. Michael's smile falters. "The queen doesn't care about your power plays, Mr. Bersa," I continue. "She cares about getting Corona's lights back on. So I suggest we focus on that, unless you'd prefer to discuss your . . . management style with the Council directly?"

Pride shines in Brigid's eyes, and I fight a smile. "Get used to feeling out of control, Michael," she sneers. "The War Letters exposed who the real criminals are. You and your Epsilon friends are outnumbered now. The Nebula will take control, and you'll have to surrender it to us and Stellan."

"The day that happens, I will be six feet under," Michael replies in a cold and unyielding voice. As I suspected, the Epsilon won't sit back and let the Nebula take over. But the Nebula are ready to fight dirty, if they must. Michael and the rest of the Epsilon would rather die than give up power, and the Nebula will die trying to obtain it.

"That can easily be arranged," Brigid mumbles.

"Brigid, stop," I warn. Her smile slips.

I glare at Brigid. She's allied with Stellan, and I don't need her to make this worse. Her involvement will only muddle an already complicated situation.

"Listen to him, girl." Michael leers. "He won't always be here to save your pretty little neck."

I step between Brigid and Michael. Brigid's more than capable of putting Michael in his place, but I can't risk Eddo's fury if she loses her cool and lands a blow to Michael's smug face, as much as I wish I could let her. I need to keep this powder keg from igniting.

"Mr. Bersa," I say. "Can we just—"

"You're fired, Dimitri. Let this be a message to your entire crew—show up tomorrow, or you'll all be replaced. And, Wilder? You can tell Queen Leigh that when the power stays off, it's because your amateur attempt at playing peacemaker made everything worse." Michael rolls back his shoulders.

"You arrogant—" Dimitri's face flushes with rage. He storms toward the control room door, slamming it hard enough to rattle the soot-covered windows.

Heat builds in my palms—power itching to be unleashed—and the ache is almost unbearable.

"Where exactly do you plan to find a new plant manager on such short notice?" I demand through gritted teeth.

Michael's upper lip curls. "If Dimitri wants to apologize, his job is still here. If not . . ." He shrugs. "Maybe the Crown and Council can send me a qualified replacement."

"You're making a mistake."

"No, what happened here today is your fault. I thought you were here to make things better?"

"I am," I say.

"I'll believe it when I see it." With that, Michael gives Brigid one more dirty look and leaves.

I groan. How can I prove anything when both sides are working against me? Have I betrayed the Nebula by being with Leigh? Is our love blinding me to the harsh realities my people face? Cooperation is the only path to a better future.

It must be.

"Hey," Brigid says softly, touching my arm. "What happened to Dimitri isn't your fault."

"He fired him, Brigid." I pinch the bridge of my nose. "I was supposed to fix this, but I made it worse."

"I know. But it'll all work out."

I shake my head. Dimitri would rather die than apologize to Michael.

"You could use some cheering up," Brigid says. She nudges me with her shoulder and smiles. "I'm meeting Ry and the Erinye sisters for drinks at Furies. Do you want to join us? My treat. It'll be fun! Like old times. Don't let Michael Bersa ruin our reunion."

"I can't." I sigh. "I still haven't found Stellan."

Brigid's grin widens. It's genuine, reminding me of when we first met, before feelings got involved, and things between us were still simple. My chest tightens. Sex ruins everything. "Come out with us, and I promise Stellan will still be there tomorrow."

"Brigid . . ."

"One drink, and I will introduce you. He's a friend; he'll listen if I tell him about you. But Gianna stays home."

CHAPTER TWENTY-THREE
LEIGH

I OVERSLEPT after last night's dream, delaying my trip to the lunchroom. Ravi is the last person I want to see, but he might be the only one who can explain what's happening to me. But if I tell him about the dream, will he think I'm cracking? He could tell Alden, who would exploit any weakness. I have to be very careful how I describe what happened.

Thinking back to the nightmare—me, strapped down, moments from a horrifying procedure—sharpens my determination. It's clear Janus wants me off the throne, and I believe she's using Stellan to do it.

Ravi sits alone at the large table, absorbed in reading an article on his tablet. Despite the tempting aroma of coffee and fruit, the pit in my stomach doesn't ease.

"Where's Alden?" I ask as I take my usual seat, which happens to be across from Ravi. He doesn't pause his reading, leaving me to tighten my grip on my fork while an attendant fills my glass with iced tea.

"He went out while you were sleeping."

I sip my drink. "Out where?"

"Breakfast."

My eyes narrow. If he's making more messes to clean up, I need to know about them now. "With whom?"

Ravi sets the paper aside, his gaze finally meeting mine. He takes in my attempt to look presentable, but his eyes linger on the dark circles betraying my sleepless night. Makeup can only hide so much.

"Rough night?" His question is simple yet grating.

I stab my fork into the salad. "You could say that."

The clink of metal against the plate is unnaturally loud in the quiet room. Ravi assesses me. His attention is sandpaper against my skin.

"What?" I challenge.

"Tell me about your dream."

My spine collides with the back of my chair, the hardwood unyielding against my tense muscles. "H-how did you know?"

Ravi raises an eyebrow, then plants his hands on the table as if preparing to dissect my mind. "You have the look of someone touched by the unexplainable," Ravi says, his voice level. "So, tell me about your dream. What did you see? Or *who* did you see?"

My heart stutters. How did he . . .

Ravi smiles. It's scary how disarming it is. "Don't worry. Every Lunar Witch experiences it eventually."

"Experiences what?" I whisper.

"Dreamwalking."

I set my fork down. Dreamwalking? "What does that even mean?"

Ravi sighs. "Don't you understand the breadth of your abilities? Lunar Witches possess the gift of dreamwalking. It allows us to navigate and influence the dreamscapes of others. To analyze the subconscious."

A sharp inhale. So, this is not me losing my mind?

"How do I know whose dreamed I entered?" I ask before I can help myself.

Ravi shrugs. "There are always clues. Tell me what you saw."

I hesitate. Have I already said too much?

"Leigh?" Ravi nudges again. "Dreams might reflect hidden fears or desires or even serve as omens."

"You think what I saw reflects someone else's desires?" I ask. My heel taps a nervous rhythm against the floor. Janus reigned supreme in the dream, orchestrating events with cruel precision. If that's true, does it mean her hunger for my position is, too?

To know for sure, I must enter her dreams again.

"Could I do it on purpose?" I ask. "Enter someone else's dream?" Now that I know it is a dream, maybe I can coerce Janus into giving answers. It's as if she's working with Stellan and Beatrix to dethrone me—to cause a rift among the Council to make herself more appealing.

"I wouldn't advise it," Ravi says carefully. "Accessing the subconscious can be dangerous for you and the person whose dream you've entered. The mind is often volatile, and you could get trapped in the dream." He pauses, considering his next words. "I'm happy to teach you more about your magic, but we should start with the basics, like shadow manipulation. Or talking with ghosts. Have you ever crossed anyone over? There's an expiration date for how long a ghost can remain in this realm before their visitation rights are revoked."

I hesitate. The prospect of mastering my magic is tempting, but prioritizing the exposure of Stellan's mole before they strike again is paramount. Still . . . this could be an opportunity to unravel his and Alden's plot, to peel back their intentions like the layers of an onion.

Before I can even respond, Alden strides into the room. Far from hungover, he's as crisp as a daisy in a tailored suit. He's even freshly shaven. His cologne—a complex blend of spice and pine that I *refuse* to admit I enjoy—fills the condensed space.

"Good afternoon, party people!" Alden says.

As the staff rushes to accommodate his needs, I cross my arms. "Where have you been?"

With a guarded grin, Ravi dives back into his article, unfazed. The tapping on his screen softly counterpoints my heart pounding. "Well, while you were catching up on your beauty rest—you look radiant, by the way—I had the most enjoyable breakfast."

"I didn't realize you knew anyone that would bother to take you out?" I say.

"I do." His response is cryptic.

I huff. "Well, quit leaving me in suspense. Did you meet them last night?"

Alden settles into the seat beside me. He steals a tomato off my plate. I scowl.

"Janus."

I strive for a nonchalant air, desperate to mask any indication of the burgeoning tension between Janus and myself, acutely aware of Alden's scrutinizing gaze.

"Huh, didn't realize you two were chatting," I say, ignoring the unease creeping up my spine. The hell? Why wasn't I invited?

Alden sighs. "Janus reached out after yesterday's failed luncheon. I'm surprised you didn't know, given how close you and your Council are."

My jaw hardens while Ravi pretends to be absorbed in reading, but he hasn't turned the page. He's hanging on to every word, a silent observer in this dangerous game. Alden thinks he's caught me in a lie.

"What did you two discuss?" I ask.

"All sorts of things."

"Such as?"

Alden snags a crouton, the loud *crunch*—like the splitting of bone—in his mouth sending a jolt through me.

"You know," he drawls, "last night's . . . adventures are catching up with me. Think I'll grab a nap. Wanna join?" He shoots me a wink, and I can't quite place the look in his eye.

"I'd honestly prefer suffocating myself with my pillow."

Alden yawns, then says, "Suit yourself."

"My offer still stands to practice magic together," Ravi says.

"That's a great idea!" Alden claps. I frown. I don't like them teaming up against me. "Do spells, read each other's cards, or whatever you witches do in your spare time, then we can go out tonight. The three of us."

Alden leaves the room.

I inhale a deep breath, hating that Alden spent time with Janus. If those meetings are going to keep happening, I need to uncover Janus's plans sooner rather than later. Ravi may not want to teach me about dreamwalking, but I will convince him to.

"Sounds great," I say to Ravi. He blinks as if he can't believe I agree. "I'll meet you in the gym in an hour."

After Alden's fingers violated my uneaten lunch, I no longer have an appetite. With a quiet, determined exit, I leave the room, my heart a drumbeat urging me toward action.

CHAPTER TWENTY-FOUR
LEIGH

SITTING cross-legged in the palace gym, wearing my workout clothes with my hair pulled into a high ponytail, I glare at Ravi. He's across from me, mirroring my posture, eyes blissfully shut.

"I can feel you staring at me," Ravi comments, his eyes still closed. "Are you having trouble connecting to your root? If so, you may need to identify what's blocking you."

I glower, even though he can't see me. This meditation session is agonizing. I need to learn how to use my magic to infiltrate dreams. But Ravi dodged the topic of dreamwalking altogether. First, he said he wanted to show me how to harness the shadows. I managed to impress him by creating shadow figures that resembled barking dogs and hissing snakes. Now, he's trying to get me to ghost whisper by connecting to my body's *subtle realms* and unlocking the seven *primary energy centers*. Ugh. I'm bored out of my mind. Besides, I can already talk to ghosts just fine.

I need to learn about dreamwalking so I can figure out my enemies' plans, but I'm afraid to press him too hard. I don't want him to guess what I'm up to. If he doesn't bring it up soon, I'll have to. We're running out of daylight.

He takes a deep breath. "You took suppressants for a year. That had to have taken a toll on your psyche. Reflect on how you feel now that you don't take them anymore to create a clearer pathway between you and the beyond."

I scoff. "I am not here to talk about the repercussions of suppressants."

Ravi cracks a lid. "Why are you here?"

I frown. My interest in Ravi begins and ends with Alden. I see him seated on my throne every time I close my eyes. It's a constant, infuriating reminder of his true allegiance. *His* allegiance to *my* rival. He claims to be a distant cousin, but his true loyalties lie elsewhere. And this "training"? It's my insurance. My way of making damn sure he doesn't double-cross me.

"I am here to learn what you can teach me," I say.

"Well, that requires getting to know you a bit. Why don't you tell me about your mother?"

My father's invisible presence hums nearby, radiating unease like my own.

"What about her?" My voice carries a sharpness I hadn't intended.

"Where is she?" Ravi probes.

"At home."

"She doesn't live here with you." His words don't come out as a question.

I can't help but laugh. She would never. Though it's clear Ravi isn't amused. His features remain neutral. "No, she doesn't," I admit.

He nods solemnly. "I see."

"And what exactly do you see?" I snap.

Ravi exhales slowly. "Leigh, I'm not trying to attack you. I am trying to help."

I'm tired of snap judgments, people lying to me, and people trying to control me. He is collecting information to share with Alden. Why else would he ask me something so personal? My mother's whereabouts have nothing to do with my powers.

"No, you're judging me. My parents weren't perfect, but they did their best," I retort.

Sorry, I project to my father's lingering spirit.

Gwyn Raelyn was a fantastic father, but he had his secrets. He never prepared me for the possibility of ascending the throne. It's not like anyone plans for their death without some forewarning, but still, I was left clueless about how to rule. And now, here I am, grappling with the consequences, and he is a ghost making up for lost time.

"My parents weren't perfect, either," Ravi admits. His brown eyes hold a deep sadness, and I feel bad. Almost.

"Were your parents Lunar Witches?" He nods at my question. "And they taught you how to use your magic, despite the consequences?" Again, he nods. "Weren't they scared?"

"My parents spent time in an asylum, Leigh," he reveals, and I flinch. Images from my dream return. I can't imagine living in such a place. "That's how they met and why they taught me about magic. They wanted to overcome the stigma that the Lunar Witches were something to be feared. We aren't evil."

We aren't, but I'm not the one who needs convincing. The world does.

"Was your mother or father related to Ivah?" I ask. Ravi barely suppresses a smile. I roll my eyes. "I am not saying I believe you."

"My ma," he finally says.

"How'd she die?" The question slips out, unbidden. I'm supposed to be learning to dreamwalk, but I can't help myself. Other than Selene, I've never actually known another Lunar Witch. It seems like we're all cursed with the same kind of pain.

Ravi hesitates, then asks, "Can we talk about something else?"

My heart aches. I know how hard it is to talk about this kind of thing. "I'm sorry," I manage to say, though it feels inadequate. Words don't bring people back.

"I buried her years ago in Glaucus." His voice is steady, but I sense an underlying sorrow that echoes my own.

I let out a slow breath, fiddling with my sleeve. "My grandmother is actually there now. It's also where . . ." I pause. I don't want to discuss Psyche Psychiatric. That chapter of my life has nothing to do with Ravi.

"I know your family had you committed," Ravi says.

I bare my teeth. "Have you been keeping tabs on me?"

"You're my family and a queen. And, I might have done an internet search or two."

I release a strangled laugh. Dammit, Ravi . . . I do not *want* to like him. I can't afford to. But something about his presence puts me strangely at ease.

"You mentioned in your television interview that you concealed your magic by taking suppressants," Ravi says. "Will you tell me who gave them to you?"

Something in his posture tells me he already knows the answer.

"An orderly helped by giving me medical grade suppressants. I tried off-market ones before I left Borealis, but I ran out when I got to the hospital. And then, I couldn't hide my true nature. But that's all I will say."

"Was it Anselm Raymor?"

I open my mouth several times. How the hell does he know that?

"We're friends," Ravi says. "Anselm helped smuggle us suppressants when we lived in Glaucus. He's one of the good ones."

I nod, my scalp prickling. I don't like that Ravi knows so much about me, especially my time at Psyche Psychiatric, while I know next to nothing about him.

"You said 'us.' Do you have siblings?"

A flicker of surprise—or perhaps guilt—crosses Ravi's face, as if he's let something slip that he didn't intend to reveal. Dammit, we've veered way off topic, but now I must know what he is hiding.

"A brother or a sister?" I press. Perhaps it isn't him who wants my throne. Maybe it's his sibling.

Ravi shifts, unable to meet my gaze. "We should get back to the lesson . . ."

I shake my head and ask, "Is he or she dead, too?"

Ravi grits his teeth. "No, my sister isn't dead."

"But? Why isn't she here?"

Ravi tears his fingers through his dark hair, and I tighten my hands into fists. Yeah, it doesn't feel good to have your scars prodded, does it? I can't think of any good reason why he would keep information about this sister from me. I want to shake the truth from him.

"What magic do you want to focus on?" Ravi deflects. "You asked earlier about dreamwalking. Though it should be avoided at all costs, meditation is the easiest way to enter someone's dream."

"Ravi—"

"We aren't talking about her. It wouldn't change anything."

My hackles rise. None of this adds up. Ravi has secrets, and those secrets are connected to his sister. Too much is going on beneath the surface. "If you can't be honest with me, then we're done here," I state, rising to my feet.

Ravi stands his ground, flinty eyes meeting mine. "You can't have it both ways, Leigh."

"Excuse me?"

"You can't keep things from me and expect me to divulge myself to you."

With that, he turns and walks briskly out of the gym. I gape after him, feeling strangely guilty for no good reason. Clearly, he's not going to teach me about dreamwalking, so I'll have to take matters into my own hands, like I always do.

CHAPTER TWENTY-FIVE
DESIREE

MY CRAMPED CORNER inside the vampire dormitory feels like a silk, lace, and leather storm amidst hundreds of polished mahogany coffins. Several vampires flit about in a blur as they prepare for their nightly shift at the club. Their chatter whirs low amidst the rustle of elaborate fabrics. Other, more languid vampires meticulously dress for the evening's breakfast.

Pulling on my leather mini dress, I catch snippets of several conversations about the wolves' surprising visit last night. Some marvel at how Alden and his friends defied ingrained preconceptions. I think Alden's plan for coming to Little Death was to divert attention away from himself and the Balam attack by making friends with his enemies.

Anger surges through me in response. I never got the chance to question Alden before Vane unceremoniously threw him out. I think he was wandering in the Nest's tunnels to find Vyvyan so he could finish what he so callously started.

Vyvyan is the other topic of conversation in the dormitory tonight. No one has seen her in days, and many believe she's fallen ill. No one knows the truth. My empty stomach clenches with guilt. I am directly responsible for her current situation. If I don't solve this case, I'll find myself friendless and, perhaps even worse, homeless.

With a groan, I eye my reflection in the mirror, weighing if I should change as I clutch a pair of well-worn jeans. My bare feet sink into the plush carpet, attempting to ground me amidst my racing thoughts. Dressing to go out with an ex-boyfriend is always a delicate dance, especially when said ex might possess crucial information that could aid in my quest to find Vyvyan's would-be killer. Alden stays with Leigh at the palace, and Jaxson and Leigh are close. Jaxson may have heard or learned things that could significantly benefit my investigation. Despite everything, I can't deny I'm also excited to spend time with Jax. He mentioned wanting to apologize. But for what, exactly? Our messy past or our complicated present?

Whatever. The dress stays. It does wonders for my cleavage.

I grab my favorite tube of burgundy lipstick and am just about to apply it carefully when the dorm doors swing open with unnecessary force. Vane waltzes in as if he owns the place. I jump, smearing color across my pale face.

I curse under my breath. He'd better not be here for me. The last thing I need is to show up late and risk Jaxson leaving before I even get there.

As I wipe away the errant lipstick with a tissue, I can't help but notice it's the very same deep shade as Vane's shirt. I scowl. He's also deliberately left several buttons undone, providing a tantalizing glimpse of his sculpted chest. Heat rises to my cheeks, and I curse myself for looking. He's disgustingly attractive, but so is the devil himself. Vane managed to get under my skin last night after accusing me of essentially whoring myself out to Alden rather than focusing on helping Vyvyan. Then, as if to drive me mad, he'd caged me against the wall, and I'd fought the overwhelming urge to kiss him senseless.

If he's here to poke fun at me for it, I don't want to hear it.

All over the room, the other vampires have fallen silent. As Vane bypasses them, heading for me, eyes lock on me with varying degrees of animosity. Red flares prick at the edges of my vision. Vane's presence here will only make things infinitely more complicated between Misty and me.

Vane follows my gaze, and his brow furrows. "Leave us."

Every vampire departs without a second glance, the echo of their footsteps fading.

"Is that what you're wearing on your date?" Vane questions.

I snap the cap back on my lipstick. "Are you the fashion police?"

Vane's eyes narrow on mine in the mirror. With every inch he closes between us, my heart pounds in a wild, erratic rhythm against my ribs, threatening to break free. When his hands finally come to rest on my bare shoulders, the sheer heat of his touch feels like it's searing itself into my exposed skin. He swiftly spins me to face him, leaving me with little opportunity to react.

"Watch your tone, Desiree." His gaze drops provocatively, sweeping over my bare feet. "You can't possibly leave without shoes."

Vane rifles through my scattered belongings, presumably searching for shoes. I glance at the ornate pocket watch on my vanity to check the time. If I don't leave in ten minutes, I'll be late.

"Why are you here? Is Vyvyan okay?" I ask.

Vane examines a pair of towering platform heels before decisively setting them aside. He analyzes my vast shoe collection with an almost unsettling intensity, as if he genuinely believes the right pair could somehow reveal the identity of Vyvyan's attacker.

"Vyvyan's fine."

I purse my lips. "Are there any new symptoms I should be aware of?"

"No."

"So, you're here . . . why exactly?" I ask, attempting to inject a note of defiance into my voice, despite the tremor I can't entirely suppress.

"I came to apologize for my behavior last night," Vane states, finally looking up from my shoe collection. His gaze is intense, almost penitent, but I can't shake the feeling that there's more to his visit than a simple apology tour.

I raise an eyebrow. "You, apologizing? Did Hell freeze over when I wasn't looking?"

"Here." He rises to his full, imposing height, and holds two pairs of shoes. "Which ones?"

I point, perhaps too eagerly, to the lace-up boots in his right hand. The buttery-soft material practically begs to be caressed, and I can't deny the style's visual appeal against the backdrop of my dress.

"Great choice. Now, sit, and I'll lace them for you." I blink. "Now, Desiree, unless you want to be late for your date."

With narrowed eyes, I begrudgingly sit on an upholstered ottoman beside my bed.

Vane hands me the shoes before kneeling.

I slip one foot inside, then the other. They are beyond comfortable, familiarly molding to my feet. A faint scent of Misty's favorite perfume still clings to the leather. They were a gift from her last year. She claimed they made her legs look short, a sacrifice I happily benefited from. The memory sparks a small, sad smile on my face.

"Can I ask you a question?" Vane's hands drift over my calf. As he carefully pulls the laces, his deft fingers brush against my bare skin, sending shivers up my spine that I desperately try to suppress. "Why do you want to be here, Desiree?"

My breath hitches, a strangled sound, as he expertly ties a bow at the top of my thigh, just inches beneath my skirt's hem. Heat builds low in my core, and unbidden images flash through my mind: Vane on his knees before me, his face buried between my thighs. My pulse throbs in my throat. Vane's lips curve into a knowing, predatory smile, as if he can taste the direction of my impure thoughts, the dark fantasies swirling beneath my carefully constructed composure.

I squint at an empty coffin across the room, trying to banish the provocative image from my mind. Vane used me, discarded me, and shattered any illusion that what we shared was ever real. Still, my cheeks continue to burn.

"This is my home," I finally reply.

"But you had a home," he says. "A family."

I love my family, but being a vampire is forever. The connections I make here will last an eternity.

"So did you. I told you the night you Turned me—I want this life."

After tying the second bow, Vane's fingers linger. My breath stalls as his thumb traces a slow, deliberate pattern on my upper thigh, making my skin burn and tingle with a thousand tiny sparks. My thighs part unconsciously.

"Maybe after tonight, you'll feel differently," Vane says.

"Doubt it."

Vane smiles, and I melt entirely. The empty dorm screams temptation. Gods, I want him—*need* him. It would be so easy to surrender to this ache.

But his eyes are guarded, unreadable. He's hiding something. And I can't trust him. He's hurt me enough.

"There's a whole world of possibilities out there waiting to be discovered. Other Nests, other people . . . potential mates," he murmurs, meeting my gaze.

I swallow hard, my throat tight. Why is he prodding me with suggestions to leave? While touching me, as if he cares about me? What a cruel way to mess with me. "Vyvyan," I say, my resolve crumbling with each caress. "I'd need her permission . . ." I gasp when his fingers move higher, my cheeks flaming at his effortless power over me. Drowning in his presence, consumed by him, feels like everything I've ever craved. Damn him.

"You can do it. Leave tonight and never come back," Vane insists.

Through my desire-clouded mind, one thought breaks through. "But the case?"

The change is stark, like a candle snuffed. Vane recoils. "You disappoint me, Desiree."

I blink. "Excuse me?"

Still sporting a scowl, Vane stands. The intimate moment shatters like glass. "Vyvyan will want a full play-by-play after your time with Jaxson."

The room spins. I am such an idiot. Was that seduction a tactic? To unbalance me before I go see Jax? To control me? Or is he trying to stop me from finding Vyvyan's killer?

The door opens and then slams shut just as suddenly.

"I forgot my gloves; one second," calls a familiar voice. Misty appears and then halts when she sees Vane and me. I'm still seated with my thighs parted, Vane lording over me. It is and isn't what it looks like.

For fuck's sake. She always has the worst timing.

I stand, fearing what she's about to assume. Vane crosses his arms with a lethal, breathtaking grace. I slide around him, rush to my jewelry box, and clutch my grandmother's pearl studs. Their gritty texture is a balm in my shaking hand.

I slip the earrings into place. "You can tell Vyvyan I'll be back before sunrise. Have someone meet me at the entrance," I tell him, loud enough for Misty to hear.

Vane's frown deepens, but he nods sharply. "Okay." His tone is clipped and businesslike once more. "She will be pleased to know you are following orders. And I will meet you afterward."

He's going to *pick me up* from my date? "Absolutely not," I say, but Vane has already turned his back on me. The muscles of his shoulders flex beneath the expensive dress shirt. He gives Misty a curt nod, strides past her, and leaves the dormitory.

Misty places a hand on her sequined hip. "Lover's quarrel?"

I grab my purse. "Have a good shift," I toss over my shoulder as I brush past her.

I told Misty there was nothing between us, yet here I am, caught with Vane. I refuse to turn and see her hatred. Vyvyan's attacker holds the key to the Nest's safety, which eclipses everything else tonight—even the tangled mess of Vane and Jaxson. Even my messed up relationship with Misty. Whatever the cost, I will see this case through. Everything else can wait.

CHAPTER TWENTY-SIX
WILDER

THE RESIDUAL WARMTH from the setting sun clings to my skin as I navigate Tyche Street to Furies.

"Slow the fuck down, will you?" Gianna gripes, almost tripping in her heels.

"I told you to wear sensible shoes," I reply, rounding another corner. The scent of spices and simmering street food wafts through the air, tempting my growling stomach. It's been months since I've had my favorite layered rice dish, a regional specialty which can only be found in this part of Corona. But we are already late, and we'll have to eat when we get there.

The extra time I spent at the Bersa Power Station documenting the damage for Leigh and the Council put us behind schedule to meet Brigid, Ry, and the sisters. The first round of images I sent through text were blurry, so I spent extra time documenting the scene again as if it were a magazine shoot. When Janus called to press me for more updates on the power restoration, I gave a vague answer, promising more concrete information once the engineers and Michael finished their assessments. But the truth is, I need to find Stellan Navis first. If anyone can talk some sense into Dimitri and his former crew, it's him. I need to convince him that the Nebula can still fight for equal rights without resorting to sabotage and keeping the city in the dark.

I need Brigid's help to get to Stellan tonight, so I'll be extra agreeable and hope she introduces me. I'm not sure why she waited so long to mention she knew him, but I had a feeling. Brigid specifically told me not to bring Gianna. But if I really want to end the conflict between Epsilon and Nebula, I have to start with my own friends—even if it means dealing with Brigid and Gianna's mutual hatred.

"These are sensible shoes," Gianna insists defiantly. "But they are designer."

I roll my eyes. "What, do you want me to carry you?"

Gianna stops dead in her tracks and lifts her arms. "If you insist."

I shoot her a look that says, *"Fuck, no."*

"Are there no cars in this city?" she huffs.

"Considering you cussed out our last taxi driver, I am not taking my chances."

Gianna's scowl deepens. "Do you need to eat or something? Or are you upset about how things went down at the plant? You never told me what happened. Did you manage to get them to—"

I spin around to face her, my patience a thinning rope. "Look, things went a little sideways, but everything will be sunshine and rainbows once Brigid introduces me to Stellan. We just need to ensure tonight goes smoothly."

Gianna inhales sharply. "Stellan and *Brigid* are connected? On second thought, maybe I don't want to meet this Stellan guy after all. I'll learn about my father another way."

I can't help but laugh. "Come on, be nice. Brigid is trying to help."

"Help?" Gianna scoffs. "Yeah, help herself back into your pants."

My insides rebel against being with Brigid when I have Leigh. "It's not like that. She's just being a good friend." Does she seriously think I'd rekindle anything with Brigid?

Gianna rolls her eyes, clearly unconvinced. "Right, because 'good friends' always go out of their way to introduce you to their journalist buddies while giving you bedroom eyes."

I sigh. "You're impossible, you know that?"

"No, I'm just looking out for you," Gianna retorts. "Brigid has an agenda."

I pause. I'm not naïve; I know what type of person Brigid can be when she wants something. While I was documenting the scene at the power station, she was busy texting. I bet she didn't waste a second informing the Erinye sisters and Ry about my run-in with Dimitri and Michael. Knowing her, she spared no juicy detail, probably painting me as the Council's errand boy and making it her mission to "uncorrupt" me, ensuring our friends stay firmly in *her* camp.

But Brigid *was* there for me after Isolde cheated on me, and I thought Desi died. Even though we're not on the same page right now, I need her to trust that I'm here to help, not to make her life worse by pushing some Epsilon agenda.

"Come on, we are almost there," I say. "I know a shortcut up ahead."

We enter an alley lined with ornate metal lanterns, their geometric cutouts promising intricate shadow-plays when lit. Now, powerless and dark, they offer only emptiness, punctuated by the fleeting shadows of stray cats darting between our feet.

I slow down. The hairs on my neck prickle.

"So," Gianna muses, oblivious to my unease, "I have this idea of going to the library tomorrow to research my birth father. I want to see if there are any articles about him or his family. Do you think I'm chasing ghosts?"

"That's nice," I reply. A glance around the alley reveals nothing amiss, but an unsettling stillness hangs in the air. Is it just in my head?

"Yeah, and then I'm going to strip naked in the square and do an interpretive dance."

"Cool." I pause. "Wait, *what?*" I rotate, and Gianna's eyes narrow— before flying wide at something over my shoulder.

A cold, sharp object presses against my throat. Great. Fucking perfect.

"Move, and you'll bleed out right here on the pavement," a gruff voice threatens. The voice is familiar, but I can't pinpoint it.

"Um, W-Wilder," Gianna whimpers.

Two figures emerge from the darkness behind her. Both men wear scarves around their faces. One drags a menacing metal chain across the pavement with an ominous scrape. The other brandishes a sharp knife, its blade glinting in the dim moonlight.

I want to shout for Gianna to run, but I know it's futile. Those impractical heels would never carry her far.

"If it is money you're after, we don't have any," I tell them.

The two men close in, barking at Gianna, who shrieks in response. One even dares to sniff her hair. Sparks of electricity flicker at her fingertips. I shake my head, silently pleading with her not to escalate things. A sting lances up my throat, and I realize I've accidentally pressed the knife at my throat too hard, breaking the skin. Warm blood trickles down my neck. I frown deeper. The stain will be a bitch to get out of my shirt.

"Keep your money. We want you to deliver a message," the man behind me says. His voice clicks in my memory.

"Dimitri?"

The former power plant manager stiffens behind me. "Tell your queen that if she doesn't give Stellan what he wants, then the next time we see each other, you won't be lucky enough to leave without a scratch."

I want to point out that I am already bleeding, but semantics. "What exactly do you want me to say to her? The queen doesn't respond well to threats."

"Tell her that Aurora no longer bends to her will," one of the masked men adds as he strokes Gianna's head. Her lip recoils.

I exhale slowly. Now that I recognize Dimitri, the situation is less dire. He's angry, but I doubt he has the balls to harm a Blade irreparably. However, the presence of weapons and magic among the group still makes me uneasy. If I mishandle this, Gianna could get hurt.

"What does your wife think about you knifing people in the dark like some sort of common criminal, Dimitri?" If I can keep him talking, I can distract him enough to free myself, grab Gianna, and get the fuck out of here.

"Shut up! Don't bring my wife into this!"

"But your actions reflect on her."

The knife digs deeper into my skin. I swallow a sigh. He is pigheaded.

"Do you agree to our terms or not?" Dimitri growls.

"What happens to *us* if I refuse?" I ask, my gaze fixed on Gianna as a tremor runs through her body.

"Then we will send one or both of you back to Borealis in a body bag."

I laugh, and Dimitri tenses. "You'd kill us? Certainly, Stellan is against cold-blooded murder."

Dimitri laughs. "You have no idea what Stellan wants."

It's clear they've taken Stellan's words and twisted them to justify violence. It's what I feared. "I plan to ask him that when I speak to him," I say.

The man petting Gi's hair shakes his head. "Stellan would never talk to you, traitor."

"Why? I am a Nebula, the same as you. She is, too."

My Nebula mark is on display, as is Gianna's. What more do they want?

The two men holding Gianna eye her as if truly looking at her for the first time. One of them tilts her chin with the tip of their knife. "Say, don't I know you?"

"No," she says, averting her gaze.

"Yes, I do. You are Elio's daughter."

The other man whistles.

Gianna struggles harder against her captors, but they tighten their hold. "Don't be rude. We are just being friendly with you, little Epsilon princess."

"Leave her alone." I jerk toward Gi, but a second blade tip is at my side then.

"New bargain," Dimitri says with glee. "You let us take the girl, and we will take you to Stellan right now. Prove to us that you are one of us."

My blood runs cold.

"W-what?" Gianna screeches.

"What will you do with her?" I ask to stall. I'll fight tooth and nail before letting them take her, but I need to find a way out of Dimitri's grasp without Gianna ending up disemboweled.

"Use her to send a message to all Epsilon that a new age has come," Dimitri says, and I snort, failing to cover up my laugh. He sounds like a cartoon villain. "You don't believe me?"

One of Dimitri's accomplices pulls a gun. My lungs seize. A Solar Witch, not a Cosmic one. *Shit.* Cosmic Witches don't have magic to power firearms, making them less lethal in hand-to-hand combat. Why did I leave my own gun at home? The gun's barrel digs into Gianna's temple. She cries out.

The heat of my anger rises to my palms. "Let her go!"

Dimitri snorts and presses his knife deeper into my trachea. "If you even think of calling your element, my friend's bullet gets buried in that girl's brain. Got it?"

I clench my fist, suffocating my flames. "I'm going to enjoy making you suffer."

"She'll be dead before that happens," Dimitri says. "What is she to you, anyway? She's Elio's daughter. Her dad has ruined so many Nebula lives."

Bile rises in my throat. Revenge may be their thirst, but Gianna's blood won't wash away what Elio did.

"Please," Gianna gasps out. "Let me go. *Please*. Elio isn't my father."

I have to get her out of this.

"You're right," I lie, the hard words sharp in my own throat. "She means nothing to me." Gianna's breath hitches. "Take her. Do whatever you want with her. But take *me* to Stellan." When Dimitri doesn't move, I snarl, "We have a deal, don't we?"

"If there's any funny business, shoot her," Dimitri tells his friend.

As Dimitri's grip on the knives loosens, I seize the opportunity. Before he can blink, I've grabbed his wrists and twisted them behind his back. I shove him forward, putting his body in front of mine as a shield.

As Dimitri struggles against my hold, the masked man's finger twitches on the trigger at Gianna's brow. "What are you waiting for?" Dimitri shouts. "Shoot her!"

I press my knives harder into Dimitri's side. "If you even *think* about pulling that trigger," I warn the other man in a low growl, "I'll bury these knives so deep Dimitri will need surgery to dig them out. And trust me, his death will be on your hands. The next sunrise you see will be through the bars of a cell."

The gunman exchanges a nervous glance with his chain-wielding companion. Their bravado cracks. They know they're outmatched, and that Dimitri's death will be laid at their feet. Slowly, almost reluctantly, the gunman lowers his weapon.

I don't loosen my hold on Dimitri. "Give her space."

The masked men back away from Gianna.

"Gi, walk toward me slowly," I say without taking my eyes off the masked man's gun.

Tears stream down Gianna's face as she shuffles unsteadily toward me. Once she's securely at my back, I make my move. I slam the butt of one knife into Dimitri's temple, knocking him unconscious—my element flares. Flames lick at my fingertips, reflected in the wide eyes of the remaining criminals.

They turn and run.

I'm about to unleash the full force of my fire when a stream of water whistles past me. I spin and find four figures racing toward us from the far end of the alley. A fierce surge of relief floods me. *They're here.* With a flick of Alec's wrist, one of the masked men is encased in ice, frozen mid-scream. The other man is quicker. He bolts down a side street, firing a shot back. We all duck for cover, and by the time I straighten, he's gone.

Brigid rushes to my side to help me up. Meg and the fourth person— my old friend Ry Nieman—hurry after the gunman.

"You're hurt," Brigid says, her voice as chilling as death.

I shake out of her hold. "I'm fine." My pride stings more than my wound.

"Doesn't look deep." Her fingers ghost over my throat.

"It isn't."

"What do you want to do with him?" Alec nods toward the unconscious Dimitri.

I pull my phone from my pocket. "I'm phoning in the attack."

Brigid grabs my wrist. "What will you say?"

I gape at her. "The truth? He attacked us. They threatened Gianna."

Brigid's grip tightens. "If you send Dimitri to prison, you make an enemy of him and likely dozens of other Nebula who are his friends. Dimitri is just angry he got fired; he wouldn't have hurt her." She glares at Gianna. "If you had listened to me and left her at home, none of this would have happened."

"Dimitri wanted to hurt Gianna as a message to the Epsilon, and you want me to look the other way?"

"Gianna may be a Nebula, but she didn't grow up as one," Brigid sneers.

I stumble back. Where does this viciousness come from? I don't recognize her anymore. "So that makes what happened to her tonight okay?"

"Of course not," Alec chimes in, always the voice of reason. "None of this is okay."

"Goo—"

"But if you turn these people in, it could be seen as siding with the Epsilon," Brigid points out. "Stellan won't like it. He may not want to meet you."

"Are you fucking kidding me?" I say, my voice rising with each word. "This isn't about choosing sides. It's about distinguishing right from wrong." If Stellan can't see that, he is more detrimental to society than I thought. "We can't just attack people because they grew up differently than we did."

"You're different," Brigid mutters.

I bite back the childish retort that *she's* the one who's different. Even back then, I would have called this in. Ry and Meg return.

"Did you catch him?" Gianna asks, her voice thick with tears. Meg shakes her head, and fresh tears spill down Gianna's cheeks.

Alec wraps her arms around her. "I am so sorry they scared you."

Ry pulls me into a tight hug. "Still getting into trouble without me, I see." His chuckle is dark, but it draws a half-smile from me. Despite being several inches shorter than me, Ry's built like a tank, all muscle and brawn beneath his curly blond hair and deceptively youthful face.

I sag against him as I hug him back. At least someone in this city is glad to see me. No one can replace Jaxson, but during my time here, Ry and I became as close as brothers. I missed him fiercely.

Ry steps back, and Gianna rushes into my arms. For a moment, I'm frozen, as still as the ice encasing Dimitri's accomplice, but then she whispers, "Thank you," and I thaw instantly. I hold her close. She's Leigh's best friend. If anything had happened to her, Leigh might never have forgiven me. *I* might never have forgiven myself.

"What happens now?" Gianna asks, pulling back to glare down at Dimitri.

"How about we walk you back to the garrison while Wilder and Ry deal with him?" Meg proposes. Behind her, Brigid quietly seethes.

Gianna searches my eyes. I nod. She'll be safe with them.

After they leave, I call Commander Eddo to report the attack; Brigid be damned. Ry sticks with me, and when the call is over, we lean against the caged front of a spice shop, awaiting the familiar siren of approaching officers.

Ry breaks the silence first. "Is there something going on between you and the Epsilon girl?"

I let out a heavy sigh. "Gianna is a Nebula."

Ry cracks a grin. "I don't care what she is, as long as she's single."

"She is. I'm with Leigh."

"That's right," he says. "Does that mean I have to call you *Prince* Wilder?"

I laugh. "Call me prince, and you'll wish you were in Dimitri's place."

Ry's smile dims a bit. "Despite what Brigid thinks, I'm glad you're back. So is she. She just doesn't know how to express her feelings. At least not verbally. She thought you'd return, and the two of you would pick up where you left off. She's not used to being told no."

I shift my weight. Now she isn't going to introduce me to Stellan. She'll purposely keep us apart. That's Brigid all over—hot one minute, an arctic blast the next.

"Do you know what her deal is with Stellan Navis? Are she and Eddo loyal to his cause over the Council?" I ask Ry.

"Stellan is friends with all the Nebula in this city. But if you really want to know what all the fuss is about, see for yourself at his next rally."

I push off the wall. He's making a public appearance? "When is it?"

My friend shrugs. "He's speaking at Trinity Square in two days. It's not a secret."

I harden my stare on the dusty pavement. Brigid made it sound like getting in touch with Stellan would be harder than getting into Little Death.

"I'm going," Ry says. "You should come, too. Bring Gianna."

"If you and Meg fight over her," I warn, "don't come whining to me when Meg ultimately kicks your teeth in."

Ry straightens, a mischievous glint in his eyes. "Please, there's no competition."

The wail of approaching sirens grows louder, and I draw a deep breath, steeling myself for the fallout. Eddo won't be happy, and neither will Michael Bersa when he learns he'll need to replace his plant manager on short notice. That apology he wants won't happen anytime soon.

CHAPTER TWENTY-SEVEN
DESIREE

"I'M SO sorry I'm late." Jaxson's smile lights up as he presents me with a flower. Its intricate star-shaped petals glisten under the soft light of the backup generator powered streetlamps. The sweet, earthy scent of the blossom cocoons us. "For you."

It's a white oleander—my favorite. He remembered.

I accept the flower that matches the tattoo on my shoulder, twirling it between my fingers. Part of me still cares for Jaxson, but my heart *had* to move on after he left. Except, the longer he smiles at me, the more I regret I ever did.

I'm a vampire. We don't belong together. It's unfair to let him think otherwise.

I pinch a velvety petal between my fingers. "But they aren't in season. Where'd you get it?"

Jaxson's grin spreads wider, warm and inviting like a sunbeam. I have to look away, not wanting to get lost in that easy comfort. Unlike Vane, who scowls and plays with my attraction, pulling me close only to cruelly withdraw, Jaxson's smiles are genuine and free. I remind myself, though, that those smiles aren't special; he gives them to everyone. This isn't a date. I need to focus on proving to Vyvyan and Vane that I can solve this case, and that starts with Alden Lupas. Why is he in Borealis, and how does he fit into what happened to Vyvyan?

"Can't a guy have his secrets?" Jax muses.

"Fine, leave me guessing," I say.

"Maybe if you are super nice to me, I'll tell you all my secrets."

"You forget I already know all your secrets."

"Then that means we get to spend all night talking about you."

"You have me until dawn," I state, unwilling to miss my curfew.

"Right," he says as we maintain steady eye contact. "Gods, you're so pretty."

I roll my eyes, ignoring how my heart skips a beat. "Come on, loverboy, I'm starving."

Inside Blue Sparrow, Jaxson and I sit across from each other. Soft music plays in the background, a gentle melody that seems to wrap around us like a sensual embrace. I bury my face in my menu. The vampire-friendly options include ox-blood soup, lamb's blood casserole, and ethically sourced witches' blood warmed to ninety-eight degrees. My fangs ache.

"I know what I want," I announce, closing my menu.

"Me too," Jaxson replies, staring right at me.

Bats flap in my belly. "So, what do you know about Alden?"

Jax sips his water, the ice cubes clinking against the glass. "Ouch. Should I be offended that you want to discuss another guy on our date?"

I chew my bottom lip. "This isn't a date."

"You mean to tell me you got all dressed up for our non-date? Right."

Jaxson's gaze drifts down, lingering on my chest, on the swell of my breasts pushing against the fabric of this dress—a dress I wouldn't have dreamed of wearing back in high school. He narrows his eyes. I take a steadying breath. "What?"

"The sight of you breathing goes against everything I thought I knew about vampires," he says.

I smirk. Vampires are very misunderstood. "So long as we drink blood, our bodies resemble yours."

Jax wets his lips. "That's good to know."

"Behave."

"Only because you asked so nicely."

"Okay, so Alden . . ." Jax's gaze is heavy with more unspoken words.

I sigh. "What now?"

"What's wrong with Vyvyan?" he asks.

A cold dread seeps into my bones. "What do you mean—"

"No one has seen or heard from her since before the blackout. Is she sick?" Jax's next question is laced with skepticism. "Do vampires even get sick?"

"Vyvyan's been busy," I say defensively. Too defensively.

Jaxson leans forward. All the heat of our flirtation is gone.

"Fine, she's recovering," I say. It's the truth, and it better be enough to get him off my case.

"Desi, don't underestimate me. You're here because you need something, and I'm guessing it involves information. Quid pro quo, right? Tell me about Vyvyan, and I'll answer whatever questions you have about Alden. Though discussing another guy sounds about as appealing as a root canal, but for you, I'll manage it."

My brows dip below my bangs, a frown tugging at my lips. Jax might have valuable information I need to help Vyvyan, but he won't give me what I want if he senses I am lying. "Vyvyan got hurt. She's recovering."

Jaxson scratches his jaw thoughtfully, the scrape of his stubble against his fingers filling the silence between us. "Hurt how?"

"Does it matter?"

"If you want to know more about Alden, it does. Because what I know about him is juicy."

"How juicy?" I press.

"Like you'll be journaling about it along with how handsome I look tonight, *juicy*," he says, drawing out the last word with a teasing grin.

I laugh softly. Journaling was my refuge growing up, a place to pour out every fight, every bad day, expelling the anger and loneliness so I could process it all. But I haven't felt the need to write since moving into the Nest. I had Misty to talk to, before . . . well, before everything fell apart. Now, I'm starting to think I need that journal more than ever.

"I don't believe you," I challenge.

"That makes two of us, sunshine."

"Well, then, I guess we are at an impasse." I reach for my purse. "I guess I better get going."

"Sounds good to me. We can skip dinner and get right to the fun stuff."

I pause. "Such as?"

"Let's get the hell out of here and go back to my place," Jaxson says, a mischievous glint in his vibrant eyes. "I have a single now, which means we don't have to pretend to be quiet anymore." He raises an eyebrow, and heat crawls up my neck. Dammit.

My clothes suddenly feel confining. Jaxson's place had been our escape back then, a haven from my parents. We often found the room occupied by his roommate at the garrison, but that never stopped us from finding ways to touch. I'm sure his roommate was well aware of what was going on. After all, life as a Blade didn't afford much in the way of privacy, which only made our encounters more exhilarating.

"What about dinner?"

"Don't worry, I still plan on eating." Jax's grins devilishly.

Chills dance along my skin. I cross my legs, but the pang between them refuses to subside. Fuck, I'm a mess. First Vane, now Jax? I'm overwhelmed by flashbacks of my last few months as a witch, torn between trying to commit to Vane and the difficulty of letting Jax go.

"We are just friends," I say.

"We've always been friends. That didn't stop us before."

"It did." His friendship with my brother and the unspoken bro code stopped us from crossing more lines than we already had.

Jax studies me. "Are you seeing someone?"

"No," I say halfheartedly as I search for the waiter.

"What about Vane?"

"What about Vane?" I ask, and my hackles rise.

Jax notices. "He's your sire, so doesn't that make you his?"

I growl a low warning that rumbles in my chest. "You are toeing a dangerous line, Jaxson Foster-Reid. I belong to no one."

Jaxson smiles a satisfied grin that makes my blood boil. "Good."

"Grow up, or I'm leaving."

"No, I'm sorry. I'll behave," Jax says. I sit straighter. "Okay, so let me get this straight: Vyvyan's recovering because she was hurt, but don't all you vampires have super healing abilities? What hurt her so badly for it to take days to heal? Answer truthfully."

A knot forms in my throat. I can't tell Jaxson the truth, but he won't help me if I say nothing. My week is almost up.

"Do you promise to keep it a secret?" I ask.

Jaxson offers me his pinky in a childish gesture that makes my heart ache with nostalgia. It's what we did as kids, Jaxson, Wilder, and me. "I promise."

I gesture for Jaxson to lean in closer to me. He does. "Someone summoned Balam to kill Vane and Vyvyan the night of the blackout."

"Fuck. Are you serious?"

I scan the restaurant for signs of eavesdroppers. Satisfied that no one is listening, I say, "Yes."

"Who knew they were leaving the Nest?"

I shrug. "The Council."

Jax is silent for a moment, his eyes distant. "Then why are you asking me about Alden?"

"Because Balam's daemon signatures were paw prints."

He considers my words before realization widens his eyes. "You mean, like wolves."

"Wolves and vampires have been enemies for hundreds of years. The conflict escalated when Vyvyan refused to challenge the witches' decision to force the vampires underground. Many vampires refused to comply and headed north into Lua, seeking refuge in wolf territory," I state. Jaxson nods, his expression grim.

"The vampires' encroachment on wolf lands heightened tensions. Fiercely protective of their territory, wolves saw the vampires as a direct threat. Skirmishes broke out, with both sides suffering losses," I continue. "Wolves view vampires as unnatural, soulless creatures, while vampires see wolves as primitive, ruled by instincts. The cultural differences and territorial disputes have made peaceful coexistence nearly impossible."

"But Alden was at Little Death the other night. Did something happen?"

"Alden got caught wandering the tunnels, heading into the Nest. I think he was trying to get to Vyvyan to finish the job." While my voice rises with excitement at the possibility of being right, Jaxson is shaking his head.

"But Alden wasn't in town during the blackout. His train got in days later. Maybe the tracks you saw were from a large dog?" My jaw hardens at Jaxon's statement. "Alden didn't sneak into Corona, make his way down to Borealis, attack Vyvyan, timing it perfectly with a blackout, then make it back to Lua, only to arrive as if nothing happened a couple of days later."

It does sound absurd when he says it like that, but I was so sure it was Alden.

"How else would you explain the prints?" I ask.

Jaxson clicks his tongue. "I think someone is trying to throw you off their scent."

"Like whom?"

"Someone on the Council?"

I groan. He sounds like Vyvyan. "There are sixteen members on the Council, including Leigh. It'll be like finding a needle in a haystack."

Bennett and a few other councilors were at Little Death the other night. Other than Bennett's terrible reaction to the Allure, he seems harmless. My brother has told me a little about him. How he is Leigh's ex, how he betrayed her with Eos, only to win her and the country back with a heartfelt apology. He may be slimy, but he doesn't seem to be the type to risk his life or job by raising daemons to hurt Vyvyan and Vane.

What motive would he have?

"Desiree? Earth to Desi, anybody home?"

I blink. "Sorry?"

"What do you want to eat?" Jax lifts his gaze. The server's expectant eyes are on me.

I open my menu, pointing to what I want. "The blood we have on hand tonight is B positive. Does that suffice?" the waiter asks.

"Sure." To me, blood is blood. I've yet to have any that has rocked my world.

I glance at Jaxson, wondering what his blood type is. Would it taste sweeter because it's him? My mouth waters, a dull throb pulses through my gums. Jax winks. I quickly glance away.

Once the waiter finishes, we give him our menus, and he goes to relay our order to the kitchen.

"What are you thinking about?" His voice is low and teasing, as if he already knows.

"Nothing. Just how pissed I am about hitting a dead-end." I uncross my legs, accidentally bumping Jaxson with my foot. His gaze smolders. My breath catches in my throat from the heat burning in his eyes. I stare at my lap, my fingers twisting my napkin.

"You know," Jaxson ponders, his tone contemplative. I lift my gaze. "If you want to know who attacked Vyvyan, all you need to do is raise the daemon that did it."

My head falls sideways. "That's a thing?"

"Let me help. I remember how to do it. We could ask for the check, get the ingredients we need tonight, and have the answers you need by morning. Balam isn't like the Harborym. So long as you are calling the shots, he can't hurt you."

The idea I could have answers has my body thrumming with anticipation, but my curfew looms over my head like an executioner's ax. If I am not there by morning, Vane will lock me out. He wants me to fail, and this is the perfect excuse for him to banish me. Maybe I can table this idea, present it to Vyvyan, and meet up with Jaxson tomorrow, though the idea of putting him in danger has sweat dotting my brow.

"Not tonight."

Jax frowns. "Just say when."

I nod. "Thanks."

"Anything for you."

I take a deep breath. If he means that, then he owes me the truth. "Jax, at Little Death, you mentioned wanting to have this dinner to apologize. What exactly are you apologizing for?"

Jax's hands disappear beneath the table, his gaze intense. "For wasting so much time, Desiree. From the moment I learned you survived that car bombing, I should've been by your side. Every single day since we met at the loft in November, I've wanted to ask you out, but I let my doubts hold me back. I wasn't sure if you wanted the same thing."

He leans forward. "But I'm done waiting—done being passive. I thought I lost you, and it nearly destroyed me. Now that you're back, I will fight for you, for us. You're it for me, Desiree. You're the one."

His words hit with the same amount of shock as defibrillator pads. He didn't say, "I love you," but the sentiment is crystal clear. It took nearly losing me for him to realize how deep his feelings were and how rare our connection is.

And he's right. Jax and I are a force to be reckoned with. We keep each other safe and grounded. Unlike Vane, Jaxson is a sure thing without constant games and secrets. Jax is my best friend; even if we don't have a future together, we have this moment.

It may be time to let go of my hurt and enjoy the present.

CHAPTER TWENTY-EIGHT
WILDER

AFTER GIVING our statements to Eddo and the other Blades in the alley, Ry and I climb into a taxi to head back to the garrison. As the car pulls away, we watch from the window as a delirious but conscious Dimitri gets put into the back of a squad car. The Blades then call in a van to transport his frozen accomplice.

Pockets of city lights blur past us, and Ry and I fall into easy conversation, catching up on his life in Aurora since I've been gone. He laments the practically nonexistent dating pool, which leads him to ask about Gianna and, inevitably, Leigh. Ry's relentless teasing fills the car, warning me not to let Brigid see the undeniable smile that appears whenever I speak about Leigh. But I'm done hiding. My friends mean too much to me to conceal something as significant as my relationship with them. It's time to prove that.

When we arrive at the garrison, we hang our jackets in the foyer.

Ry's eyes sparkle with mischief. "Come on, Alec texted that the girls were in the courtyard. You can't bail on that drink now."

Exhaustion tugs at my limbs, urging me toward the stairs leading to my room. But the sound of laughter is impossible to resist. The day's events still weigh heavily on my mind, especially Brigid's attempt to control my access to Stellan. Her manipulation leaves a gross taste in my mouth. But more than that, I need Ry and the others to understand that despite my life in Borealis, they still matter to me. They're still my family.

"One drink," I concede.

Ry's grin is infectious as he claps me on the shoulder and steers me out into the warm night air.

"No, you're wrong, Brigid. Dead wrong! That's not what—" Alec cuts herself off as she sees Ry and me. "Hey! Perfect timing. Brigid was trying to convince us she wasn't hammered at the Mayoral Ball last year when Janus Dyer visited."

"I wasn't," Brigid insists.

Meg and Alec lock eyes. Then Alec's laughter bubbles like a gurgling fountain as her drink sloshes onto the plush outdoor couch. The rich aroma of spilled whiskey mingles with the heady scent of jasmine from the nearby trellises.

Gianna laughs along with everyone else, but her laugh is a hollow sound devoid of genuine mirth. I half-expected to find her barricaded in her room, but it seems she prefers the company of others to facing the demons that lurk in the solitude of her thoughts. I understand her choice completely. My friends have a way of helping you forget the bad stuff. It's what made living here so easy the first time around.

I'd arrived broken and scarred, my soul battered by the shitstorm I'd left behind in Borealis. But they'd given me a chance to start over, to be the person my dad never wanted me to be. I flourished here and maybe Gianna can, too, if she doesn't let the acts of three idiots dictate her future.

"That's funny, Brigid, because I remember seeing you take several shots on an empty stomach, no less," Alec reminisces, her voice taking on a dreamy quality as she transports us back to a memory from ten months ago. Before Dad had killed Sinclair, life had seemed good, or at least, I'd thought it was. Little did I know that, shortly after, I would meet Leigh, and she would turn my world upside down. Living in Aurora, I'd been happy, if not aimless. It wasn't until I returned to Borealis and chose to compete for Domna that I found something worth fighting for.

Alec continues, "Remember? Everyone was there. Stellan covered the event, wandering around, and trying to get quotes from the inebriated guests. Janus was the only person who deigned to speak to him."

That's right. Stellan had been there, but I didn't pay him much notice. He'd been a beat reporter for the mayor's office, observing from the shadows for a long time, waiting for his opportunity to strike. Stellan had been quiet, if not nosy. I believed he was harmless, but after what Dimitri did tonight, claiming it was to further Stellan's cause, I fear Stellan's use of violence will push people to their limits. I glance at Gianna. More people will get hurt in the process.

Meg draws from a long, ornate pipe connected to an intricately designed water vessel. Swirling patterns and glowing runes adorn the glass. "Ah, yes," she says, exhaling sweet, tobacco-scented smoke into the air. "Phe wore that hideous gown."

"Yes! And Brigid, who wasn't wasted, tripped and fell into the fountain," Alec recalls, her voice rising in pitch as the story progresses. "You were floating around like a jellyfish in all that taffeta!"

My smile freezes on my face, cracking around the edges. That party . . . it was just a few days before the call, before Marlowe told me my dad was in prison, and after that my sister was dead. I remember Marlowe's voice, the way she stayed on the phone for a full hour while I tried to grasp the impossible. How could I live without my sister? My twin. My other half, whom I left behind when I moved to Aurora to deal with my problems instead of being there for hers. I fight the wave of grief that threatens to drown me, one jagged, painful childhood memory at a time. My chest tightens, as if a vise grip wound around my lungs. Suddenly, each breath feels stolen, a desperate gasp for air.

Ry squeezes my shoulder. "You good?"

I force a nod.

He gives me a closed-mouth smile before sitting beside Gianna. Meg frowns into her drink.

Brigid's cackle cuts through the tension. I sit across from her on one of the upholstered floor pillows. "Papa was so mad! I couldn't understand why. It's not as if I fell on purpose."

"Please! Eddo had a good reason to be angry!" Alec screeches. "The water made your dress see-through. Everyone saw your pierced nipples!"

The girls and Ry erupt into another fit of laughter, but I know what's coming next.

"When Wilder tried to pull you out, you yanked him in with you, tux and all," Meg adds. I groan at the memory. I had promised myself nothing would happen again between Brigid and me, but I broke my word that night. "Eddo about blew a fuse."

Brigid's gaze meets mine, and the intensity in her eyes makes my lips flatten into a grimace. "That was a great night, wasn't it, Wilder?"

I avert my gaze, feeling Leigh's presence even in her absence. Things were different back then. "I'm heading to bed," I announce, rising.

"But it's not even midnight," Brigid protests.

I shrug. "It's been a long day."

Gianna sets her untouched coffee on the low table and declares, "I'll come with you."

Eddo gave her a room across from mine. It's small, but it does have a window overlooking the courtyard. It's no Najma Hotel, but it also didn't seem to have been occupied for some time, so Eddo was being an ass for not getting it ready for her sooner.

Alec whines, "You can't go yet, Gi! I haven't even asked you all the burgeoning questions I need to know."

"Like what, Alec?" Brigid asks, a slight edge to her voice.

"Like where Gianna bought that dress? It is so chic."

"You probably can't afford it," Brigid says, her tone dripping with disdain.

Alec scoffs. "Bitch!"

While Alec and Brigid bicker, I tell Gianna, "You should stay if you want." It's good for her to be around other Nebula who don't want to cause her harm.

"Yeah, stay!" Alec chirps.

Gianna's gaze flicks between me and the others, lingering the longest on Brigid.

"Have some fun," I encourage. Gi smiles, nods, and then sits back down beside Ry.

He leans in, lowering his voice conspiratorially. "Do you want to hear the story about how I accidentally shot Commander Eddo in the ass?"

"Aren't you a sniper? That's what Alec said," Gianna asks.

Ry's smile is wide and infectious. "That's why it's a good story."

A gentle breeze wafts through the courtyard, carrying the heavy promise of rain with it. The palm fronds rustle and whisper as if sharing secrets of the impending downpour. I can almost hear the water rushing down the streets and smell the petrichor as it mingles with the sand and debris that will inevitably clog the storm drains. It's time to go.

"Wake me if there's news about Dimitri's accomplice. The one that got away," I tell Ry.

He nods, his eyes never leaving Gianna's face. "Will do."

I leave the courtyard, and seconds later, footsteps tap behind me. Brigid's hand grips my upper arm, her touch searing my skin through my sleeve. My room is to the left, and hers is to the right. We've been through this routine countless times.

"Brigid, I'm exhausted," I firmly tell her.

"Can we talk a bit? It feels like I angered you with how I handled things earlier."

"You think so?"

A flush of color rises in her cheeks. She hurries to explain. "I'm sorry. Having you back . . . it's been a whirlwind. Stellan is a good guy, but not everyone takes his message the same. I just didn't want Dimitri's actions to reflect on him or the Nebula who follow him. You know how the media likes to twist things."

I fold my arms. "The media or Stellan?" They are one and the same.

"That's not fair."

"Why didn't you tell me about Stellan's rally? You made me think I needed you if I wanted an audience with him."

Brigid drops her gaze. "I wanted an excuse to spend more time with you. Having you here has been difficult. You're the same, yet different, and I'm just trying to figure out where I fit."

"Fit?"

"In your life."

"We're friends, Brigid."

She steps closer. "What if I want more?"

"Brig—"

"Just hear me out." I turn away, but she yanks me back to face her. "After you left, I realized something."

"Brigid, stop."

"I love you, and I can't just switch that off. You make me feel seen, important, and on equal footing. None of my other partners have ever made me feel that way."

An uncomfortable tightness fills my chest. None of her other partners were Nebula. She dated Epsilon, whom she thought were better than her because she didn't think highly of herself. "We agreed to keep things casual, and now you're telling me you love me, all while knowing I'm with someone else. How is that fair?"

"I should have held onto you tighter," she offers.

I sigh. Brigid was my distraction. It was never serious for me. But it's my fault if she got the wrong impression.

"Brigid, I'm sorry, but we never should have crossed those lines. It wasn't fair to either of us. We were hurting." The light in her eyes dims. "You are important to me, but I am not in love with you and won't ever be. I'm sorry." Gently, I withdraw myself from her grasp.

Brigid blinks, her eyes glistening with unshed tears, before taking a deep breath.

"It'll never last," she says. "Leigh's queen and queens marry princes or wealthy Epsilons. You're a Nebula, Wilder. You have a chance to get a fresh start here. Don't throw away your future for her. If you're going to Stellan's rally, you'll see he is trying to make changes for us. He deserves your support. So do I. Meet me there, and I will introduce you. I wasn't lying. He is my friend, and so are you."

Her words sting, hitting a nerve I'd rather not acknowledge. Sure, I've had my doubts, and I'm not blind to our complications, but Leigh and I have been navigating this mess together since day one. We've fought tooth and nail for every moment we've shared. I'm not ready to give her up. Brigid's offer to introduce me to Stellan is genuine, but comes with strings attached. The more favors she does for me, the more she'll expect in return.

"Goodnight, Brigid," I mutter, stalking to my room.

I close the door and let out a shuddering breath. The room is dark, the only light comes from the soft luminance of the moon filtering through the window. Collapsing onto the mattress, I sink into the soft comforter and pull out my phone.

My thumb hovers over Leigh's name. I want to call her, hear her voice, and tell her how much I miss her. But for some reason, I hesitate.

The sound of laughter drifts in from outside, causing an ache in my chest. I'm an outsider in a world I once loved—a world that filled a hole in me. But that life is gone now, and I'm not the person I was then. I've changed, grown, and found something worth fighting for.

I hit the call button.

CHAPTER TWENTY-NINE
WILDER

"HEY, STRANGER," Leigh's sultry voice breathes into the receiver, prompting my smile.

"Hey," I respond as I unlace my boots.

"You sound tired."

My boots thud on the worn wooden floor as I kick them off. "It's been a long ass day," I admit with a ragged exhale.

The patter of rain against the windowpane intensifies, accompanied by the mournful howling of the wind. I picture the others scurrying indoors to continue their revelry but I'm relieved to be alone.

"Want to talk about it?" Leigh asks.

I hesitate. Aurora is a disaster, from the chaos at the power station to the brutal attack in the street. But telling Leigh feels like an unbearable burden. She might spiral, convinced that Stellan sent those thugs after Gianna to hurt her. I'm still far from understanding Stellan's motives, let alone confirming his involvement in the attack. No, I decide I can't risk it right now.

I told Leigh I was here to turn on the power and convince Stellan to stop sowing division. He hasn't posted a new article in days, which works in my favor, but I'm afraid of what he might say at the rally and who he will anger next.

"I'd rather talk about your day." I roll onto my side. The prolonged silence that follows sets my nerves on edge. I almost hear Leigh biting her lip. "Is everything okay? If something happened, you could tell me." The hypocrisy tastes acidic on my tongue.

Another pause, and then Leigh laughs, but it rings hollow and strained, like in the days before she came out as a Lunar Witch. "I'm just missing you."

I don't believe her. Something's troubling her, and her not wanting to tell me has me thinking the worst. But pressing her further might only push her away.

"I miss you, too," I confess, my voice strained. "Like so fucking much."

"Oh, yeah?" Leigh teases. Fabric rustles on the other end of the line.

Is she in her room? I picture her lying on her bed, dressed in silky pajamas, twirling a strand of her long hair around her delicate finger. Suddenly, the distance between us grows into a physical ache. If only I could reach through the phone and pull her onto the bed with me.

"Yeah." My voice lacks the enthusiasm her teasing deserves.

I truly miss her.

"Make anyone cry today?" I joke.

Leigh sighs. "Not yet, but there's still time." I smile as she adds, "Alden is as tiresome as ever. He went to breakfast alone with Janus. Can you believe that?"

"Why? Did you two have plans?" I ask, trying to keep the jealousy from seeping into my tone, but it's a struggle.

"Queens marry princes," I recall Brigid saying. Alden is a prince.

"No, but we haven't had a chance to agree on anything, nor have we discussed peace terms," Leigh says. "I've tried to, several times. It's like he is purposely stalling. All he does is flirt with me. Not to mention, he almost got me in trouble with the vampires. And then he tries to pass Ravi off to me like some sort of gift, which I mean, I am grateful for the help with my magic, but every time I turn around, I fear he'll stab me in the back. And now Alden is going out with Janus without me. I mean, what the hell is that all about?"

I'm gripping my phone so tightly that I'm surprised it doesn't break. The image of Alden licking Leigh flashes before my eyes. The urge to tell her to send him home is overwhelming, but I know an alliance after years of animosity between our countries would be a monumental achievement for her. Besides, I have no room to talk, not with Brigid batting her eyes at me at every opportunity.

"It sounds like you have your hands full," I say.

"Yeah, but you know the worst part?" Leigh says. "I'd rather my hands were busy doing something else."

I'm adjusting my arm behind my head to get more comfortable when I groan at her suggestive tone. Though it comes out sounding more like a growl. "I wish I were with you."

"I wish I were naked with you, too, baby." Her voice, a mere whisper, sends a jolt straight to my groin, every inch of me responding to her invitation. The image floods my mind: her lying beside me, her lips on mine, the heat of her body pressed against me as I grip her ass, breathless, seeking that intense friction between her thighs. I bite my lip, trying to regain composure.

Fuck. I want her.

"What are you wearing?" I ask, but then she laughs, breaking the spell. "What?"

"That line is so cliché. 'What are you wearing?'" She mimics my deep voice, and I can't help but smile at her playful attempt. "You can get more creative than that."

"I don't know. I've read some pretty cringy and *cliché* lines in some of those romance books you like. I mean, where do some of these guys get off with their alpha male bullshit?" I think of the entire shelf she has dedicated to taboo romances. I know because I might've borrowed one or two. For science, of course.

"I happen to think it's hot," Leigh retorts, her voice sultry. "You can tell me to get on my knees and take it like a good fucking girl anytime you want."

"Promise?"

Leigh laughs. "Cross my heart."

We continue our playful banter, and my worries melt away faster than butter in a hot skillet, but fatigue tugs at the edges of my consciousness. If it meant I could talk to Leigh longer, I'd tape my eyes open, but sleep is falling over me like a weighted blanket.

"Wilder," Leigh's dream-like voice drifts through the phone. "Are you awake?"

"Yeah . . ." I mumble, fighting to stay present.

The next thing I know, I'm on the rooftop of the Aurora garrison. As I gaze up at the vast expanse of the star-studded sky, the cool night air caresses my skin. The February moon is full. It seems close enough to reach out and touch.

The distant hum of the city below drowns out by my heart's slow, rhythmic beating. This rooftop has always been my sanctuary after grueling days on the field, where I can lose myself in the vastness of the cosmos and remember that my troubles, like how to keep the Nebula and Epsilon from tearing each other apart, are fleeting in the universe's grand scheme.

The soft rustle of fabric draws my attention, and I see Leigh approaching. She is an ethereal vision in a flowing gown that waltzes in the gentle breeze.

My heart twists. A dream, then.

Her beauty steals my breath away. It still amazes me that she's mine.

But as she settles beside me, a flicker of uncertainty gnaws at the edges of my mind. If the day ever comes when I'm forced to let her go, I know it will shatter me. Having just found her, the thought of losing her is unbearable. I silently vow to fight tooth and nail to keep her by my side—propriety be damned. Queens marry for love sometimes, don't they?

"Are you hiding from me or your troubles?" Leigh asks softly. Her violet scent envelopes me like a soothing balm. "Where are we?"

"Aurora," I reply. "I'm not hiding. I'm . . . contemplating."

"How to rule the world?" she teases.

"More like my role in it."

Leigh sighs. "Sounds fun. Can I join?"

"It's not a party without you."

Her smile widens. "You sound like Gianna." Leigh tilts her head back and releases a soft gasp. "Do the stars always burn this brightly in Aurora?"

"Always. Less light pollution means we get this killer view."

Her exhale is reverent. "Wow." She hugs her knees to her chest. "No wonder you like it here so much. It's breathtaking."

I roll onto my side, propping myself on an elbow to study her. "Is that jealousy I detect, princess?"

"I feel like I'm keeping you away from your one true love," she chides with a hint of melancholy. "Aurora is beautiful. I can see why it means so much to you."

A soft chuckle escapes me as I flop onto my back once more. "I love it here, but Aurora no longer loves me back."

In this dream-like realm, my words flow freely. Here, with Dream Leigh, I can bear my soul without the risk of shattering my heart. Free from the pressures of reality, we can simply be ourselves, two souls intertwined in a moment of perfect understanding.

I thread my fingers through her silken locks and draw her face closer. Our lips meet, and her soft sigh has me tightening my grip. If only we could freeze this moment. Here, I could hold her forever, shielding her from the cruel realities that await us beyond the veil of dreams.

As we part, the words tumble from my lips. "I love you."

Leigh's smile is radiant. "Do you mean that, or is this part of your dream?"

I blink. "It's the truth . . . but, also, I *am* dreaming. Aren't I?" A note of uncertainty creeps into my voice. "Aren't I?"

Sitting up abruptly, I pinch myself. That hurt. Why did that hurt? "What's going on?"

"You're asleep," Leigh explains, a mischievous grin on her lips.

"So, this is a dream?"

"Yes, but it's more like lucid dreaming. I haven't quite figured out its mechanics yet."

A lump forms in my throat. "Wait, are *you* real?"

"Real enough."

I swallow. What the hell is happening?

"I'm dreamwalking," Leigh clarifies. "While you're asleep, I can enter your dream and see what you see. But this time is different from the last. I tried to reenter the person's dream I visited the first time, yet ended up here with you. It's different, though. You seem more aware, more . . . you."

Tentatively, I reach out and touch her cheek again, marveling at the familiar peachy smoothness of her skin. "I'm confused. How can you do this?"

"Ravi," she states simply. Leigh shrugs in a noncommittal gesture. "He's teaching me about my magic. Or he was . . ."

Holy shit, she's inside my dream.

It hits me like a bullet to the chest. Leigh is in my subconscious, and I just confessed my love. Again.

And she didn't say it back. Again.

Glancing sidelong at Leigh, I struggle to find words.

"Honestly, I'm not entirely sure how I got here," Leigh admits, seemingly oblivious to my inner turmoil. Her touch on my forearm sends a jolt of warmth through my veins. "You must have been thinking about me when you fell asleep. And then, suddenly, I was here."

That's an understatement. Leigh is always on my mind.

"Is it as real for you as it is for me?" I ask.

"More. When I entered Janus's dream, I woke up covered in dirt. At least, I think it was her dream. That's why I agreed to let Ravi train me—so that I could do it again. Except he refused to teach me about dreamwalking in depth, and this time, I'm in your head instead of hers."

I balk at the revelation that Leigh invaded Janus's dream. I agree with Ravi; being inside Janus's head, where she is most vulnerable, is not a good idea for Leigh. She could misconstrue something, leading to potentially lethal outcomes. However, I know that if I lecture her now, she will only get angry. It's best to share my thoughts when we are both awake and can have a proper discussion. Pushing my concerns aside for the moment, I ask, "In the other dream, was it similar to this?"

The world around us seems to shimmer, the edges blurring like a watercolor painting.

Leigh shivers. "None of you were as you are in real life."

"I was in Janus's dream, too?" I press.

She nods, avoiding my gaze. My chest tightens.

"Why won't you look at me?" I urge, my voice calm despite the dread coursing through me. The thought of hurting her, even in a dream, is unbearable. "What did I do?"

"It doesn't matter. It wasn't real," Leigh murmurs, hugging her knees tighter.

My jaw clenches. Whatever transpired, it was real enough to leave a mark on her.

I touch her chin, tilting her face until our eyes meet. "Leigh, I'm sorry."

"Why apologize? It wasn't you."

"Because whatever dream me did, it hurt you."

Leigh's shoulders slump, and I hold her close as she whispers, "I wish you weren't so far away. I wish Stellan Navis didn't exist and that Alden would go home and take Ravi with him. Why can't this be real life and everything else be a dream?"

I tighten my embrace, wishing I could shield her from the world. "Because if this were real life, we'd never grow. We'd stay like this forever."

"That doesn't sound so bad."

I kiss her head. "Leigh, you're a new queen. Everyone faces challenges when they start something new. Trust me, you'll get the hang of it." Her smile doesn't quite reach her eyes. "Look at what you've already accomplished. I mean, you're owning your magic. That's incredible."

"Yeah?" she asks, a glimmer of hope.

"Yeah." A thought strikes me, and a smile tugs at my lips. "If this is my dream, does that mean I have control here? If I wanted us to be at the beach instead of in the desert, could I make that happen?"

Leigh shrugs, a playful gleam in her eyes. "I'm not sure how it works, but maybe?"

Holding her close, I close my eyes, conjuring the memory of a long-ago family vacation to Nereus. It was my favorite trip before my Emergence, Mom's promotion to Altum Healer, and Desiree's struggles at school. I picture the tropical beach town, the endless expanse of azure sky, the sun's relentless heat, the gritty sand between my toes, and the distant crash of waves against the shore.

Leigh's gasp prompts me to open my eyes. We are sitting on a deserted stretch of pristine sand. The sun hangs high in the cloudless sky, its warmth enveloping us like a hug. The ebb and flow of the waves is almost enough to lull me back to sleep, but I'm already dreaming.

"It worked," I breathe.

Leigh arches a brow. "A bikini?"

The tiny black string bikini she's wearing sets my blood on fire. The small triangles barely conceal her curves, and the slinky bottoms seem more suited for lounging than swimming. I groan. She is perfect.

But if I keep staring, I won't be able to resist pouncing on her. And while I'm hurting to have her, I'm also eager to explore this dream world we've created.

Springing to my feet, I flash her a challenging grin. "Race you to the water."

"Wha—"

Before she can finish, I take off toward the inviting waves. Her startled cry and laughter rings in my ears. Sand flies beneath my feet as I sprint, not slowing until I'm knee-deep in the welcoming sea. I plunge beneath the surface, the water surprisingly pleasant, like a soothing bath.

"Is it cold?" Leigh calls from the shore.

Emerging from the depths, I stride toward her, grinning. In one swift motion, I scoop her into my arms. My laughter drowns out her protests as I toss her into the waves. Leigh vanishes beneath the turquoise surface, only to resurface, sputtering and wiping the saltwater from her eyes.

"What the hell?" she yells, but amusement dances in her eyes.

"Come on, princess. Don't tell me you can't swim," I tease, earning myself a face full of water.

"I can swim," Leigh retorts.

I ignore her, pulling her close. "Don't worry, I've got you. You're safe with me."

She wraps her long legs around my waist and encircles my neck as my hands find her hips, toying with the strings of her bikini bottoms. "I said I can swim," she repeats, a smile tugging at her lips.

"Then you can let me go," I challenge, but her grip tightens.

I'm acutely aware of every inch of her skin pressed against mine, every point of contact setting my insides ablaze. I kiss her chin, trailing kisses over her jaw and throat.

But then she asks, "Is everything okay in Aurora?"

I freeze. I consider lying, or at least omitting the truth, but it feels wrong in the raw honesty of this shared dream.

"It's not," I admit, and her chin lifts. "But it will be. They're working on restoring power, and I have plans to see Stellan soon."

"There hasn't been an article in a few days. Maybe Stellan's given up on me?" A hopeful note colors Leigh's voice.

"Maybe," I say. But deep down, I doubt it. Something tells me Stellan is just getting started.

"Okay, enough talking," she says as the water laps against our entwined bodies. "Time for you to kiss me."

She doesn't have to tell me twice. I capture her lips, savoring the taste. My fingers dig into her skin as I pour all my pent-up longing into this perfect moment.

Her tongue rolls with mine, and I lose it, kissing her with a desperate desire as if her very essence is the air I need to breathe.

"Wilder," she gasps, my name a breathy plea on her lips.

I tug at the flimsy strings holding her bikini together, my self-control fraying at the edges.

Her mouth latches onto my neck, her lips and tongue leaving a trail of heat as I carry her out of the water. I lay her down on the compact sand. As I settle between her thighs, my hips thrust against hers, desperate for friction, for the mind-blowing release only she can give me. I'm fucking obsessed with her, my thoughts consumed by her intoxicating scent and the way she's always soaking wet, ready to take every inch of me. The mere thought of her has me by the balls. She's a drug I can't quit.

"Fuck, I've missed this." I groan as she tugs my shorts down my legs.

"Same."

Leigh unties the strings of her top and tosses the scrap of fabric aside. She lays bare before me, a goddess in the flesh. Every man's ultimate fucking fantasy come to life.

If this is a dream, I never want to wake up.

But somewhere in the distance, a voice calls my name as I slowly ease inside her, and with each passing second, Leigh's warmth fades. Her body grows less substantial in my arms. She's slipping through my fingers like sand, and I can't stop it.

With a groan, she rolls her hips. "Don't wake up. We are just getting started."

"I'm sorry," I whisper, desperation clawing at my chest. "I can't help it."

"Dammit."

"Revisit me?"

I jolt awake, blinking rapidly as I try to orient myself. Ry's face swarms into view. "What?" I snap, my voice rich with sleep and my skin hot with arousal.

Ry takes a step back, a hint of apology in his eyes. "We found the guy who had the gun on Gianna."

I sit up, all the heat draining out of me. "And?"

My heart rate accelerates as the fog of sleep dissipates, replaced by a growing sense of urgency. I remind myself that I'm in Aurora on a mission for the Crown. I need to stay focused.

"He's at the precinct."

I nod, pushing aside the lingering ache of leaving Leigh behind in my dreams.

I toss the blankets aside. "Can we question him? I want to know if they're working with Stellan or simply fanatics."

A knowing grin spreads across Ry's face. "Dreaming about your girlfriend?"

I shoot him a pointed look as I reach for my boots. "Shut up."

"Hey, it's okay. Sometimes I make out with my pillow, too. It's good practice."

"Grow up," I growl. "Text Eddo to hold the prisoner until we get there."

Ry's expression turns serious as he follows me out of my room with his phone in hand.

CHAPTER THIRTY
LEIGH

SEATED in my usual chair inside the audience room, my heart pounds with anticipation and a touch of dread as I wait for Janus. I've been dying to know what she and Alden discussed during breakfast yesterday. Alden hasn't said a peep. All he wants to do is go out as if he could supply me with enough alcohol to get me to forget I hate him. It hasn't worked, and neither have my attempts to get him to talk about Janus or how to maintain peace between our countries.

My phone chimes, and I set down my teacup to read the incoming text from Pallas.

> **PALLAS**
>
> Janus plans to meet Beatrix Marks at the kelpie race.

I choke on my spit before reading his text again. Janus has a confirmed meeting with Beatrix. It's bold to meet the anti-monarchist in such a public space, or that's its brilliance. With so many people around, no one will be paying close enough attention. Alcohol will be free-flowing, and everyone will be watching the race.

It's the perfect setting to commit treason. I kick myself for not finding out sooner.

I've been trying to slip back into Janus's dreams. Though I have zero regrets about entering Wilder's subconscious, only that he woke up entirely too soon and left me frustratingly aroused, I still would have liked to peek inside Janus's subconscious. What is she planning with Beatrix, and how does it tie to Stellan and Alden? I will use this time to find out.

The creak of the doors echoes through the room like a harbinger of the coming confrontation. Janus sinks into a clumsy curtsy before me. I cock a brow. Is she nervous? My attention snaps to the heels of her boots. They look new. I open my mouth to welcome her, but a giant yawn escapes.

Janus lifts a brow. "Didn't get much sleep last night?" she asks. Her smile is colder than the icy breeze rattling the branches outside.

The chill of another winter day in Borealis seeps into my bones, and I find myself longing for the warmth of Wilder's dream, the searing heat of his embrace, and the sun-drenched surroundings of Nereus. All of that is a world away from the frigid reality that surrounds me now.

I reach for my black tea. "I've slept better," I say, my tone clipped.

I set my cup down. The delicate clink of porcelain against the saucer echoes in the room, a fragile sound amidst the tension thickening the air. Like last time, Janus remains standing, her presence looming over me. The act sets my teeth on edge. It is as though I'm under interrogation, and she's the inquisitor, ready to bombard me with questions and pry the truth from my unwilling lips.

"Take a seat, Janus. It strains my neck having to look up for so long," I demand.

Begrudgingly, Janus settles into the seat across from me.

"How have things been?" I ask, keeping my voice carefully neutral. "Any new developments? Visitors I need to worry about?"

"No, and the only visitor you need to worry about is Alden," she says with a clap of her hands.

I force myself to maintain my smile, breathing through my nose. "That's good. I wondered if the blackout would allow dangerous outsiders to slip our notice. But it sounds like you have everything under control," I press, reaching for my tea again to occupy my restless hands. They itch to wrap around her throat and shake her until she has no choice but to yield answers.

"Thank you, Your Majesty, but I want to ask you something," Janus says. "It has been weighing on my conscience for days."

I quickly swallow my tea. "Go on."

"As you know, Alden and I had breakfast together after you failed to attend our luncheon. As Simon Lupas's enforcer, he is the one to champion the king's armies, and he promised that if Lua has access to Corona's resources, then Lua and Corona can be friends."

"He told you that?" I blurt out, heat skirting up my neck. I've been in Alden's company for days, and he has never outright asked me for resources. But Janus spends a morning with him, and he spills his guts?

Janus meets my gaze head-on, her eyes glinting with pity. "He told me a lot of things, but mainly, we talked about you."

"Me?" I sit straighter. "What about me?"

Janus flinches from the bite in my tone. "As queen, you have the final say, but to ensure Lua's needs are met, Alden and I discussed the best way to ensure peace is if you two get married. That way, as prince consort, Alden and Lua will never need to invade Corona because you two will be husband and wife. I hoped to speak to Queen Jorina about this before bringing it to your attention, to get her advice on the best way to approach you, but I haven't been able to reach her."

The world tilts on its axis. My vision blurs. *Married.* The word sinks into my skin like poison, seeping into my veins, and spreading through my body like wildfire.

"Wow, it seems you two had quite the meal." My voice sounds foreign even to my ears, too high-pitched and brittle.

A hint of satisfaction plays at the corners of her lips, a smug certainty that curdles my blood. "We did, Your Majesty."

"I will not marry Alden." The words are cutting and sharp like glass when they leave my mouth. "In case you forgot, I am seeing someone."

"Leigh, Wilder is a Blade Commander," she says with a sigh, as if that negates the depth of my feelings.

"So?"

"There's marrying beneath your station, and then there's marrying him."

Red-hot anger surges through me, and I grip the arms of my chair so tightly I fear I may tear the upholstery. "I beg your pardon?" I say through gritted teeth. "Did you not marry a Nebula woman?"

Janus's expression hardens. "I am not a queen. My marriage holds no sway over peace."

"This is unbelievable. You can't just auction me off like some broodmare!"

Janus shakes her head. "That's not what I am doing. I am doing my best to keep our borders clear of invaders."

I scoff as Janus goes on to add, "Would marrying Alden be so terrible? I find him to be an exemplary young man. You may not love him, but you could do much worse as a political alliance. Besides, his story about other nations reportedly showing interest in conquering us doesn't sit right with me. He is a warrior, and with the extra defenses, we can focus on fixing our internal issues. We can unify the factions, and then we can allocate time and funds to projects like your Lunar asylums."

My hand clutches my stomach as a wave of nausea rises inside me. The thought of bearing Alden's children, of them ruling in my stead, sickens me. But so does the idea of other invaders eyeing us like a center-cut sirloin.

But what about Wilder? He loves me.

"Stop it," I say, my voice cracking. "I won't do it."

"Leigh, please. At least think about it." Janus's mask of patience does little to conceal the calculation in her eyes.

Every fiber of my being rebels against the idea.

"What would your grandmother say? Or your father?" Janus presses.

"They both would rather shoot themselves in the foot than let a wolf sit on a witch's throne," I snap.

Janus gives me a look that says, *Get real.*

You need to consider all options, Leigh, my father's ghost pipes up. My breath catches, and I shove him out of my mind. This can't be happening.

"What about your mother?" Janus adds.

I scoff. Mother would love to marry me off to a prince. She never warmed to the idea of Wilder. A Nebula, who carries a gun and has tattoos that are visible in a suit, is a man who represents everything she despises.

Janus nods like she can sense what I'm thinking. "Talk to Cynthia. And your grandmother while you are at it. I told Alden we would give him an answer tomorrow. I invited him to watch the kelpies with me and the rest of the Council."

I grimace. Janus is handing me over to our enemies—a sacrificial lamb to be slaughtered on the altar of political expediency. I know what would happen if I said no. Any failed talks of peace will be my fault. Janus will scheme behind my back more, and the Council will fall in line behind her, a united front against me. Stellan will catch wind of my failed nuptials and write about it, and my mother will tell me she told me so in a smug reminder of my inadequacy.

"Talk to Wilder," Janus says, and I blink. "He's an understanding guy, and I think if you told him you had to put your country first, he would understand."

That's it.

"Why were you at the hospital the night of the blackout?" I demand.

"It's personal." Janus stands with her attention on the clock. She curtsies. It's a mocking gesture. "Tomorrow. At the races."

The door clicks shut, and I groan, chucking my teacup against the wall. It shatters into a million pieces, leaving a brown stain on the carpet my grandmother would wring my neck over. But she's in Glaucus, and something tells me that if she were here, she'd agree with Janus.

Leigh, relax. You don't need to decide right now, Aradia's ghost says faintly, as if she's miles away. She is a distant comfort in the face of my despair. Still, I jolt, having not heard from her since before the first dreamwalking incident.

"Where have you been?" I ask, but once again, there's no answer.

I bury my face in my hands, the sense of isolation akin to drowning. I can hardly breathe. Janus wants me to give Alden my answer tomorrow, but I've had no time to digest this new information. He's been planning this since his arrival, and it makes sense why he's been so reluctant to talk to me. He wanted to win Janus to his side. But their alliance won't be strong once I expose her for conspiring with Beatrix Marks tomorrow at the races. Then I'll get the rest of the Council to investigate her and Stellan's possible relationship.

CHAPTER THIRTY-ONE
WILDER

GIANNA, Ry, and I weave through the bustling streets, dodging honking taxis on our way to Trinity Square, where Stellan Navis is rallying supporters outside the Auralite Library. Ry thinks we can ambush him after his speech, but with the crowd's size, I worry something might go wrong. I hope I'm mistaken, and I can talk to Stellan first without taking Brigid up on her strings-attached offer to introduce us.

I want to ask him about Dimitri and his thoughts on his followers threatening to kill an innocent woman because of her affiliation with Epsilon. Gianna, who came to Aurora to uncover her past, has faced one roadblock after another. The gunman claimed during our interrogation the other night that he was following Stellan's orders. Stellan may not be the peacemaker Brigid claims he is, but rather a warmonger in the making.

"Let's get as close to the stage as possible," I say as Ry takes Gi by the hand, ensuring we don't lose her short stature to the crowd.

Over a thousand people have gathered to hear Stellan speak. It's impressive, especially considering his lack of formal political training. He connects with people on a visceral level. Dressed as a civilian, I have my gun tucked into my waistband, prepared for any outcome. Although several Blades are on duty, they're stretched too thin to manage a crowd of this size if things go sideways.

"That might be the most stunning piece of architecture I've seen," Gianna exclaims.

We've found a spot to stand, sandwiched between several smiling Nebulas. I haven't seen many Epsilons, but that doesn't mean they aren't here.

"Yeah, the Auralite Library is a testament to time—a relic from the past that commands respect and admiration," Ry yells. "It took two decades to construct, even with the aid of magic, and once reigned as the tallest structure in Aurora."

Gianna shades her eyes to get a better look. At dusk, the setting sun reflects off the building's mosaic glass, creating a kaleidoscope of colors in the square. It's where the city holds the Harvest Festival each year. I went while living here, forced out of my cocoon by Brigid, the Erinye sisters, and Ry. We had danced and partied under the stars, but the atmosphere was less hostile than today.

Someone screams, and my hands itch for my weapon.

"Easy," Ry mutters to me as Stellan steps out from the library doors, his arm raised above the cheering crowd. People scream for Stellan like he's a celebrity. He settles behind a Lucite podium at the center of the stairs leading from the library down to the square, dressed in a cream-colored linen suit that enhances his olive skin. Nearby, a Nebula witch wipes away tears as she jumps up and down, waving at him.

"Ladies and gentlemen, friends and comrades," Stellan begins, magically amplifying his voice to be carried with the wind. "For too long, we, the people of the Nebula, have suffered under the oppression of Epsilon witches. Our powers, our heritage, and our very existence have been scorned and persecuted by those who claim superiority over us. But no more!"

I cross my arms as I listen, bracing myself for the dread, but Stellan's words strike a chord. It's as if he's speaking directly to me, his message resonating with a clarity that cuts through the crowd's noise. Each word he utters has me holding my breath.

Stellan continues, "Today marks the dawn of a new era, a turning point in our history. We stand united, not as victims but as warriors, rebels, and champions of our destiny. We will no longer cower in the shadows, bow to the Council's whims, or be second-class citizens in our land."

The crowd swells, and so does my chest. Stellan's words are everything I've wanted to hear my entire life. He makes it sound so easy to seize the day and demand control over our destinies. As much as I want to believe it, I know it's not so simple. Seizing power doesn't mean taking it from someone else by force. We can't go from being oppressed to becoming the oppressors ourselves.

A smile spreads across Gianna's face. "The crowd loves him."

"Together, we will carve out a new destiny for ourselves and ensure that never again will our people be subjected to the horrors of persecution," Stellan announces.

I arch an eyebrow beneath my sports cap, skepticism creeping into my thoughts. How does Stellan plan to accomplish that? If overthrowing the Epsilon were that simple, Nebula would have done it years ago. His words, while inspiring, seem to gloss over the harsh realities we face.

"But let us not forget the role of our young queen in this struggle," he continues. "She may have shed light on the Nebula's innocence in igniting the First War and the terrible oppression that was enacted upon us because of this lie. Yet, this action alone is not enough. The queen has yet to fully embrace the cause of justice and hold the Epsilon accountable for their crimes against us."

My frown deepens. While containing a kernel of truth, Stellan's words paint an incomplete picture. Leigh is trying to make amends for the mistakes of her ancestors, but she doesn't have sole control over the country. Her hands are often tied, constrained by the system she's attempting to change. Stellan's oversimplification of the situation leaves me questioning his understanding of our complex political landscape.

Then, Stellan's piercing umber stare locks with mine across the square. I freeze.

"But there are those who aim to stand in our way," he says, pointing directly at me. The weight of the crowd's collective gaze settles upon Ry, Gianna, and me. We've become the focal point of his speech. How does he know who I am unless someone like Dimitri told him? "Among us are those who, despite being Nebula, would rather maintain the status quo. And to that, I say, hell no. We will not let anyone stand in our way. Will we?"

The crowd jeers.

My heart splinters as Stellan's words wash over the crowd, each syllable a carefully crafted weapon aimed at our very existence.

Ry tenses behind Gianna. "This took a turn," she mutters.

I nod. Yeah, it did.

I place a reassuring hand on her shoulder. She leans into my touch.

The weight of countless hostile stares settles upon us, and I meet each one with a defiant gaze, refusing to be cowed. But even as I stand my ground, the same sense of unease I felt the other night slithers up my spine.

From the nearby alleys, figures emerge like spiders, their movements fluid and purposeful. I squint against the sun's glare, my blood running cold. A group of men who seem born and bred in violence flank Michael Bersa, their scarred faces a tapestry of brutality. They wet their lips, a predatory gleam in their eyes, as if the thought of a fight ignites their nerves.

I whip my head in the opposite direction, my breath catching at the unmistakable glint of gold. More Epsilon men. Their tattoos are proudly displayed as they encircle the crowd like a pack of wolves closing in on unsuspecting prey. The air grows heavy, and I can almost taste the suspense on my tongue.

But something doesn't add up. The Epsilon haven't made a move or unleashed the violence I expected. Instead, they stand motionless, listening to Stellan. A flicker of doubt bubbles to the surface. Did I misjudge the situation? Could they also be here to seek enlightenment?

Stellan's voice rises and falls, each word a masterful stroke on the canvas of the crowd's emotions. I was bracing for trouble, prepared for the worst. But maybe I overreacted.

I refocus on Stellan's speech, keeping my peripheral vision trained on the nearest Epsilon, never losing sight of their position.

"To ensure peace and prosperity for all Nebula witches, I propose a future where we no longer answer to the Epsilon. We will create an enclave ruled by the Nebula, making Aurora and her surrounding towns sovereign! I have the backing to make this a reality. All you must do is vote for me, and Aurora will be its own country!" Stellan says.

A numbness overtakes me.

Stellan wants to rule Aurora, not just as mayor but as president, maybe even as a king. If Aurora becomes an enclave with its own rules and government, the Nebula will be free to do whatever they please. They'll no longer answer to Leigh or the Council.

I sense the hostility radiating off the Epsilon in droves. If Stellan's promises become a reality, they will pay taxes for their business and homes to Stellan and his Nebula government. The Nebula will be in charge, and the Epsilon will be forced to accept that or leave.

Cheers erupt in the crowd, but a few boos come from the Epsilon.

"Ry," I say as a few Epsilon bare their teeth. "Get Gianna out of here."

Ry takes Gianna's hand, but she digs in her heels.

"Be careful," she says to me.

"You fancy yourself a king!" an Epsilon woman shouts at Stellan, who shakes his head.

I snap my focus on Stellan as the men with Michael Bersa hurl profanities. Epsilon voices rise, each obscenity a verbal dart aimed at Stellan's composure. The nearest Nebula retaliates, insults flying back. The groups inch closer, and my muscles tense for a fight. The crowd shifts around me. It's only a matter of time before the fragile peace shatters, unleashing chaos. The Blades brandish their weapons.

"We won't let you take our businesses and drive us out of our city!" another Epsilon screams.

"Now, settle down." Stellan tries to manage the crowd, but a Nebula man throws the first punch, sending the shouting Epsilon businessman to the ground.

For a moment, no one moves. Stellan's taken aback expression hangs in the square. I think the worst is over, but in an instant, the fallen Epsilon's friends retaliate, throwing fists, kicking, biting, and summoning magic.

"Go now," I tell Ry, and he tugs Gianna.

I push through the crowd to Stellan, frozen, his mouth agape as the carnage unfolds.

"Stop, please, all of you, if you could just listen . . ." Stellan pleads, but the fighting drowns out his words. He wipes the sweat from his brow, his eyes darting across the scene, but he doesn't intervene. There isn't much he can do. Stellan is a journalist, not a fighter.

Two Epsilon men storm the stage, and Stellan's guards conjure a magical barrier around him. But their efforts are short-lived as the fight escalates. Within moments, Stellan's men lie battered and bruised, blood pooling beneath them on the stone steps. Stellan backs away, arms raised in surrender.

"Please," Stellan begs, his words falling on unhearing ears.

I push against the sea of bodies that separate me from Stellan, desperation fueling every move. If the Epsilon harm or, even worse, kill him, the consequences will be catastrophic. The Nebula will rise against them in droves, their anger and grief igniting a fire that will consume the city. The Council will have no choice but to intervene, transforming Aurora into a war zone.

The Council will never believe that Stellan genuinely cares for the Nebula. Though his message was not well-received today, he remains a beacon of hope for the Nebula's fight for change. If Stellan falls, so does the chance for a peaceful resolution.

The Epsilon men close in on Stellan, each step taunting him.

I shove a burly man out of my way and race up the steps. An Epsilon man lands a brutal punch to Stellan's face. I reach for my gun. More Epsilon men apprehend Stellan, who opens his mouth, likely to beg for his life or reason with them, but they silence him with a swift kick to the gut.

Doubled over and gasping for air, Stellan falls to his knees. One attacker reaches into his jacket and pulls a gun from the holster, aiming at Stellan's head. Stellan's eyes widen.

"The only way more people will follow you is in a funeral march," the gunman sneers, his finger tightening around the trigger. Mine tightens as well.

He inhales, and I do the same. Before the gunman can exhale, I fire. The resounding bang leaves my ears ringing as the man pointing a gun on Stellan falls to his knees, crying in agony. His blood stains his shirt where my bullet buries itself deep in his rear deltoid, just as I intended.

For a moment, the world seems to hold its breath. The Epsilon restraining Stellan stare at me in open-mouthed horror before releasing him and vanishing into the uproar. Sirens blare through the square, heralding the arrival of reinforcements.

I exhale. So much adrenaline courses through me that my limbs tremble. I quickly approach Stellan Navis, hunched over and shorter than expected. He carries himself like a larger man.

"We need to get you out of here before they arrest you for inciting violence," I say as I pull him up from the blood-stained steps. Gratitude shines in his one good eye; the other is swollen shut.

"Thank you," Stellan whispers, shaking.

I nod. This choice to save him will have consequences. My attack on an Epsilon man will be broadcast all over the country. Leigh will see it, and people will question if I'm on Stellan's side. However, I am positive now that Stellan is our best hope for finding a peaceful resolution to this conflict between the factions, and I'm willing to do whatever it takes to make that a reality.

The violence continues as I yank Stellan into an alleyway. He leans heavily against me, his breath coming in short, pained gasps. His hot blood seeps through my shirt.

"We need to find somewhere to stitch you up and lie low," I say. "The Council will order the Blades to find instigators in the uprising, and we can't risk getting caught in the crossfire."

Stellan nods, his face ashen and drawn.

I adjust my grip on him, taking more of his weight. The adrenaline that fueled me during the fight is fading, replaced by bone-deep exhaustion. But I can't afford to rest yet. I just pray that when Leigh watches the footage, she trusts that I rescued Stellan for her sake. I'm convinced that if Stellan and Leigh meet, this fantasy of an enclave will disappear, and they can stitch this fraying country back together.

CHAPTER THIRTY-TWO
LEIGH

I STEP out of the car, and the salty sea breeze whips through my hair. It carries with it the excited chatter of a crowd and the distant neighing of kelpies. I feel the weight of Alden's persistent glances as he steps out onto the racetrack grounds behind me.

"You're drooling," I remark dryly.

"You look yummy."

"They have food inside the clubhouse." I brush past him, eager to escape his presence. I need to find Janus and Beatrix Marks. If I can prove they are working together, I can present my findings to the Council, which will force Janus to admit she is Stellan's mole. My hope is that this will reunite the Council, and, more importantly, save me from marrying Alden.

Alden grasps my arm. "What's wrong?" His tan coat and orange-hued scarf make his blue eyes even more striking.

I pull out of his hold as Ravi stops beside us. Alden gives him a nod to head inside. Ravi tries to meet my stare, but I refuse to acknowledge him. He must've known Alden's intentions to marry me. Telling me would have been a wise move to win my trust.

"Did you have plans to marry me all along, or was it a spur-of-the-moment idea with Janus?" I snap, my voice low in case any photographers are nearby.

Alden smiles. It isn't cruel or cunning, but resigned. "You silly girl, you ruined the surprise. I was going to ask you. But now the cat is out of the bag, we might as well discuss it."

My jaw hardens. "That's right, you should have asked me, but you didn't. Were you afraid I'd say no, so you had to force my hand?"

"You can always say no." Alden crosses his arms.

I exhale slowly to quell my anger. "You should have talked to me first. Not Janus. Instead, she blindsided me yesterday, giving me an ultimatum —peace or Wilder."

It's not fair.

Alden sighs. "I am surprised you didn't see this coming, Leigh. As a single woman in her early twenties, it was only a matter of time before your Council began pressuring you to get married. You are the last in line for the throne. How else did you expect we would ally with Corona?"

"Not through marriage," I say, and he frowns. "We could forge a treaty. Or—"

"Leigh, a strategic marriage between us would be a politically astute move. Several leaders of neighboring countries, including my father, perceive a Lunar Witch as a threat to their security. Not to mention, control over Corona means access to your ports in the east and your oil reserves in the west. As a war strategist, I could help strengthen your borders and project an image of power to deter potential invaders," he explains.

His words cause my throat to constrict. It feels as if I've swallowed gravel.

I scowl. "You've left no stone unturned."

"I am nothing but thorough," Alden says, then his eyes sparkle. "And charming."

"I have a boyfriend," I remind him, but the words sound weak after he's outlined how ripe my country is for invasion.

"A marriage is a strategic alliance, Leigh. Keep your boyfriend. I have my affairs back home, anyway."

My face pinches. "That's messed up on so many levels."

He shrugs. "Welcome to politics."

I can't even speak. There has to be another way. Janus can't just broker my marriage like some trade deal. My country's future can't hang *only* on who I marry. If the Council and I were united, and Stellan ceased writing stories that sow division, we could consider allocating more resources to our military. However, our priority would be to address the issue of Janus and her potential role as a mole.

"I can't wait forever, Leigh," Alden says. "My father expects an answer soon, or he will demand I take your country by force. What will it be? Me or war?"

I don't bother responding; I just head for the clubhouse.

"You have two days! Then I expect an answer!" Alden calls, and I give him the finger without so much as glancing back.

I don't like that guy, my father's ghost grumbles.

"Join the club," I respond.

Alden follows me to the clubhouse, unease spreads through my body like a poisonous vine, wrapping tendrils around my heart before squeezing. The thought of telling Wilder about Alden threatens to drown me. Will Wilder understand my position, or will he fight it? As queen, I must prevent war at all costs, even if it means making personal sacrifices. But the idea of Wilder not accepting that decision fills me with dread. If I could, I'd remove the crown off my head and stomp on it.

Conflicting emotions rage within me, each one battling for supremacy. The desire to protect my kingdom is a constant presence, but it's intertwined with the bitter realization that my happiness may be the price.

THE KELPIE CLUB is alive with excitement on this picturesque winter day. The sun shines over the unique circular racetrack, where kelpies race through a shallow, water-filled channel. A cacophony of cheers and shouts rises into the air. Inside the clubhouse, where the Council and other elite members and visitors observe the race, the vibrant colors of the jockeys' silks captivate me through the open windows, standing out against the shimmering water.

With the blast of the starting horn, the first racers surge forward, their reversed hooves churning up the water as they gallop. But these races are not for the faint of heart—the rules are brutal, reflecting the wild and untamed nature of the kelpies. As they thunder forward, the mythical creatures possess the ability to summon floods and manipulate the currents within the track, adding an element of danger and unpredictability to an already thrilling spectacle.

As I circle the VIP lounge, Alden snakes an arm around my waist. I attempt to wiggle free, but he digs his claws into me, drawing the attention of a few Epsilon corporation owners and Council members in the room. The Council members' behavior is telling; while some mingle, many seem uncertain of whom to trust and keep their distance. It's clear that our vulnerability to invasion is on full display. However, Alden seems oblivious to the strained atmosphere, focusing solely on me.

"What are you doing?" I hiss. I don't want people to get the wrong idea about us.

"This is our first public appearance. I'm cementing our alliance," Alden says.

"Do you have to be so handsy?"

He glances down at me with a smirk. "Physical touch is my love language."

My stomach roils, but I tamper down the need to puke, choosing to escape.

Across the room, I spy Janus with her wife, Daphne, partially concealed by the crowd. But she's not talking to her wife or their companions. Instead, her eyes focus on a sandy-blonde-haired woman across the room. Beatrix Marks. Though her features are hidden beneath a wide-brimmed hat, I would have bet my life on it.

"Excuse me." I move toward Beatrix, but she slips out onto the covered balcony and down the stairs to the racetrack level before Alden can protest or ask where I am going.

Outside on the covered balcony, servers offer me warm refreshments along with dozens of different kinds of canapés. I refuse them all, smiling at people waving for my attention as I search for Beatrix, who has mysteriously vanished.

When I look back at where Janus was standing inside by the ice sculpture, I spot her wife alone. I've lost them both. I consider asking around to locate them, but I'm wary of drawing a crowd. When I confront Janus, I want it to be just us.

Deciding to check the stables—the perfect place for a private conversation—I turn to go down the stairs, hurrying before Isolde can follow me. However, as soon as I reach the steps, I run into Bennett as he ascends them. My eyes widen as they meet those of a stunning brunette.

"Leigh," Bennett says, his posture rigid. "You remember Corvina Miller?"

All I can do is nod as Corvina pierces me with a guarded gaze. The last time I saw Corvina was at my brother's engagement party, where—drunk off my ass and pissed Fynn was marrying someone he didn't love—I gave a speech in which I told the entire party he was in love with someone else. Her. Corvina. A twinge of guilt pierces my chest. There have been so many things I've wanted to say to her over the years. I've practiced an apology a dozen times, but I was too chicken to visit her after Fynn's death. Too ashamed.

"I am happy for you," I say quickly, trying to get away.

Bennett's ears turn pink. "Leigh. Slow down . . . Let's—"

"It's good to see you, Leigh," Corvina murmurs. "You're looking well since the last time I saw you—more sober at least."

My legs shake.

I glance back at Bennett, and my throat tightens. He had ample opportunity to tell me he was seeing Corvina. Instead, he ambushes me at a public event, probably so I couldn't cause a scene. Does he think that little of me now? "You look well, too, Corvina, but I need to go."

"Leigh," Bennett says. "Have a drink—"

"Look, I'm trying to find Janus. Have you seen her?"

Bennett's eyes narrow. "I saw her go down to the winner's circle."

"Great."

With one final glance at the sneering Corvina, I race to find Janus as if my feet had wings.

As I make my way toward the winner's circle—a circular pool cordoned off from the main track, complete with a sponsored backdrop perfect for capturing celebratory photos—I clutch my phone, the camera open and ready to document any interaction between Janus and Beatrix. To my surprise and disappointment, the area is deserted. Frowning, I decide to investigate the stables, like I had initially planned.

I keep walking as the crowd thins, their excited chatter fading into the distance until I find myself alone on the concrete path. An unsettling sensation prickles the back of my neck, and I can't shake the feeling that someone is watching me. Before I can turn to look, the heavy sound of footsteps pounding against the pavement reaches my ears, sending a jolt of adrenaline through my body.

Instinctively, I run, not daring to glance back at my pursuer. But my heels betray me, slowing my pace to a frustrating crawl. I'm not fast enough. A solid body collides with mine, knocking the wind from my lungs. I open my mouth to scream, but a gloved hand clamps down, stifling my cries. The pungent scent of leather fills my nostrils, and panic rises in my chest.

The memory of Wilder dragging me into an alley to evade Nyx during the Harvest Festival flashes through my mind. Still, this time, there's one crucial difference: Wilder is in Aurora, and I'm utterly alone, at the mercy of my unknown assailant.

I struggle against my captor's iron grip, thrashing and twisting my body to break free. My mind races with questions. Who is this person? What do they want from me?

As they drag me into the shadows, away from the crowd's prying eyes, my hope dwindles. Darkness engulfs us, and the sounds of the racetrack fade into the distance, replaced by my pounding heart in my ears. With each passing second, the shadows seem to stretch forever, and I can't help but imagine the worst-case scenarios.

As my captor's grip tightens around me, forcing my hands behind my back, cutting me off from my magic, I close my eyes and pray for a miracle. But deep down, I know I can't rely on anyone else to save me. If I make it out of this alive, I'll have to find a way to save myself.

I refuse to give up without a fight, and continue to struggle against my captor's grip.

CHAPTER THIRTY-THREE
WILDER

STELLAN and I race down the street, our hearts pounding in sync with our footsteps as we navigate the labyrinth of narrow alleyways to avoid the squad cars or violent Epsilon. The sun—an unforgiving adversary—beats upon us, and sweat trickles down my temple as we pause behind a building, straining our ears for any sign of pursuing Blades or vengeful Epsilon. The memory of the gunshot—the bullet tearing through flesh to protect Stellan—replays in my mind.

I don't regret my actions, but the weight of the consequences presses heavily on my shoulders.

When the coast is clear, I urge Stellan forward. We take off running again, our breaths sawing in and out as we push our bodies to their limits. The relentless heat saps our strength, and I silently curse our lack of stealth. In moments like these, I wish I had Leigh's shadows to cloak us from view.

Despite the chaos and violence in the square, Stellan's pleas for peace replay in my head. He wants a better future for the Nebula, one free from the cycle of oppression and retaliation. If he's willing to negotiate with Leigh, find a common ground, and work together toward a peaceful resolution, then the bloodshed that stains our hands today can be the catalyst for change.

"In here," I say to Stellan as I rap sharply on the rear entrance to Furies.

No answer.

I'm sizing up a window to break to get us off the street when the door cracks open, and a wide-eyed Meg appears. Her gaze switches between

Stellan and me. She presses against the door, giving us enough room to slip inside.

We navigate through the cluttered stockroom before stepping into the main room, which is strangely lit and quiet in the off-hours. The stale smell of spilled beer and cigarette smoke clings to the drapes. As I settle the older man into a solitary wooden chair, the floorboards creak beneath my feet.

Meg approaches in her cat pajamas, clutching a dish towel and a bottle of antiseptic. Turning my hat backwards, I saturate the towel, and its sharp, medicinal scent fills my nose.

"I'm no healer, so this is going to hurt," I warn Stellan. Before he can protest, I press the damp towel firmly against the deepest cut on his face. He curses, his legs kicking out reflexively. "Don't be a baby. I saw you take a beating like a champ back there."

Stellan snatches the rag. "You're lucky you aren't a healer; you don't have a gentle touch or bedside manner."

I laugh. "If you think this hurts, maybe I should have left you in the square. Was it your intention to rile the Epsilon up to attack?"

Stellan scoffs. "I wasn't inciting violence."

I glare at him. "You had to have known the idea of annexing Aurora from the rest of the country would anger many still loyal to the Council and the Crown. Not to mention the old ways."

Stellan's eyes flash. "I knew it would, but I didn't say it to incite a riot," he begins, his tone laced with a bitter edge as he sits tall, defiance in his posture. "I hoped it would make more people excited by the possibility rather than angry."

Stellan spits a mouthful of blood onto the floor by my foot.

I scowl. "You want a safe space for Nebula to start over. That is admirable, but it'll never happen. You can get a million signatures on a petition, and the Council will still push back. You'll have a war at your door if you follow through on your plans."

"I'm not looking to start a war." Stellan sighs. "But I also feel it is in the Council's best interest to let us go free."

I inhale through my nose and exhale out of my mouth. "Aurora is too valuable."

Stellan remains silent as he dabs at his wounds with the antiseptic rag, wincing each time the fabric contacts his battered face. The wound is deep, but it doesn't require stitches like I thought. Despite the pain etched into his strong features, there's a certain youthfulness about him, suggesting he's in his late forties.

His eyes capture my attention—they hold a trusting nature that feels familiar, putting me at ease in his presence.

Meg, standing nearby, frowns. "I'll get a mop and bucket. We need to clean this mess up before we open. There's blood everywhere."

"It's a bar, Meg," Stellan calls as she walks away.

She flips him off, and my eyes widen at the unexpected gesture. Brigid isn't the only one who shares a close bond with Stellan. "Next time, go soil someone else's!"

"You tried to get the rioters to stop, proving you care," I point out to regain Stellan's attention.

He shrugs. "Violence isn't the answer, but neither is rolling over and playing dead."

"That's not what I'm doing," I retort, my voice steady but firm. "I haven't forgotten or forgiven the hardships my family and I endured, but not all Epsilon are the problem. If you got to know Leigh as a person rather than just the wearer of the crown, you'd see she's trying to make a difference. But she can't when your articles make it impossible."

Stellan's gaze meets mine. What does he see when he looks at me? Earlier, he viewed me as part of the problem, but that was before I risked everything to save his life. Does he now recognize me as someone like him? Someone willing to fight for change, but not at the cost of innocent lives? Someone who believes there must be a better way, a path that doesn't lead to more bloodshed and suffering if only we dare to seek it out?

"I know the queen has had it hard," he says, and I nod. That's an understatement. "Lunar Witches in this country have had it just as bad as the Nebula, and in some cases, even worse, what with the burnings and asylums. But Leigh is still a royal. Her magic doesn't erase hundreds of years of lies. It doesn't mean she cares about *us*. If the Nebula don't control our destiny, Wilder, who is to say the government won't keep lying to and manipulating us?"

I pause, considering the implications of Stellan's words. I've witnessed the injustices the Nebula face daily. A separate Aurora could provide a haven for many, offering them a chance to experience true freedom for the first time. But at what cost? The price of war is too high, and the consequences are too devastating to bear.

The scars of oppression run deep, not just for the Nebula, but for the Lunar Witches. We've all suffered under the weight of discrimination and prejudice. But I know no one is more devoted to the truth; no one more committed to changing things for the oppressed than Leigh. If I could get Stellan and Leigh in the same room to sit down and talk, I'm certain they would see that they have more in common than they realize.

"I want you to talk to Leigh," I say.

Stellan shakes his head. "She'll tell me no."

My nails bite into my palms. "Give it a go, for the Nebula people, for peace."

"With the enclave, we won't need her approval."

I resist the urge to roll my eyes. "Corona isn't just going to let you secede without pushback. Ivah failed to turn Aurora into a free state, and many Nebula died in the process, so what makes you think you will succeed?"

Stellan gives a cryptic smile. "Not *what*, but *who*?"

I raise a brow. Is he referring to his source on the Council? "What does that mean?"

"You're asking the wrong questions, Wilder."

"Wilder is on our side, Stellan," Meg says, reappearing with a bucket and mop. She stares at Stellan. "His notions are misplaced, but love will do that to a person."

I shift uncomfortably. I'm in love, not lost.

Stellan sizes me up. "I understand your predicament more than you think. But you're fighting for the wrong team. Our values are the same. I could use someone with your strength and hunger for justice working for me."

I shake my head. There are no *teams*. When will people get that?

"I'll pay you kindly for it."

"I'm a Blade. I can't be turned or bought."

I'm not Marlowe. Nor am I my father.

Stellan laughs. The sound echoes around the quiet bar. "I'm asking you to help me. Help *us* start over," Stellan says.

"I'll tell you what," I say. "I'll consider working for you if you agree to a meeting with Leigh. Think about it, Stellan. You want to prove you'll do whatever it takes to fight for the Nebula people? Then at least give them a chance for peaceful change."

Stellan mulls over the possibility. "I see now that what happened today is a microcosm of what could happen if we aren't selective about who we have on our side. We need people who understand the fight. We need people who will go down swinging, and who aren't afraid to get their hands dirty." His gaze drops to my bloody knuckles.

As I watch Stellan prepare to leave the bar, wincing as he retrieves his phone to send a text, a sense of urgency grips me until I can barely breathe. If he leaves, I might not get another chance to speak with him. I need him to agree to meet with Leigh, and I need that commitment now.

"I need your answer," I say in a steady voice. At my words, Meg pauses. The mop and bucket she's been using halt, the water inside swirling under her magical command. She looks up, her eyes darting between Stellan and me, sensing the gravity of the moment.

I remain seated, my gaze locked with Stellan's.

"Will you meet Leigh?"

My heart pounds in the delay of his response. The silence stretches between us, heavy with the weight of the decision that hangs in the balance. If Stellan agrees to sit down with Leigh and find a way forward, then we can avoid the bloodshed and suffering that seem all but inevitable

But if he refuses, if he walks away now, then I fear that the cycle of violence and oppression will continue. More lives will be lost, and more hearts will be broken. I don't move a muscle.

When Stellan grins, his teeth are sharp.

"Why not? Now, if you both excuse me, my ride's here." He reaches the door, giving me one final glance. "Wilder, I'll be in touch soon. In the meantime, tell Leigh I look forward to meeting her."

My only response is a nod before he adds, "By the way, your blind faith in Leigh is inspiring, but I'm not sure you know who you're dealing with."

"What does that mean?" I call after him. But the door rattles shut.

CHAPTER THIRTY-FOUR
DESIREE

VANE and I walk side by side toward Vyvyan's chambers, our footsteps echoing against the stone floors. Everyone in the Nest is asleep, but Vyvyan requires a check-up before Vane tries once again to turn her back into a vampire. I plan to use our time together to plead my case to find the killer by raising the Balam. It is a surefire way to apprehend the killer and keep living here.

My fingers trace the silver necklace hanging around my neck.

"Will you stop fidgeting? You are making me nervous," Vane chastises, his voice tight with an emotion I can't place.

It is the most he's talked to me since my date with Jaxson. As we approach Vyvyan's bedroom door, I adjust my attire, pulling up the neckline to avoid showing too much cleavage—Vyvyan always comments on my appearance.

Just as I smooth my skirt, Vane grabs my hand.

"Relax, you look fine," he orders.

I yank my hand from his, my skin tingling where he touched me. "I don't get you," I reply. The words hang between us like a challenge.

Vane's grin widens. "What's not to get?" he asks.

"This." I gesture between us, the movement sharp. "You say you want nothing to do with me, yet every time I turn around, there you are."

Is it because he senses I'm about to uncover his secret? Alden might not have been in Borealis the night of the attack, but perhaps Vane planted the prints to cast blame on the wolf. It was sheer misfortune that Alden came to visit right after.

"Do I bother you, Desiree?" he asks.

I put some distance between us, my fingers twitch betraying my unease at his presence. My evening with Jax was enjoyable, and I refuse to let Vane ruin it by playing mind games with me. "We should go inside."

I raise my hand to knock, but he says, "Wait."

My hand falls to my side. Vane steps forward, pushing open Vyvyan's ajar door. The hinges creak. We exchange wary glances. Vyvyan always keeps this door locked.

"Vyvyan?" Vane's voice rings through the unsettling quiet as he pushes the door wider and steps inside.

I follow and collide with his rigid form as he stops beyond the threshold.

"What's wrong?" I ask, but Vane doesn't answer. Instead, he rushes to where Vyvyan lies sprawled on the floor.

I gasp, the sound sharp in the silence.

Vyvyan's room is a catastrophe, strewn with clothing and shattered furniture. The torn curtains surrounding her four-poster bed mirror the disarray of her attire, the fabric hanging in tattered shreds off her shoulders. The air stinks of spilled liquor and the metallic tang of blood. All the smells threaten my upchuck reflex.

I rush to Vane's side—my shoes crunching broken glass—as he pulls Vyvyan's limp body into his arms. She is a small, fragile figure amid the wreckage, a bloody mark on her lip stark against her ebony skin. "Is she . . ."

Vane shakes his head grimly. "She's alive but unconscious."

A huge breath escapes me. "What the hell happened? Was she attacked?"

I search the room for daemon tracks. Nothing.

"The scent of her blood is fresh." Vane's tone hardens with a hint of malice.

"M-maybe I can catch them?"

I shift to rush out the door, determined to find the assailant once and for all, but Vane grabs my wrist. His grip is firm yet gentle.

"Don't go. I may need your medical knowledge. I'm sure they're long gone by now."

I nod, swallowing hard. What else am I good for?

"Vyvyan," Vane murmurs, his voice laced with a tender affection that sends a flush of warmth through me despite the grim circumstances. He handles her with such gentleness it is a wonder that I suspected he could ever raise a hand to her in hate. "Wake up." With tender encouragement, Vyvyan stirs, cracking open an eyelid with a pained groan. Vane releases a choked sob, his relief tangible. "Thank the heavens."

Vyvyan weakly licks her bloodied lips and then winces. I search the nearby bar for an intact glass among the shattered stemware. Once I find one, I fill it with water from a pitcher and hand it to Vane.

"Drink," he instructs. She complies, her throat moving as she swallows the water, droplets escaping the corners of her mouth. Once she's finished, Vane lifts her effortlessly into her expansive bed, which is large enough to accommodate half a dozen people.

"Who did this to you?" I ask.

Vyvyan flinches at the sound of my voice.

Vane's muscles are tense as he releases Vyvyan, who manages to sit up alone, her movements stiff. As he steps back, I cautiously move closer, but Vyvyan watches me with narrowed eyes, her gaze accusatory. She's scared of me.

"Vyv," Vane prompts.

She points directly at me and declares, "You."

The word knocks the air from my lungs.

"This is your fault," Vyvyan states, each word a sharp slap.

I grip my chest as if I could calm my pounding heart. "Mine? I just got here."

"Vyvyan, Desiree didn't do this," Vane says.

Vyvyan shakes her head.

"He's right," I blurt. But a chilling thought occurs to me. Did Jaxson tell someone that Vyvyan was vulnerable? He promised he wouldn't. Bile rises in my throat.

"Vyvyan, tell us what happened," Vane urges as he drapes a blanket over her shoulders.

"Someone broke into my room," Vyvyan replies, her voice husky with exhaustion, each word seeming to take immense effort. "I didn't get a good look at their face before they used me as a human punching bag."

"Was it a witch or a vamp—" I ask, but Vyvyan's frosty glare stops me.

"They weren't as strong as a vampire, so I'm guessing it was a witch, but the whole thing is a blur. They hit me in the head. I think they wanted to kill me."

Vane and I exchange a tense look. How did a witch infiltrate the Nest?

"Are you sure it was a witch? Could it have been a wolf?" I ask. Alden breached these tunnels before. Perhaps while we were all sleeping . . .

Vyvyan shakes her head. "You'd smell him if a wolf were here."

I shake my head, my thoughts racing. "That Ravi guy is always with him. He's a witch? They could be working together."

"That's a fair point," Vane declares. "I will sound the alarm. See if the other vampires saw anything."

Vyvyan grabs his hand. "Get rid of her."

I blink, taken aback. "But, Vyvyan, you shouldn't be alone."

Vyvyan's menacing laughter interrupts.

"You don't understand. I want you gone—out of sight for good. I wish I were a vampire so I could have the strength to dispose of you myself. I am in this vulnerable position because of you and your toxic blood."

"I am trying to help you," I plead.

Vyvyan snarls. "Help me? Look where your help has gotten me. I am *human*. You are a waste of space and a threat to our kind. You are behind this. Did you do this as a revenge stunt after outing you to Misty?"

"No—"

"Then you must want me out of the way," she screeches, "so you can have Vane!"

My breath sputters as I search for the right words.

"That's absurd," Vane says.

"Is it?"

"Vane hates me. You told me yourself," I say.

"You pathetic girl, when are you going to wake up? You aren't wanted," Vyvyan declares, backing me into a corner with her words. "I want you gone—dead and buried!"

"Please, don't. My family will wonder what happened to me. They'll—"

"I thought we were your family?" Vyvyan sneers.

"Vyvyan, you're being unreasonable," Vane cuts in, his voice tight with tension. "What happened here has nothing to do with Desiree. She's trying to help you by solving the case."

I gasp, not needing him to defend me. "I know how we can find your attacker. We can summon the Balam and ask who controlled it that night. We—"

"You want to put more of us in jeopardy by raising the daemon powerful enough to almost kill me?" Vyvyan screeches. "You'd put the rest of the coven in jeopardy, all for what? My approval?"

I resist the urge to shrink beneath the mountain of clothes strewn across the floor.

"It's dangerous, but if —"

"You selfish girl," Vyvyan snarls. "You only think about yourself."

I step back. No matter what I say, Vyvyan wants me gone. My only option is to accept her decision and hope I can someday regain her favor. Even if it means packing up everything I own and leaving the only place I call home.

Vane raises his hands placatingly. "Vyvyan, let's stop pretending this is about Desiree —"

"I'll go," I say. They both look at me. "I'll leave tonight. I'm sorry for all the trouble I've caused, but I promise I'll do everything possible to make it up to you."

I turn on my heel to go, my vision blurring with unshed tears. Vyvyan's door slams behind me like a final judgment.

A moment later, a hand grasps my arm. The coolness of the grip sends a shiver through me.

"Desiree," Vane says, his voice tight. "Where will you go?"

I shrug, trying to appear nonchalant despite the turmoil inside. "My brother's loft. He's out of town, so it'll be empty."

Vane nods, his eyes searching mine. "And the Balam? You aren't thinking of summoning it, are you?"

If it means finding out who wants to kill Vyvyan so I can regain her favor, then yes. But I lie. "No."

Vane's shoulders relax. "Good."

Before he can say another word, I turn and leave him and the Nest behind.

CHAPTER THIRTY-FIVE
LEIGH

I THRASH AGAINST MY ATTACKER, contorting my body in a desperate attempt to break free from their unrelenting hold. As I struggle, I try to catch a glimpse of their face, searching for any identifying features I can use against them later.

My mind catalogs every detail I can gather. The strength of their grip, the size of their hands, the scent of their skin—anything that might give me a clue of who they are.

A car parked in the employee lot behind the stables comes into view. Its trunk gapes open like a dark, hungry maw. Panic surges through me, and I buck with renewed desperation. If they shove me into that trunk, I'm done for.

Then my attacker hoists me up as if I weigh nothing. I resist, pressing my high heels into the bumper to lean back from the trunk. Their reflection flashes briefly in the shiny paint job of the car: clad in a black mask, eyes hidden behind dark lenses. Who could be behind this brazen attack in such a public setting?

The image of Janus's face springs to the forefront of my mind. She disappeared with Beatrix right when I arrived. Could this be her doing?

Suddenly, a gust of wind, like a squall torn from the pages of a fantasy novel, surges forward. The force knocks my attacker and me off our feet, sending us sprawling onto the gravel path.

"Let her go!" Janus's commanding voice cuts through the day. "Guards!"

My attacker scrambles to their feet with inhuman agility.

I reach for their ankle, but my fingers graze empty air as they leap behind the car's wheel. The engine roars to life, drowning out my frustrated cry. As the car speeds away, two pairs of footsteps crunch across the snowy, gravel path.

I roll over just as Janus blocks out the sun above me. She's flanked by a woman in a hat. Beatrix.

"Are you hurt?" Janus asks, her voice soft as she reaches out a hand.

I flinch away from it, glancing between the women. My throat tightens with unshed tears and unspoken accusations. I went looking for Janus, then got attacked. She might have spooked them away, but that doesn't mean she wasn't somehow involved.

Janus follows my line of sight, unease furrowing her brow. "Leigh, this is Beatrix Marks."

Beatrix offers a small wave and a tight smile. "It's nice to meet you."

"Are you conspiring against me?" I blurt out, my voice hoarse.

"Perhaps you both need some privacy," Beatrix suggests.

Janus nods, and Beatrix walks off to intercept the approaching guards, which include a tight-lipped Isolde, who glares at me. I pitch it right back. It's not as if I asked to be kidnapped.

"We need to talk," Janus says.

"Yeah, we do," I say, trembling.

I stand without her help, ignoring the shake of my legs. We need to air our grievances.

The president folds her arms. "Beatrix is in town to tell me that her father died." I blink at the information. "I know her family's politics are divisive, given they were staunch Nyx supporters, but he was a nice man and close to my parents growing up," Janus continues, her voice softening. "For a while, during my teen years before Ama and Father died, I thought I wanted to join his party. You might already know that, given you've been having me followed."

I cross my arms over my chest. I won't apologize for due diligence. She's been acting shady.

Janus narrows her eyes. "Leigh, I caught Pallas snooping through my house the other day on the baby monitor."

"Baby monitor?" I ask. Janus doesn't have kids.

She hesitates, then sighs. "Yes, Daphne is pregnant, and we were testing out the merchandise. The feed showed him *in my house*."

I shake my head. "I didn't ask him to break into your house."

Janus purses her lips. "Perhaps not. But you had him follow me."

I open my mouth to protest, but what's the point of lying? "Can you blame me? He uncovered the truth about your meeting with Beatrix."

"Beatrix and I are not working together."

I scoff. "You should have told me that the moment she stepped foot in Borealis."

A flicker of regret crosses her face. "Maybe so, but we have bigger things to—"

"You met with Alden without me to *sell* me into a marriage," I snap, my pent-up suspicions tumbling out one after the other. "And why won't you tell me what happened to you the night of the blackout?"

"I deeply regret how I handled the situation with Alden. It was a lapse in judgment on my part."

Janus makes me sweat for a minute, the silence stretching taut between us. Finally, she says, "Hebe. Daphne had some complications, and we rushed her to the hospital to see Doctor Dunn."

"Why didn't you just say that?" I demand.

Janus sighs, her shoulders sagging. "Because we weren't ready to tell anyone about the pregnancy. Not after . . ." She swallows.

"What?"

"Not after you poisoned me with the Harborym venom!" Janus yells, her composure finally cracking.

I stumble back a step. "I apologized," I say weakly, knowing it's insufficient.

"On national TV, never to me," Janus says, and I shrink. The hurt in her eyes is genuine. But I never got a chance to apologize to her personally, not with how poorly our first audience went.

"It was a misunderstanding. I didn't know Don would use it on you."

Janus's hands ball into fists. "And I didn't know if I could trust you. Your uncle lied to us all. You lied to us about your magic. I was protecting my family."

"I was protecting my people!" I fire back. "Someone is betraying us, telling secrets to Stellan to divide us, and you—"

"You think that's *me*?" Janus scoffs.

"You disappeared during a blackout. What else was I supposed to think?"

Janus laughs with so much disbelief and disgust that, despite myself, I can't deny it—she's not the mole.

We stand there, two leaders at a crossroads. But I refuse to back down first. She might not be the enemy I thought she was, but she lied to me. I was right not to trust her.

"Leigh, I'm disappointed in you. You can't just run around assuming the worst of people and leading secret investigations with your friends."

"Well, when people stop betraying me, then I will."

A professional coolness masks the hurt in her eyes.

"It seems we should be worried about whoever just tried to have you *abducted*," she says. My throat tightens at the reminder. "Did you see their face?"

"No," I murmur. Just then, Alden bursts out from the growing crowd the guards keep at bay. He trots over, accompanied by Ravi.

"What happened?" he gasps, trying to pull me into an embrace. I push away from him as cameras flash in the distance.

Was *he* the one behind my attack? What purpose could the wolves have for kidnapping unless they're trying to goad us into war? But why do that now if they're trying to arrange a marriage alliance?

As I try to storm off, Isolde intercepts me. "There was an attack," she breathes. "In Aurora. It just got called in."

I straighten. Wilder. "What happened?"

"Stellan got hurt."

Isolde's words send a chill down my spine. "Is he—"

"Wilder saved him, but he shot a man," she whispers. The ground no longer opens beneath my feet when Isolde adds, "Wilder wouldn't betray you."

I nod, wanting desperately to believe her. There has to be an explanation.

As if on cue, phones start pinging in every person's pocket—a telltale sign of a new article from *The Tower Tribune*. My heart squeezes, and I reach for my phone, but I must have lost it in the attack. Isolde hands me hers.

The Tower Tribune

SCANDAL ROCKS THE MONARCHY

Scandal Rocks the Monarchy: Fynn Raelyn's True Parentage Revealed

By Stellan Navis

AT a peaceful rally for my campaign earlier today, I was attacked. An Epsilon tried to silence my quest for justice. But the truth will not be silenced. I come to you from a safe and secure location with a new, inciting story.

In a stunning revelation that threatens the stability of our royal institution, my favorite trusted source has presented information that could redefine the Raelyn family's lineage. It has been disclosed that Fynn Raelyn—previously believed to be the son of the late Prince Gwyn Raelyn and heir to the throne—is the offspring of Don Raelyn, the former Heir Apparent's brother.

This source, who has proven reliable in the past, alleges that the truth has been a closely guarded secret within the palace, stemming from a long-concealed affair between Queen Mother Cynthia Araceli-Raelyn and Prince Don Raelyn. This affair challenges the legitimacy of Fynn's position and casts a shadow over Queen Leigh's rightful claim to the throne. Could Don be her father as well?

All the air empties from my lungs. Around me, the excited sounds of the racecourse are shifting into something sharp and accusatory, whispers turning into hisses of shock as people read the article.

"Leigh?" Isolde's voice cuts through my shock.

I look up at her. "Get me out of here."

I need to see my mother.

CHAPTER THIRTY-SIX
LEIGH

IT'S NOT TRUE, please. Tell me it's not true. *It can't be.*

"Mother?" The crack of my voice rings in the cavernous foyer.

The moment I step into my former family home, a wave of unfamiliarity suffocates me. In the last year, my mom got rid of every piece of furniture that existed here when my father and brother were alive, replacing warm, comforting pieces with cold, modern designs. The walls, once adorned with cherished family photos, now bear the cold stare of black-and-white images captured by renowned photographers. Strangers, celebrities, and high-fashion pieces have replaced the smiling faces of my loved ones. Their lifeless eyes follow me as I navigate the hallways, each step echoing with memories that are like distant whispers.

Hot anger churns inside me. Mom has been a ghost for months since the truth about Don being the Magician came out. She left, leaving me to pick up the pieces of our shattered lives alone.

It's like she's trying to erase any memory of Father, Fynn, and me.

I follow the scent of mother's rose perfume toward the sitting room. I need her to say it. I need to hear her say Stellan is lying. Fynn can't be Don's son. It would destroy everything. It would destroy *me.*

My mother couldn't have had a relationship with my uncle. She despises Don, and he loathes her in return. But there's a fine line between hate and love, isn't there?

I shake my head. No, I couldn't have misread their interactions for twenty years. Mother needs to tell everyone. She must kill the story before it spreads.

I find my mother seated near an easel, painting a beach scene.

Haunting strings of a violin drift from a nearby speaker as the news plays silently on the TV in the background, its flickering images flickering revealing she's heard the story about Fynn.

"Are you going to tell them it's not true?" I ask.

Her magic swirls murky water around her paintbrush, the colors bleeding together like the secrets and lies threatening to drown us all.

"Hello, Leigh." Mother sighs. "I had a feeling I'd see you today."

I scoff. If that's true, she could have picked up the phone and saved us both the hassle of me coming here. I should be at the precinct giving a statement about my failed kidnapping or calling Wilder after what happened at the rally in Aurora, not here.

"Well?" I prompt.

Mother refuses to meet my gaze. She can pretend Don doesn't exist all she wants, but the world outside these walls won't. Stellan's accusations are spreading like wildfire, and she's at the eye of the storm. One word from her—just one—calling him a liar could shatter his credibility. His followers would start to doubt, his influence would wane, and this nightmare could end. It's time for her to step up and *do* something to help me.

Be kind to your mother, Father's ghost warns, appearing beside me. He stares between me and my mother with watery gray eyes.

She doesn't seem aware he's here. Mother never glances in his direction. Is he concealing himself on purpose?

You two need to talk. I will only get in the way, Father explains to me.

"Stellan's article—I know you've seen it." I gesture wildly to the TV as reporters speculate about Stellan's words and what they mean for the monarchy. "The accusations are outrageous, and it's on every channel." I pick up the remote with a shaky hand and scroll through channel after channel for emphasis while my mother pointedly stares at her painting. "They are saying Fynn is Don's kid." Mother's ice blue eyes finally meet mine. I'm struck by how devoid of emotion they are. I squeeze the remote. The plastic creaks under the pressure. "Some people might question if I am, too."

Mother returns to her painting. "Now that's just ridiculous," she says.

"You are Gwyn's daughter. Anyone can see that—you two are so much alike. So headstrong in your beliefs. Heaven, help anyone who stands in your way. Even as a child, you were steadfast in your ways. I'd tell you no, while Gwyn would say yes. It was—"

"I know I am my father's daughter. I can see his ghost. But that doesn't mean people won't speculate. What about Fynn? Are you going to let Stellan tarnish his memory by linking him to that . . . murderer?"

Slowly, Mother sets her paintbrush down and faces me. "Leigh, there's something you must understand." Dark circles bruise under her eyes. Has she been sleeping? "When I discovered I was pregnant with Fynn, your father and I were already getting married. We made the choice not to say anything about Don or—"

"Wait. *What?*" I shriek. Her words steal my strength.

I grip the back of the sofa and notice my father still hovering nearby, hidden from Mother. When our eyes meet, he doesn't cower or flinch.

"You knew?" I say to him, my voice breaking on the words.

He nods, and my world shatters like crystal.

"Of course I knew," Mother responds, thinking I am talking to her. "I had been in a secret relationship with Don before your grandparents betrothed me to Gwyn. We were having fun and hadn't been the most careful."

"You speak as if you and Don broke a rule or two, not as if you were having *sex* with your husband's brother!" The words explode from me. Mother cringes, but I can't find it in myself to feel guilty. Not when every revelation is another knife in my back. Stellan will have a field day with this.

I came here expecting—*needing*—her to debunk Stellan's lies. Instead, she's confirming the unthinkable: she and Don had a relationship. My father knew. He helped her hide it.

My mother and Don.

The words are like poison in my mind. All those years I watched them trade barbs and cold shoulders across dinner tables and family gatherings. Was it all just an act?

"I was never unfaithful to your father, Leigh. I called things off with

Don months before my first date with Gwyn. Three months before we were betrothed."

I clutch at the hollowness in my chest. It's like a chasm threatening to pull me and everything around me into a sunless void. So Stellan was right about Fynn, after all. But the question remains: how did he know?

"Who else knew about you and Don?" I ask.

Mother purses her lips and rises from her stool. "Sit down, you are upset—"

"Of course, I am upset! I just learned that you had a relationship with my uncle! The man responsible for my father and Fynn's deaths! Do you have any idea how this could ruin our country?" I exclaim. As my mother drifts past me, her perfume envelops me, tightening like handcuffs. This woman lied to me for my entire life. Even my father lied to me.

We thought we were doing the right thing, Father's ghost says.

The right thing would have been telling me the truth years ago. Instead, I had to learn about my family's secrets alongside millions of strangers, watching my life unravel in real-time on social media. The humiliation burns deep, horror clawing at my insides. And now, standing here in my childhood home, facing my mother's guilty silence, I've never felt more utterly, completely alone.

My mother collapses on the pristine white sofa in her matching white dress. White is the color of purity, perfection, and honesty, but it no longer suits her.

"Sit with me, Leigh. We need to talk." Mother's voice cracks, a sound so unfamiliar I flinch. I perch on the edge of the couch beside her, my spine straight, muscles tense—ready to flee at a moment's notice.

Father's ghost sits close to Mother, his ethereal presence a mean reminder of all the secrets between us. She can't see him, can't feel the comfort he's trying to offer her, but I can. And it burns. She's had twenty-four years to live with this truth, while my world is shattering. My nails cut into my palms. Hot tears of rage blur my vision. Is this why my father came back? Not for me, but to keep watching over my mother and her secrets?

I swallow the golf ball of grief in my throat and say, "Start from the beginning."

Mother nods, her eyes glassy. "Don and I were in the same year at Sussex, and every girl had a crush on him. Unlike your father, who preferred the company of books, Don was the life of the party. We should never have fallen for each other. There was a rumor that I would marry Gwyn one day, but Gwyn was four years older than me, and we hardly had anything in common. He was already performing his princely duties and was not interested in me, so I wasn't interested in him."

"You sound naïve." I cringe at the cruelty in my voice.

Mother's eyes flash with a hint of the fire she keeps carefully hidden beneath her cool exterior. "Leigh, I was eighteen. You try to control a hormonal teenager. I couldn't with you."

"We aren't talking about me."

"No, we aren't," Mother agrees with a sigh.

"Anyway, Don and I had our first friendly conversation at a Yule party a year before my engagement to your father. Your father ignored me. He was too busy with his friends and appeasing his future councilors, who all wanted a word with the future king. But Don made time for me. I'd been a wallflower, dressed up like a doll to resemble everything my parents were told your father wanted, but it wasn't your father who noticed me. Don and I spent the whole night talking about the impossible expectations of our parents. I had never felt so *seen*."

Bile inches higher and higher. My uncle brought my mousy mother out of her shell.

"After the party, Don and I were inseparable," she continues. "But, to avoid disturbing the fragile peace between our families, we carried on secretly. As the months ticked by, the more besotted we grew, the more risks we took to be together. Our meetings were often spur-of-the-moment and reckless."

I groan. "I'm going to hurl."

Leigh, Father chastises as Mother's cheeks flush.

I ignore him. How he sits composed while Mother spills her heart out about her intimate relationship with his younger brother is beyond me.

"If you and Don were together, and you were pregnant, why did you not marry *him*?" I ask.

Mother shakes her head. "Don never knew. Knowing the scandal would disrupt the realm, your father and I kept it between us. We raised Fynn as ours and promised each other that we would never speak of it to anyone again."

"Stop lying," I say.

Someone told Stellan. Either Mother is the mole, or she confided in someone. That someone is my rat; the traitor in our midst.

Mother pales. "Leigh, I wouldn't—"

"You've been lying to me my entire life. Someone told Stellan about Fynn, which means you or Father told another person about your secret. Who?" I stare between my parents, my gaze accusing.

Once I unmask the mole's identity, I can get the Council to stop pointing fingers and listen to me again. They will reunite once Stellan no longer threatens them, and they will hear me out when I say marrying Alden doesn't secure peace for our nation. There are other ways to do that.

Mother follows my gaze to where Father sits. Her eyes widen. "Is Gwyn here now?"

My father scowls at me. "You have no right to be angry," I tell him.

Mother blinks. "What's your father saying?" she asks, but I refuse to look away from Father.

We made a mistake, Father's voice is firm.

My smile is unkind. "A mistake is forgetting to take out the garbage. What you two did changed everything! Fynn was never the rightful heir to the throne. Yet you lied to me and everyone about it to protect your secret." I was always meant to be queen, and my family was intent on never telling me.

My mother bursts into tears, covering her face with her paint-crusted hands, shoulders hunching.

"Did Fynn know?" I ask.

"No," Mother says, while my father says, *Yes.*

My jaw sets. I don't know whom to believe.

"Leigh, you were never meant to know," Mother exclaims.

"So that makes it okay?"

Mother cries harder.

"You made me feel that my becoming queen was *stealing* from Fynn." I focus on my anger to keep my tears at bay. "I almost gave up the crown to Don because I didn't think I deserved it. But it's been mine all along."

I lift my hair off my neck. The room is boiling. It is too full of secrets and lies.

"None of this is okay," Mother wails. "But, Leigh, I have no idea how Stellan found out."

"I do," I say. "It was Don. Even from prison, he is still calling the shots."

Mother's eyes bulge. "You're mistaken. Don never knew about Fynn."

Father nods.

"But do you know for sure?" I lean forward. Mother's hands fidget in her lap.

As the Magician, Don had access to many secrets. It's possible that someone in Eos somehow found out about Fynn and reported their findings to him. Alternatively, Fynn might have confronted Don about his true parentage, even though they were never close.

Don might not be the one contacting Stellan directly, but he could have a loyal supporter on the Council who is leaking information on his behalf.

I think of all the letters at home, unopened on my bedside table. Could Don have warned me this would happen? Is there something about Fynn penned on those pages?

"Don couldn't have known," Mother says with conviction "In the months leading up to my wedding with Gwyn, Don got back together with Lilura di Siena. The night he found out I was pregnant, he announced his intention to marry Lilura, but she called off the engagement shortly after. Don was dealing with quite a lot when Fynn first came into the picture. Questioning mine and Gwyn's timeline was not his top priority."

My chest tightens. I try to control my breathing, but each exhale comes out short and ragged. I never knew Don had been engaged to Gianna's aunt. Our family history is overflowing with more scandals than Tsilah Cemetery has bodies. People are furious about Stellan's articles, and I understand their anger, but how can I prevent these explosions when I'm constantly blindsided by the past?

"We need to confront Don," I say. "If he's behind the information leaks to Stellan, we must get him to confess or reveal who his accomplice is. Once we have that information, we can go public with it."

My eyes lock with my mother's. "Think about it. If we can expose Don's involvement and the identity of his informant, we can take control of the narrative. We can show the people that we're not hiding anything and are willing to be transparent about our family's past to build a brighter future."

"No! Stellan is trying to tear our country apart by discussing my private business. I will not help him by indulging in the gossip mongering."

I balk. "You are helping him by saying nothing. If you come clean, you can clear *my* name and any questions about my rule. You can help me regain control of the Council."

Mother glares at me, her jaw set. She will weather this storm, holed up away from prying eyes, thinking it will all blow over. Except it won't.

"I won't do it," she says with finality.

"You're making a mistake." I rise on jellied limbs.

"You know I love you, L-Leigh." Mother's voice cracks.

"Then tell the truth. Regain our people's trust. Regain *my* trust."

"My silence is protecting you."

My heart is as heavy as lead as I turn and stride for the front door. Mother doesn't call after me. Fine. I'll find my own answers.

My father follows. *What are you doing?*

I take my belongings from the housekeeper. "Sorting the mess you made," I reply.

How? Father asks.

Stepping outside, I shrug my coat on. "By talking to the person responsible for ruining all our lives."

I slide into the back seat of my car and shut the door at my father's look of horror.

"How'd it go?" Isolde asks, meeting my gaze in the rearview mirror.

294

"Terrible."

"What did your mom say about your brother?"

"I need time to process. Please take me home." The words come out calm, controlled, even as my mind races ahead to Don's letters and the conversation I need to have with Ravi.

I don't have to see Don in person if there's a way to astral project into the prison. Isolde drives along the familiar road to the palace. I stare out the window, watching the world pass by in a blur of colors. How did my life get so wrecked?

CHAPTER THIRTY-SEVEN
DESIREE

HOURS AFTER VYVYAN'S DISMISSAL, I shift my duffel bag higher on my shoulder and text Jaxson with one hand, asking him to meet me at Wilder's loft. If his offer to help me raise the Balam is still good, I will take it. This might be my only shot to prove myself to Vyvyan.

The door to my old apartment groans. As I step inside, the aroma of garlic and ginger wafts over me, transporting me back to the nights Wilder would cook for us when my parents didn't come home. I drop my bag by the door, taking in Wilder's changes to the space.

The floral couch I once snagged at a yard sale is gone, replaced by a sleek gray sectional that looks like it belongs in a magazine. An industrial coffee table sits atop a patterned rug, and I notice that the mismatched outdoor table and chairs are absent. I cross my arms. Wilder has developed a knack for interior design, or he's had help. Judging by the decorative pillows and scented candles strategically placed throughout the room, I'd bet on the latter.

While I appreciate the aesthetic appeal of the renovations, my heart splinters. Nothing reminds me of the life I once had in this apartment.

I bought this place on my own after finishing my residency at the hospital. It was meant to be my first step into the world as a true adult—a symbol of my independence and hard work. But life had other plans, and I gave it up. After Vane turned me into a vampire, I bequeathed the apartment to my brother, hoping it would serve as a haven for him if he ever needed it. The neighborhood isn't the best, but the building had recently undergone renovations, and the purchase didn't put too much of a dent in my savings, which Wilder inherited as well.

The clanging of pans snaps me out of my reverie. I'm not alone. My vampire senses pick up on a heartbeat in the kitchen. I step inside, each footfall measured and deliberate. A witch with striking purple hair stands at the stove, tossing noodles in a sizzling pan. He's wearing headphones, and the faint strains of melancholic music seep from the buds.

Pallas Lyra is here, in the apartment. The former Nyx member, who helped diffuse the capitol bombing and earned Wilder's respect—and his friendship. The personal touches around the place suggest he's living here with my brother. Bursting in unannounced like this . . . I should have called first. The clatter of a pan on the stove draws a smile. While I crave the constant chaos of the Nest, what if Pallas wants his space?

My phone buzzes in my hand.

JAX

I'm in the neighborhood. Be there in ten.

I cram the phone back into my jeans.

"I hope you made enough for two," I shout.

Pallas stiffens, then turns to face me. His eyes widen as he takes in my oversized hoodie, baggy jeans, and well-worn boots. Then, a small smile spreads across his freckled face. He points his spoon at me. "You must be Desiree."

I raise an eyebrow. "What gave me away?"

"Family resemblance." He grins.

As I smile in return, my fangs are on display, but Pallas's heartbeat remains steady. He returns to his stir fry, and I decide I like him.

"Twins often look alike," I say as he switches off the burner. He opens a nearby cupboard and retrieves plates from the shelf where I had once planned to store the cups. It takes a moment for me to adjust, reminding myself that I am merely a visitor now; this is no longer my home.

Setting his earbuds on the counter, Pallas says, "It's more than that. You two carry yourselves the same. As if you're entirely comfortable in your skin, a confidence that can't be faked."

I snort. Wilder might be confident, but me? I've always been a fish out of water. As a witch, no matter how hard I tried to be people's friend, they still disliked me. At least as a vampire, I've tasted acceptance—a taste I'll savor forever, a taste I'll do anything to get back.

I glance at the clock above the stove. It's only been five minutes. Jax isn't late.

"You don't have to make me a plate," I tell him.

Pallas gestures to the mountain of noodles. "I made enough."

"I'm on a strictly liquid diet these days."

A flush colors his cheeks as he laughs, and I can't help but join him. I haven't experienced such kinship with a stranger in what feels like forever, not since Misty. The thought cuts me short.

"Well, you can at least sit with me while I eat," he offers, sitting at the small bistro table in the corner. "Unless you're here to eat me, in which case, I'd prefer a quick death."

"Careful, that almost sounds like an invitation."

Pallas shrugs. "After today, I'd almost welcome it," he says amicably, but his words have a tinge of sadness.

I settle into the seat across from him. "Care to share? I'm always eager to hear a good story, especially one that ends with a death wish."

Pallas chews a mouthful of food. "I don't see the harm in telling you, given you're Wilder's sister."

"What happened?"

"I got into trouble and am being sent to Aurora because of it—a banishment disguised as a favor."

I nod, a strange sense of camaraderie washing over me. I understand what it's like to have nowhere to go and live off the generosity of others. It's often charity that comes with a price.

"If it makes you feel any better, I also got banished," I offer.

Surprise ignites in Pallas's eyes, and he sets aside his fork. "Sounds like there's a story there."

I size Pallas up, considering how much to reveal. Given that I'll return to the Nest soon, I see no harm in commiserating with him. After all, there's a chance we may never see each other again.

"Someone summoned a daemon to murder Vyvyan," I say, deadpan, gauging his reaction. Pallas blinks once. "Vyvyan hates me, and to get back into her good graces, I told her I'd find her attacker, except they got to her a second time before I got to them. I had no choice but to leave the Nest willingly or get thrown out on my ass."

"Not much of a choice, huh?" Pallas says.

I smile. "Not at all. But Jaxson's helping me find the attacker, return to the Nest, and reclaim my place." Pallas laughs, and I fold my arms. "What?"

"That's what Jaxson said, huh?"

Before I can answer, there's a knock on the front door. It creaks open. "Anyone home?" Jaxson calls out.

My eyes close, unable to hide my relief. No matter how tough things get, I can always rely on Jaxson to come through in a pinch.

"In here!" I answer.

A second later, Jaxson appears in the kitchen, which is far too small for three people. But Pallas is almost done eating. Jaxson nods to him in greeting, unsurprised to find him here, telling me they have stayed in touch since I saw them together at Little Death. Before I can dwell too much on what that could mean, Jaxson kisses me on the head, and warmth spreads through my body, chasing away the cold that has lingered since leaving the Nest. He then inspects the leftover noodles and fixes himself a plate.

"I hear you're helping Desiree return to the Nest," Pallas asks. There's a slight undertone to his words that I can't quite place. Teasing?

Plate in hand, Jax spins to face us. "You sound surprised."

"Only because I know there are other things you are supposed to be doing while Wilder is away. Have you even tried to find Marl—"

"Wait," I say to Pallas. "You never said what you did to warrant a one way ticket to Aurora."

Jax goes quiet as Pallas's face falls. "I wiretapped and broke into the president's house."

While I gasp, Jaxson mumbles, "Dumbass."

Pallas and I glare at him. He's never had to resort to desperate measures to get what he wants. Things come easily to Jaxson. If he'd try a little harder, he'd have the world at his fingertips.

"She found out?" I ask Pallas.

"Yes, Janus confronted Leigh about it. I guess I violated a few laws. Leigh is sending me to Aurora to keep me out of Kratos." He takes another bite. The sound of his grinding teeth fills the room.

I may live underground, but even I know that Pallas's family and friends are in Kratos, and his testimony helped put them there. Our country owes him a lot, yet we repay him by sending him packing. This is why I don't miss being a human. They don't value loyalty.

Pallas sighs and turns to Jaxson. "Did Soter catch the person who attacked Leigh?"

Wait. Leigh got attacked?

"No, but we have the city surrounded. No one is getting in or out of Borealis without Soter's knowing," Jax replies.

I stare between them. "Am I missing something?"

"Leigh almost got kidnapped earlier today," Jax replies.

Well, shit. "Are there any leads?"

"A few. But none that are tangible."

"What does Wilder think?"

"No one's heard from him, not since . . ." Jaxson trails off, sharing another guarded look with Pallas.

I groan. They are keeping things from me, and I hate it. "Since when? Where is my brother?"

"Did you like your flower?" Pallas asks, changing the subject.

"*What?*"

"He means the flower I gave you on our date," Jax supplies.

I frown at him. It wasn't a date.

"The dahlia?" I ask. "Jax never said it was from you."

"You're a jerk," Pallas says to Jax, but he's smiling as he says it.

Jaxson smirks. "You like that about me."

I glance between my ex and Pallas, suddenly reminded of their history.

Jax and Pallas shared much more than a kiss during their visit to Little Death. I got an eyeful of them with their tongues down each other's throats before I hurried off to deliver drinks, trying to process what I had just witnessed. Leigh had grabbed me while in search of Vane, but she'd been with Wilder, and I was so paranoid he'd recognize me that I finished my shift early and returned to the Nest. However, upon my return, I was immediately summoned to the throne room for Zev's trial.

I glance at Pallas, noticing his purple hair, and my heart constricts. It's the same shade of the girl the two of them were also with that night. Selene? It must be for her.

"So, Desiree, with a kidnapper on the loose, if I don't return to the streets soon, Soter may fire me, and I don't need another reason to hate him," Jaxson says. "What did you want to ask me?"

I sit straighter. "I want to raise Balam."

Jax blinks, then he nods slowly. "Okay. I'll just need to make some calls for supplies."

"How long will that take?" I ask. We have to do this as fast as possible before the attacker strikes again.

"Desiree," Pallas snaps. "Your plan is to raise a *daemon*? Fuck that. Fuck Vyvyan. Just come with me to Aurora."

I blink as Jaxson's jaw hardens. "What would I do in Aurora?"

The sun shines there three hundred and sixty-three days a year. I've heard the vampire community is tiny and wary of outsiders. They also answer to Vyvyan.

Pallas shrugs. "We don't know each other, but take this chance to start over."

My gaze falls to the kitchen floor. Pallas makes it sound so easy—a fresh start, a new beginning. But is that what I want?

I glance at Jaxson, whose eyes are intent, waiting to see how I'll answer, and my heart restricts. I don't want to be alone.

"I'm staying."

Jaxson barely manages to hide his smile behind another bite of food.

Pallas shrugs and gathers his belongings. He touches my shoulder and says, "Be good to Jax," before leaving me in the kitchen with my ex.

"I have to run, too," Jaxson announces as he scrapes leftover food into the trash. "I'll text you when we can pick up the supplies. Shouldn't take more than a day."

I nod but say nothing. Am I making the right decision?

"Don't worry, it won't be like when Leigh raised the Harborym," Jax says, mistaking my silence for fear. "The Balam obeys its summoner. You'll be completely safe with me." He pinches my chin, forcing me to meet his gaze. "I'm glad you stayed, sunshine."

"Same."

But then his attention falls on my painted lips.

Jax wants to kiss me. Is that what *I* want, though? Fresh from the Nest, I'm hardly at my strongest. Yet, my fingers ache to grab his uniform, pull him close, and meld our breaths into one.

The other night, he told me how he felt about me. I should stop pining for what was and start living for what could be.

I don't want to have regrets.

He clears his throat. "Maybe watch some TV and consider how you want to tell me about what—"

I grip his jacket, rise on my toes, and press my lips to his. It's like coming home.

Jaxson wraps his arms around me, tugging me until I am pressed against him. I open my mouth to deepen the kiss, but Jaxson pulls away with a smile. "As much as I hate to say it, I really have to go."

I blink. "Oh, okay."

"But we should talk."

Unable to talk, I nod. What the hell did I just do?

After I release him, Jax leaves, and I am truly alone for the first time in ages.

I toss my phone atop the coffee table, flipping on the TV. The sounds of fucking saturate the space. A porno blazes in the dim living room light. I shriek, hastily trying to turn it off, but I somehow turn it up. The last thing I need is for that nosy pink-haired neighbor to knock on my door again.

The last time I was here was with Vane, weeks before I became a vampire. We'd been spending all our time together, and I was so excited to show off my big-girl purchase to my vampire boyfriend. At least, I wanted Vane to be my boyfriend, but he never asked, nor had we had sex yet. I'd wanted to change that to finally close the chapter of my life titled *Jaxson*.

I didn't have keys to the loft at the time, so we broke in by jimmying a window over the fire escape. I showed him all 1,200 square feet, deciding to turn it into a game by removing an article of clothing each step of the way until I was completely naked in the living room. I didn't have to beg. We ended up screwing on the hardwood floor. After months of pent-up desire, we hadn't held back, and the neighbors called the authorities.

With a shake of my head to dislodge the memory, I turn off whatever program Pallas had been enjoying, but it does nothing for the throbbing need surging through me. Personal space was a luxury in the Nest, but here, in this suffocating solitude, the walls pressed in close. It was almost intimate.

I fall back onto the couch. Lifting the edge of my hoodie, I pop the button of my jeans and slip my hand beneath the elastic of my panties, my fingers finding the warm, eager wetness below. A shock of pleasure jolts through me at the first touch.

My back arches, a surprised gasp escaping me, loud in the stillness. I start slow, circling my aching clit, then pick up the pace. Jaxson's image— his tender expressions and solid, inviting frame—fills my mind, heightening the intensity of each caress. The mounting pressure pushes me toward the edge until the dam bursts.

I cry out, lost in ecstasy, as my body shudders. But as I float back down, it's not Jaxson's name that slips from my lips in a breathless whisper. It's Vane's.

A pang of something complicated stirs within me. I tell myself it doesn't mean anything. It's just lingering memories from being in this place. But the truth is written in my racing pulse's insistent thrums.

No matter how much I hate him, I'm not over him.

Rolling over, I groan. Vane ruins everything. "Leave me alone!" I scream my shame in the pillows, wishing I could bury my feelings just as quickly, smothering them until they die.

CHAPTER THIRTY-EIGHT
LEIGH

BACK AT THE PALACE, I rip open Don's latest letter from prison as I wait for Ravi to return from whatever errand he's running this late. My fingers tremble as I quickly scan the documents for any mention of Fynn or Stellan. I find a whiny message that reeks of desperation. Don apologizes for trying to steal my throne and for the deaths of his brother and Fynn— his nephew, contrary to Stellan's claim that Fynn was his son. His words are meaningless until I confront him face-to-face. I crumple the letter and toss it into the overflowing wastebasket with the others.

"Your Highness, Mr. Deyanira is back. He's in the gym," my equerry announces from the doorway.

"Thank you."

Kicking off my high heels, I storm out of my room. I leave behind my phone, which is inundated with hundreds of missed calls and texts from the Council, Gianna, Wilder, and the press. I can't focus on them right now —not until Ravi shows me how to astral project into the prison.

If I were to request an official visit, there's a risk that the press could catch wind of it, and I don't want anyone to know I saw Don until I can wrangle the truth from his lips. I need to know who he has working for him and why he leaked the story about Fynn to Stellan. Is he trying to buy his way out of prison?

When I enter the gym, the scent of sweat and the faint hum of energy greets me. I spot Ravi, clad in loose-fitting sweats and a matching gray shirt. His eyes are closed, and his chest rises and falls with each breath. I sit across from him.

Tread lightly, cautions my father's ghost. But I push him away. I am not ready to face him after what happened at my mother's. He's had twenty years to come clean about Fynn.

"I need your help." My voice cuts through the silence. Ravi remains unperturbed, as if I were a mere whisper in the wind.

I study him, my mind racing with questions. Did he know about Alden's proposal? If he did, why didn't he tell me? Unless . . . that's what he was trying to tell me that day in the throne room when he advised me not to accept Alden's request to visit. Perhaps he knew what Alden's intentions were, and for some reason, he didn't want me to agree to them.

But Ravi and Alden are close friends, so wouldn't he want me to marry his friend? It would make many people happy, not to mention secure peace between our nations. So, what would Ravi gain from my saying no to the proposal? There must be something more to this, a missing piece of the pie.

"I know you can hear me," I persist. I tap my fingers against the cushioned mat. "And I'm not leaving until you show me how to astral project."

Still, Ravi does not respond. A flush creeps up my neck, amplified by the restless murmurs of my ancestral ghosts stirred by Ravi's presence. They are as confused by him as I am.

"Ravi!" My voice reverberates off the gym walls.

His shoulders collapse. "Leigh, whatever it is, I am sure you can figure it out yourself, or there's someone else you trust more than me to help you," Ravi says, his eyes opening. The concern in them makes my breath stall.

If he had known about Alden's proposal, he wouldn't be worried about me. Unless . . . he's concerned about Stellan's article, which is none of his business.

"I want to astral project," I say. He scoffs. "I came damn close to doing it again the other day, so I promise I won't take too much of your time."

He pinches the bridge of his nose. "The last time I tried to help you, it didn't end well."

I square my shoulders. If he remains within the palace, he's obligated to assist me. He also promised. But I am desperate enough to beg. "Please."

Ravi sighs. "Have you been practicing your meditation like I asked?"

"Yes," I lie.

A slight frown tugs at his lips. "Your aura betrays you."

I narrow my eyes. "How?"

"It's all red."

"I thought red denotes leadership, passion, and groundedness," I mimic his deep voice.

"It can, but on the opposite spectrum, it means anger, fear, over-sensitivity."

"Can you not?" I say, not meeting his gaze. He sees right through me, which wouldn't scare me if I knew who he was here for. "I'm not angry. But I will be if you don't stop judging me and help me get what I want."

"Okay," Ravi concedes with a nod. "So, you want to astral project."

"Yes."

"Where?" Ravi states as he sips his water. The sound of his swallowing is loud in the quiet room. He wipes his mouth with the back of his hand.

I don't meet his eyes as I reply, "No where in particular."

"You're lying. Your aura is a muddy-yellow." Ravi's voice comes out gentle, almost conciliatory.

My jaw drops. I can't tell him about Don. He could tell Alden, who might withdraw his proposal after hearing about Fynn, especially if he suspects I'm a bastard-born child. But Ravi is still here, which means Alden is as well. This suggests that the proposal is still on the table.

My muscles tense at this notion. I am neither relieved nor upset, but I am glad that I haven't missed the chance to secure peace for our borders. Keeping the possibility of the alliance alive is crucial.

"Fine," I say, contemplating a lie to get him to teach me what I need to know. "I want to visit Wilder. I haven't heard from him since the rally, and I need to be face-to-face when he tells me what happened."

Ravi's eyes narrow, but then he sits tall. "Fine. The fourth layer of the aura is the astral body. It's the layer that you project out into the world. Tell me what you felt when you harnessed this magic the first time."

I swallow. I hate talking about Thayer or anything having to do with That Night. I now know I am not to blame for my father and brother's deaths, but after blaming myself for so long, those feelings still surface. The shame makes me want to endure dozens of purification rituals, but I force myself to stay seated. My magic isn't dangerous. I can be a better leader if I know how to use it.

"When I did it the first time, I was only able to project a few feet before . . ." I take a deep breath, "before the witch who killed my father and brother attacked us."

Ravi nods. "That's understandable, but you must forgive yourself for what happened. It is the only way to move forward and use your magic easily. When we link an experience with shame, it is hard to access those reserves." I frown. Maybe I've already failed before I've begun. "But don't worry, with a little self-love, you can send your spirit anywhere. All you have to do is connect emotionally to the person or place you want to see."

When I think of Wilder, missing him is a physical pain in my heart. Not seeing him after being able to *feel* him in his dream has been maddening, but I didn't want to risk something happening to him if I visited him again. I wasn't entirely lying when I said I wanted to know what happened at the square in Aurora with Stellan today. Several councilors have sent me messages questioning Wilder's loyalties. I've deleted them all.

He's with me. There is an explanation.

"The astral layer connects the three lower and three higher auric layers, acting as a bridge between solid and spiritual energy," Ravi continues, his voice low and authoritative. "When we astral project, we send a carbon copy of ourselves through the spiritual plane. The energies from the spiritual and physical plane make contact, causing you to appear visible to the naked eye. You will feel connected to your physical self, but you cannot make physical contact with others. It'll be like you are a ghost."

"How long does it last?" I question.

Ravi shrugs. "Depends on the wielder."

So, a powerful witch can hold on to the projection, while a less powerful might not have as much control. I will lie in the middle; my magic is still untested and raw.

"How do we start?" I ask, my eagerness bleeding into my voice.

Ravi lifts a brow. "Do you fully accept your powers? You aren't afraid of the consequences after what happened before? It's important that we clear any negativity before we start."

I inhale a cleansing breath. Using this ability feels like opening old wounds, but I meant what I said. I am no longer ashamed of who I am or what I can do.

"My magic is a gift." He continues to study me. "I mean it. I've made great strides to forgive myself for what happened after my Emergence. I can do this. *Please* help me do this."

With a curt nod, Ravi straightens. "Sit tall," he instructs, and I do. The mat cushions my hips, and the crown of my head reaches toward the ceiling. "You begin by expanding and contracting your aura. You must learn to access your magic even while others are in your space. Their energy frequencies will engage with yours, but the goal is not to let it affect you. First, close your eyes." My eyes shut.

"Breathe in slowly." I inhale, and the air cools in my lungs.

"Imagine your breath starting in your root, then flowing through your body, out of the top of your head. Think of it like a blow hole as if you were a whale or another aquatic mammal." I laugh, but when Ravi doesn't join me, I know he is scowling without opening my eyes. "Once breathing and visualization are down, you will expand your aura. To practice, astral project by thinking of me."

I play around with the exercises for several more minutes, with Ravi's voice guiding and instructing me until his words grow distant. My focus turns all the way inward, and my magic stirs within me as I conjure an image of Ravi's face.

Suddenly, I am weightless, my essence no longer tethered to the earth.

I still feel like me, my breaths continuing to come and go.

"You did it," Ravi says. A whisper in the stillness.

Ravi still sits on the floor as I stand in my astral body several feet away. Pride shines in his eyes. He cradles my human body in his arms, his touch gentle yet secure. His hold is a promise of protection that both comforts and unsettles me. He won't let anyone harm me while I am so vulnerable.

I hang out in my astral form for a few more minutes, stretching my magic to see how far it will go, flexing it like a muscle until I am sure that, if I tried, I could be with Don at the prison. Closing my eyes, I return my consciousness to my body. Then, I open them again. I'm in the gym, resting in Ravi's arms.

"That was amazing," Ravi says as I pull out of his embrace. His warmth lingers on my skin. I try to smile, but his grin falters when it doesn't reach my eyes.

"Thank you," I say without meeting his stare, afraid of what I might find there. This connection growing between us is dangerous. The gods know I could use a friend, but too much has happened, and he is still loyal to Alden.

"You are a gifted Lunar Witch," Ravi says. "But even so, you know you can't astral project into Kratos, right?" I freeze, and he shrugs. "After the article, it's not a big jump to believe that's where you want to go."

I hug my body as if my arms are a shield. It's no secret that Don betrayed me, but I still don't want to talk about him with Ravi. The sooner I get out of here, the better. "I don't expect you or anyone to understand."

"I know all about being deceived, Leigh. We aren't so different, you and me. You'd see that if you only gave me a chance."

I want to believe him, but I can't.

Ravi sighs. "Wards make it impossible to astral project into the prison. I'm sorry."

"Excuse me." I rise with my heart in my throat. I head out the door with Isolde hot on my heels. I need to get to my room to make the painful request to Warden Grey. My heart sinks.

One way or another, I'm talking to my uncle.

CHAPTER THIRTY-NINE
WILDER

I HOLD the Aurora garrison door open for two Blades before I shove my way inside. The smell of lemon-scented cleaner and old stone grounds me after the shitstorm I uncovered at Furies. Ry had texted, telling me it was safe to return home. The Council was initially angry about the shooting, but after reviewing the circumstances—that I was undercover, on duty, and saved a life—they acknowledged the man I shot would make a full recovery before serving his prison sentence. Technically, I did everything by the book. Still, the reality weighs on me—I shot a civilian. Even though they'll recover, I discharged my weapon against someone who wasn't military. I know how it must've looked, but the Council isn't what has my blood heating in my veins; it is the article Stellan wrote about Leigh.

How fucking dare he write that bleeding shit about her after he agreed to meet her?

Now, how am I supposed to get Leigh to agree to come here? Leigh will laugh in my face.

I've tried calling her several times, but I keep getting her voicemail. Gods, she must be reeling. My chest aches with how much I wish I could be with her right now.

With my phone pressed to my ear, I try her again, needing to hear her voice.

I head toward my room, but before I ascend the stairs, Eddo calls out, "Wilder, wait a minute." I freeze, unsure if he is coming over to yell at me after shooting that Epsilon, or if it's something else. He's probably pissed he didn't do it.

"Not now," I begin.

Eddo lifts a brow. "Now, hold on a minute. I wanted to congratulate you on how you handled the situation in the square today. You saved Stellan's life." He playfully jabs me in the arm. "I knew the real you was still in there. You just needed to be reminded of who you are, and if anyone could do that, it was Stellan. Where is he?"

"I don't know," I grumble as I'm forwarded to Leigh's voicemail. If I did know where Stellan was, I would wring his neck for publishing that article after our talk. Not enough to cause any real damage, but enough to leave a mark. It's the least he deserves when he looked me in the eye knowing he had that article about Fynn queued up while we were talking. He knew it would hurt her. He just couldn't help himself.

"Well, I am sure he is fine," Eddo remarks, and I frown.

Yeah, thanks to me. It's not as if I want Stellan to suffer, or that I've changed my mind about him being the answer to securing peace between the Nebula and Epsilon, but I can still be pissed that he hid this article from me. He dangled it like a carrot before he left Furies, too, taunting me about whether I knew Leigh or not. I should have known he had one more trick up his sleeve.

"You made us proud today," Eddo adds.

I blink. It's the first time Eddo has treated me with respect for the time that I've been here, and it's because he thinks I've chosen sides—his side. My desire to make my old mentor proud roots me where I stand, but my determination to fix this country has me giving him my back as I aim for my bedroom.

"Where are you going?" Eddo calls.

"To call my girlfriend," I reply.

Eddo scoffs. "Brigid is looking for you!"

I ignore him. Oh, so now he wants me around his daughter. Fuck him, and fuck that.

I kick my door closed and lock it, not wanting Brigid to come rub my nose in Stellan's article and say she told me so, that Leigh has more secrets than a diary.

Such a scandal will be hard to recover from. Leigh will have a challenging time convincing the public of Stellan's lying—*if* he's lying. The implications for her reign, our relationship, and the kingdom are staggering. I can almost feel the crown's weight pressing down on me, though I'm not the one who wears it.

My phone vibrates in my hand, and I groan.

> **BRIGID**
> Are you okay?

> **WILDER**
> I am fine.

> **BRIGID**
> I've been looking for you since the riot, and then when I read that article . . .

I frown at the screen. She is always weaseling her way into places she doesn't belong.

> **WILDER**
> It's a lie.

> **BRIGID**
> I'm sorry, babe, but do we know that for certain?

I exhale. This conversation is over.

> **WILDER**
> I appreciate your concern for my well-being, but I'm in the middle of something.

I am about to call Leigh again when another text from Brigid lights up my phone.

> **BRIGID**
> Just . . . be careful, Wilder. This situation is more complicated than any of us realized.

I know. But at the same time, I know nothing.

Exhaustion weighs me down, and I sink onto the edge of my bed. I rub my eyes to clear the fog. I'm beyond tired—physically and emotionally drained.

With a curse, I toss my phone aside and lie back on my bed, staring up at the ceiling fan. I may not be cut out for this boyfriend stuff. Juliette bullied my sister, Isolde cheated on me, and Brigid, who wasn't a girlfriend but was the closest thing I've had to a healthy relationship, which is saying something, throws my words back in my face. I did tell her Epsilon and Nebula shouldn't date, and now those words taste like ashes in my mouth. But that's the coward's way out—a way to avoid the difficult conversations and the painful truths.

I focus on the ceiling fan's oscillation, watching as it goes round and round in a never-ending cycle that mirrors my relationship with Leigh. No matter how hard we try, we never seem to outrun our issues.

I reach for my phone and stare at the blank screen. The cursor blinks expectantly, waiting for me to pour my heart out in a text. My fingers move slowly across the keyboard as I try to articulate the depth of my feelings.

WILDER

> Leigh, I know things are hard right now, and I can't imagine what you're going through. But I want you to know I'm always here for you. No matter what happens or what anyone says. Talk to me . . .

I pause, my thumb hovering over the send button. Is it enough? Will my words bring her comfort or add more fuel to the fire? I hesitate, doubt creeping in like a fucking jewelry thief.

Without hitting send, I close my eyes, setting my phone aside. I could wait and give her space to process the news about Fynn. But I want to give Stellan an answer soon. Now that he's publicly announced his intentions to turn Aurora into its own country, we need to act fast to keep things civil. I need to convince Leigh to trust him, even though she trusts no one, not even me.

"Hey," a soft voice says beside me.

Nearly jumping out of my skin, I find Leigh perched on the corner of my bed, staring at me.

"What a day, huh?" she asks.

"What the fuck. You're *here?*" My heart nearly bursts as I lunge to hug her, only to fall right through her and smack my face on the fucking floor.

Leigh stands with one hand covering her mouth as she barely stifles a laugh.

"What the hell?" I ask, and she smiles. It's the best thing I've seen all day. Warm and radiant like her.

"I'm here, but not really here," she says.

"Am I dreaming?" I ask as I rub my bruised forehead like it could ease my bruised ego.

Leigh's been through hell, and the first thing I do is tackle her. I'm such an idiot.

"No. I am astral projecting."

Well, fuck me. I know she's done it before, but I didn't know she could do it again.

"How?"

Leigh shakes her head. "No time for questions. I am unsure how long this is going to last."

"You are here because you saw the news. The Council has cleared me, but in case you had any lingering doubts, I promise, Leigh, I didn't save Stellan because I've turned my back on you. I—"

"Wilder, I believe you, but Stellan needs to be stopped."

I blink. "Those are menacing words for a queen whose entire regime is based on peace."

Leigh grunts. "He started it."

"The article. Do you want to talk about it?"

"No, I don't want to talk about Stellan at all. I don't want to talk." Leigh paces before me, her body reminding me of a hologram. Real-looking, but not.

I push myself off the floor. "Well, considering I can't touch you, we have nothing to do but talk."

She groans. "Did you talk to Stellan? Did he tell you where he got his information today?"

"No."

"Did he tell you anything?"

I sigh. "Come to Aurora and ask him yourself."

Leigh stares at me. "What?"

"Stellan's agreed to meet with you. I am sure you heard the news about wanting to annex Aurora into an enclave?" I say, earning a nod from Leigh. "Well, I convinced him to speak to you. A conclave, if you will. A chance for the two of you to air your grievances and get on the same page. You want the same thing: justice for the Nebula, a new world founded on peace and understanding. I think you two could work together to unite the factions."

Leigh taps her lips with her forefinger. "Hmm. I am willing to meet with him if he takes the article down about Fynn."

I open my mouth to tell her I will do my best to get him to remove it, but Leigh adds, "And only if I can astral project. I have too much going on in Borealis to leave."

I shake my head. "Stellan won't go for that. He'll see it as an insult." He fancies himself a leader, and his pride would take a hit. If he and Leigh are going to work together, they need to speak face-to-face. Shake on it.

"There's no way I can leave." Leigh sighs. She sits on the bed. It doesn't dip beneath her.

"What's twenty-four hours in the grand scheme of things?" I sit beside her.

"I'm needed in Borealis."

"Why? Hot date?" I tease, but Leigh flinches. My jaw clenches as she hides her face behind her hair. "Leigh?"

"I am fixing things, Wilder, I swear."

Despite the warmth in the room, goose bumps prickle my skin. What isn't she telling me?

I open my mouth to ask, but Leigh sighs, and the excessive amount of pain I see reflected in her gaze keeps me silent. "I wish you could hold me."

If I could hold her, I'd never let her go.

"You know you can tell me anything, right?" I offer.

"Hmm," Leigh deflects. Her tone is mischievous. "Just because you can't touch me doesn't mean we can't make the most of our time together."

"I thought you had too much going on in Borealis to be here?"

Leigh leans closer to me. Her bare shoulder should be touching mine if she wasn't thousands of miles away. I take in the sight of her dress. Her breasts spill from the heart-shaped neckline, enticing me to take a bite. I want to. Fuck, I want to do *more* than that.

Leigh is everything I want wrapped in a tight, blonde package.

"What are you thinking?" Leigh asks, her voice a throaty whisper.

"How that dress would look a thousand times better torn to ribbons," I sigh.

"Oh, yeah?"

"Yes."

"I like this dress, so I won't tear it apart, but . . ." She bites her lip. "Close your eyes." I frown, and she laughs. "That's an order, commander."

I do as she says, but nothing happens. The longer nothing happens, the more I fidget. "Leigh? I feel stupid. What—"

"Open them," she says after a long silence. I obey, and my heart falters. The dress is gone, and she's lying back on the bed, clad only in her underwear. Her hands move rhythmically over the comforter. "What do you want to do to me?"

"What are you doing?" I ask, but she shushes me to play along.

"Everyone is downstairs," she continues. "If we are quiet, we can have some fun."

I sigh as she sits up and crawls toward me with a taunting smile. "Come on, Wilder. Don't you want to play with me?"

My laughter is a throaty grumble in my chest. "Yes."

Her smile blinds me. "Good."

"How do you want to do this?" I ask. I am completely at her mercy.

"Well, for starters, you are wearing entirely too many clothes."

Eyes locked on hers, I pull my shirt over my head. Her gaze is ravenous, like a caress across my chest and abs. My dick hardens, straining against my zipper. This is happening.

"Now what?" I ask.

She shifts, now on her side, head propped on her hand. "Touch yourself," she commands. "Let me see what you do when I'm not around."

She rolls onto her stomach, offering me a view of her ripe ass, practically begging to be touched. "C'mon," she whispers, "I'll show you what I do when I'm alone, missing you."

I unbutton my pants. Leigh groans, her hips undulating as if we're already joined. I'm captivated, unable to tear my gaze away. Soon, I forget what I'm supposed to be doing, lost in the sight of her parted lips, the little whimpers spilling from them.

"Does that feel good, baby?" I ask.

Her eyes close with a nod. "Y-yeah."

"How wet are you?"

"Very."

"Show me."

Leigh stops dry humping the mattress, rolls over, and shimmies her cheeky blue panties down her thighs. She flings them across the room, gone as if they'd been erased from existence. Lying back, she parts her thighs, displaying just how wet and willing she is.

"Fuck. You're a dream. Keep touching yourself," I demand, my hands clenching into the sheets. It's a painful torture knowing I can't touch her.

Leigh gasps, slipping her hand between her legs. Her fingers trace up her slit before circling her swollen clit. She sighs as if I'm the one touching her, and I harden more. It's fucking excruciating.

"With my eyes closed," Leigh breathes, her voice laced with a desperate edge, "it's your fingers I feel, sliding inside me . . ."

My pants hit the floor, and Leigh's moan is pure, unfiltered hunger. Her eyes lock on the glistening bead of precum clinging to my tip. "Oh, fuck," she gasps, her fingers moving even faster.

"Shh, the walls are thin here," I chastise, though I fucking love it.

I don't want any of the other Blades hearing her like this. The sounds she makes are for my ears.

"S-sorry, I'm not used to being quiet unless you cover my mouth with your hand."

I shake my head. The need to possess her, to consume her with every sense, is a tangible force. "You like it when I do that, Leigh?"

"Mm-hmm."

She moves faster, spreading the wetness around as I grip myself and begin to jerk off. Her thighs are a mess, glistening with her own arousal as her slippery fingers disappearing completely inside her. Her breaths come faster, ragged and desperate, her chest heaving with each gasp.

I grit my teeth, the sight of her driving me wild. "Tell me, Leigh," I growl, "Tell me how much you like it."

She's getting close, but I refuse to let her come alone.

"I love it," she admits, the word a shaky exhale. "Gods, yes. It's . . . it's too much, even like this. I feel you *watching* me."

My hips thrust up as she cries out, my muscles tensing with each movement, the bed creaking beneath me. "Wilder, I'm so close."

"Fuck," I growl. Leigh pants, and the sound sends shivers down my spine, and my dick twitches in my hand. I adjust my grip, focusing every last bit of my will into mirroring her rhythm.

Leigh watches me with nearly black eyes before she rolls over, face down on the blankets. Her hand is buried between her legs, one knee propped higher to spread herself wide. Her ass rises and falls as she writhes against the sheets, her back arching and neck straining. Her moans send jolts of pleasure through me, from the top of my head to the tips of my toes. My blood rushes in my ears.

"Right there, just like that . . . yes, Wilder. Fuck, so good." Her body bucks against the mattress, the sheets rustling with frantic abandon as she spirals closer to the edge, imaging it's me fucking her rather than her hand. I let her cries wash over me, fueling my own desire, imagining every detail of her body beneath me.

I'm stroking myself raw as her ethereal curves drive me to the brink of insanity. I'd give anything to grab those hips and sink into her tight heat from behind, claiming her hard and deep the way I know she loves. The angle always hits just right. But I can't, and she knows it. Her magic makes me watch, makes me ache to my core. That perfect ass bouncing on nothing when it *should* be slamming back against me. It's torture. I'm stuck with my unsatisfying grip while she smirks over her shoulder. Untouchable perfection.

"I like having your eyes on me," she breathes.

"Better than my hands?"

Leigh's limbs tremble, her thighs quivering. "N-no."

"You know what you're doing to me, don't you? Driving me crazy from a thousand miles away." My pace quickens, desperation coloring my tone. "Gods, Leigh, that's not fair. You're going to make me explode just watching you."

Her eyes glaze over, and I know she's reached her peak. I quicken my movements, my heart pounding in my chest, my skin slick with sweat, my breath coming in short gasps.

My abs clench with each stroke, my balls drawing up tight against my body.

A few more seconds tick by, and her moans switch to cursing, her voice rising in pitch, her body tensing. "*Fuck.*"

Leigh screams into the covers, her body shuddering, her hand still moving as she rides out her orgasm. I savor the image to conjure the next time the urge to draw hits me. Leigh coming is the prettiest thing I've seen, and I want to capture it on paper to immortalize the moment.

"Shit." I shudder at my release leaving me breathless and spent, my cum spilling over my hand and onto my stomach. I stroke myself through it, prolonging the sensation, my eyes squeezed shut, my mouth open in a silent moan.

I open my eyes to see her reaction, but I'm alone. The room is suddenly cold and empty without her larger-than-life presence. I swear I smell the lingering scent of her perfume and arousal in the air, a ghost of her essence. My hair is damp and stuck to the nape of my neck, and my skin is cooling in the aftermath.

Groaning, I rise, eager to take a shower. My girl is a fucking goddess.

CHAPTER FORTY
LEIGH

THE NEXT DAY, I hoist my biggest purse over my shoulder. It's packed with a disguise—a red wig, sunglasses, and a dark overcoat—I will need to slip into Kratos Prison without alerting the press. My heart pounds as I race down the palace steps. Isolde is waiting outside with a car to covertly whisk me to the prison.

Don must be Stellan's source. The letters in my wastebasket claim he wants to be a family again, but I know better. My uncle wants my crown—he always has. What better way to discredit my claim to the throne than to undermine my leadership capabilities and my brother's legitimacy by selling intel to Stellan? Today, I will make him admit it.

As I pass the billiard room, the rich scent of aged whiskey and cigar smoke wafts out. Pool balls collide with a sharp crack. I glimpse Ravi sinking the eight ball into a pocket, but Alden's piercing blue eyes are fixed on me, ignoring his loss. A breath lodges in my throat, and I quicken my pace. Gripping my bag until my knuckles turn white, I've barely taken a few steps before Alden's voice cuts through the air like a knife.

"Where's the fire?" he asks, his tone businesslike and devoid of the flirtatious charm he usually uses with me. The sudden shift in his demeanor prickles my skin.

I pause, my chest tightening as I turn. My gaze meets his. The warmth that used to reside there has been replaced by a chillier, more calculating look. He's read the article about Fynn. I had hoped to avoid talking to Alden until I spoke to Don and the Council. If Alden decides that invading Borealis is more worthwhile than marrying me, I don't know what we will do. Our kingdom is not equipped to go to war, especially when our people are divided.

"Hi, Alden," I manage, steadier than I feel. I tap my heel in anticipation of leaving.

Isolde is waiting, and time is of the essence. Warden Grey gave me a very small window to talk to Don. It's hardly enough time, but letting that man bully me is a necessary evil to fixing the cruelty embedded in this country's bedrock. Each minute is precious.

"Are you avoiding me, Leigh? We haven't talked since you stranded me at the races yesterday." Alden circles me with a predatory smile. I resist the urge to step back.

"I've been busy, and you were hardly stranded," I reply. Some of my guards stayed behind to ensure the prince returned to the palace.

Alden frowns. "I heard you visited Cynthia. How is Mommy Dearest? I am sure she is disgusted by the rumor regarding her courtship with your uncle. It seems I've arrived just in time to save your family from ill repute." He slips his hands into his pockets, then pulls out the moonstone. Ravi told me it belonged to his dead mate, Tanith. He palms it like a worry stone.

I exhale. His offer still stands. That's good. I need more time to figure out how to counter it.

A shiver slides down my spine. How does he know I visited my mother? Only a few select staff were aware. A pit hollows my stomach. How deep does his influence run in my home? Maybe he's outstayed his welcome.

"I still have time left before I owe you an answer," I say, "so if you will excuse me, I have to go."

"Go where?" Alden appraises my outfit, but nothing indicates I am going to Kratos. My disguise is in my bag. Even so, when I meet Ravi's gaze, his eyes have a knowing look. I scowl. Did he tell Alden I wanted to astral project into the prison?

When I don't answer, Alden says, "Tick-tock, Leigh. I'd love to return home with good news. My father may be ill, but he loves weddings."

"Alden, I need to go," I repeat, turning to leave.

"I'll miss you while you are away," Alden calls, and I wince.

"I am sure you will find a way to entertain yourself," I call out as I hurry toward the stairs.

"Aw, I've done that already today."

I grimace. "Ew."

As I approach Isolde outside with the car, I steel myself. I will not be a pawn in anyone's game. Not anymore.

I am the queen, and it's time I started playing like one.

CHAPTER FORTY-ONE
LEIGH

A COMMUNAL SUBMARINE transports Isolde and me from Poseidon's Wharf to Kratos Prison. It jolts as it arrives at the underwater unloading dock deep beneath the waves of the Starless Sea. An eerie silence follows the engine's shutdown. A metallic taste coats my tongue as reality settles in. In a few minutes, I'll be face-to-face with my uncle. I'm done with him trying to control me.

Besides Isolde and me, the five other passengers unbuckle their seatbelts in resounding clicks. The captain's voice crackles through the intercom, announcing our arrival in a tone as cold and detached as our metal surroundings. Isolde adjusts her hat, which hides her cobalt hair.

As I study her, she brushes her fingers against the brim of her hat. Though I was annoyed with Wilder for assigning his gorgeous ex to guard me, I admire her take-no-shit attitude. She's fiercely independent. I once thought she was selfish for cheating on Wilder, but spending time with her has shown me otherwise. She's been there for me this past week in ways no one else has, and I am grateful for her help and discretion.

"You ready?" she asks me.

I nod. "Let's get this over with."

We both appear as civilians as we enter the prison. I'm disguised in a red wig, an artfully styled headscarf, sunglasses, and heels. We sign fake aliases on the visitors' log. A guard eyes me, and I quickly look away. My disguise feels like a flimsy shield against the press, but I refuse to risk ending up as front-page news two days in a row.

"Visiting center is this way," another guard calls. The group shuffles toward him. "But before we go, may I remind each of you that the people you are about to see may be your family and friends, but they are also convicted felons. Make smart choices."

After a murmur of agreement, we walk through the alloy lobby toward the visitors' center. Bubbles form outside the thick windows.

When the visitors make a left, following the guards, Isolde and I turn right, aiming toward Warden Grey's office. He's granted me fifteen minutes of unchaperoned time with my uncle.

I plan to get Don to admit that he's been supplying Stellan with information about the Council and me. Then I will go to the capitol with the name of his accomplice so I can end Stellan's crusade and obtain the Council's support in presenting Alden with a peace treaty instead of a marriage. But as we draw nearer to the warden's office, doubt creeps in like an oceanic fog. Can I trust Don to tell the truth? Can I trust the Council to listen?

"This is it," Isolde announces. She flashes her badge to the men stationed outside Warden Grey's door, and they let us inside.

Warden Grey's office is enormous, with floor-to-ceiling windows peering into the inky blackness beyond the sea floor. Occasionally, a fish or two swims by, their bioluminescent bodies creating neon, fleeting patterns in the darkness. The room has polished surfaces and sharp angles, as cold and unforgiving as the warden. I'm curious what Bennett's grandfather must have been like before his son and daughter-in-law died. He'd been kind to me over the years, but after my last visit here to meet Moran Dunn, any warmth between us got snuffed out like sunlight trying to penetrate the miles between the ocean floor and the surface. I can't say I miss it.

"This place gives me the creeps," Isolde says, her face practically pressed against the thick glass. "It's unnatural not to see the sun."

I nod. The lack of natural light must cause a Solar Witch discomfort. She adjusts her borrowed blazer with both hands, which does a poor job hiding her weapons.

"Is there a reason you are studying me like a book?" she asks without turning around.

I laugh. The girl has eyes on the back of her head.

"How many times have you been here?" I ask.

When she faces me, Isolde's lips spread into a thoughtful, straight line. "Maybe twice? Most of the guards are Sea Witches, not Blades. The Blades who work here do so voluntarily. What about you? You handled the submarine ride like a champ."

I settle into Warden Grey's leather seat. It dwarfs me, and the hinges groan as I lean back.

"Once with Wilder," I answer.

Isolde's attention fixes on me. "To see Moran?"

I nod. "How long did you and Wilder date? And no, this isn't his new girlfriend sizing up his old one. I am genuinely curious. I know you could break me like a toothpick."

Isolde is beautiful, and it sounds like Wilder genuinely loved her. Did she not feel the same way? As someone struggling to admit my feelings, I want to understand hers.

Isolde laughs. It's a rare sound. "Nine months. In the last year of Blade training."

I raise a brow. Who was Wilder when he was with her? They seem better matched than we are. "What happened?"

"I am a female Nebula Blade. I had a lot to prove," Isolde replies. "The Nebula Solar Witches in my family aren't fighters. They don't strive for much at all. Still, I wanted to make something of myself after my Emergence, so I enrolled at the Blade Academy and got good scores, but I worried it wasn't enough. I worried that *I* wasn't enough. What would happen to me after graduation if I didn't get any job offers? I loved Wilder, but Soter had connections, and I thought I could use them to my advantage.

"At first, I only intended to befriend him, but Soter can be charming when he wants to be, and Wilder drifted away the closer we got to graduation. He had been worried about having to work for his dad. I knew my behavior was wrong and should have been there for him. I've been trying to atone for it since."

She hangs her head, and I say, "What you did was wrong, but it doesn't define you."

The door opens with a hydraulic hiss, yanking my attention. Don enters the room with two armed guards. A gasp lodges in my throat.

He looks the same, but different. The suave man I loved and looked up to all my life was gone, and in his place is a man as harsh as his true nature. They've shaved his hair close to his scalp, and thick facial hair covers his cheeks and jaw. But his eyes are the same. Sapphire, same as Fynn.

My eyes sting, but I refuse to cry. He doesn't deserve my tears.

Don stumbles to a halt. My heart threatens to break out of my chest.

"Leigh?" he asks, his voice rising.

Heat courses through my veins, causing my hands and arms to flex. This isn't the man who would take me out for ice cream when my parents fussed over Fynn. That man is a myth. This man is a criminal, through and through.

I gesture to one of the empty chairs across from me. "Take a seat, Don."

He doesn't move, still gaping at me. One of the guards forces him into a chair. "I am so glad you finally came," Don says as his guards leave.

Isolde shifts behind me. She's the only guard allowed to witness this exchange. I'm not stupid enough to be alone with the Magician. There are still tricks up his sleeve.

"This isn't a friendly visit," I tell him before his attention traces my face to take in my disguise. I can see the wheels turning in his mind, trying to decipher my intentions.

"Still, you're here. I have so many things I want to say to you, starting with 'I'm sorry.'"

The pretty words hang between us, piercing like a lightning bolt. Too bad my father and brother are still dead.

My hands clench into fists. An apology won't undo his crimes as Eos's Magician, and it doesn't overwrite the lengths to which he went to subjugate the Nebula by keeping the War Letters a secret. It can't make up for the lies he told me to try and get me to give him my throne. The Epsilon started the First War, and he manipulated and killed his own family to keep it a secret.

"Am I supposed to forgive you?" I ask, my tone laced with venom.

He swallows. "Please. I've changed."

My edged laughter causes a wince from him. "I trusted you. No, more than that. I loved you." A sob thickens my throat, but I refuse to release it. I loved him. It's the truth, and he spoiled his love for me entirely. Now, I cannot even say the words to the man who matters most to me. Wilder deserves it, but I am broken. This man *broke* me.

Don hangs his head, but I refuse to feel sorry for him. He's still the architect of our family's destruction, even now. I need to remember that.

"I am sorry, Leigh. Please, believe me," he says. "I swear I never meant for Thayer to harm you. He was meant to take the letters and bring them to me, but that's it. Your father was working with Chiron. I was scared Nyx would turn against him and use the letters to instigate war. My goal was to maintain peace, but everything got out of hand. I see that now. I've had so much time to think, and I miss you, Leigh. I never meant to hurt you. Please, let me make it up to you."

"You want to make it up to me?" I ask. He shifts, the magic-binding manacles around his wrists clinking against the desk. "Thayer almost killed me, too. If Wilder hadn't found me, I would have bled out beside my father and Fynn on that pavement. Yet you want to *make it up to me?*"

"I am so sorry. I had no idea you'd have your Emergence and Thayer would feel threatened."

"So, it is my fault my father and brother are dead?" I sneer.

"No!"

"Their blood is on your hands. Not mine."

I can feel my father and Aradia's ghostly caresses, but they don't speak. This is my fight. Not theirs.

Don sniffles. It is a pathetic sound. "I am repenting for my sins."

"Don't lie to me," I snap. "I know you're still pulling strings from down here. I know you're still trying to take my throne." The first tear falls. It trails down my cheek before landing on my lap. Fuck. I told myself I wouldn't cry.

"I don't know what you're talking about," Don says. "I can't do anything from in here."

I laugh. "Don't pretend you don't know; you're the one who told Stellan about Fynn. Now you've put my mother in a corner, *again*."

Don blinks. "Wait, what?"

"She told me everything after Stellan published his article with the information *you* fed him."

Don blinks again. "Leigh, I am at a loss here. Who is Stellan? The writer?"

I slap my hands on the table, causing Don to jump. "Stop lying! You know who he is, and you've been selling him information about Council members and our family to sow distrust. Thanks to you, people are questioning my rule. They've lost faith in their queen. Which I'm sure is exactly what you want." I'm seething, heaving with breath, but Don's face remains blank. Fury roils inside me like a volcano ready to erupt. "What did you expect to happen? That you'd tell Stellan the truth, make people doubt me, and put yourself on the throne as some savior of the people? News flash, uncle, you are in fucking prison!"

Don still doesn't answer me. I groan, burying my face in my hands.

"Leigh, this is absurd," he finally mutters. "You're right. I *am* in prison. How could I—"

"You threatened me. You said that my ruling would bring instability."

"I did say that, but—"

"You are still trying to weasel your way onto the throne!"

"No."

"Yes!"

"No," Don protests. His eyes blaze with an intensity that catches me off guard. "That's not true, not to mention impossible. I've been imprisoned here for months. I cannot speak to anyone outside the family, nor are you talking to me. I made many mistakes by lying to you, but I promise I've changed. I go to the confessional every day, and I have written amends. Didn't you read my letters?"

I read them, but I didn't believe them. Men like him don't change.

"You are the Magician. You have led Eos for years, which means you are good at cheating the system," I spit. The frustration rolling off Don in droves is almost tangible. "Tell me how you are sending information to Stellan."

"As much as you refuse to believe me, I am not sending this *Stellan* information," Don replies evenly. The sincerity in his voice gives me pause, but I quickly push the doubt aside.

"Who on the Council is working for you?" Don shakes his head, and I take a deep breath to keep going. "Are you also going to deny that you didn't know Fynn was your son?"

Don stills. What little color he has left leaves his cheeks. But I've been fooled by him before, and I won't let it happen again. "Fynn isn't mine."

I roll my eyes. *Liar!*

"My mother told me you got her pregnant. How did you find out Fynn was yours?"

Don opens his mouth several times before whispering, "Fynn isn't mine."

I appraise him. No wonder Don played cards so well. "My mother said you announced your intention to marry Lilura di Siena the same night she learned she was pregnant with Fynn. Coincidence or were you trying to rub your relationship in her face because you knew Fynn was your child?"

Don takes a deep, shaky breath. "I loved your mother, even after she broke things off. The night she and your father announced they were pregnant, I lost my damn mind. I told everyone I was marrying Lilura to hurt her back. Lilura later broke off the engagement because she found out I still cared for Cynthia. For good reason, I suppose. It was wrong of me to use her like that. But I swear Fynn's not—I didn't—" He chokes off, seemingly overwhelmed by emotion. Could it be that Don Raelyn has a heart?

I rub my temples. If he did, he wouldn't keep hurting the people he continues to claim to love most.

But if Lilura broke off her engagement to him because she knew about my mother, would she have suspected the truth about Fynn's parentage? If she did, did she ever tell anyone? Maybe Maria or her favorite niece, Gianna?

"I had no idea Fynn was mine," Don repeats. "If I had, then I wouldn't have—"

"Sent Thayer after us?" My question has him cowering like a small child. "Your orders killed your brother and son. All for a crown never destined to be yours." My voice cracks as flashes of That Night return in a flurry. Fynn's expression as the world shifted around us. How he reached for me seconds before he died. My lungs refuse to inflate.

Water spills down Don's cheeks. He doesn't wipe them away. My uncle chokes on his grief, and the display is almost too much to bear. A part of me clings to my memories of him. Of whom I thought he was. But that man was never real.

"I'm s-sorry," Don blubbers.

I wither from his remorse. For the first time, I doubt Don is leaking information to Stellan. He looks gutted and pitiful, wailing over the child he didn't know he had. The child he *killed*. It's the perfect ending for his villain story, but I don't have it in me to gloat over his tears. I feel sorry for him, and the realization shakes me.

"You really didn't know, did you?" I ask.

"No." A lifetime of regret and pain fills that single word.

I look at Isolde, signaling with my eyes she should take me home. My uncle is not my mole. He won't save me or Corona.

Isolde moves to the door to alert the guards that we are finished.

Don's face flashes with panic. "Don't go yet. Stellan's article—tell me what it said."

"Why?" I rise to my feet.

"Because I can help you." The desperation in his voice is unmistakable.

I pause, staring down at my pitiful excuse for family. Don doesn't deserve my forgiveness. And yet, a small, weak part of me wants to believe he's sorry.

"The guards are here," Isolde tells me. "Should I let them in?"

"No, Leigh, please, don't go," Don beseeches. More tears fall freely down his cheeks.

More of mine threaten to fall, too.

I glare at him. "You thought peace could be secured with lies, deception, and murder, but that wasn't your first mistake. Now, you will remain here until the end of your days, going over all your crimes, starting with my mother, and ending with me." I watch him shiver, and then say, "Goodbye."

CHAPTER FORTY-TWO
DESIREE

THE SUN SETS as Jaxson and I leave the occultist shop filled with black market relics disguised as a condemned bakery in the Burned-Over District. The fading light casts an ominous glow on the weathered exterior. We almost have everything we need to summon the Balam daemon. I glance at the list on my phone to see what's left to gather.

18 black candles blessed under a full moon and rubbed in minotaur lard ✓
Chalk ✓
Matches (which we don't need, thanks to Jaxson) ✓
Cup of salt ✓
Blood Offering
Protection charm or Sunstone Bullets
The summoning spell ✓

"What are we missing?" Jaxson adjusts the heavy box in his arms.

Through my cat-eye sunglasses, I peer at the veins straining in his forearms. "The blood offering and the protection charm. Unless you think you can get sunstone bullets?"

"Soter's been counting the inventory at the precinct. If we take them, he'll have questions," Jax says.

"I'd rather not get you into trouble."

He nods. "You said you can handle the charm, right? We don't have to buy anything?"

"Yes, I can." Despite the confidence in my voice, uncertainty gnaws at my insides.

Fortunately, all the herbal ingredients we need for the protection charm are stored in my mom's apothecary at home. She's inevitably still at work, despite the hour. And the spare key still hidden under the mat—a habit I once found unsafe but now feels like a lifeline. Accessing them won't be a problem. Jaxson initially argued that we don't need the charm, insisting that Balam lacks Harborym's notorious violent streak. But knowing what it did to Vane and Vyvyan, I refuse to gamble with Jaxson's life. Caution is a small price for the safety of those I hold dear.

"Okay, let's go," Jax says.

"Let's drop those off first." I gesture with my chin at the candles.

"Good thinking, sunshine."

I smile wickedly, and Jax returns my grin with smoldering eyes. The kiss we shared the other night was a tantalizing preview, and I'm desperate for more. I crave to have his lips devouring mine, his hands exploring every inch of my body, igniting a firestorm. More than kissing, I long to feel his skin against mine. Creating new, erotic memories with Jax will surely obliterate any lingering thoughts of Vane. I'll be able to return to the Nest unbothered.

We leave the daemon-raising supplies inside a cobweb-infested crypt at Tsilah Cemetery, surrounded by the random belongings of an extinct Epsilon bloodline. We will return before midnight to prepare for the ritual. I haven't ruled out Alden, or one of his entourages, as a suspect.

Despite his flirtatious behavior at the club, I'm unconvinced the wolves have truly abandoned their hatred for vampires. I know when people are messing with me, and Alden's actions feel insincere, as if he were acting.

As we approach Mom's house, laughter spills into the street, mingling with the soft instrumental music inside. Is Mom home? I texted her earlier telling her I planned to stop by, but she had not replied. Her silence, juxtaposed with the liveliness inside her house, has my phone resembling a dead weight in my pocket.

Jax faces me. His brows furrow. "Sounds like a party."

I stare at the closed door. Mom doesn't do parties. She's always been the type to work tirelessly on one project before moving on to the next, rarely taking the time to revel in her achievements.

Growing up, I could count the number of times my parents celebrated an anniversary on one hand. It's not that they didn't love each other, but they were too obsessed with their careers, leaving little room for festivities. Wilder and I had to plan our birthday parties in high school, and we considered ourselves lucky if our parents shared a slice of cake with us.

I finish twisting the key in the lock, and as I do, the door swings open, revealing Juliette's blazing blue eyes. She folds her arms, her sleek green dress hugging her small curves.

She meets my gaze. "Oh, it's you. I thought you were the delivery guy." Her bored gaze then roams over Jaxson behind me. The heat of his body against my back comforts me.

"What are you doing at my house?" I ask. More laughter erupts behind her. I attempt to peer inside, but she blocks my view with a smirk.

"Celebrating," she says. "And I don't recall either of you being on the invite list. So, bye." She attempts to close the door in our faces, but I wedge my foot in the door. "Desiree, please, know when you're not wanted."

I stifle a vicious snarl for propriety's sake. This is my mom's house. *Juliette* is the one who doesn't belong. I need to get into Mom's apothecary. Curating those protection charms to raise the Balam rules out my former friend's self-importance.

"Move, Juliette. I need to grab something," I say in the most amicable tone, though it still comes out as a sneer. Her knuckles turn white the harder she grips the door. Fine, it's time to use the big guns. "Mom!" I yell.

"Stop that." I open my mouth to scream again. "Fine, but be quick," Juliette says, as if she has authority in my house. Juliette steps aside, and I gesture to Jaxson to follow me.

As Juliette closes the door, she sighs. "I'm having dejá vu seeing the two of you together. All that's missing is Wilder." She gazes toward the street as if she might find my twin standing there. Except if he were here, he would have bulldozed past her the second she opened the door.

"You're lucky Wilder isn't here. After what happened the last time you set foot in this house, he wouldn't hesitate to make you leave," I say, and she blanches.

Juliette was here the day of Wilder's Emergence. They were

hooking up, and he set her on fire—accidentally, of course. When I asked her to leave so Wilder and I could cover up the evidence, she got violent. I was used to her cruelty, but Wilder wasn't. That was the end of their relationship and the continuation of Juliette's vendetta against me, which lasted throughout school, and the years after at Hebe.

I leave the foyer to head toward the downstairs apothecary in the cellar beneath the stairs but pause as I pass the party. Hebe staff fill the family living room, all dressed in fancy attire instead of their usual scrubs. I hardly recognized them.

Mom notices me and breaks away from her conversation. My eyes land on a fancy script sign that reads, *"Congratulations on Funding for the Cure."* My nostrils flare.

It better be about the cure for some rare, exotic disease.

Despite my poor efforts to dissuade her, it seems Mom has continued her research for a treatment. Little does she know that the answer to her prayers is in this room. My blood is the cure for vampirism, but that's a secret I will take to my future grave.

"Desiree?" Mom asks. Her maroon dress, which I told her to buy last year on one of our rare shopping trips, shimmers under the soft light.

Jaxson halts beside me. He locks eyes with a few guests, who take in his faded jeans and hooded sweatshirt. He smiles at them as if his street clothes were as expensive as their suits.

"I'm sorry, honey, but what are you doing here?" Mom kisses my cheek, and I smell alcohol on her breath.

"I apologize, Doctor Dunn. I tried to stop them, but they didn't listen," Juliette chimes behind us with false sincerity.

Mom's features soften toward Juliette, and her green eyes fill with a mix of surprise and something else I can't quite decipher. Praise? "That's quite all right, Juliette. Desiree and Jaxson are welcome to be here. It's because of Desiree I began researching a cure."

I exhale, crossing my arms. Mom's wasting her time.

"Chiara, congratulations on your achievements. You look radiant," Jaxson says.

Mom, who has always loved Jaxson, blushes. "As pleased as I am to see you both here," she begins, and I peek at Jaxson from the corner of my eye.

He winks when Mom isn't looking, a small gesture of support that warms my skin. Jax is the only person who has ever made me feel like the most important person in the room.

"I wasn't expecting you. You should have called. My research isn't public knowledge. Sorry, Jaxson, but I must ask that you keep it a secret."

"I texted," I say through my teeth.

Besides, Vyvyan and Vane already know about her research—Vane is the Secret Keeper—but they've been too preoccupied to deal with it.

Mom purses her lips. "Well, since you are here, let me introduce you to some people."

Mom reaches for my hand, but I pull it away. I have no desire to let her parade me around the party as if I'm okay with this—as if she's doing this for *me*. Mom is doing this for the clout. Her career took a nosedive after Dad's arrest. She's trying to regain what she lost and pretending it's for me to win brownie points.

"I came here to use your apothecary," I tell her, and Mom's head falls sideways. "It is important."

Juliette's eyes darken before she mumbles, "Ungrateful."

I glare at her. She is getting on my last nerve.

"Of course," Mom replies. "But make it fast. We are serving dessert soon. Join us."

I nod, but Mom forgets I don't eat cake. The thought leaves a hollowness in my chest.

Instead of embracing who I am, she wants me to change.

As we enter Mom's apothecary, the familiar scents of drying herbs hanging from the ceiling envelop me. Their leaves rustle softly when the heater kicks on. Jars reminiscent of those in the spectacle shop Jaxson and I visited earlier line the shelves. Each container holds various herbs, spices, medicinal ingredients, and psychedelic mushrooms.

The sight of the mushrooms triggers a memory from my apprenticeship at Hebe. Jaxson and I came down here after researching the benefits of mushrooms. That was shortly after Wilder left for Aurora. I'd wanted to make a mushroom tea. However, I inadvertently grabbed the wrong kind, and we spent the rest of the evening laughing uncontrollably while hallucinating on the couch, the world around us melting into a kaleidoscope of sounds and shapes. Our drug-induced euphoria led to us skinny dipping in the canal. Unfortunately, swimming in the canals is illegal due to boat traffic and water quality, and our excursion got called to the authorities. Dad made us sleep off our high at the Blade Precinct.

I smile. We've had some good times together.

I gather the necessary ingredients and add them to a stone mortar before grinding everything together with a pestle. Jaxson hovers nearby, his presence both comforting and distracting when he picks up the jar of mushrooms, a coy smile on his face. My chest flutters at his playful expression. Meeting his gaze, I wiggle my eyebrows at him, a silent acknowledgment of the connection that seems to grow stronger with each passing moment.

"Remember—"

Juliette enters the apothecary. "Are you two finished yet?"

My shoulders practically touch my ears, but I don't turn around. "I'm in the middle of creating a dressing, so no, I need five more minutes," I snap.

Juliette scoffs. Her heels snap behind me. "We don't want you here, Desiree. This is a big night for your mom. And you bring drama wherever you go. Or was it your intention to ruin my party?"

My hand clenches around the pestle. "I didn't ruin anything, and it's my mom's party, not yours."

"That's what I meant."

I roll my eyes. Sure it was. Fucking egomaniac.

"Juliette, shouldn't you be schmoozing upstairs? Your perfume is giving me an allergic reaction," Jaxson says.

I soften, knowing he always has my back. When we were in high school, he'd always jump headfirst into any fight if he stumbled upon kids bullying me. It was one of the reasons I fell for him. He was my knight in ripped jeans and a faded hoodie, always ready to defend me. With a smile tugging at my lips, I return my focus to the pestle.

Juliette laughs. "I should be, but I'm down here babysitting you."

"Go away, Juliette," I grouse.

"Make me, Desiree."

I face her. "Are you trying to pick a fight with me?"

Juliette's grin is cruel. "You annoy me so easily, Desiree. You may be a vampire now, but not much else has changed, has it? You still yearn for attention, desperately clinging to Jaxson's side. He's the only person who can stomach your presence for more than five minutes." She takes a step closer, her eyes narrowing. "This is why I'm here to clarify one thing and one thing only. The two of you don't scare me. In the grand scheme of things, you are nothing."

"You're a bitch, Juliette," Jaxson says, and I nod in agreement.

Juliette faces Jax. "Oops. Did I strike a nerve? I get why you went for Desiree, Jaxson. She's pretty and all that, but she's also easy. And you never had much ambition, did you? Is that why you're here tonight, rather than helping protect the city from all the political *drama*?"

Jaxson's jaw hardens. "Walk away, Juliette."

"I'm just getting started. I heard you turned down the opportunity to compete in Domna Trials in Glaucus. Was it because of Desiree?"

I gasp. He didn't tell me that. Why didn't he say anything? Being Domna is a huge deal. The fact he made such an impression that another commander in a different city chose him to compete is impressive. Jax should at least consider it. He'd have so many opportunities but also a lot more responsibility. My throat thickens. It's making much more sense why he didn't share the good news.

A nagging suspicion grows in the back of my mind. Could I have influenced his decision to put his future on hold? Perhaps he's worried about leaving me behind or feels obligated to stay by my side. Suddenly, another thought strikes me. If Jax competed and won, he'd leave Borealis. He'd be hundreds of miles away, starting a new life in a different city. My heart sinks at the idea of being separated from him.

Jax glances sidelong at me before answering. "Why do you care so much about what I do?"

"I don't. I'm trying to make a point. You two cling to one another because you fear the unknown," Juliette comments.

I shake my head. "If that were true, why did I become a vampire?"

"Because no one alive likes you."

"I like her," Jaxson says, standing taller.

"You don't count."

"Why?"

Juliette's little laugh is pure evil. "Because you are her shield. You like her because it makes you feel important. Loving her gives you a purpose in a world where you are aimless. You are a Blade, but you aren't Domna. You are her friend, but you aren't her boyfriend. She chose to be a vampire, yet you pined for her when you thought she was dead because you were too afraid to let her go."

"I love her," Jaxson growls.

"That's not love. That's *fear*."

I let out a breath and close my eyes.

She's right. Goddammit. Juliette is fucking right.

I'm holding Jaxson back from finding true love and happiness. His feelings for me are preventing him from meeting someone with whom he can spend the rest of his life. Our relationship is built on mutual fear of rejection.

By pining for me, he never has to risk being rejected by someone he truly cares about. The worst part is that I enabled this behavior. Juliette may be a bitch, but I am equally at fault for allowing this dynamic to continue.

A stone settles in my gut.

"You've always been cruel, Juliette. Cruel and jealous." My voice trembles with barely contained rage. "All you crave is attention, and you turn into a brat the second someone takes it from you."

Juliette laughs, harsh and mocking. "I am not jealous."

"What did I ever do to you?" I ask. The words burn my throat on the way out. I've pondered this for almost a decade.

Juliette groans. "You always played the victim. It was annoying as hell, and it still is. No one wants to be around someone who tries as hard as you, Desiree. It's embarrassing."

"You turned everyone against me!" I screech.

"Because you wouldn't leave me alone!"

"You went after my brother and now my mom. I think *you* can't leave *me* alone."

Juliette's eyes widen. The color drains from her face.

I've finally cracked her stony exterior. She picks up a book and throws it at me. I duck as it crashes through the glass window above my head. Glass fragments rain, landing in my protection charm, rendering it useless.

A primal snarl tears from my lips and I lunge toward Juliette, my vision tinted red. Jaxson steps in my way, grabbing my shoulders and holding me back from snapping Juliette's head off.

"Don't," he says as I thrash against his hold. "Don't give her the satisfaction of stooping to her level."

I snap my fangs at Juliette, who pales. "She's tormented me for years, and it's time for me to teach her a fucking lesson."

"I know, but not here, not now," Jaxson grunts, struggling to hold me back. My vampire strength proves a formidable match for him.

Mom barrels into the room along with several other healers.

Jaxson adds, "There are too many witnesses."

"What is going on down here?" Mom asks.

A few guests glare at me from behind her. Their gazes shift from a trembling Juliette to Jaxson with his hands still on me, to the broken window, to me. The reality of the situation sinks in, and the red haze of fury slowly dissipates. Is that what Juliette wants? To make me look like the bad guy?

Juliette sobs, her shoulders shaking with exaggerated grief. She buries her face into Mom's shoulder, and Mom freezes before wrapping her arms protectively around my aggressor. The gesture is a knife to my heart.

"She attacked me, Chiara," Juliette cries.

Mom gasps. I want to curl up in a ball and disappear from the disgust in her eyes. She has never looked at me like this before. Like I am a monster that doesn't belong, a creature to be feared and reviled.

"You win, Juliette," I finally say. I run from the room. Upstairs, I race for the front door and fling it open to be swallowed up by the night, to disappear into the darkness and never be seen again.

I am halfway up the street when I can barely see through my tears.

"Desiree, wait up!" Jax calls.

"Jaxson, please, leave me alone," I say through sobs.

But he reaches me before I can argue further. "You don't mean that," he says.

I can't be with Jax, no matter how much it hurts to think that. We're fundamentally different, like opposite seasons—he's the embodiment of summer, full of warmth and life, while I'm the harsh reality of winter, cold and empty inside. As strong as it may be, our love is a crutch, preventing us from growing and achieving our true potential.

As a vampire, I'll never be able to give Jax the life he deserves. He deserves a partner who can walk alongside him, pushing his dreams and aspirations. Someone who yearns to see him succeed with a loving family and children to cherish.

This knowledge shatters my heart into a million pieces, but I know I can't be that person for him. My sole purpose is to return to the Nest.

It's time for Jax to see the truth. I'm not the girl for him. Letting him go is the hardest thing I'll ever do, but it's the only way to set him free and find the happiness he deserves. He would never do the same for me. That much is clear, or he would be in Glaucus right now.

"You're such a hypocrite," I say.

Jax's eyes widen. "How?"

"You always solve your problems with your fists, yet now that I have the strength to fight my battles, you won't let me. Why? Too scared I won't need you?" I know I'm taking out my anger at Juliette on him, but I can't stop. I'm shaking like a leaf from head to toe.

"Maybe when we were kids," he says, "but things are different now. We can't go around hurting people because we feel like it. That's not who we are."

I shake my head. Nothing has changed since we were kids. We are older, that's it. We are still clinging to each other because there's no one else.

"You don't know me," I say, turning on my heel to leave.

"So, it's like that?" Jax shouts.

I spin to face him, my hands on my hips. "Like what?"

"Is it that easy for you to walk away from me?" His words punch me in the gut. "I said I love you, Desiree. Doesn't that mean anything to you?"

I shrug, even though my heart sinks. Of course it does. "You had it right when you dumped me. We are not meant to be together. I'm not good enough for you."

"Stop saying things like that."

"You need to let me go. Move on with your life!" I say, and he flinches. "You have your future at your fingertips. We couldn't be more wrong for each other if we tried. I'm a *vampire*."

Jaxson's eyes search mine. "So? There are ways around that."

I scowl. "If you mean the *cure*, then—"

"Your mom is brilliant, Desiree. If there's a cure, she'll find it." I scoff. If he only fucking knew. "You can be a witch again. We can be together, *really* together. Wilder doesn't care, and I was a fool for letting you go. All I want is another chance," he says, cupping my cheek.

I lean into his touch, savoring the feel of his skin against mine. Then I push him away, my heart breaking with the action. "What if I don't know what I want?"

"There's someone else," he says, accusingly. "Is it Vane? He's your sire, but I saw the anguish in your eyes when you talked about him. Do you love him?"

Jaxson deserves better than me. He just needs a push before he sees it. "Yes."

Jax recoils as if struck. "Are you lying?"

"I'm not! And I will never take the cure and ride off into the fucking sunset with you." My entire body trembles. "Forget me. Forget you love me. I am not worth it."

The silence stretches between us, heavy and suffocating.

"You're angry at Juliette. This isn't you." I shake my head, but he adds, "I'll give you some time to cool off before we raise the daemon."

"I can do it alone," I snap after him.

"We are in this together," Jaxson replies without turning around. "I'll see you in a few hours. I expect an apology."

I stare after him long after he disappears, my feet rooted in place. If I chased after him, he might push me away for all the harsh things I said. I'm already alone; I don't need his rejection. A bird can only stay in the nest for so long before learning to fly, and I want Jaxson to soar, even if it means leaving me behind.

CHAPTER FORTY-THREE
WILDER

I PEEL OFF MY JACKET, and the canvas material of my uniform falls to the floor. Next, I tug my shirt over my head and let it drop next to the coat. I go to my chest of drawers and yank out a plain white T-shirt. When I glance outside, a few lights are on in the buildings across the street, but most businesses and homes are still rationing energy with the generators. By tomorrow, though, the grid should be back up and running. After several hours of discussions with Michael Bersa today, I finally got some assurance. He'd be back in production by morning with Dimitri's replacement. One win, at least.

The piercing ring of my phone jolts me from my thoughts. Stellan's name lights up the screen, and I frown. I've been waiting for this call all day. Since Leigh refuses to meet in person, I need to convince Stellan to meet her as an astral projection.

If he does, they might reconcile their differences and keep Aurora on the Corona map. But after Stellan's explosive article about Fynn, negotiations will be like treading on thin ice, with each step shattering the fragile peace. He needs to take down the article before they talk—if they talk at all.

"Stellan."

"Ah, Wilder, I hope you have good news for me," he replies. In the background, papers rustle. "Are you ready to join my team of freedom fighters?"

I put him on speakerphone so I can put on a shirt. "I haven't decided yet." The only way I'd work for him is if he and Leigh teamed up together.

"But if you want me to keep thinking about it, rather than flat out refusing, I suggest removing the article before we get into it."

"Which article?" Stellan's feigned innocence has me frowning at my reflection in the mirror.

"Don't get cute. You know which article," I growl. The silence on the other end is maddening. I can almost see Stellan's self-satisfied smirk. "It's libel."

"Is it?"

I cross my arms and lean against my dresser, unsure what to think. Leigh didn't tell me anything last night. Instead, she distracted me with sex. She needed the distraction, and I was too eager to give in to her when I should have pressed her more. I take a deep breath to ebb the frustration within me, knowing she doesn't trust me enough to confide in me.

"Writing about her family is a sure way to get on her bad side before you two have a chance to be friends," I tell him.

There's murmuring on the other line, followed by the soft thud of a closing door. When Stellan speaks again, his voice is low and conspiratorial, a snake's whisper in the dark. "I get my information from a very trusted source, Wilder. They have it on good authority that Fynn is Don Raelyn's son, which questions whether Leigh is, too. Not much is known about Lunar witchcraft. Just because she summoned Gwyn's ghost doesn't mean she is his heir. And maybe I don't want to be Leigh's friend."

I glare at my phone. What the hell? Leigh is the rightful monarch. Stellan is stirring up trouble.

"Did you ever have any intention of meeting with her? Or were you just dicking me around until your article came out? Because I don't get the sense you want to collaborate," I demand. "Who even is your source, anyway?"

Stellan's laugh is like nails on a chalkboard. "A good journalist never reveals their sources, Wilder."

"A good journalist also doesn't fuck up their career by not fact-checking said sources," I retort.

"You're angry."

"No shit. Leigh isn't forgiving, and you aren't making her reign any easier." The words come out in a rush. "If you could take a step back and view the situation from all sides, you'd know Leigh wants the same thing as you. Justice for the Nebula; peace in Corona."

Stellan exhales loudly. "It's not my job to make it easier. Neither is it yours. She inherited a trainwreck, and if she and her family intend to keep secrets, then my goal is to uncover every one of them. If what I wrote about Fynn wasn't true, why hasn't anyone issued a statement?"

His question hangs between us like forbidden fruit. I don't have an answer because Leigh didn't tell me anything. I pinch the bridge of my nose.

"You seem like you need a minute," Stellan muses. "Should we recess and convene later?"

As my phone dings, I open my mouth to ask him about the astral projection. It's a text from Leigh. My breath stalls.

LEIGH

I'm coming to Aurora tonight. I'll sleep on the train. Set up the meeting with Stellan. Make it early. I need to be back in Borealis tomorrow before midnight.

Holy hell. Leigh's coming to Aurora. What made her change her mind? You know what, it doesn't matter. She is coming, which means, things are finally heading in the right direction.

A surge of anticipation courses through me, a potent mix of excitement and nervous energy. Leigh, *here*? In the same space as me, not just an astral projection or in my dreams? The possibilities are endless – and intoxicating.

"Wilder?" Stellan prompts.

I clear my throat. "Leigh agreed to meet. If you mean what you said at the rally about peace and are willing to do whatever it takes to ensure that it lasts, then you will meet us tomorrow at Furies at ten o'clock in the morning. Don't be late."

No sound comes from Stellan's end. I think I've shocked him. He's a small-time reporter running for mayor and gets a one-on-one with the queen. Maybe he is having a heart attack. The thought brings a grim smile to my face.

"Hello?" I ask.

"I'll be there."

"And the article?"

I leave my room to scrounge up whatever is left over from dinner in the kitchen. As I descend the stairs, a warm evening breeze rustles my hair, carrying the scent of blooming flowers.

The aroma is a welcome change from the sterile, stale air that had been clinging to my room. I pause on the last step, drawn to the open doorway. Instead of heading straight for the kitchen, I veer off course and step out into the balmy night.

"When Leigh revealed the letters, she proved that, as Nebula, we must demand better. We must demand the *truth*. Let Leigh address the article's validity. Until then, I won't take it down. If you can't accept that, perhaps this meeting is a bad idea," Stellan says.

I take a deep breath. He's right, but airing family secrets fans the flames of discord. He is doing more harm than good for our people.

"You're playing with fire," I point out.

Stellan's response is quick. "Imagine if the Council's predecessors hadn't covered up the truth about the First War, and the Labor Laws never existed—would you have enrolled at the Blade Academy following your Emergence? Or would you have pursued another path? As leader of this new enclave, I plan to give all Nebula a *choice*. I'm not the bad guy. So if that is playing with fire, I'll happily burn."

Outside the common room, I pause where a movie's muffled sounds filter through the door. Gianna is curled up on the couch, the flickering light casting shadows across her face. The sight of her sends a pang through my heart. I can only imagine the pain she's going through as Fynn's former fiancée since that article was published.

Maybe Leigh opened up to her about Fynn. Perhaps they spoke about what Leigh and I couldn't.

"Stellan, you don't know the first thing about running a country," I say. "You need Leigh, and Leigh needs you. I'll see you tomorrow."

I hang up the phone, then I text Leigh back.

> Meeting scheduled.

> Leave your door unlocked.

> I'll pick you up.

We need a moment alone before we meet with Stellan—a chance to align our thoughts and strategies—and I don't trust us being able to have that conversation in my room and keep our clothes on. If I am driving, I'll have a better shot at keeping my hands to myself. More importantly, we need to have a heart-to-heart before we have sex again. The secrets between us create a chasm I fear will soon become insurmountable if we don't address them.

Leigh texts back a playful wink face emoji, eliciting a smile that tugs at the corners of my mouth. This could be massive if she's really had a change of heart. At a minimum, knowing that she'll be *here*, in the flesh, is progress.

When I step into the common room, Gianna doesn't move. I sink into the couch opposite her. "What are you watching?" I ask.

With a subtle flick of her wrist, she uses her Cosmic magic to pause the program. A brooding, pale-faced actor freezes mid-sentence, his chiseled features etched with a tortured expression. "Some vampire romance."

"Is it any good?" I ask. I'll ease into asking about Fynn.

Gi shrugs. "I think the main character is based on Prince Vane."

I chuckle. "So, what? He's a romance cover model reject?"

A faint smirk plays on her lips, a glimmer of her former self shining through the cracks in her newest mask. A mask that tells everyone that life in Aurora has been great, despite being attacked, and nearly killed. "Slow your judgment. Someone may look at you with all those tattoos and piercings and think you're a bad boy cliché."

I examine my inked hands and forearms. "Are you kidding? These are works of art. It's not as if I got barbed wire or biomechanical designs."

"I think Ry has a series of gears tattooed on him," she says.

"He does." I laugh, and it feels good. I haven't laughed much in recent days.

Gianna snorts, a sound so unexpected that it makes me laugh harder.

"Where is he?" I ask. Ry's been trailing after Gianna like a lost puppy since she arrived.

"He went somewhere with Pallas."

I nod, noting the slight change in her tone, the way her eyes flicker with an emotion I can't decipher.

Pallas arrived yesterday. Eddo took one look at him, huffed, and walked off, leaving me to deal with yet another one of his issues. Pallas hasn't told me what he did to get sent here, but I know it has to do with Leigh and what she was up to that day in her kitchen. I doubt it is legal. Eventually, I'll get it out of him, but for now, I focus on the broken girl before me.

"You and Ry have been spending a lot of time together," I remark.

Gi lifts a brow. "Yeah, so? He's nice."

"So is Meg when she wants to be," I say carefully. My friends have made it their mission to see which one of them Gianna will fall for first.

"She is."

"Pretty, too."

Gianna's eyes narrow. "I never pegged you for a gossip."

I blink. It dawns on me that I've annoyed her, which wasn't part of the plan. "I'm sorry. I know they both like you, and I wanted to see if there's a chance you returned either of their feelings. I thought that if you can't find information on your birth father, then maybe a winter romance wouldn't be such a bad idea. I didn't mean to upset or pry into your personal life."

Gi sighs. "Look, ever since my Emergence, my future has been meticulously planned. First, it was Fynn, and then Hammond Bishop—

always someone who could provide the best financial security for me and my family. I've never had the luxury of choosing a partner based on genuine attraction or connection. Honestly, I don't know where to begin when it comes to dating without first assessing what they can offer me."

Gianna fidgets with the hem of her linen shirt. She inhales a deep breath, her voice a whisper as she continues, "I'm pathetic, right? A shallow, calculating girl who can't see beyond the superficial?"

"You are not pathetic. You are just . . ." I consider how to say what I want to without sounding like an ass, but I also believe Gianna would appreciate the honesty right now. Her entire life has been a lie. "Lost."

Gianna nods. "Yeah. That sounds about right."

"Can I ask you something about Fynn?" I ask as gently as possible. I need to know more about what I might be walking into when Leigh arrives. It would be enormously helpful if Gi knew whether the rumor was true.

"What about him?" Gi asks.

I drape an arm across the back of the couch to appear more casual, though my heart is pounding so hard I'm sure Gianna can see it.

"Stellan's article—has Leigh confided in you?" I ask.

"No." She shakes her head. "She hasn't, but I've been thinking about Fynn a lot."

"Oh?"

"I didn't think Fynn is Don's son. He never let on if he was, but our engagement wasn't profound. He didn't tell me anything worthwhile. He was too besotted with his ex to pay me much attention." I raise a brow. "Oh, come on, you must have heard the rumors."

"Sorry, no."

Gi sits straighter. "Fynn was seeing this Nebula girl, Corvina. They were in love, based on what I gathered. But he dumped her and asked me to marry him, likely for propriety's sake." She gives me a sympathetic look, but I refuse to show any emotion. Leigh and I will cross that bridge when the time comes. *If* it ever does. "I felt sorry for the girl but said yes to the proposal, regardless. Anything to obtain an ounce of approval from Elio." She says her stepfather's name like a sneer.

"Where is Corvina now?" I make a mental note to look into her, to unravel the mystery of Fynn's past and the secrets he took to his grave. Maybe he confided in her before he died.

"Corvina isn't a danger to Leigh."

"How do you know?"

"We went to school together. The girl is a mouse."

Yeah, but mice still have sharp teeth.

"I'm sorry," I say after a beat, and Gianna's brows dip. "Fynn was your future husband, and though there was no love between you, it still must've hurt when he died, and again, it must've been tough to call off your engagement to Hammond."

Gianna tips her head back and laughs, but there's no humor. "Calling off my engagement to Hammond was the easiest thing I've ever done. But do you want to know the hardest?"

"What's that?"

"Coming here to be turned away at every turn. I thought I'd finally get answers about my family by talking with Stellan, but he hasn't had time for me, and then the riot at the rally happened, and—" She cuts herself off with a groan that tightens my throat. "I'll never know where I belong."

"Maybe Stellan doesn't have all the answers."

She nods solemnly. "Maybe."

"I'm going to see if we have any leftovers from dinner. Hungry?" I ask.

"I ate." Gi waves her hand, and the screen returns to life.

I take that as my cue to leave. As I go, I glance back at Gianna. She quickly wipes an errant tear off her cheek. *Fuck*, I wish there was more I could do for her.

"Leigh will be here in the morning," I say to better her mood.

Gianna's eyes widen. "She will?"

Something about her worried tone gives me pause. "I thought you'd be excited."

Gianna swallows. "I am. I just wasn't expecting it. Do you know why she's coming?"

I hesitate. If I tell her about the meeting with Stellan, she'll probably want to come. But if she comes, Stellan may be less inclined to cooperate with Leigh. I can't take that risk.

"I miss her," I say, and Gi makes a gagging noise. "Why don't you give her a call? She has a long train ride."

Gianna doesn't reach for her phone. "No, that's okay. I will see her when she gets here."

Baffled by her response, I walk away. What the hell was that all about?

CHAPTER FORTY-FOUR
LEIGH

THE POLISHED SURFACE of the mahogany table reflects the opulence of the royal train compartment. Despite the late hour, Janus sits across from me. I summoned her here to establish a chain of command at the last minute. Unexpectedly, she brought Bennett to act as a "witness" to our discussion.

My knee bounces. I'm so close to stopping Stellan and uncovering his accomplice. Victory is practically within reach.

"You could always send a Council member to speak to Stellan in your place, Leigh," she offers. "Bending to Stellan's will is beneath you."

I sigh. The Council isn't trustworthy right now. One of them might be Stellan's mole, and the rest want to marry me to one of our enemies.

"I need to speak with Stellan directly," I say.

"How will you get him to confess who he's working with?" Janus asks as a train attendant glides into our compartment. She places a delicate porcelain cup before me. The steam carries the sharp, citrusy scent of lemon.

"I have my methods," I say. I don't expect Stellan to drop his campaign and work with me. Instead, I am using the meeting as an excuse to visit Gianna.

As much as it pains me, I need to consider the possibility that Gianna betrayed me in exchange for the truth about her family, Stellan knows who they are. Gianna's connections to the Council, including her former engagements with Hammond Bishop, Fynn, and her aunt's failed engagement with my uncle, place her in a unique position to gather sensitive information. It's possible that either Fynn or her aunt told her that Don was Fynn's real father.

The idea that someone I've trusted my whole life could prioritize her own needs over our friendship is like a knife sliding between my ribs. But it wouldn't be the first time someone I loved betrayed me. I cannot allow personal feelings to cloud my judgment. I must uncover the truth, no matter how hurtful it may be.

"Do you have an idea who Stellan's informant is?" Bennett asks, looking up from his electronic notepad.

I narrow my gaze at him. "Let's stay focused on why you are both here. Shall we?"

Bennett nods, but there's hurt in his eyes. If he wanted me to confide in him, he should never have lied about Corvina.

Janus sits taller. "If another crisis or natural disaster occurs in your absence, the chain of command will be me, followed by Keris Telfour."

I nod.

"I want you both to watch Prince Alden while I am gone. If he asks, you will tell him I've been tied up in meetings, but I will have my answer regarding his proposal tomorrow night," I say. Janus and Bennett exchange a look that tingles my fingers and toes. "What's the look?"

Janus removes her reading glasses with deliberate slowness. She folds them carefully.

"I hope your answer to him is yes," she says. "The Council unanimously supports the marriage. It'll establish long-lasting peace between our countries. There have been whispers about more paw prints breaching the northern border."

"Did my grandmother tell you that?" Why isn't she talking to me?

"No, she's been indisposed, but the Blade Commander there contacted Soter Telfour about it today," Janus says. "Which is why I must emphasize how King Simon and Prince Zeus will have no choice but to back off if you are married to Alden. He controls Lua's armies. We can't forget that they are still a threat despite Alden being here. The new paw prints at the border to prove it. The wolves are getting restless. You need to put an end to their threat." Her magic has the potted plants lining the compartment's walls rustling, their leaves curling with the sensations of hostility.

I grit my teeth. I had no idea there was a unanimous vote for me to marry Alden. "I understand that's what you think, yes. But I am still determined to find another way. Alden doesn't want to marry me as much as I don't want to marry him."

"He talks about you as if he wouldn't mind," Bennett says.

I roll my eyes. It is all an act.

"You might use this time in Aurora to ask Wilder to remain there. He will not disobey a direct order if he's as loyal to you as you claim. That way, you will no longer hesitate to do the right thing, Leigh," Janus says, with Bennett nodding in agreement. "The Council and I still are wary of him after what happened with Stellan in the square. You'd be doing the right thing by cutting him loose."

My hands itch to wrap around their throats. Wilder isn't the problem. Alden is. "He did nothing wrong."

Janus glides her tongue over her straight teeth. "Leigh, I am not trying to antagonize you."

I sip my tea, eyeing her above the rim. If that were true, then why is she backing me into a corner with this proposal? Her threat is there, even if it is a veiled one.

"To ensure the Council is represented in your talks with Stellan, I would like Bennett to accompany you to Aurora and sit in on your meeting."

I scoff. "That's not necessary."

Janus holds up her hand. "It is nonnegotiable. Bennett will attend the meeting to ensure Stellan understands he will be met with force if he continues his harmful discourse and rhetoric to turn Aurora into an independent nation."

It takes all my willpower to keep my jaw from dropping. "Threatening him won't win us any favors with the Nebula." Stellan will only double down about us being the enemy.

"Plenty of Nebula are still loyal to us."

I sigh. The Nebula won't stay on our side long if Stellan continues to threaten us and we threaten him back. It's a game of cat and mouse, and I am done playing. It'll only end in bloodshed.

"I'd prefer if Bennett didn't come to Aurora," I say.

"Leigh, I am an asset. My presence will help make negotiations with Stellan smoother," Bennett says, and I almost laugh.

The last time he tried to help me, he made a deal with the Magician to join Eos, and in exchange, he spread lies about his grandmother's health, claiming she had dementia when she was in great condition. No, thanks. I'd rather take my chances than rely on him again.

"After what happened at the races, we need to do what we can to keep you and this country safe," Janus says. I cringe at the conjured memory. The phantom scent of kelpie's sweat and fear fills my nostrils. "Or have you already forgotten you were almost kidnapped? There's safety in numbers. Don't fight us on Bennett's presence at this meeting, and I will keep Alden occupied until your return."

I frown at my tea. Bennett's presence will make matters more complicated. He and Gianna are friends.

Pick your battles, Leigh, Aradia warns. I push her away, but she's right. I can deal with Bennett.

"It doesn't seem like I have a choice," I say.

Janus smiles. "You always have a choice. Just ensure it is the right one."

"Fine," I relent. Janus sits straighter, satisfied with her victory. I focus my ire on Bennett. "You better tell Corvina you're leaving Borealis with me. I'd hate for her to get the wrong idea about your involvement in this mission." Bennett balks, but I rise from my seat, ignoring his reaction.

Maybe I can convince the railroad engineer to leave early. I'd love to surprise Wilder and fuck the frustration out of my system, riding him until the only thing I can think about is the damning friction between my thighs.

Turning to Janus, I open the door and say, "Janus, thank you for your time. I trust you can see yourself out?"

"One last thing, can I not convince you to bring more guards than just the blue-haired Blade?" Janus asks.

I shake my head. If I bring more people, my departure will become public knowledge. I don't want Alden to find out, and Isolde is good at her job. "I'll be fine."

"As you wish." Janus's tone is clipped, barely concealing her annoyance at my dismissal.

Janus bows her head, and I follow her from my train car. Once she's out of sight, I press my spine against the hallway wall to take a deep breath. This trip to Aurora must go smoothly if I am to escape this marriage. Otherwise, I fear my last name will be Lupas. The thought sends me into a tailspin, a premonition of a future I refuse to accept. I will protect my kingdom and heart, no matter the cost.

CHAPTER FORTY-FIVE
DESIREE

HOURS after my explosive argument with Jaxson, I enter the tomb inside the abandoned mausoleum to raise the Balam. I bite my fingernails. Soon, I'll have proof of who hurt Vyvyan.

As I step into the crypt, light flickers up the stairwell. I freeze when I see the candles we dropped off arranged in a perfect pentacle with Jaxson at their center. The flames dance, casting sinister shapes over the pilfered stone coffin at the back of the room. Slowly, I shake my head.

He's here. After I hoped he had enough of my drama.

I only meant half of what I said earlier, the words born out of frustration and fear. I haven't stopped thinking about it because when Jax leaves, I'll be disgustingly alone. Jax is my only friend; without him, I'd have nothing.

"Hi," I mutter.

Jax lifts his gaze from the spell in his hands. "Hi."

"You set up without me."

Everything matches the diorama from what Zev gave Leigh and Wilder in October. Jaxson's lines are as straight as an arrow, and the chalk circle he drew is symmetrical.

Guilt pricks behind my eyelids. "Look, Jax. About what I said earlier. I'm sorry for being such a bitch. Juliette made me so mad, and she . . ." Juliette had a point, but that doesn't excuse how I hurt him. I still want us to be friends.

Jax shrugs. "It's okay. I get it. I'm not enough for you anymore."

The pain in his voice is sharp enough to cut me open. I love him, but I don't need him as a crutch anymore, and he doesn't need me. He has everything he needs inside of him to stand on his own. If it is meant to be, we will find a way back to each other. But we each have a lot of growing to do.

"Becoming a vampire was the first decision I made for myself," I say. "No laws dictated my worth. As a vampire, I had friends. My wanting to get back there doesn't mean I don't love you. You're my best friend, Jaxson, but maybe it is time for us to become the people we were meant to be?"

Jaxson stares at me for a long moment.

I glance at my boots after the silence stretches for an uncomfortable amount of time. More words bubble up my throat, desperate to fix things, to mend the rift I've caused before he does what I ask and walks away for good.

What we had was special, even if it didn't last, and I don't want to lose him. I'm unsure how I'd survive another loss. We are star-crossed lovers in every sense of the term—destined to burn brightly but never together.

"You were destined for greatness, Desi," Jaxson finally says.

"You, too, Jax."

Jaxson steps toward me with his hands in his pockets. "You're right."

I exhale. I knew we'd get past this. We always do. "Good."

He stops before me. "It's why I can't stay," he whispers, pulling a bundle of herbs from his hoodie pocket. "I went back to that Lunar witch's shop and paid her for this after you didn't get to make one at your mom's house."

I take the protection charm with trembling fingers. "If there's only one. Why are you giving it to me?"

Regret fills his gaze. "I'm leaving."

"Huh?" I squeak. It's what I *asked for*, but I hadn't expected him to leave so soon. Panic starts to bubble up in my chest. Did he get called into work?

"I heard what you said, and you're right. I need to start living my life and not be afraid to start over, even if that's without you. I accepted the invitation to compete in the Domna Trials in Glaucus. The competition begins tomorrow. I'm on the last train out tonight."

I take quick, shallow breaths. "When will I see you again?" My voice sounds pathetic even to my own ears. I told him to go, to put himself first, and it's what he deserves. It's what I wanted. So why is my soul tearing apart?

Jax shrugs, and I notice a backpack in the crypt's corner. Fuck. Is this it?

I force a watery smile. "I'll miss you."

"Not as much as I'll miss you."

A sob tears from my throat, raw and aching, and Jaxson folds me into his arms.

I bury my face in his chest, breathing in his citrus scent, clinging to him like I could fuse our bodies forever, and it's exactly like the night he broke up with me. He held me then as I cried too and told me it had to be that way to protect Wilder.

More tears fall, hot against my cheeks, and he shushes me, his hand rubbing soothing circles on my back. "It's going to be okay, sunshine."

"Will it?" I ask against his shirt. Once again, Wilder is gone, and no one is here to help me survive the loss of Jaxson a second time.

"You could come with me," Jaxson whispers. His breath is warm against my ear.

I pry myself away to peer into his eyes. Is he serious?

"I know you have the vampires, but what if you left all that behind and started over with me? Maybe in another city, we can make it work . . ."

I push away from him. "Move with you to Glaucus?"

Jax nods.

"But Balam . . ." My gaze shifts over the black candles at my feet.

If I don't go through with this ritual, we may never uncover who wants Vyvyan dead. If I leave, I may never be able to patch things up with Misty. She's angry now, but that anger hides her hurt. She was my friend. Don't I owe her an explanation? Maybe this time, she'll listen.

"I c-can't," I say.

Jaxson's smile drops. He extracts the spell from his other pocket. "Then you'll also need this."

I take the folded paper as if it were Jaxson's breaking heart.

"Take care of yourself, Desi." Jax's lips press against mine in a final goodbye.

The kiss tastes of a past tinged with regret and youthful longings—a heart I thought I'd outgrown. It ends before I can succumb to the urge to pull him closer, to cling, to rewind.

Jaxson turns away, grabs his bag with a practiced hand, and ascends the stairs without a backward glance. Each step is a nail hammered into the coffin of my foolish hopes.

To keep myself from chasing after him, I dig my heels into the worn stone at my feet. I remind myself, fiercely, that I *will* see him again. This isn't over. Our story isn't finished, not by a long shot.

The silence that engulfs me is suffocating, a stark reminder of my solitude. I have no one to turn to, and there is no safety net to catch me if this plan unravels. If everything goes sideways, I'll be left with nothing—no friends, no boyfriend, no job, no home. I can't keep relying on Wilder's generosity, leeching off his kindness like a parasite. Eventually, he'll tire of my constant need and cast me aside like everyone else.

I let a single tear slip free before I take a deep breath.

"Fucking get ahold of yourself, Desiree," I tell myself. "You made your choice. Now, buck the fuck up, and summon the daemon to go home."

I unfold the spell and commit the words to memory.

Then I squeeze my protective charm for luck and stand before the pentacle, my back facing the stairs.

As I open my mouth to begin, footsteps scrape on the stairs. Slowly, I turn, hope flaring in my chest at the expectation of seeing Jaxson. But it's not Jaxson waiting at the bottom of the stairs.

It's the Balam.

Three sets of eyes, each a flaming inferno, bore into me, searing my soul, and stripping me bare. The daemon takes monstrous form: three heads perched upon one trunk, one of a man, another of a bear, and the third a ram with twisted, curling horns.

I stumble back, blindly retreating into the summoning circle, my boots scuffing the chalk and blurring the carefully inscribed lines beneath my feet. The daemon smiles then, a predatory display that bared rows of jagged teeth, sending a frigid chill rushing through my veins.

"H-how?" I gasp.

It moves toward me with the grace of a warrior—silent, the air shimmering with heat in its wake. It's naked, a grotesque display of power and dominance.

I didn't summon it . . . someone else did.

The thought hits me like a punch to the gut. It's here to silence me, to extinguish my life like a fragile flame, and a creeping dread settles deep in my bones.

"Call it daemon's intuition," Balam's human head replies in a guttural rasp.

I scoff, trying to project disdain even as my heart hammers against my ribs. I scramble to the opposite side of the coffin, using the cold slab is a meager barrier between us. What was I *thinking*?

But I am powerless against this daemon. Even as a vampire, with enhanced strength and speed, this entity could crush my bones to dust beyond repair, scatter my essence to the winds. I force my voice to remain steady. "What do you want?"

"Does it matter? They want you dead, and I am here to fulfill their wish." Balam drifts closer. He stands between me and the stairs. A sinister grin plays on its grotesque features. He knows I am trapped.

I trip over a lifted stone, catch myself on the coffin's edge, and the rough stone bites into my palms, drawing blood. *Fuck.* The protective charm slips from my grasp as Balam closes the distance. Bile coats my tongue. He reeks of Sulfur and lard.

I have no choice but to run. If I can slip past the daemon without it catching me, I can stay alive. With a deep breath, I turn on my heel, dashing toward the stairs. The daemon is much larger than me, but I pray I am faster than it is.

Balam's taloned feet scratch against the cold stone, a sound that grates on my nerves like scraping metal. His claws tear the back of my shirt, grazing skin, a painful, burning line. A cry tears free from my throat, raw and involuntary. I hit the pavement hard, jarring my wrists in the process.

Tears prick my eyes, blurring my vision, but I have to move, *have to*. To remain still is to die. I crawl toward the fractured edge of the circle, toward freedom, as Balam looms over me, a nightmarish mountain of flesh and bone.

As if I weigh no more than a bag of cotton, the daemon flips me over with contemptuous ease, and I stare up into its hideous faces, a trinity of death.

"Goodbye, Desiree," Balam whispers.

"P-please, don't do this. I—" I rasp. "I pose no threat to anyone."

"It's what I've been ordered to do. You are a threat," the Balam growls, and I tremble.

"I'm not!"

The Balam's grip on my shoulders tightens, drawing more of my blood as his nails dig into my skin. I scream. But maybe someone will hear me. "I am but the messenger. The one who calls me laments this necessity. Your essence stains this world with what should not be and so it must depart. To ensure harmony is returned to its rightful state."

Tears trail down my face, hot and stinging. What the hell does that even mean?

"You don't have to kill me. There must be a mistake. I've hurt no one."

The Balam cocks its head. "Are you not a vampire with the power to unmake other vampires? Are you not the witch who hid the War Letters rather than exposing their truth? Silence is damning, Desiree Dunn, and so are you."

I jerk against the daemon's hold. He clings tighter. "Please, stop. Take me to your master. We can work this out!"

"What a pathetic creature you are," the daemon taunts. "No wonder she wants you dead."

She? My cold heart stops beating.

The Balam leans closer, its leathery, wet bull nose touching me, the contact searing my skin. "I'll make this qui—"

I headbutt the daemon, putting all my strength behind the blow. A satisfying *crunch* reaches my ears. The daemon wails.

Black goo, thick as tar and burning with unholy heat, pours from one of the daemon's faces, splattering across my face. It sizzles on contact, eating away at my skin like acid. Taking advantage of its disorientation, I plant my feet against its chest and kick with every ounce of strength I possess, my thigh muscles screaming in protest. The force sends Balam staggering back.

I roll away, limbs tangled and clumsy with terror, then stumble as I try to move on my hands and knees, my abused wrists screaming in agony. Pushing myself to my feet, ignoring the fire scorching my face, I charge for the exit. My feet thwack against the mossy pavement, a frantic rhythm paired with the daemon's wailing. Every breath burns now, but escape is my only focus.

I am so close to freedom when a gigantic force collides with my back. I sprawl on the floor, knocking over candles. Flames catch on the tattered remains of a drape on the crypt, spreading quickly.

But it's not enough. Balam's massive hand closes around my shoulders, the grip like a vise, lifting me as easily as a ragdoll. Then I'm thrown against the unforgiving stone floor, the impact stealing my breath. Over and over, my head slams against the ground, each hit a jarring explosion of pain as the inferno roars higher, licking at my exposed skin. Spots dance across my vision, blurring everything into a swirling mess of light and shadow.

I'm losing the battle, my consciousness slipping away as the heat of the flames turns unbearable, searing my skin.

On the next sickening throw, something cracks. A sharp, splintering sound echoes in my skull before the unbearable agony blossoms, stealing the rest of myself. Blood, hot and thick, pours down my face, blinding me, filling my eyes and mouth with the coppery taste of death. This is it.

"Desiree!"

The sound of my name is a lifeline in the darkness.

"Get off her!"

The daemon crashes into the far wall. I gasp for breath. My broken body screams in protest, but I know if I don't move, I'm dead.

Twisting sideways, I claw at the blood-slicked floor. The stench of my burning flesh makes me gag. Through the haze of smoke and blood, I see two figures grappling, their silhouettes a dance macabre among the infernos.

A final shriek fills my ears, piercing and agonizing. I fear the worst as I collapse into a broken heap.

"Desiree," a melodic voice calls out to me. "Desiree, can you open your eyes?"

I force myself to obey, fighting against the pull of oblivion.

"That's it. Stay with me," the voice says again, soft and encouraging.

My eyes flutter open, and I blink thrice. Am I dreaming? I'm cradled in Vane's arms.

"Vane," I croak. "How did you—"

"Shh." Vane brushes a bloody strand from my face. Even bruised and battered, I lean into his touch, ruining his nice clothes beyond repair. Eager for a hint of affection when I thought I had none. I never thought he would be the one to save me, but against all odds, here he is. He's not a knight like Jaxson; he's an avenging angel. "Save your strength."

He lifts me easily. I claw at his shirt, but my strength bleeds away with the blood. Too much blood has been lost to heal, too broken to mend. Darkness presses in. This might still be the end.

We emerge from the tomb, and the frigid night air caresses my battered face. Vane kneels in the brittle grass. Weeping headstones watch.

"Balam," I croak. "Did you—"

"It's not dead," Vane says. "But it's wounded, just like you. And you're not healing fast enough."

Exhaustion tugs at my eyelids. Blood is the key to accelerating my recovery.

"Here." Vane's blood-slicked wrist hovers before my face. The scent is similar to an irresistible siren's call. "Drink."

I search his eyes, seeking for any glimmer of deceit. Does he want to share blood with me despite knowing the consequences? Drinking his blood will forge a bond between us, tying him to me for eternity. I'll be able to know how he feels at any given moment. Why would he want me to experience a one-sided bond that puts him at a disadvantage? He hates me.

"Why?" I gasp, the question a fragile breath between us.

Despair shadows his eyes. "Seeing you in pain . . . it tears me apart."

My gaze locks onto his wrist so I don't have to read too deeply into his words. The gash left by his fangs is already beginning to mend. If I drink his blood, does that mean he will take me home?

I latch onto the wound, my lips sealing over the torn skin, and I suck, his essence exploding on my tongue—rich, heady, and intoxicating. I swallow, and each gulp is a river of molten silk, liquid fire igniting my senses and awakening my body. His blood courses through me, healing my wounds, knitting bones back together, banishing pain and exhaustion, and replacing it all with a surge of power, strength, and vitality.

Vane sighs, his body melting against mine, his arm tightening around my waist, holding me close as I lie in his lap. A primal moan vibrates through me, through him, as my tongue dances across his skin, savoring his taste, relishing the feel of him hardening beneath me.

Fuck. He tastes delicious. I could drown in his blood.

Vane's mouth finds my neck, his lips a whisper against my skin, his breath a searing caress. He captures my earlobe between his front teeth. Each swallow is greedier than the last. I arch against him, pressing closer, craving more. Him. Us. More.

"That's enough," he says, his voice low and rough, but I can't let go. The need is too strong, the hunger too deep. I grind my ass against him, eliciting a hiss from his lips. "Desiree, *please*. Not here."

His plea pierces through the haze of desire, forcing me to stop. Releasing his wrist is like trying to break bones with my bare hands. It takes every ounce of strength to let go, to pull away, to separate myself from his taste and from the hard press of his body against mine.

I open my eyes to find a thirst, need, and desire that mirrors my own. His half-lidded eyes, glowing red in the darkness, are a temptation I yearn to lose myself in.

My tongue skims my bottom lip, savoring the lingering traces of his blood. The urge to mark and make him mine pulses through me, but I know these thoughts are not entirely my own. It's the blood's influence.

"Thank you," I breathe, the words are inadequate. He saved my life. It makes no sense, considering I thought he wouldn't mind if I died.

Vane doesn't answer. His attention drifts toward the north entrance. His unease ripples through me like a mirage.

"The groundskeeper is coming to inspect the blaze," he says, then picks me up, and whisks me away from the cemetery. I let him take me only because he's bringing me back to the Nest.

CHAPTER FORTY-SIX
DESIREE

MUCH TO MY DISAPPOINTMENT, we return to Wilder's loft. The elevator ride to 2B is a suffocating journey, with the confined space amplifying the unspoken words between Vane and me. With Vane's blood coursing through my veins, I'm painfully aware of his proximity. Every inhale sends goose bumps racing across my skin, and every exhale draws a silent whimper from my throat. Thank fuck Vyvyan was unconscious after I fed her my blood. I'm shaking with need.

I flick on the loft's lights and storm straight to the bathroom. Though the torn skin on my face has knitted together, the blood remains. I grab a towel and wet it, the cool water a welcome relief as I clean the caked blood from my skin.

Once I get most of it off, I return to the living room to deal with Vane. Why the fuck did he bring me here instead of the Nest?

Dropping onto the couch, I wince as the cushions press against my formerly tattered body. The metallic scent of blood fills my nostrils as I peel off my torn shirt. The fabric clings to my healed wounds, but it doesn't stop me from tossing it aside. In just my bra and jeans, I swipe at the dried blood on my chest and stomach. I'm positive my back is a web of scratches and bruises.

Vane stands stiffly near the window, his silhouette outlined by the few city lights working in this area of town. When he turns to face me, his eyes roam over my exposed skin, lingering on my curves.

A flush creeps up my neck. What does he see when he looks at me now? He's given me his blood, completing half the bond. We already had a connection due to him siring me, but now that he's given me his blood, I am overly aware of him. The difference is that the sire bond doesn't amplify attraction, unlike the blood bond.

With his blood coursing through my veins, the desire to erase the distance between us is paramount above all else. His hands clench and unclench at his sides. Is he angry or having trouble keeping himself from touching me?

When I gave my blood to Vyvyan, she wasn't a vampire long enough to experience the full effects of the blood bond before my blood turned her human. But now, I can sense the powerful connection that Vane's blood has forged between us. It's a sensation I've never felt, both exhilarating and terrifying. Is this what Vyvyan would have felt if my blood weren't poison? I choke on a laugh. She would have hated that.

"Let me help you." Vane stalks toward me.

I freeze in place. He takes the towel from my hand, and when his fingers brush against mine, a jolt of electricity rips through my body. He kneels before me as he did before my date with Jaxson to help with my shoes, his eyes never leaving mine as he wipes blood from my skin, his touch surprisingly gentle.

I'm so used to his callousness that I close my eyes, losing myself in how his fingers brush over my skin, leaving fire trails in their wake. I bite my lip, stifling a sigh, as he works his way up my arms, across my collarbone, and down my chest.

It's not real—this behavior toward me, this kindness. He might have given me his blood, but only because, as my sire, my pain must've felt visceral to him. Soon, the effects will wear off, and the maddening need to touch and be touched will dissipate, or at least, I pray it will. Vane doesn't care about me; he only cares about Vyvyan and himself.

"Vane," I whisper, my voice barely audible over my pounding heart.

He looks up at me, his eyes brimming with desire, and I know in that moment that I'm lost. I'll never be able to resist him, no matter how hard I try. Not anymore.

I stifle a dark laugh. Was his intention to ruin me for anyone else?

"I'm confused," I say, taking the towel. I can't think with his hands on me.

"About?" Vane replies, still on his knees.

"Why did you save me?" I ask.

"I'm your sire."

I blink. "So?"

"When a vampire turns another vampire, a bond forms between them," Vane explains. "The longer two vampires spend in one another's company, the stronger the bond becomes. It's why you always want to be near me, even when you don't. As your sire, I have a unique connection to you. I can sense your presence and your emotions, even from a distance. It's like an invisible thread ties us together. I felt a disturbance in that connection tonight, a sense of danger and distress emanating from you. It was as if you were leaving a trail of breadcrumbs to follow, guiding me to where you were. That's how I knew you were in trouble and how I was able to find you."

"And what about now?" I ask. "Do you feel it, too? This . . . pull between us? Is it the sire bond or the blood?"

He's silent as he studies me. There's conflict in his eyes. "Both," he admits. "I feel the pull. But that's nothing new. I feel the desire to be with you. To touch you. Every. Damn. day. The blood only demands I do something about it."

I gasp. Is this why he can't seem to leave me alone? Now that he's given me his blood, will his proximity get worse? If it does, will we spend eternity in agony? Vyvyan doesn't want us near each other. I've done a good job at keeping my distance, but that was before.

A humorless laugh escapes my lips. "Why not let the Balam finish me off? It would have saved you the torture of being near me when I returned home."

Vane interlaces his fingers in his lap. "But that's the thing, Desiree. You're not returning home. The Nest isn't safe for you."

My eyes narrow. "Excuse me? You don't get to make that decision for me. You're not Vyvyan. I didn't *force* you to heal me. You offered. So, face the consequences of your actions."

I pause, waiting for him to respond, but he remains unreadable. Daemon blood mats his white-blond hair, causing it to stick up in various directions. "You and Vyvyan have nothing to worry about. Your blood flows through my veins, but I will keep my distance if you do. We've done it before. We can do it again."

Vane groans. "Desiree, please, just let this go."

I grit my teeth. Let this go? He made me this way. "No. I'm going home! I'm a vampire. It's where I belong."

Vane's gaze darts around the apartment. "Why can't this be your home?"

A tingling sensation spreads through my chest. I'm not taking in enough oxygen. "This is Wilder's home. Not mine."

Vane groans. "I'm sure if you wanted it, he'd—"

"Why are you doing this? What did I do to make you hate me so much?" I demand.

My whole life has been a cycle of rejection and heartbreak. No matter how hard I try, how kind, smart, or confident I am, no one seems to like me. No one except Jaxson, and now he's gone. People only ever want to use me, or hurt me, just like Vane. He gave me his blood to make me yearn for him, to exert one more ounce of control over me. It's a calculated move, designed to manipulate my emotions and bend me to his will.

But if I bend anymore, I'll break.

Vane's eyes widen. "Hate you? Desiree, I don't hate you."

"Then why push all my buttons?" I yell. "Why keep me at arm's-length, only to swoop in and save me when I'm at my lowest? Why keep me from the one place I am truly meant to be?"

He leans closer, reaching out as if to console me, but then hesitates, letting his hand fall back to his side. "Because I'm afraid, Desiree."

I scoff. "What . . . are you afraid of me?"

He closes his eyes, taking a deep breath. "Yes."

The air leaves my lungs. "Why?"

"I have a strict set of rules I follow, and you manage to break every single one."

Vane's hands claw his knees, and he's beside me on the couch in the blink of an eye. He's so close I can smell the daemon blood mixed with his sultry scent. I should be disgusted, but I find myself inhaling deeper.

"There's something you should know. Something I've kept secret."

I wait, but he doesn't go on. A dull ache spreads.

"Vane, quit mess—"

His mouth crashes against mine, tearing a whimper from my throat. Time freezes and so do I. I'm too shocked to respond, until his tongue brushes against lips, seeking entrance, demanding submission. My heart whispers a warning. But I cave, parting my lips, allowing him entrance.

Tears prick my eyes as our tongues tangle in a sensual dance. His taste is as intoxicating as I remember, a heady elixir that makes my head spin and my soul sing. The blood bond makes him act this way, and my traitorous heart wants to pretend it means more than it does.

Whatever. I'll enjoy it before I let myself regret it.

I crawl into his lap, straddling him. My thighs tighten around his hips, my core pressing against his growing hardness. The need to be closer consumes me. Vane crushes my body against his, his hands roaming over my hips and waist. My starved body blossoms for his touch. I roll my hips, causing us both to groan.

"Faster," Vane begs. "*Please.*"

I continue my slow, taunting movements. He doesn't deserve to get what he wants. But the second Vane's teeth brush against my neck, against *his* mark, a white-hot fire ignites within me, burning away my anger, leaving only a raw, pulsing need.

No, my mind screams, even as my body arches toward him, betraying my resolve.

"Vane," I breathe, the name a prayer on my lips, a confession of my weakness.

"I've fantasized about this for so damn long," Vane whispers with his hands on my breasts. "Every time I saw you, all those tight little dresses you wear and that barbed tongue of yours—"

I lick his throat, nibbling and sucking, as a groan rumbling from deep within him as I mark him. *He hurt me.* The thought flickers, a dying ember in the inferno of sensation. We're chest to chest, the friction of my clit against the hardness in his pants building, building. *He betrayed me.* But the words are meaningless now, lost in the rising tide of pleasure. *He* . . .I can't even remember what I was going to think. All I can feel is *him*.

"Unbutton your shirt," I demand, fumbling with the buttons. Impatience gets the better of me. I tear the fabric open, revealing his beautiful chest.

"I liked that shirt," Vane pouts.

"Boohoo." I circle my tongue around his nipple, the inferno between my legs burning brighter with each swipe. I grind against him harder, needing, *craving* the friction. The thought of being naked, skin against skin, sends a molten rush through my entire body. He sighs happily. "Take me," I whisper against his skin. "Now."

I've had a hell of a night, and the heat of his body, the way he's looking at me, the barely contained hunger in his eyes, is sending me spiraling.

His desire wraps around me, tight as a coil, and my own mirrors it, escalating until it's the only thing I can feel. At this moment, sex is the only answer, the only language I can understand. If I don't have him now, I might just explode.

I reach for my bra, but Vane's hands are already there. The straps fall away, and I pull the confining fabric off, gasping at the sudden freedom. His gaze burns into me, and his hands are on me instantly.

"Exquisite." With one hand kneading my flesh, his other hand unbuttons my jeans, and dips inside my panties. He finds my wetness, then moans low in his throat. I'm on fire. I haven't burned this hot since the last time he took me to his bed. A flash of memory. Hurt. Anger. Then his fingers on my clit. Pleasure. So much pleasure. I forget. I surrender.

My breath catches. His fingers . . . *Gods, his fingers.*

"I crave you like this," Vane murmurs. "At my mercy."

Just as I'm about to beg for release, Vane whispers, "I love you."

My heart stops. What am I doing? This is the same man who cast me aside without a second thought. The same man who chose Vyvyan over me every time. "No." The heat, the urgency, the desperate hunger—all vanish, leaving a chilling emptiness in their wake.

Vane lifts a dark brow. "No?"

"I'm not falling for this again. Stop messing with my head!"

How could I be so stupid? I am letting him touch me, letting him get under my skin. *Again.*

Mortification engulfs me. I retreat, arms crossed, longing for the shield of clothing. *Idiot.*

"I never wanted to hurt you," Vane says as I rise off him. He reaches for me, fingers trembling. "Desi, please. Believe me."

I grab a blanket. "Believe you? How can I when all you do is hurt me?"

"What about tonight?"

I laugh. "Tonight meant nothing."

I lift my chin, wrapping the blanket around me like armor. Vane's chest rises and falls. His hands clench into fists. "If that's how you feel, then I will see myself out."

"I hope the door hits you."

Hurt flashes across Vane's face. "Goodbye, Desiree. You won't see me again."

My heart lurches painfully in my chest, and for a split second, I consider reaching for him. But I force my hands to stay at my sides. A voice screams in my head to stop him, but pride locks the words in my throat.

Without a second glance, he walks out the door. I stand there, stunned, his words echoing in my mind.

He would probably love never seeing me again, especially after I just drank his blood. But too bad for him, I'll see him at the Nest tomorrow.

After what the Balam said, I'm pretty sure I know who attacked Vyvyan.

CHAPTER FORTY-SEVEN
WILDER

I SLIP my phone into my pocket after Soter's early morning call, a knot forming in my stomach. He'd updated me about a fire in Tsilah Cemetery and rumors of daemon activity, but right now, I'm grateful to focus on something else. Leigh's train arrives soon.

I know Leigh will be furious about Stellan's article on Fynn. But she needs to see past her anger—there's too much at stake for the Nebula. That's what this meeting is about. If the two of them can drop their grudges for five damn minutes and focus on Aurora. . .

These thoughts collide in my head like stray bullets, a chaotic mix of dread and determination. Distracted by my racing mind, I exit my room and immediately run face-first into Brigid. She gasps, losing her balance, and I barely manage to catch her to keep her from falling.

"Woah, sorry," I say, steadying her.

Brigid laughs, but there's a bitter edge to it. "In a hurry to get Leigh?"

"I don't want to be late." I retreat into my room. She follows me.

We haven't spoken in person since before she sent those damning texts about Stellan's article and Leigh. She believes Leigh knew about Fynn, but that's because she wants to think the worst about Leigh to justify her hatred for all Epsilon. If she's here to try and convince me that Leigh is bad news, I don't want to hear it.

Brigid sighs. "Am I not worth five minutes of your time?"

I sigh, sensing she won't let me leave until she says what she came here to say. She's in a dress instead of a uniform—something she only ever did when trying to impress me. "Is there something I can help you with?"

Brigid dangles a pair of car keys before me. "I thought I'd offer my

company. She probably has a lot of luggage. My car has all that room."
Brigid smirks, her eyes glinting with a suggestive look. A blatant attempt
to remind me of her car's spacious backseat.

I clench my jaw, unamused by her transparent efforts to worm her way
inside my head. It's a cheap move, using our history to manipulate me. I've
made it clear I've moved on, and her constant attempts to undermine my
current relationship only piss me off. I'm not interested in her or revisiting
a closed chapter of my life.

I narrow my eyes at the keys. "I am good. Thanks."

I need time alone with Leigh before the meeting. We've been keeping
secrets from each other, and it's time we confronted our lies. I love her and
want to clarify that I'm there for her in every way, not just physically. We
need to talk honestly about our relationship and where we stand before
facing Stellan. I don't expect Brigid to understand.

Brigid frowns. "What's your problem? I thought we were friends."

"We are, but you clearly want more," I reply.

"That doesn't give you the right to treat me like trash. Unless you are
afraid of being alone with me." A sly smile plays on her lips as she toys
with the locket clasped around her neck. She never takes off her mother's
belongings. Brigid's mother disappeared when she was seven years old.
Up and vanished, and no amount of Blade resources have been able to find
her. Her constant need for affection might directly result from being
abandoned at a young age.

"Brigid. Stop."

She grips her keys tighter. "Tell Leigh to return to Borealis. Take Stellan
up on his offer. She's not right for you."

I grit my teeth. "This conversation is over."

"You're making a mistake." Brigid crowds me. I shuffle back. "Think of
what backing Stellan could mean for you and your family." She purses her
lips, her eyes taking in the sparse furnishings. "Being a Blade isn't enough.
You're made for bigger things; Stellan can help you, not Leigh. Only a
Nebula can understand another Nebula."

I shake my head. Stellan's heart is in the right place; I respect his call
for more opportunity for the Nebula. But he can't deliver on that promise

without support. Leigh *can* be that support. Keeping the country together is my top priority.

I take a deep breath. "Brigid, it's over. Let it go."

"You were the one who said she was a grenade with the pin pulled," Brigid snaps. "Remember, you said that she was a disaster waiting to happen your first week here?"

I wince. Over a year ago, the night Leigh's family was killed, I found her lying bloody and bruised in the earthquake's devastation. Despite her injuries, she clawed at me. She spat that I couldn't help, and I took it personally. Her rejection cut deep—not because I was angry, but because it confirmed my deepest fear: I wasn't good enough for someone like her. A Blade would never be worthy of a royal. I felt inadequate, insignificant.

When I arrived in Aurora the next morning, I told Brigid and the others some not-so-nice things about her. But I was unfairly channeling my insecurities into harsh words. The moment I saw Leigh again more than a year later, despite everything I'd said, I was drawn to her like a moth to flame. All those feelings of inadequacy were still there, but so was something else—something stronger.

Leigh is not the tyrant Brigid wants her to be.

"I did say that, but—"

A gasp pierces my ears, and I follow the sound, my heart breaking when I see Leigh standing in the doorway, her mouth slightly agape. She overheard my admission about calling her a disaster, but she has no idea that those words came from feeling worthless in her presence, not from genuine dislike. She doesn't know how her actions that night affected me, how they made me question my place in this world.

I move toward her, desperate to explain, but she shuffles back, her eyes wide with what I suspect is hurt and confusion. I blink, shaking my head, trying to make sense of the situation. How is she here already? She wasn't supposed to arrive for another hour.

"Leigh, let me explain," I say. I can fix this. I must fix it before she runs out on me and potentially on Stellan. She needs to know I didn't mean what I said back then. I was a different person. "I don't know what all you heard, but I promise—"

Leigh holds up her hand to silence me. "Is she the girl Moran mentioned that day at Kratos?" She glares at Brigid, whose persistent smile tells me she's relishing in Leigh's anger.

I shake my head, momentarily thrown. "What girl?"

"Your dad mentioned you had a girl in Aurora."

Brigid grabs my arm. "You told your dad about me?"

I run my hands through my hair. This is *not* what we needed to talk about. "Leigh, listen to—"

"Where's Gianna's room?" she asks coldly.

"Across the hall," Brigid answers. "But I saw her in the courtyard."

Leigh nods. "Thanks. I'll let you two finish your conversation." Leigh gives me one last look. It's filled with so much hurt.

I trip over my feet chasing after her. "Wait, Leigh!" We need to talk.

She's keeping secrets, not me. Brigid means nothing to me. My plan with Stellan requires us to be united, but our relationship needs mending. It might not last much longer if she doesn't give me a chance to explain.

"Wilder, let her go," Brigid says, halting me.

"Did you know Leigh's train got in early?" I whirl to face her.

Brigid shrugs. "Papa told me she changed her train reservation to arrive sooner from Mensa Station."

"You make me sick."

Brigid pales. "You don't mean that."

"Brigid, we *were* friends, but right now? Looking at you reminds me of everything wrong in this world."

Her eyes swim with tears. Brigid's been hurt one too many times. But I am no longer supporting her. She believes Stellan will fix all her problems and that his promises of a free Aurora will allow her to get revenge on all those who've wronged her in the past, including her mother. She doesn't see how Stellan's plans won't work without Leigh.

I leave Brigid crying in my room, just as I did when I left Aurora for Borealis in September. But I'm not walking away from a chance at love this time. I'm walking toward it.

CHAPTER FORTY-EIGHT
LEIGH

THE MORNING SUN casts long shadows across Aurora's bustling streets. The scent of roasted chestnuts and spices wraps me in an exotic embrace. Gianna walks next to me, having reluctantly agreed to go on a walk so that we can talk.

After stumbling on Wilder and Brigid, I needed some fresh air. I'm not hiding from Wilder, but I can't face him now. His words stung. He said I was an unpinned grenade, which hit home. I *am* unpredictable, and I've made plenty of mistakes, but honestly, that's not the real reason I walked away.

Seeing him with Brigid devastated me. The look on her face was a painful reflection of my own. She's in love with my boyfriend, and he knows it. He never told me about her, a fact that twists the knife of my own deceit. I lied to him about Alden, desperately trying to uncover Stellan's mole, appease the Council, and find another way before he learned about the proposal.

I'm running out of time. Alden expects my answer tonight. If I'm wrong about Gianna, I might have to marry him to save my country. And the sickening truth is, it's my fault. My lies have backed me into this corner. My desperation. My stupidity.

Wilder will forgive me for walking away from him today.

He won't forgive me for agreeing to be Alden's wife.

I won't forgive myself.

Nor will I survive if my actions push him back into Brigid's wide-open arms.

No, this ends now.

I stride purposely down the street lined with towering date palms, Gianna beside me and Isolde training behind. I glance at Gianna, but she's barely met my eyes since we left the garrison, and my jaw hardens. If she's Stellan's mole, I don't know how I'll handle it.

After the events of last year and the terrible things I said about her and Fynn at their engagement party, I thought we had moved forward when we both admitted our secrets to one another—her being a Nebula and me being a Lunar Witch. We have a rocky past, but at the end of the day, she's my closest friend. No matter how bad things have been, we've always found a way back to each other. But this? I am unsure how I can get past it. It also sucks because part of me wants her to be the mole just so that I can move forward with my plans. We'll deal with the aftermath when shit hits the fan.

"What did you want to talk about?" Gi asks.

I release a forceful breath. I practiced what I would say to her on the train and concluded that if she told me the truth, I would do my best not to get angry. But dammit, I am pissed. Gianna's been through so much, and I understand the lengths a person might go to for information about their family. I raised a daemon to get Eos to give me the War Letters and almost killed Wilder in the process. This self-sabotaging dynamic between us needs to stop. We're practically siblings, the closest thing either of us has to family, and we need to remember how much we care for each other.

"We've been through a lot together," I begin. "I understand why you did it, if you did, but I need you to tell me the truth and stop. Please, too much is at risk, and I am running out of time and options."

Gianna glances sidelong at me. Color has returned to her cheeks. I hope her time away from Borealis has been good for her. "Stop what?" she asks.

I war between needing to sit down and not being able to sit still. "Have you been telling Stellan stories about me and the Council?"

Gianna halts in the middle of the busy street. So do I.

"*What?*" she gasps.

"You came here to glean information from Stellan about your father. Did you use me to do it?"

Gianna's mouth opens and closes. Betrayal flashes in her gaze, but I hold strong. I've had people lie to my face and smile while doing it. I want this moment to be different.

"Leigh, are you asking me if I am Stellan's source?" she asks.

I nod. "Yes. You live with me. You are friends with several Council members. Stellan has something you want, and I know you are tenacious. So, please tell me because I need to be armed with the truth when I see him in an hour. If Stellan isn't stopped, our government will remain divided, and—"

"Leigh, you are my best friend, but sometimes I want to wring your neck."

"Is that a yes?" The hair on my nape lifts.

"Being queen must not be easy," Gi says evasively. She's about to tell me the truth, and though it's everything I need right now, I am suddenly afraid to hear it.

"You are the queen, the top of the food chain," Gianna continues, "yet you are always watching your back, ready for someone to stab you in it, but that person isn't me. I swear on our friendship. And if that isn't enough for you, you'd be happy to know I've yet to speak to Stellan. The first and only time I saw him was that day in the square before chaos broke loose and Ry dragged me away. I've spent most of my time here, alone, being held at gunpoint, or with Wilder."

My breath hitches. Did she say gunpoint?

"Please, Leigh, I've done some shady stuff, but I'd never intentionally hurt you," Gi says. "You're the only family I've known."

I press my hands against my temples. Goddammit. I believe her.

I've known her long enough to recognize her sincerity. But if she isn't the mole, then who is? Fear grips my heart like a vise. Gianna is my last lead. "But Stellan . . ."

"Stellan has the information I need, but I would never use you to get it. Your friendship and my conscience aren't worth it," Gianna adds.

I drag my nails down my cheeks. "Then who is working with Stellan?"

I see him soon, and my bargaining chip to get him to listen just went out the window.

Gi's attention drifts up the street. "Maybe you should have this conversation with Wilder."

"Maybe," I say, but how can I look him in the eyes? Tonight, I'll likely have to accept Alden's proposal. If I don't, it means war. But Gods, I can't lose *him*. No wonder my grandmother never remarried. Love is a weakness.

Gi shakes her head. "You are so untrusting, Leigh, but neither Wilder nor I have ever faltered in our loyalty to you. Talk to him. He loves you and will listen."

I open my mouth to offer an excuse, a reason why he shouldn't love me. Don betrayed me. My mother lied to me. My grandmother won't even call me back, preferring to hide away in the mountains. But Gianna, my best friend, has forgiven me even after I thought the worst of her. Maybe Wilder will, too. Maybe he can even help me figure out a plan B with Stellan.

Swallowing, I square my shoulders. "So what do you think of Brig—"

Cold metal bites the flesh between my shoulder blades, exposed by my strapless dress.

Gianna's eyes go wide. She throws up her hands as she takes in whoever is behind me, holding me at gunpoint. She whimpers, barely audible over the ambient noise of the city.

"Keep quiet, start walking, and don't stop until I tell you to," a woman's voice hisses in my ear. "Move, now."

I try to glance behind me for Isolde. But the blue-haired Blade is nowhere to be seen.

Gianna walks first, her steps hesitant. I follow. To an outsider, it must look like we are out on a stroll. A few people walk past, their faces a blur of indifference or hidden behind scarves to block out the ever-present sand and dust. No one bats an eye.

"I'm so sorry I brought this danger to you, Leigh," Gi whispers. Somehow, she believes this is her fault. But I know it's mine. Whoever attacked me at the kelpie races must have followed me to Aurora.

Fuck, Janus was right. Being out here in a new city without the entirety of my guard, I've thrown myself into the lion's den.

"Turn here," the abductor commands. Gianna and I obey, turning down a narrow street that must double as a weekend bazaar. Empty wooden stalls line the sides, leaving a walkway in the middle. "Stop here. Now, slowly, face me with your hands high so I can see them. Any funny business, one or both of you will have a bullet between your brows."

I swallow hard. When I turn, I come face-to-face with a woman dressed head to toe in black, a scarf covering obscuring her features. But her eyes—a striking midnight blue—pierce through me.

"You attacked me at the races," I say. It's a guess, but this person and my attacker have similar strong builds.

The kidnapper nods. "I wasn't trying to hurt you."

"You two know each other?" Gi squeaks.

"What do you want?" I ask.

"Isn't it obvious? She's here to murder us," Gianna says.

"Who are you?" I ask. The abductor uses her free hand to unwrap the covering around her face.

I gasp. Marlowe Wilkes, the former Borealis Blade Commander and current fugitive. She's wanted for attempting to blow up the capitol to liberate the Nebula people in Nyx's name. Her face is gaunt, her opalescent skin now suntanned and drawn, but her red hair and sharp features are unmistakable.

A wry smile twists Marlowe's chapped lips. Gianna's jaw drops.

"Wilder's been looking everywhere for you," I say. But of course, she already knows that.

Marlowe shrugs. "It's easy to evade arrest when you taught the people hunting you all they know. And it's good that I found you first because I have vital information about the wolves' strategy."

"What strategy? You mean Prince Alden's proposal or the prints breaching our borders?" I ask. Gianna glances at me, but now isn't the time for an explanation.

"Their plot goes much deeper than a simple proposal or border control issues, Your Majesty," Marlowe says.

I blink. Sunlight reflects off the gun's barrel. "What do you mean?"

Marlowe narrows her eyes. "First, I need your word that you will pardon me for my crimes. I made a mistake with Nyx, but I'm trying to make up for it. To do that, I need your word you won't send me to prison."

I laugh. "You have a gun pointed at my head, blackmailing me by withholding information vital for national security, and yet you want me to believe you've changed?"

"Yes."

My face tightens. "You betrayed Wilder with that bomb. He would despise me if I took away his chance to arrest you."

Marlowe's grin falters. They were close. Closer than commander and subordinate. She was a friend. Her betrayal gutted him. Before he left for Aurora, he'd been tearing himself apart trying to find her and get answers about her betrayal. "My offer is final. And I promise you want to know what I know. Your grandmother's life depends on it."

Time stops. "My grandmother is in Glaucus."

"Is she?" Marlowe taunts.

"Leigh, what the hell is going on?" Gi asks, with her arms still overhead.

"Talk, Marlowe," I growl. My patience is wearing thin. "I'm supposed to be somewhere, and if I don't show up, Wilder will come looking for me. When he finds you, he will arrest you. If you want me to pardon you, you better speak fast. I'll judge whether what you say is worth your freedom and Wilder's ire. Is my grandmother in danger?"

"You need me on your side. I can help, but I need that pardon. Wilder will understand."

"Don't trust her, Leigh," Gianna says, glaring at Marlowe. "Wilder *hates* her."

The former commander grits her teeth. "Leigh, forget about Wilder for a minute and take a second to consider how you need me. Snakes surround you, and the longer you don't see that, the closer you are to being bit," Marlowe says, and my stomach hardens as if she doled out a punishing blow.

She has me backed into a corner. If my grandmother is in danger, I can't risk her life.

I take a deep breath. "Fine. What do you know?"

"The wolves have your grandmother. Prince Zeus breached the northern borders and has Queen Jorina as his hostage. He's in Corona along with a sizable army."

Gianna grabs my arm. Her long nails—needing a manicure—dig into my skin as I gasp.

"Zeus is here. And he has my g-grandmother?" My mind races, connecting the dots. Were his footprints the ones Janus was referencing last night? The thought of my grandmother in the clutches of that monster sends a chill down my spine.

I can barely process the information, my mouth going dry as I imagine the horrors she must be enduring. My grandmother is at the mercy of a ruthless prince. The fear is paralyzing, but I know I can't let it consume me. I must save her, to get us out of this mess.

"Tell me everything. Did you see Zeus?" I demand. "If he is on the move with an army, that means Alden has given them the order to invade. The troops from Lua answer to Alden, the younger prince and enforcer. However, I am convinced that people would have noticed a foreign army crossing into our lands."

Marlowe sighs, her expression grim. "Alden's armies can transform into wolves. Under the cover of night, they could have easily slipped past our patrols undetected. But to pull off an invasion of this scale, it must have been in the works for a long time."

I'm staring without seeing. For the wolves to have entered Corona, Alden must have orchestrated this invasion behind the scenes. He's been lying to me from the start.

A scream bubbles up my throat. Alden's proposal, his charm offensive —it was all a ruse to keep me distracted, to prevent me from noticing the signs of the impending attack. And like a fool, I fell for it, too caught up in my feelings to see that Alden's talk of invasion was not just talk.

"He played me," I whisper. I clench my hands into fists at the shakiness in my voice.

How could I have been so easily manipulated, so willing to believe in a future that was never meant to be? I should have trusted my instincts and seen through his deception from the beginning.

"We need to inform the Council immediately. Zeus could be heading straight for them," I say.

"They aren't," Marlowe tells me. "The wolves are on their way to Aurora. Stellan's been working with them. He is nothing more than a puppet. They are backing his campaign and money-rolling his enclave. In return, he's letting them establish their war camp outside Aurora before marching on Borealis."

"Stellan is working with the wolves?" I ask, but several shouts steal Marlowe's attention. I follow her gaze, seeing an altercation among several men at the other end of the bazaar. They are yelling at each other, and it is evident by how they get in each other's faces that they will go to blows. Soon, the Blades will arrive.

"Time to go." I face Marlowe again, who has put her face covering back on.

Gi gapes. "Leigh, your meeting with Stellan started five minutes ago."

I groan, grabbing her hand. "Come on, we need to get to Furies."

"What are you going to do when you see Stellan?" Gi asks.

I grind my molars to dust. Stellan has some serious explaining to do. Until we talk, though, I can't jump to conclusions. I need his information, the details about Zeus and Alden's army, and confirmation of their arrival time. Only then can I formulate a plan to notify the Council and negotiate my grandmother's rescue.

"Marlowe, are you coming?" I ask.

She nods. "Go ahead. I will meet you there."

I'm looking forward to telling Janus and the others that a wedding with Alden never would have protected us. We've always been vulnerable. It's time we face the truth and take action to defend our kingdom.

LEIGH'S FUCKING LATE.

I check my watch for the umpteenth time, my foot tapping on the floor. The clock above the bar mocks me, its hands crawling at a snail's pace. I'm running out of excuses for Leigh's whereabouts. She's not answering her phone, and Stellan is ready to leave, his impatience evident in the tightness of his jaw.

Stellan sits at a table surrounded by ten or more men, focusing on the door. Alec's lips are pressed into a thin line. She and Meg have done me a favor by hosting this meeting, but Leigh's glaring absence speaks volumes.

Did she go back to Borealis? Or is she lying dead in a ditch somewhere?

I bring my phone to my ear again. My muscles twitch with each unanswered ring. Just as I'm about to hang up, Leigh bursts through the door with Gianna behind her, their faces flushed. Relief fills me to the brim, but there's no time for questions because Leigh is rushing toward me, and anger is burning in her eyes.

"You won't believe what just happened." Leigh grips my arm as if to pull me away, but Stellan's been waiting nearly twenty minutes. Whatever she wants to say, it can wait. I'm not going anywhere.

"Tell me later. Stellan's waiting," I say. Leigh frowns, glancing behind her. I follow her gaze, but there's no one there—Is she waiting for someone?

After the Brigid fiasco, I searched for Leigh, wanting to make things right between us. Instead, I found Bennett sitting with Pallas in heavy silence at the kitchen table. Bennett informed me he would be attending the meeting with Stellan as a representative of the Council. I agreed to find him when it was time to leave. However, I went without him at the last minute. Bennett doesn't need to stick his nose where it doesn't belong. Leigh and Stellan must come to terms with each other before the Council gets involved.

I lead a glaring Leigh toward Stellan.

"Well, this will be interesting . . ." Leigh's words trail off as Stellan rises from his seat.

He grins, and Leigh stiffens in my grasp.

"Your Majesty," Stellan says. Leigh bares her teeth, and I suspect I was right about her coming here to confront him, not to collaborate. But we all *need* to work together.

"Say something." I nudge her. She scowls at me.

Alec meanders around us, cautiously carrying a water pitcher and two glasses. She sets them on the table before Stellan, her hand trembling as she pours.

"Please, sit," I say. "We need to do this for the sake of our people."

She hesitates for a moment, her eyes never leaving Stellan's. I can see the wheels turning in her head, a calculated plan forming behind those fiery eyes. Finally, with a curt nod, she sinks into the chair opposite Stellan.

"Fine," she says, her voice sharp as a blade.

I take my seat beside her, suddenly uneasy. I know Leigh, and I know that look in her eye. She's on a mission. Something happened, something big, and I'm in the dark.

"Thank you for coming," I say to Stellan, keeping my tone neutral. "We have differences, but we all want what's best for our people. Shall we begin?"

Leigh leans forward. "Yes," she says, her voice dripping with disdain. "Let's begin with the truth, shall we?"

"That is my specialty," Stellan replies, challenging.

Leigh snorts. "Hardly. You hide behind your computer, using your keyboard to crumble a regime, but you aren't the brains behind your master plan. You have made a huge mistake."

I blink. What is she talking about?

"By mistake, do you mean creating a safe place for the Nebula people after your people persecuted us for a war we didn't start?" Stellan mocks.

I place my hand on Leigh's shoulder. *Come on, Leigh, work with me.* We all want the same thing.

Stellan reaches for his water glass.

"It's funny," Leigh muses.

"What is?" he asks before taking a sip.

"How do you expect me to believe you are operating with the Nebula people in mind when you're sacrificing the same people you claim to care about to the wolves?"

I balk.

Stellan sits straighter. "How do you mean?"

"Well, first, you are working with Lua to ensure your enclave happens while leaving the rest of us at their mercy. They are on their way here, aren't they? When are they scheduled to arrive?"

A hush falls over the bar. Is she serious? Stellan said he had help, but the *wolves?* What did he promise them? Or what did they promise him?

My hands shake under the table. This changes everything.

If Stellan works with the wolves, he's not just a political opponent— he's a traitor to our people. I glance at Leigh, a tremor coursing through me, fueled by my rising unease. Why didn't she tell me about this before?

I take a deep breath. We can fix this.

"Stellan, is this true?" I ask, my voice tight with anger. "Are you working with the wolves?"

Stellan's eyes meet mine, a challenge in his gaze. "I think it's time we had a *real* conversation, don't you?"

"Yes," I growl through my teeth. "I think it is. But let's be clear. If you work with the wolves, you're not betraying the Epsilon but all of us. The Nebula people included."

"Yeah, Stellan," Leigh snaps, "tell him how they promised you could be king of an enclave if you let them use Aurora as a home base for their *invasion* of Corona."

I gape at Stellan, but he doesn't so much as flinch. "I do not want to be king. I am not your uncle." Leigh scoffs. "I stand by my promises. The New

Aurora will be a democracy. Prince Zeus and Prince Alden gave me their word."

I wait for him to continue, to tell me he's joking, but he doesn't. Is this a nightmare? He's helping another country invade ours to achieve his own ends. He never planned to negotiate with Leigh; by the looks of it, she never intended to collaborate with him either. I suspected as much but held onto the hope that I could convince her. I thought . . .well, my thoughts are irrelevant now. Stellan lied, and Leigh will never forgive him.

"Did you think King Simon or his sons would let you rule unchecked?" Leigh sneers. "You're trading me in for a new monarch who will never trust you."

I stand, turning away from them. How did this go so sideways?

"All I want is a better world for the Nebula," Stellan says calmly.

That's all we all want, not just for the Nebula but everyone. How does inviting a war to our lands achieve that?

"I've reread your articles dozens of times," Leigh says, "trying to unmask the person feeding you information, but I came up short. I even spoke to my uncle to ensure it wasn't him."

The pain in her voice hits me like a punch. She swore she'd never confront Don again. Why didn't she tell me? Is this what she was doing in Borealis behind my back? Did she think I would disapprove? My energy depletes. Will she ever stop keeping secrets?

Stellan huffs a laugh. "My source tried to refuse me because they thought it would be too obvious. But it seems that is not the case." Leigh scowls. He's trying to get under her skin, and it's working.

"Who is it? They deserve to go down with you!"

Stellan grins. "Why? It's too late to get out of your marriage proposal —not that Alden wanted you anyway."

The ground falls out from under me. Marriage proposal? What is Stellan talking about? And why does Leigh look like she's been caught red-handed?

"What proposal?" I ask. Was she considering marrying Alden?

The thought sends a cold wave over me, but I force myself to take a deep breath. We're here to negotiate peace and find a way forward for our people. Whatever is going on with Leigh and this marriage proposal can wait. We need to convince Stellan to call off the invasion before the wolves arrive.

"Stellan." I keep my voice controlled. "When are the wolves set to arrive? Is there any way you can call them off? Tell them you no longer want to pursue the enclave. Tell them you and Leigh will fight if they don't back off."

Stellan's eyes narrow. "I made promises I intend to keep."

I shake my head. "And what about the Epsilon—the civilians caught in the crossfire? Are they just collateral damage in your grand plan?"

Stellan leans forward, his gaze intense. "The New Aurora will be a haven for all, where everyone can live in peace and prosperity. But sometimes, sacrifices must be made for the greater good. The Epsilon have a choice: follow us or be left behind. The wolves are on our side, Wilder. You have nothing to worry about unless you refuse to join me."

A chill runs down my spine. Sacrifices, greater good—this rhetoric has been used to justify countless atrocities throughout history.

I glance at Leigh, hoping to find an ally in this fight. But she's still reeling from Stellan's earlier comment, her eyes distant and unfocused.

"Where is Zeus? Did you know he took my grandmother?" Leigh asks him.

Stellan smiles. "I understand you are worried about her safety, but so long as you agree to their terms, Queen Jorina will remain safe, I'm sure."

"And if I don't, are you saying they'll kill her?"

Stellan clears his throat as Meg gasps. "It's been a pleasure, Your Highness, but our time is up. I am sorry it had to be this way. You seem nice, just born into a difficult circumstance."

Stellan motions to his men and thanks the Erinye sisters for their hospitality. His footsteps echo as he strides toward the door.

Panic rises in my throat, its coppery tang sharp on my tongue. I have to stop him. But he brought a dozen armed men with him. He came prepared, while I had not.

"Stellan—" I start, but Gianna steps between him and the exit. Her short frame is no match against his much larger one. Stellan blinks, surprise flickering across his face.

"Move, girl," he growls, but Gi stands firm, her chin lifted in defiance.

"You are making a mistake," she says.

Leigh rises to her feet. "Gi, don't," she warns, but Gianna ignores her, her gaze locked on Stellan.

Stellan scowls at Gi. "I disagree. Epsilon like your father—"

"*You* are my father. And as your daughter, I am begging you not to do this. Don't turn your back on Leigh. You can't trust Zeus," Gianna declares.

The room falls silent.

I grip the chair, staggering from the impact of Gianna's words. Stellan is her father. I had assumed he had information on her father's identity because of his role as a journalist, not because he was the man himself.

Stellan stares at Gianna, his eyes wide with shock. His mouth opens and closes as he struggles to find the right words.

I stand there, my world rocked to its core. Stellan betrayed us, Leigh betrayed me, and Gi kept the truth from me. I am an idiot for believing I could fix things.

I look at Leigh, searching for some sign of remorse, some hint of the woman I thought I knew. But her eyes focus on Gianna and Stellan, and her expression is unreadable.

Did she know about this? Was this another secret she kept from me, another lie in a long line of deceptions? What is left of my resolve disappears. I trusted her and believed in her, and now I don't know what to believe anymore.

Stellan has a daughter, an Epsilon-raised daughter, which somehow changes everything and nothing simultaneously.

Stellan's face crumples. For a moment, he looks lost, like a man adrift in a storm-tossed sea. But then his expression hardens, and he shoves past Gianna, his movements jerky and uncoordinated.

"I have to go," he mutters.

"Wait!" Gianna cries, but Stellan's guards block her from getting to him. The door slams shut behind him with a sense of finality.

The following silence is deafening, broken only by Gianna's soft sobs.

Leigh slumps back into her chair. "That was a disaster," she murmurs, and I can't help but agree. But it's her fault, too; her secrets and lies have brought us to this point.

"You could have tried harder," I snap.

"*Me?*" Leigh laughs, the sound hollow and acidic. "Did you not hear me? Zeus has my grandmother! Stellan's helping him!"

I shake my head. "How do you even know that?"

The door opens, and I expect to see Stellan standing there, maybe with a change of heart, but I jerk back as if I've seen a ghost.

The sudden onslaught of rain has made her red hair longer and plastered to her face. Instinctively, I summon fire to my palms. "Marlowe?"

Marlowe offers me a smile. I see red.

The last time I saw her was at the Domna Trial. She had plans to blow up the capitol. After I forfeited the competition, she'd skipped town, knowing I'd leave that arena and come for her. She abandoned Nyx's cause and left her scruples. I shake my head, not believing that she's here to turn herself in. She wants something.

"Wilder, before you do anything stupid, you should know I am here to help you," Marlowe says.

The fire in my palms flares brighter, the heat licking my skin. "You betrayed me. You made me believe I could be Domna and we would fix things together. Instead, you just planned to use me to aid in a terrorist attack. You knew Chiron kidnapped Leigh and locked her in that vault, yet you said nothing! *Why?*"

I trusted her, believed in her, and she used that trust to further her agenda, to manipulate me into becoming her pawn.

"Tell me," I demand, searching for a glimmer of the person I once thought she was. "Tell me why you tarnished everything we stood for. Tell me why you are here now."

"I saw no other option to make things right for the Nebula," Marlowe says, running a hand over her face that's lost some of its fullness. The dark bags under her eyes tell me she's been troubled these past few months.

Some of the fight drains out of me. "None of us knew what the letters said. You kept things from me, Wilder, like how you and Leigh had teamed up with Chiron to find the letters. Even though I was in charge, I also expected more from you."

I scoff. She can't fault me for her actions. "I should arrest you."

"I am under Leigh's protection. She gave me immunity in exchange for the information about her grandmother and the wolves."

I look at Leigh. She pardoned Marlowe? My girlfriend is a stranger.

"Wilder, Zeus has my grandmother. Marlowe told me about Stellan's duplicity."

"Believe it or not, I am here to help," Marlowe argues.

"This is un-fucking-believable!"

Leigh flinches.

"Save your freak out for later," Marlowe begins. "While outside, I overheard some of Stellan's men talking. The wolves are here. Zeus and his brother's troops arrived an hour ago. Stellan's gone to see them."

Leigh's mouth hangs open. More tears fill Gianna's eyes. The sisters swear.

Wolves in Aurora? I am living in a goddamn fucking nightmare.

"I need to warn Eddo and the other Blades," I say, my voice steady.

Leigh stands. "I'll notify the Council."

I nod, pushing aside my resentment for now. "Good. We don't have much time. If Stellan and the wolves join forces, it could be too late. We should move fast before they can consolidate their power."

Determination hardens their expressions. Even Marlowe is ready to fight, though I am hesitant if we can rely on her. She may run again the second things don't go in her favor.

"Let's go," I say, resolve strengthening. "We have a city to save."

We'll deal with our personal issues later. Right now, Aurora needs us.

CHAPTER FIFTY
LEIGH

WHEN WE BURST into the Aurora garrison, the heavy wooden doors slam against the stone walls with a bang that startles several uniformed Blades and their leader, Commander Eddo.

The commander takes in our rain-soaked clothes and worried expressions. "What the hell happened to all of you?" Eddo asks over the distant thunder rattling the windows.

I eye the Blade Commander. Wilder can bring him up to speed. I need to find a phone charger to call Janus. I need to tell her Lua invaded and have her order Soter to detain Alden at the palace before he becomes aware I know about his brother being in Aurora. If we can use him as leverage, we can avoid going to war altogether. It's a risky plan, but our best chance at preventing bloodshed.

"Did you know Stellan had an agreement with Zeus Lupas?" Wilder asks, marching straight to the commander in the large foyer. Eddo's eyes widen.

I peel off my sodden jacket and say, "I need a phone charger, or can I borrow someone else's phone? Mine is dead."

"I knew Stellan had friends in high places," Eddo says, scratching his head, "but I swear I didn't know it was Zeus."

Both he and Wilder ignore me.

"I knew," Brigid says smugly, entering the room.

I roll my eyes. Of course, the girl trying to steal my boyfriend knew about Stellan's misdeeds. How trite.

Pallas appears by my side and hands me his cell phone. "Thanks," I mutter.

"You realize that's treason, right, Brigid?" Wilder asks. Brigid sighs.

I don't stay to hear the rest. My footsteps sound harsh as I walk toward the courtyard for privacy. Once there, I dial Janus's number with trembling fingers, praying she picks up.

I shut my eyes as fury directed at Alden and myself fuels me. I knew he would betray me, yet I allowed it to happen by foolishly believing I could outsmart him. My fists clench. Alden will pay for his treachery, and I will see to it that he answers for every lie, every false promise, and every moment he spent deceiving me.

The call fails, and I sigh, redialing Janus's number, when I hear stomping to my left.

"You fucking bitch!" Isolde charges Marlowe.

Gianna grabs Isolde's shoulders, stopping her.

"Release me," Isolde demands in a growl. "She is a wanted criminal. She also attacked an officer!"

Marlowe frowns at the bloody gash on Isolde's forehead. "You should see a healer for that wound, Faez."

Isolde throws her weight against Gianna, but Gianna pushes back. "You can't touch her. She's under Leigh's protection."

"You better be joking," Isolde says to me.

I clutch my phone tighter. The phone stops ringing after the first ring, and Janus's sharp voice fills my ear. "Hello, this is President Janus Dyer."

"Janus. It's Leigh. We need to talk," I say. "I just found out that—"

"Ah, I heard the good news. Congratulations," Janus warmly interrupts.

I blink. "For what?"

"Your engagement. When I spoke with Alden, he told me he would travel back to Lua to share the good news with his father."

"What? There's no engagement." My knuckles turn white around the phone. "Did he leave?"

But then Janus speak in a hesitant voice. "Yes. Not long after you—he and Ravi left together."

Black dots dance in my vision. Alden left Borealis. He is on his way here to join his troops. If he left after me, he's probably *already* here. I lean against a pillar for support. My terrified expression reflects in the puddle of water at my feet. "Did he say anything else? Anything about his plans or intentions?"

"No. Leigh, you're scaring me. What's going on?"

"You shouldn't have let him leave!" I exclaim. "Zeus invaded Corona, using Alden's troops. He is here in Aurora, and they have my *grandmother*. Alden was distracting us this whole time." I gasp. "I told you he was bad news!"

"You can't trust Alden," Ravi told me his first night here. Did Ravi know what Alden planned to do this entire time? I need to talk to him. Maybe he knows what Zeus is planning. I wasn't willing to listen before, but now I am.

"Zeus likely wouldn't have invaded if you had agreed to Alden's proposal," Janus replies tightly.

I gape at the phone. "Are you serious? If that was the case, they would have waited until I refused him to move their troops. Did you not hear me? They're *here*, in Aurora, already. They've made their base camp here." If we had negotiated for peace, like I'd wanted, maybe we could have found something to appease Zeus. But no, the Council insisted on falling for Alden's farce of a marriage proposal and focused all their attention on that.

I watch a Blade with curly blond hair enter the foyer, heading straight for Gianna as she converses with Isolde. He says something that makes Gianna's eyes widen before they flicker to me. The temperature in the room drops.

I take a deep breath. "We need to figure out a plan on how to handle Zeus and Alden. Stellan is with them, which means they know I am here, too," I tell Janus. I'm sure they'll reach out to ask for our surrender before they officially enter the city. I want to have a plan before I receive Zeus's summons. "You need to call an emergency war meeting with the Council."

Janus sighs, and the sound grates on my already frayed nerves. "Leigh, there's no time for that. If Alden is joining his troops, their next plan must be to march on Borealis. I need to prepare. If the capital falls, so will the country."

I want to throw the phone across the yard. "Make time, Janus. What about the innocent people in this city?"

Bennett charges toward me, his eyes are slits behind his glasses. "Where the hell did you go?"

I hold up a hand, indicating I'm on the phone. He can be pissed at me for leaving him out of the meeting with Stellan later. It was a colossal waste of time, anyway. Stellan had no plans to work together.

"Leigh, we need to talk," Gianna says to my right. I eye the curly-haired Blade at her side before covering the mouthpiece on my phone with my hand.

"I am on the phone with the president," I say as Bennett seethes beside me.

"It can't wait," Gi insists.

I close my eyes, willing myself the patience to deal with one fucked up situation after another. "Janus, give me a second," I say before muting the call. Then I turn to Gianna. "Yeah?"

"Ry just got back from scouting," Gi says, gesturing to the Blade.

In a deep voice, Ry reports, "The wolves are indeed in Aurora; they've set up camp on the outskirts of the desert, just three miles shy of the train station."

My mouth grows dry. They are closer than I thought.

"It's worse," Gianna adds, her voice wobbling. "They've taken Stellan prisoner."

"I thought they were working together?"

"So did we, but someone reported seeing a man matching Stellan's description being blindfolded and taken against his will. The call came into the precinct an hour after Stellan left Furies. I don't think it's a coincidence."

Did Stellan's usefulness expire? Or was this part of a larger plan?

"Leigh!" Janus's voice screams from the phone.

Fuck. I take her off mute, my hand still trembling as I bring the device back to my ear. "Yeah?"

"I need to address the Council, then the city," Janus says.

"Don't go yet. I just learned they're camped three miles outside Aurora.

The city will fall if we don't act fast. We need to send more Blades to Aurora."

Janus gasps, followed by prolonged silence. When she speaks, her voice shakes. "Leigh, we can't afford to saturate our army. You focus your efforts on Aurora, and I will focus on what needs to be done everywhere else."

"We need backup," I say. "How are we supposed to convince the wolves to leave if we don't have a strategy against them? They will take the city, and they'll take me as their prisoner."

Janus curses. "If that's true, then the Council and I will figure out how to get you back."

"But I am the queen. I should be involved in your decisions with the Council to keep Aurora safe. Someone working on the Council still has ties to Stellan and the wolves. We need to be cautious."

"Yes, well, you're not here," Janus snaps. "You ran off to Aurora alone, against our wishes. Your inability to listen has cost us greatly, Leigh. It pains me to say this, but I will hold a vote of no confidence in your favor so that you don't interfere with whatever we decide to do. I understand someone on the Council may be working with the wolves, but I will deal with that *my* way. We've already tried yours."

My lungs feel as if they've shrunk. It sounds like she's kicking me off the Council.

"You're going to vote me out?" I ask.

"It's nothing personal and, hopefully, temporary," Janus says.

"B-but I'm the queen." I can't believe my ears.

"And as the president, my duty is to my people. It might be too late for Aurora, but Borealis has a chance."

Tears fill my eyes. I can still save my kingdom and people if they listen and give me a chance, but with the Council casting me out, they will turn their backs on me when I need them most.

"Janus, you're making a mistake," I rush to say. "If we lose Aurora to the wolves, we lose valuable resources. You might as well give Borealis to them as a gift, complete with a pretty bow, and hand over the kingdom without a fight."

"Maybe so, but I can try to devise peace negotiations with Alden and Zeus," Janus declares. "Since Alden likely knows you're in Aurora, I suggest you have Commander Eddo take you someplace safe. I will contact him soon."

"You can't do this. I am the rightful ruler of this kingdom. I must protect it."

But even as the words leave my lips, I know they're futile. Janus has made her decision, and I can do nothing to change it. I'm over a thousand miles away. If I'm going to save everyone, I need to do it on my own.

I need to contact Ravi.

"Fine," I make myself say. "You are in charge." I hang up.

"What did she say?" Gianna asks, but I have no words.

"Leigh," Bennett snaps. "We need to talk."

"Bennett, not now."

My pulsing strides thunder as I race up the stairs to Wilder's room.

CHAPTER FIFTY-ONE
WILDER

I GLARE AT BRIGID. Is there anyone I can trust to tell me the fucking truth anymore?

"You knew Stellan was working with the wolves, yet you still supported his plan?" I ask.

Her face is ashen after hearing from Ry about the wolves betraying and capturing Stellan. "We thought . . . we wanted to believe that after everything we've endured since the First War, our luck was finally changing. We wanted to believe that the wolves would be allies."

"Are you really that naïve?" I scoff. "Aurora is too valuable. It has the Corona's richest resources. The wolves wouldn't give it up."

Brigid's eyes dart away from mine. The wolves are just outside the city, and they have Queen Jorina as a hostage. If we survive this, I will do whatever it takes to ensure Corona bolsters its borders.

"Do you know what Zeus promised Stellan to get his enclave?" I ask her. "Do you know anything about his plans from here?" When she doesn't answer, I grab her arm, my grip firm but not painful. "Come on, Brigid, talk to me. You'll be doing Stellan a disservice if you don't tell me what you know."

Brigid swallows hard, her hands trembling. "Stellan met with Zeus months ago. They struck a deal to make a free state for all Nebula in exchange for his allegiance."

My stomach churns. Prince Zeus used Stellan's fight for freedom against him. But why target Stellan specifically? There are bigger players Zeus could have approached. But then it hits me—Stellan isn't a politician. He's an orator.

The pieces start to fall into place. The wolves used him as a mouthpiece to sow discord and division within our country, ensuring we were vulnerable before their attack.

"Stellan is a good person, and he is smart. He thought the wolves were the answer to gaining our independence," Brigid says. "Please, Wilder. We need to get him back. I'm afraid of what they might do to him."

I clench my jaw.

"We will figure something out," I promise after a few moments. "But you're going to help me."

Brigid nods. "What are you thinking?"

"We need to know where Stellan got his information about the Council," I say. "Do you know who his source is?"

Brigid's eyes glint. I hold my breath as she points. "Him."

I follow her gaze. "*Bennett?*" But even as I scoff, I realize it makes perfect sense. His family has been in politics for ages. He dated Leigh. He worked with the Magician as part of Eos. He's slimy as sin.

"Yes," Brigid says. "I recognize him from the news. Stellan was so pleased when he told us he had the queen's ex-boyfriend on his payroll."

My jaw hardens. "Is that so?"

Bennett locks eyes with me. He slowly backs away. I smile because there's nowhere for him to run in this city. At least, not where I won't find him.

"Yes," Brigid says.

"Then, if he enjoys talking so much, we get him to continue doing just that," I say, stepping around Brigid. Bennett turns on his heel and runs.

Let the hunt begin.

CHAPTER FIFTY-TWO
DESIREE

IT'S EASIER SAID than done to slip back into the Nest undetected, but I do. I've been gone a handful of days, and no one notices or talks to me. I am nothing but a memory, but that's about to change.

With purposeful strides, I head for Vyvyan's chambers. If my instincts about her attacker are correct, I could leverage my way back into living here.

As I round the corner to Little Death, two vampires clad in leather hover near the entrance. I turn my face to hide behind my hair.

"Vyvyan's in a mood," one of them remarks, and I slow to listen.

"She's been in a mood," another responds with a hint of exasperation in their voice.

The first vampire leans in, lowering their voice, "Yeah, but I heard her tell her guards to give her space. She never asks for space."

With a shrug, the other vampire explains, "Vane's missing. Again."

A shiver racks my body, a cold dread settling in my bones. Has he truly abandoned the Nest? Is that why he said I would never see him again?

A sharp pang of longing pierces me, a painful reminder of what I've lost. I tell myself it's for the best. Now, bound to him by blood, carrying a piece of him within me, his presence would be a constant torment.

I felt the truth in his words when he said he loved me, a fleeting warmth in the glacial wasteland of my heart. But I force myself to dismiss it. If his love were real, he wouldn't have left. I repeat, I'm better off without him, even though his departure leaves a gaping void.

"Figures," one of the vampires continues. "Those two have the strangest relationship."

"I'll say. She's brooding over him in the throne room."

Their laughter dances through the halls as they disappear into the club. I circle back to the throne room.

I find Vyvyan alone, perched upon her throne of skulls with her cheek resting in her palm. The towering flames in the large black clay fire basins behind her crackle and pop, casting monstrous images upon the walls. When she looks up, my steps falter.

Her eyes are red again. Vane must have turned her back into a vampire, which means the effects of consuming my blood can be reversed. Maybe this means she'll hate me a little less.

"It's good to see you looking like your usual self," I say.

"You've got some nerve coming back here," she replies through gritted teeth.

"We need to talk."

Vyvyan raises an eyebrow. "I have nothing to say to you."

As I approach her throne, I avoid the trapdoor to the Eurynomos's lair. Just a few months ago, my brother stood on that door before falling into the pit to face the daemon for Zev.

"You will want to hear what I have to say," I tell her.

Vyvyan glances behind me. "Where's Vane?"

I shrug, ignoring the ache in my chest. "You're his sire, so you tell me."

Wait, is she? Technically, he's her sire now.

Vyvyan clicks her tongue. "Watch your sass, Desiree. My guards will have you detained and dismissed with a single word from me."

Despite my eternal loyalty and belief in her refuge for misfits, she has inexplicably despised me. But if I'm right about the Balam, I can prove my loyalty to her.

"I know who summoned Balam," I say.

Vyvyan's eyes narrow. "Trying to worm your way back into my good graces?"

I swallow my laughter. Good graces? She had me scrubbing urinals.

"I have no reason to lie," I say. "I just want to come home."

"I'm listening."

430

"It was you. You raised the Balam the night of the blackout, and you staged the attack inside your bedroom."

Veins stand out in Vyvyan's neck, and my adrenaline spikes. I must be right.

Everything clicked last night. During our confrontation, the Balam referred to its summoner as a "she." Vane's sudden appearance to rescue me and insistence that I do not return to the Nest made it clear he was protecting someone. Who else would he shield if not Vyvyan?

"I don't care why you did it," I add quickly. "I'm sure you had your reasons. I won't tell anyone. I want to come home."

There's a beat of tense silence, then Vyvyan says, "You're right. And do you want to know why I did it?"

I gasp, and Vyvyan sits straighter. Her beautiful face lights up with a cruel smile.

"For the vampires, but especially for Vane."

I don't dare say a word.

"You see, we've survived over a century without the help of witches," Vyvyan continues, her voice dripping with condescension. "The witches forced us underground, then later began killing us to harvest our tears."

I swallow hard, my mouth too dry.

"Together, Vane and I persevered," she continues. "We turned these tunnels into a city. But there had to be rules. No one went up to the surface without permission, and Vane did not, under any circumstances, sire any progeny."

A knot forms in my stomach as Vyvyan's words punctuate my eardrums.

"We were strongest, just the two of us. . . until you came along." Vyvyan's eyes narrow with hatred. "Vane's sensitive. He has been struggling with the idea of eternity for some time now. Nothing I did made him happy anymore. Then you stumbled into our club, and suddenly, Vane acted like his usual self, but it had nothing to do with me and everything to do with you."

The pieces fall into place. She staged the attack to drive a wedge between Vane and the surface world. She wanted to blame the witches and give Vane a reason to retreat underground with her again. The wolf tracks weren't part of her plan – they were an unexpected complication.

"He defied my orders, broke all the rules," Vyvyan continues. "When he Turned you, he came to me in hysterics—not because he betrayed me, but because he feared for *your* safety. You'd become a target as part of our family, third in line for the vampire throne."

My knees buckle. Vane went to her for help, fearing the consequences I would face. If true, it counters the monstrous image I've built of him.

"My distaste for you began when I understood Vane's love had shifted. Sharing his affections, particularly with someone as pathetic as you, wounded my pride and heart."

My mind reels. How can it be true that Vane loves me when he treated me so horribly?

"I had him devise a plan to bring you into the Nest, but to lie about your sire," Vyvyan reveals. "To ensure you wouldn't come near him, I told him he had to break you. Otherwise, you'd never give him up."

A sob catches in my throat. She manipulated Vane during his most vulnerable moments.

"When he began disappearing again—likely to escape the pain of seeing you, knowing you hated him—I devised a plan to bring him back, but this time for good. I summoned the Balam, intending to blame the witches and force us back underground, safe from their influence, where we could be happy. But your poisonous blood interfered, ruining everything."

I understand it all now – her fear of change, her desperation to control Vane, her desire to recapture what she fears she's lost.

Vyvyan flashes her fangs as she rises from her throne. "Which is why kicking you out of the Nest wasn't the answer. You must disappear. For good."

I stumble back. "What, you are going to kill me?"

I shake my head. Vane left. He looked me in the eye and walked away. If he's the obstacle between Vyvyan and me, his absence should clear the path.

"After everything—after all my loyalty—this is how you repay me? With a death sentence?" I ask.

Vyvyan shrugs. "It is for the good of the coven. Your blood is deadly."

Vyvyan may look human, but the humanity inside her is long gone.

"I trusted you. I believed in your promise of a home for outcasts. But now I see the truth. You're no better than the monsters you claim to protect us from."

The witches feared the vampires because we were different. Now, Vyvyan's doing the same to me.

"Your blood could lead to mutiny, Desiree."

Vyvyan snaps her fingers—a sound like the crack of a whip.

Her guards burst into the room and surround me. The remnants of my heart plummet with the knowledge that I'm going to die here, in this very room.

Part of me wants to beg for mercy. But a spark of defiance ignites within me. I won't go down without a fight. If I do, I might as well roll over and plunge a stake into my own chest.

I sprint toward Vyvyan. She hisses and plants her feet, but I have no intention of engaging her in combat. I launch myself at the lever that controls the trapdoor to the Eurynomos's pit. I pull with all my might, and the stone floor splits open, revealing a yawning abyss.

With a silent prayer on my lips, I leap into the inky darkness and the slim chance of survival it offers.

I hit the ground hard on my right hip. The jarring impact sends shockwaves through my body. The pit is a grim tapestry of stone, sand, and the remnants of those who came before me, their bones splintered and scattered.

Above, Vyvyan peers over the edge of the pit.

"Give it up, Desiree," she calls out. "I'll make your death quick."

Trembling from head to toe, I raise my hand, and flip her off. Then, I set my sights on the depths of the pit where Eurynomos resides. There must be another way out. Failure is not an option. I will claw out of this hellhole if necessary.

Engulfed in darkness, I limp forward, to search for an exit.

Every rustle sets my nerves on edge, the fear of the Eurynomos constantly lurking in my mind. Time crawls until, after what feels like an eternity, I find a trapdoor—a glimmer of hope. I knock, praying that someone is on the other side.

"Let me out!" I shout, pounding my fists against the barrier. The Eurynomos might hear, spurring me to bang even harder, desperate to escape before it arrives. Maybe it's been watching me all along, waiting for this moment of vulnerability, this breaking point, before it attacks.

"Desiree?" a familiar voice asks.

"Zev?" I gasp. He's Misty's sire, and Misty is not my biggest fan right now. "What are you doing here?"

"I was going to ask you the same thing," he replies.

"I need you to let me out," I plead. A long pause follows, and my breaths turn ragged.

"How'd you get in there?"

"I jumped."

"What happened?" Zev asks, almost sounding concerned.

"Please, Zev, let me out before the Eurynomos come," I plead. I whimper from a distant sound.

"It is resting," he reassures me.

"How do you know that?" His stare doesn't waver. I gasp. "Are you its handler?"

"Yes. Vyvyan's poetic justice after disobeying her."

Tears prick my eyes again. Zev betrayed Vyvyan by aiding my brother's Blade investigations and communicating with his wife through Wilder. Vyvyan, in her insatiable need for control, punished him for it. Her rules are meant to keep us safe, but they also bind us, ensuring our obedience.

"Please, let me—"

The door opens, and Zev appears, bathed in faint light that accentuates his inky hair and kohl-lined eyes. I squint, adjusting to the brightness, revealing a part of the Nest I've never seen.

"Thank you," I gasp out.

Zev nods. "You're lucky I was down here."

"Which way to the surface?" Vyvan's guards are likely searching for me.

Zev points left. "That way, but Vyvyan has the entire coven hunting for you."

Something inside me deflates. I'm a fugitive in my home.

"But I know another way." Zev takes my hand, his soft touch jarring. "Come with me."

I hesitate. Can I trust Zev? Do I have a choice? Noticing my reluctance, Zev meets my gaze. "Your brother saved my life. I owe him. I'm your friend."

Friends are scarce these days. I nod, putting my life in Zev's hands, and pray I haven't just made a fatal mistake.

CHAPTER FIFTY-THREE
DESIREE

WHEN WE EMERGE from the hidden tunnel beneath the Iron Parthenon, I'm engulfed by Equinox Park's bustling energy. Witches spill out from the evening service of the Iron Parthenon, laughter and chatter grating on my ears. The tall towers reach the heavens.

No one pays much attention to the steady trickle of people entering and exiting Little Death beneath the Parthenon's catacombs, a significant change from how things were before Leigh took the throne. But given Vyvyan's need for control, and fear of the witches, I doubt our two species will coexist much longer.

"Thank you, Zev," I tell my vampire companion. He shrugs, eyes glinting with sincerity. "Can I pass along a message for Maureen?"

"I didn't help you to receive something in return," Zev replies.

My spine bows. He risked severe punishment to help me.

"How did you know that tunnel led up here?" I had no idea another entrance existed within the park.

Zev smirks. "Vane showed me. He had a vision and said I might need it one day. Guess that day was today."

Just when I think I've heard it all, Vane surprises me. Again.

Could he have anticipated my need for help? Cared enough to intervene? Yesterday, the thought would have been laughable. But after last night, and after what Vyvyan just told me. . .I'm not so sure anymore.

"Are you and Vane close?" I ask, but fail to keep my tone casual.

Zev laughs. "Jealous?"

I shake my head. Vane could be miles out at sea. Yet, his blood sings in my veins, clouding my judgment, whispering temptations to seek him out and demand his version of Vyvyan's story.

Zev laughs again. "Relax, Desiree, Vane is all yours."

"We aren't . . . Vane and I . . ." The words catch in my throat. I don't owe Zev an explanation. "Thank you again. I hope you don't get into too much trouble."

"It was the right thing to do." Zev's gaze softens. I turn away, but Zev catches my arm. "Right now, you may feel alone, but that will change. Misty will come around. She misses you."

I disappear into the trees before more tears fall.

Alone, with nowhere to go, I wrap my arms around myself, as if to hold together the fragments of my pitiful life. Everything I thought I knew was a lie. The truth crashes over me like a tidal wave, dragging me under, threatening to drown me in despair. The Nest, the future I'd envisioned there, the foolish dream that once included Vane by my side . . . it all shimmers in the distance, like a mirage, taunting me with its impossibility.

I wish Wilder were here to tell me everything will be okay, but he's thousands of miles away. Dads in prison, and Mom is the only person left in this city genetically programmed to give me the time of day. I desperately need guidance on what to do next. Where do I go from here? I need her to tell me. I need her.

✪

The bustling atmosphere of Hebe Hospital engulfs me as I step through the main doors, bypassing the busy reception area. Suddenly, a hand grasps my arm. My breath catches, and I expect to face one of Vyvyan's guards, but it's a woman with curly black hair and ill-fitting scrubs.

"It's Desiree, right?" she asks, glancing down the hall at the male security officer. He starts our way.

Fuck. I'm not here to make trouble. "No. Sorry," I mutter, trying to step around her.

The witch slides in front of me. "You aren't supposed to be here."

I blink. "I'm visiting someone. Doctor Chiara Dunn." I shoulder past her.

"I'm sorry, but Doctor Dunn ordered you be kept away," she says, keeping pace with me.

My eyes bulge. My mom did *what*?

No. I must have misheard. She couldn't have just told me I'm barred from the hospital. The idea is preposterous. It is . . . exactly the kind of thing Mom *would* do if she thought I was a threat.

"But I'm her daughter," I say.

The healer shrugs. "Sorry."

The security officer casts a long shadow over us. His uniform is too tight. "Is there a problem here?"

I meet his menacing gaze. "No."

The healer's eyes dart between the officer and me. "This is Desiree Dunn. She was just leaving."

The officer's hand clamps down on my arm. "I'm escorting you out, Miss Dunn."

I dig my heels into the shiny floor. All I need is five minutes of my mom's time. "No, I—Hey! Release me!" My screech ricochets through the corridor.

"You don't need to make this more difficult. Doctor Dunn insists you maintain distance for your safety and that of others," the officer says. I wrench free from his grasp.

"Why?" I demand, shuddering. The memory of Mom's face at the party flashes before my eyes. She looked at me like I was a stranger. Someone dangerous.

"To protect Doctor Juliette Bird," the healer says.

Red flares at the edges of my vision. Juliette has finally succeeded in ruining me. She turned my mom against me. I *need* to see my mom.

With a burst of supernatural speed, I dash to the elevator, slipping inside just as the doors begin to close. My finger slams against the button, and I watch the floors tick by while my stomach sits heavy in my throat. I need to make Mom see the truth about Juliette. I'm not the villain here.

On Mom's floor, I hurry down the long corridor, my gaze on the ground. The black-haired healer and security guard have likely announced my arrival. Time is slipping away.

Mom's lab is easy to locate. Her name is prominently displayed on the door. As I step inside, the automatic lights flicker to life. The room is empty, but Mom's work surrounds me—books, research papers, and a square box draped with a thick cloth.

I decide to check the sign-in boards to find her when a fluttering noise catches my attention. My brow furrows. It's coming from beneath the fabric.

Hesitantly, I approach the box. The rustling gets louder. With a wavering hand, I pull the cloth away, revealing three small bats inside. But these are no ordinary bats; their eyes glow red—vampire bats.

I stagger back, horrified. These must be the bats Mom has been experimenting on, while I keep the truth hidden.

I am the key to ending vampirism. But I don't want to be.

The loudspeaker at Hebe Hospital crackles to life, and my name echoing through the halls. "Attention all staff and patients! Be on the lookout for a dangerous, dark-haired vampire named Desiree. She is on the loose within the hospital and considered a threat. If you see her, alert security immediately."

Each repetition of my name feels like a physical blow. Soon, every person in the hospital will be searching for me. Before I face my end for the second time tonight, I need to find an exit. But I am not ready to leave just yet.

The vampire bats rustle in their cage. I step closer.

"It's wrong to keep you locked up against your will," I tell them.

Vampire bats don't harm anyone; they aren't dangerous. It's a stereotype fueled by their differences.

I wince at the devastating parallel between their lives and mine.

With a scream that shatters the stillness of the lab, I sweep my arm across the countertop, sending Mom's research flying. She abandoned me when I needed her most. Beakers and burners crash to the floor. She cares more about this hospital than she ever did about me. I confront the board of her formulas, pick up the eraser, and wipe it clean. If not for Wilder, my childhood would have been a game of solitaire.

The bats squeak excitedly, their leathery wings fluttering in anticipation.

I work through the rest of the lab, leaving chaos in my wake as I prop open the refrigerator doors filled with temperature-sensitive samples.

I need my mom to feel my pain. I'm not being subtle. She will know it is me, but I don't care. It's not as if I will ever come back here.

Finally, I unlatch the metal cage and stand at the head of the room, watching the vampire bats pour out of the now-open window, their silhouettes vanishing into the night sky. At least, they get a second chance.

Tears stream down my face as I turn to the wreckage. It doesn't alleviate the pain. If anything, the pit inside me deepens to a miserable black hole.

Backing away from the destruction I've wrought, I race down the emergency stairs, and burst out onto the street with the hospital alarm blaring behind me.

As I run, I have no clue where I am going. I have no home, no support system. Nothing.

I *am* nothing.

CHAPTER FIFTY-FOUR
LEIGH

SEATED on the floor in Wilder's dark bedroom, I gaze at images from his past. Charcoal drawings of his friends—Brigid, the Erinye sisters, and a smiling Ry—adorn his walls. These people were a considerable part of Wilder's life before he met me. They all supported Stellan's plans to liberate the Nebula from Epsilon rule—my rule. The realization stings.

You haven't lost yet, Aradia's ghost reminds me.

She's right. I haven't.

I close my eyes, block out the world, and focus on breathing. I will astral project to Ravi and compel him to reveal what he failed to tell me all those days ago inside my throne room. He may not tell me anything, but if the mutual understanding we've built over these past few days means anything to him, he'll tell me the truth. How do I defeat Alden's armies?

With adrenaline coursing through my veins like liquid fire, I picture Ravi—his dark stubble casting shadows across his soft jaw, his haunted eyes holding untold secrets, and his tense physique. Pain sears my chest. We're more alike than I thought.

Ravi's voice meets my ears. "Leigh?"

I open my eyes to find myself in a drab tent with lumpy rugs underfoot. It's spacious, if not stifling. Outside, the sun is setting, and its orange rays filter through my astral form, causing me to emit a ghostly, translucent emanation.

It worked.

I stalk toward Ravi. "You let Alden deceive me. Why?" Hurt thickens my throat. "I thought you considered yourself my family."

Ravi's expression tightens. "Leigh, you shouldn't be here." His dark eyes dart toward the closed tent flap. Muffled sounds of conversation and laughter filter through from outside. "What if I hadn't been alone? You're taking a huge risk."

"An inescapable risk," I say. "I need answers. What game are you and Alden playing?"

"Alden and I are not friends," Ravi says. My mouth snaps shut. I didn't expect him to be so willing to talk. "While Zeus prepared the invasion, Alden agreed to distract you while he familiarized himself with Borealis. Alden doesn't care about conquering Corona like Zeus does. He wants vengeance."

I hesitate. Vengeance for what? Alden wasn't alive when the wolves last invaded Corona and failed.

"I never meant to hurt you, Leigh," Ravi says. "And I hate the part I played in Alden's deception, but I had no choice."

"You always have a choice," I bite out.

"Not when family is involved." He rubs his eyes; they glint with unshed tears. "My sister is Zeus's prisoner."

I gasp. "How?"

Ravi's voice is heavy with emotion. "Sama and Zeus were intimate, and she falls in love easily, always seeing the world through rose-colored glasses. She thought her heart was safe with Zeus and that she'd have a second chance of being a princess with him. So, she confided in him about our ancestry. But, as I knew he would, Zeus betrayed her and told his father, who ordered Alden to take Sama as their prisoner to jumpstart his war."

"I went to Nocturn Castle, searching for her, but they apprehended me, too. They told me they would free Sama if I helped them deceive you."

Ravi's gaze meets mine. "I agreed only because I thought I could deceive them instead. I hoped that if I told you my identity, you might help me save Sama. But you hated me from the moment we met. I realized I would never win your trust. From then on, I decided I couldn't risk Sama's life by betraying Alden. I gave up trying to convince you, but I didn't give up wanting to know you."

Gods, I made a terrible mistake. A prickling starts behind my eyes. If I had been more trusting when I met Ravi, all this could have been avoided.

I had fixated on Alden, thinking I could handle the Wolf Prince while weeding out foes within my Council. Ravi warned me about him, but I didn't listen. I had focused on Janus as the traitor after that dream, but my inability to reenter her dreams now casts doubt on everything. And Gianna . . . how could I have suspected *her*? The biggest misstep was closing myself off to Wilder, when being with him is all I truly want.

If I hadn't been so guarded, so consumed by my fears and insecurities, I could have shared what I saw in that nightmare. I could have collaborated with others, uncovering these plots before they took root. Instead, I isolated myself, choosing the path of most resistance, convinced everyone around me would eventually betray me, just like my uncle.

"What does Alden's invasion have to do with vengeance?" I ask.

Ravi rubs his eyes. "You remember Tanith?"

"Alden's mate who died?"

"Zeus is responsible," Ravi says. I cover my mouth to quiet my gasp. Alden left out that part of the story. "Zeus and his father had their eyes on Corona long before the king fell ill. They watched as your father and brother died, and when you disappeared for a year, only to return after President Sinclair's death without claiming the throne, they sensed weakness."

Shouts erupt outside the tent. Ravi brings a finger to his lips, then cautiously opens the tent flap just a crack. I hold my breath as he peers outside. Satisfied to find nothing, he lets the flap fall back into place, then resumes his position on the cot before me.

"Zeus urged Alden to make a move on Corona, claiming it was their father's dying wish to expand their territory. But Alden, wrapped up in love with the gentle Tanith, refused to leave her to go to war. Enraged, Zeus lured Tanith into the woods and had her ambushed by rogue vampires to remind Alden of his place."

I shake my head, horrified. "Did they . . ."

"They didn't kill her, but they turned her into a vampire," Ravi states, his voice tinged with regret. "Unfortunately, werewolf DNA rejects the vampire gene. They don't maintain an ounce of humanity. Tanith might as well be dead. Zeus convinced Alden that Vyvyan was to blame, since the vampires who attacked Tanith slipped from her control. Alden came to Borealis to find Vyvyan and enact his revenge."

Chills erupt through my body, goose bumps prickling my skin. I think of that first night at Little Death. Alden claimed he had gotten lost in the tunnels, but now, I see it was a lie. He was scouting for Vyvyan.

"But if Zeus is the one who set the vampires on her, why wouldn't Alden blame him?" I ask.

"He doesn't know," Ravi says simply. "Zeus threatened to kill Sama if I told him."

"We need to tell Alden the truth." My mind drifts toward the cure, hope fluttering in my chest. Chiara received the funding she needed to continue her research. If I asked for a favor, could she expedite her research?

"The truth won't change that Tanith is a vampire. She might as well be dead."

"What if there is a way to change that?"

If I can convince Alden that there's a way to save Tanith and prove to him that Zeus is the one to blame for her attack, then we might avoid war altogether.

"Where's Alden now?" I ask.

"Sleeping," Ravi says, though the sun has barely set. "It was a long journey."

"I have an idea."

Like an invisible lasso tied around my waist, a sudden tug yanks my spirit back to my body before I finish. I gasp as if taking my first breath, finding myself back inside Wilder's room.

"Leigh." Wilder hauls me into his arms, sagging against the bed, and drawing me down with him as if terrified to let me go. My heart clenches at the intensity of his care, so different from the emptiness in his eyes when he looked at me back at Furies.

He expels an audible breath before adding, "I couldn't wake you, and . . . fuck, I feared the worst."

I clutch him back, wanting to soothe the lines above his brow. He didn't lose me; I am still here, and if he still wants me, I will tell him everything. "I'm sorry for scaring you." But I am not sorry I did it.

"Where did you go?" Wilder asks.

I pull away from Wilder's embrace and notice we aren't alone.

CHAPTER FIFTY-FIVE
DESIREE

AS THE MOON SETTLES OVERHEAD, I kneel in the frozen dirt. Winter rain falls like a cascade of tears around me. The scent of damp soil and dry grass fills my nostrils. Before me, the inscription etched into my headstone reads: *"Desiree Dunn, beloved daughter, sister, and gifted healer, taken from us too soon until we meet again."*

The words blur as tears well up in my eyes, their weight bearing on me. Would all this be easier to stomach if I had indeed died? Maybe it would be better if I were dead-dead now.

No one would miss me. Wilder is busy with Leigh. Jaxson is finally living his life. My death would hurt him, but after what happened outside Mom's house, it wouldn't haunt him like before. Mom would pour her grief into her research, incurring more of Vyvyan's wrath. Vane—wherever he is—would be free of me.

I fist the muddy grass, and the icy rain intensifies as if punishing me. Tilting my head back, I allow it to wash over me, cooling the hot tears streaming down my cheeks.

Suddenly, the onslaught stops. My eyes flutter open, and I find myself beneath a large, batwing-style umbrella. The umbrella's cane rests in the hands of a man dressed in black standing opposite my headstone.

"Vane," I whisper. He doesn't smile as the rain dampens his hair and clothes. I struggle to swallow. "How are you here?"

"Someone has to keep you dry," he murmurs.

More tears spill down my cheeks. I never expected *him* to be the one showing up for me in this, my darkest hour, especially after how I pushed him away. Suddenly, Vane crouches before me in the mud, heedless of his fine clothes. The umbrella becomes a shield, blotting out the world.

I meet his red eyes, which are so warm I melt inside. "Why did you come back? You shouldn't have—" Another sob breaks free. I'm not worth his concern or pity.

Vane catches my tear on his index finger. He studies the iridescent bead, his brow furrowed. "I felt your pain," Vane admits, his voice low.

My mouth falls open. Does that mean he's been in Borealis this whole time? "Vane, I . . ."

Something unreadable glimmers in his eyes. "Come." Vane stands with his hand outstretched toward me. "I want to show you something."

I hesitate, glancing between his hand, and the headstone that bears my name, a silent reminder of the life I once had—the life I can never reclaim. Then I reach for his hand, allowing him to pull me to my feet and lead me away from the grave.

As we navigate the cemetery, the ancient trees loom over us, their gnarled branches creaking in the wind. We pass the mausoleum where Balam attacked me, its entrance now sealed with yellow caution tape. Without Vane's intervention, I would have joined the ranks of the forgotten dead, forever bound to this place. I squeeze his hand in thanks, and he offers me a half-smile, likely sensing my gratitude.

We venture deeper into the cemetery's older section, where the headstones become more weathered. Their inscriptions are barely discernible beneath the thick layers of moss and grime. The ground beneath our feet is spongy from the tears of countless mourners. Vane abruptly stops before two graves. One has a crack running through its center, rendering the name illegible, while the other bears the name "George Auchincloss" in faded, worn letters.

"My parents," Vane declares over the howling wind. The pain in his tone is palpable. Whatever happened between him and his parents, time has failed to heal the wounds.

"Your last name was Auchincloss?" My brows lift, and a sudden, inappropriate urge to laugh bubbles within me. "Vane Auchincloss?" He glares sidelong at me. I stifle my laughter, clearing my throat. "Vyvyan's name suits you better."

"Vane Alvise Auchincloss," he clarifies with a melancholy pride. "They named me after my maternal grandfather. He was a good man, and I was proud to have his name. Still am."

"Is he buried here, too?" My gaze sweeps over the surrounding graves. I want more of a glimpse into the enigma that is Vane.

Vane shakes his head. "He was a merchant Sea Witch. He never returned from his final voyage." There is a slight tremor in his voice, and I ache to take his hand. I can't reconcile the man who has treated me with such cruelty with the man bleeding emotion in front of me now.

"My grandfather was the only one standing between me and my parents," Vane confesses. His shoulders are round. "They were gamblers and used their gifts to manipulate emotions and trick people out of their money. When my abilities manifested, they forced me to join their schemes, exploiting my empathic powers to cheat. Despite his ineptitude at cards, my father used me to read his opponents, to know when they were bluffing. What he earned in riches, he equaled in enemies."

My hands clench into fists at my sides. What kind of father would use his son in such a despicable manner? "What about your mom? Did she do nothing to protect you?" I ask.

"She was too devoted to him," Vane replies, a bitter smile playing at the corners of his mouth. "She endured his cruelty long before I did."

Anger dries the tears on my cheeks. "What was her name?"

A flicker of warmth passes over his features. "Antonia. They say she was the most beautiful witch in Borealis."

I study Vane's profile. I believe it.

"Then why did she marry George?" I ask, unable to conceal the disgust in my voice.

"They were in love," Vane murmurs. "Love has a way of making you do things quite out of character." His attention flits to me, then back to the graves.

"Poor Antonia," I whisper.

Vane laughs. "Don't cry for her. In the end, she poisoned his money with arsenic."

"She what?" My gasp makes Vane chuckle.

"There's more." Squaring his shoulders, he turns from his parents' graves. As he walks away, I cast one final glance at the resting place of Vane's parents and offer a silent prayer for Antonia's troubled soul and one last "fuck you" to George. Then I hurry to catch up with Vane as he strolls up the path, entering an area so heavy with grief that even the air seems to stand still.

"This is where Antonia had me figuratively laid to rest."

I glance at him, finding his gaze focused on the graves before us. My brow furrows as I say, "But these graves are unmarked."

"Yes," Vane answers on an exhale.

"But why—" A cold dread settles in my core. "Is it because you were a vampire?"

He nods. Then his gaze bores into mine with an intensity that weakens my limbs.

"A group of thugs my father pissed off in one of his schemes beat me to an inch of my life. Vyvyan found and Turned me. When my parents found out, they refused to admit what I was or pay to make funeral arrangements for me like your mom did for you. Still, my mom brought flowers weekly to this grave until she died."

Vane's grief, a deep, resonant sorrow, strikes a chord within me through the blood bond. It's an unusual ache, the unmistakable lament for a lost mother. I ease closer, my heart heavy, and stare at Vane's grave, struck dumb that despite the century that separate us, we are buried in the same earth, united by this shared place of mourning.

Looking toward my headstone, guilt pierces me. Despite their frequent absences, my parents mourned me. They loved me. The understanding cuts me like a shard of glass. Just as Antonia loved Vane fiercely and protectively, despite his father's cruelty, my parents loved me, even though I never truly understood it. And I repaid their love with the ultimate deception—my fabricated death, a gaping wound in their lives that I carved myself.

"Why are you showing me this?" I lift my face to Vane's. Why is he sharing these intimate details of his past with me after nearly a year of lies? Even when I believed we were happy, he kept his past guarded.

His eyes fill with an emotion that takes my breath away. "I kept these details from you about who I was and where I came from because of the pain my past brings. I would have died if Vyvyan hadn't Turned me. I owed her my life," he admits. "But I am done following her rules. I once thought I would have no one if I didn't have Vyvyan. But then, I met you."

I nod, frowning at the mention of Vyvyan. That viper dangled details of Vane's supposed feelings for me like a bloody lure, then tried to kill me. He's here, yet my racing heart silences me. Did he really make me lie about siring me to protect me? I can't bring myself to ask if my suspicions were true. Another lie would crush me.

He takes my hand. "Desi, after bringing you to the Nest, I tried to keep my distance for your own good. I wanted you to have everything you were denied growing up. I was awful to you because I was furious with myself. No matter how I treated you, I still wanted you." His voice cracks. "I was terrified of what would happen to you if the others knew about us. I thought that you'd be happy by keeping my distance and making you hate me. You'd have friends. But I couldn't stay away. Your scent, your beauty . . . it was like a drug. I saw myself in you. That night, you wandered into Little Death, I had to have you. And letting you go has been the hardest thing I've ever done." He pauses, his gaze intense. "You are a dream that terrifies and tempts me whenever I close my eyes. The pull to be near you is beguiling. Your control over me makes me hate myself because I should have held you close, but I let you go. I am sorry for everything. And I will do everything I can to earn your forgiveness."

My lips part. His confession stirs too many emotions in me at once.

I pull free from his grip. His touch clouds my senses. "What are you saying?"

He exhales. "From that first meeting, you have made me feel things that no one—not even Vyvyan—has ever made me feel. I never should have Turned you. I *knew* what would happen if I did. I knew Vyvyan would be pissed and that she would make your life a living hell. But I also knew if

I didn't turn you, you would make someone else do it, and I couldn't bear the thought of someone else being your sire. It was my selfish mistake, and everything I feared came true. I made Vyvyan think I hated you, even though it was tearing me apart because I knew it was the only way she would let you have a normal life in the Nest. And it *worked*, Desi. You made so many friends. You seemed so happy. That was worth it, even if it tore me apart."

My chest quakes. It's everything I want to hear, but there are still parts of our history that don't make sense. "Okay, so after Vyvyan told everyone about us, why didn't you stand up for me?" I ask. "If your words are real, why were you still so cruel to me? You made my best friend hate me by telling Vyvyan secrets about me."

His left hand tightens around the umbrella. His knuckles turn bone-white with the force. "Desiree, please."

I shake my head. He let me take the blame for our relationship alone, leaving me to face the consequences while he remained unscathed.

"Why did you tell me about Nyx's bomb, then?" I press.

"Because I knew it would break you if something happened to Wilder."

"Yet Vyvyan took her anger out on me for leaving the Nest that night—*just* me!"

Vane's expression darkens. "You're wrong. She punished me, too."

"Oh, yeah, how?" I don't recall seeing him clean toilets.

"By hurting you."

Silence falls, heavy between us. My heart is beating so fast I'm dizzy.

"Vyvyan is my family; we've been together for over a century, but it has taken me decades to realize her deep fear of loneliness and rejection drives her to control those around her."

My hand clutches my chest as it caves. I want to believe him and trust in his words' sincerity, but the last time I did, he broke me.

"Everything I did in the Nest—the ignoring, the pushing you away—it was all to keep you safe. I see now how wrong I was. I should have just claimed you, Desi. You *are* mine. Even if it meant isolating you from the others, they don't matter. Only you do. That's why I told Vyvyan those things. She would have suspected something if I hadn't." His voice drops, heavy with regret. "I also hoped . . . that if you left the Nest, maybe we could be together. That place isn't home to me anymore. *You* are my home. I'll go where you go. Forever."

The rain intensifies, a torrent against the umbrella, mirroring the tempest in my head. He's telling the truth. The blood bond vibrates with his sincerity. Tears prick my eyes, hot and angry, but beneath that anger breathes understanding.

I shift closer, my fingers curling around his neck, needing to touch him, to believe. He leans into my touch, a silent plea for forgiveness. And the crushing weight of loneliness lifts for the first time since Misty and I shared those last laughs in the Little Death bathroom.

His methods of protecting me were misguided, but Vane's intentions were pure. He thought he was giving me what I wanted when all I ever needed was him—someone who accepted me for who I am.

I once believed that living at the Nest and having Vyvyan's acceptance were the only ways I'd ever feel genuinely happy, but that isn't true. Vyvyan's bullying tactics, which I succumbed to, were merely a means for her to oppress Vane and me. I also let Misty treat me cruelly after I made the mistake of lying to her instead of giving her the space to come to terms with my actions.

Fear of hurting those around me has always been a driving force, causing me to prioritize their happiness over mine to maintain peace. I've been tormented one way or another my entire life, and I am sick of it. Taking control of my life, without the fear of angering the wrong individuals, is a step I am determined to take.

I'll take a page from Jaxson's book and move forward. Any sane person would run after how Vane treated me, but who said I was sane? I fell in love with a vampire, for crying out loud.

"I love you." I've only ever said those words to Jaxson. I meant them then, just as I do now. But this is different. Through years of isolation and mistrust, Jaxson protected me, but Vane pursued me, fought with me, and now wants me to accept myself and show the world who I truly am, jagged edges and all.

"I've been in love with you since that night at my loft when the Blades came. It's why your actions hurt me so badly," I confess. Vane frowns, but I cup his cheek. "I'm willing to forgive you if you make it up to me."

"Anything you wan—"

I rise on my toes and press my lips against his. His taste is a heady elixir.

Vane returns my kiss with a tenderness that makes my soul sing. The connection between us resonates with a sense of belonging, a home I've never known. In this moment, the Nest, and everything in it, ceases to matter.

I slide both arms around his neck, pulling him closer. I need to fuse his flesh with mine. Vane's hard body presses against me, eliciting a groan from my lips. He drops the umbrella, freeing his hands to explore my face. His fingers thread through my wet hair before sliding down my body. In one fluid motion, he lifts me. I wrap my legs around his waist, desperate to be as close to him as possible. Vane's fangs graze the sensitive skin of my neck, sending shivers of pleasure raining over me. I arch into his touch, every nerve ending in my body awakening at his caress in a silent plea for more.

Our lips collide in a fury of tongues. The cemetery fades into nothingness. A deep growl from Vane's chest is my only warning before he peels off my leather jacket. I rip off my shirt, exposing my black bra, skin, and skirt to the elements and his blown-out gaze.

We collide, a tangle of limbs and desperate need. Hands roam, mapping familiar landscapes, seeking solace and reassurance. The world outside mirrors the storm within, ice pellets stinging my skin as the sky descends into a brooding black.

Vane lowers me into the dirt, the cold mud a welcome relief from the burning heat between my thighs. He settles between them, his weight a welcome pressure. My hands work feverishly, ripping his coat away, and the gold buttons from his shirt. A possessive sound escapes my throat at the sight of his sculpted torso. Each plane, each defined muscle, is a masterpiece I yearn to explore with my hands and tongue, devour and memorize.

Vane's hand slides between my legs, cupping me, sending shockwaves of pleasure radiating through my center. My spine arches, a helpless offering. I shudder, aware of my wetness, the slick heat mingling with the rain that sheens my skin, turning me into a living, breathing invitation.

"I know you love me, but I want you to fuck me like you hate me," Vane commands, his voice low and husky. I gasp, a broken sound torn from my throat as his fingers expertly play me like a finely tuned instrument responding to his every touch. My eyes fly open as he withdraws. His impatient fingers find the flimsy barrier of my underwear. He rips them away with a single, sharp tug, discarding them into the mud and rain. The sound of his zipper follows. His pants get caught around his ankles. A moment later, his crown probes my entrance. I writhe as his lips graze my earlobe. "I'm about to defile you in a cemetery," Vane whispers. "Where *are* my manners?"

I gasp, pushing my hips into his, inviting more than just a fraction of him inside me. It's enough to unleash the beast lurking beneath Vane's polished surface. He buries himself to the hilt. I scream at the intrusion. But he gives me no time to adjust, setting a brutal pace as he drives into me again and again.

"I . . . missed . . . you," Vane admits between thrusts. "Each day since I last had you, I imagined it was you instead of my hand."

Vane's words coat my thighs with more arousal. "I thought of you, too," I confess, my throaty voice barely recognizable. "Each time I was alone . . . touching . . . mm . . . myself."

"I know," he growls, and I stiffen. "I could—" He adjusts his position. We groan. "Feel your desire as your sire."

When his touch detonates that spot, molten heat floods me. I buck, desperate to take him deeper, to be stretched, molded around him. His relentless tempo fuels the fire until my orgasm crests. His fangs scrape my neck, a sharp, exquisite bite, and a litany of curses rips from my throat, loud enough to wake the dead.

Vane draws back to look me in the eye. "Look at me, Desiree."

Ecstasy has me in its clutches, but I pry my eyes open. "Keep your eyes on me when you come."

"Oh gods." My legs shake uncontrollably, my entire body quaking beneath him. My moans splinter apart, fractured by the overwhelming pleasure that overtakes me. Vane smiles, a predatory gleam in his eyes, as he watches me break before him, reveling in my surrender.

As the tremors of my orgasm subside, Vane continues to drive into me, a savage, possessive force that echoes our hate-filled sparring matches. He finally stills as he empties himself inside me, his forehead pressed against mine, our breaths mingling in the damp air. The rain hasn't stopped, drumming against the branches twisting above us, but the world feels washed clean, renewed.

My hands caress the tight, rippling muscles of his back. "That was perfect."

He kisses me. "You are perfect."

We stay locked together, lost in the afterglow. Kissing, touching, and tracing the lines of each other's bodies as if we had all the time in the world. And then, with a sudden, breathtaking clarity, it hits me: we *do*.

"Get dressed," I say, and Vane quirks a dark eyebrow. "We are leaving the city."

Vane studies me as if I am a different person. "Really?"

I kiss him again, slow and deep. "Let's see the world," I whisper against his lips.

Vane unsheathes himself. I rise on my wobbly feet to retrieve my ruined jacket. Dirty and the evidence of our cemetery tryst dirty my thighs. "On second thought, let's make a pit stop at the loft first."

Vane laughs. "Only if we can use the empty apartment while there."

I bite my lip. "Thank you for coming back," I say.

Vane kisses me and my entire body sings. Which direction is up? He's turned my world upside down. "I'm the one who is thankful, Desiree. That after everything, you are giving me a second chance."

I place a hand on my hip. "Who says I am? Maybe I'm just using you for sex."

Vane gives me a purely carnal look. I yelp before sprinting through the cemetery toward the loft with him chasing me.

CHAPTER FIFTY-SIX
LEIGH

CHIARA DUNN'S research is the answer to ending this war. We need to move quickly now that the sun has almost set. I reach to grab Wilder's arm and tell him this, but he has turned away from me. Before I can blink, he's marching to Bennett, who is cowering, cornered by Brigid in the back of the bedroom, his wide eyes darting to the door.

Wilder clamps a hand on the back of Bennett's neck like he's subduing a puppy, and I gape at him. "What are you doing?"

"Bennett has something he wants to tell you," Wilder growls.

I shake my head. I need to act while Alden is still napping. "Can it wait?"

"I'm Stellan's source," Bennett bursts out.

I blink once, then twice, my thoughts scrambling. Not Bennett, not again. He had already proven he wasn't the person I thought he was when he sided with Eos in October to get me an audience with the Magician. Then, he lied about Corvina, and now, he admits to being Stellan's fucking source. If this is a dream, somebody better fucking pinch me because I don't know how Bennett and I will get past this. We barely managed to do so before.

"Explain. Now."

"Corvina and I aren't dating. We work together," Bennett begins. His gaze flicks to Wilder, who frowns. His disappointment in Bennett mirrors mine. "Shortly after you rejected my proposal, she and I started talking." He pauses, swallowing hard. "We bonded over the sting of rejection from you and your brother. But later I discovered she sought my friendship because of Stellan."

I freeze, and each of my muscles tenses like a snake.

"Corvina introduced me to Stellan," Bennett continues in a rush. "They work in the same field, and she started feeding him pieces of information her editors passed on that were deemed too salacious for print. But they needed someone to corroborate their stories about the Council—someone whose word could not be doubted, so Corvina came to me. She told me working with Stellan would be worth my while. I swear, Leigh, I never intended to hurt you."

"But?" I prompt through gritted teeth.

"I've tried to talk to you about this before, but you never listen to me." Bennett's voice is so dense with emotion that chills brush over my skin. He tried to tell me? "When the guilt of helping Stellan became too much, I wanted to confess everything to you. The night of the blackout, I was ready to tell you the truth, but you were too focused on your problems to hear me out."

He inhales a deep breath, trying to compose himself. "I've been having nightmares about what would happen if you were deposed, and it terrified me. I wanted to come clean, to tell you what I'd done, but you never gave me a chance. When you asked me to spy on Janus, I agreed because I knew there was no getting through to you otherwise. It was a way for me to watch you without raising suspicion. It eased my guilt about lying to you."

My hands ball into fists. He told me he wanted to talk at the Council meeting before the blackout. Did he intend to come clean about Stellan then, only to be scared back into submission by Corvina's text? I should have pushed him to talk to me. Instead, I'd been consumed by that text from Corvina. I let it bother me more than it should. Still, I was right to suspect foul play. Corvina pushed him to become Stellan's source. But I pushed him into hiding it from me. If I had listened, maybe we could have avoided this mess.

"What did Stellan promise you?" Something he says sparks an idea. He's been having nightmares about me. Could those nightmares end with me getting my brains scrambled by a leucotome? I shudder, remembering the dream I'd fallen into last week. I thought it was Janus's, but what if it was Bennett's? That would explain why I had trouble entering it again; I'd been focusing my efforts on the wrong person.

Anguish swirls in his ocean eyes. "He told me he'd reveal the truth about how my parents died."

"I'm confused. You know ho—"

"Stellan told me it wasn't an accident. They were murdered," Bennett admits, tears rolling down his cheeks. He removes his glasses to wipe his eyes with his sleeve.

My anger dissipates like steam. The anniversary of Bennett's parents' death just passed, and from all the years I've known him and his grandparents, I know the pain of losing them was still raw for the entire family. The news of their passing had been in all the papers; Coral and Duke Grey died in a boating accident on rough seas.

I can't help but wonder if Stellan is taking advantage of Bennett's vulnerability, but at the same time, everything Stellan has written so far has been true. Why would this be any different?

"What has Stellan told you?"

"Nothing yet. That's why I wanted to accompany you to Aurora. I've given him everything he's asked for, but he hasn't returned the favor."

I nod. It makes perfect sense why Bennett agreed to Janus's request for him to travel with me. I bet he would have volunteered if Janus hadn't asked. But he isn't here to act on behalf of the Council. He is here to get the answers Stellan owes him. It's why he was so angry about missing the meeting at Furies. Bennett likely had plans to ambush Stellan there. But now, Stellan is with the wolves, and Bennett may have sold his soul for a second time with nothing to show for it.

I want to shake him, scream at him, throw him out for this betrayal. It hurts to know he'd stab me like this again. But as I look at him in his tear-filled eyes, I see Ravi hurting over his sister. I see myself withholding information from Wilder because sharing would be a burden.

Bennett is not my enemy. He is a man in pain. This wouldn't have happened had I paid attention to that earlier and listened to him, rather than used him for my own schemes.

"I need answers, Leigh. They were the people I loved most in the world. They didn't drown in that accident; they were *Sea Witches*, and I need to know the truth. I am not sorry that I made a deal with Stellan, but I am sorry you got caught in the crossfires," Bennett says. "Do you think you could ever forgive me?"

More tears stream down Bennett's cheeks, and though he lied to me, manipulated the situation with Stellan, and threw my brother under the bus, I still understand why he did it. I've been on my quest for the truth.

"How did you know about Fynn?" I ask.

Bennett wrings his hands. "I didn't. Fynn confessed to Corvina."

I gasp from the sudden, jarring clarity. It all makes sense now. Fynn must have deeply loved her to entrust her with such a dangerous secret. Could that be why he broke things off so suddenly and rushed into a marriage with Gianna? Was he trying to escape the truth and bury it under the pretense of a new beginning?

I shift toward Bennett, leaving Wilder gaping at my side. He tenses as if he will pull me back but remains still as I wrap my arms around Bennett. He stiffens at first, then crumbles. I let him cry on my shoulder, his tears soaking through my shirt as I hold back my own. I've been on my quest for the truth, and though his methods, once again, were deplorable, I can still emphasize his need for answers.

"I forgive you," I whisper, and Bennett cries harder. I clutch him tighter as my heart cracks. He's been carrying this pain for so many years. "The truth about my brother is out there, and so are Zeus, Alden, and their army. There's no time to waste on being angry."

Bennett sniffles as he pulls away from me, and though the sting of his betrayal still lingers, I have also done terrible things searching for the truth, like agreeing to get Harborym daemon venom, which was used to poison Janus.

"I doubt the others on the Council will be as forgiving as you," Bennett says.

"Probably not," I reply honestly. He winces. "But we'll deal with that later. Right now, our focus needs to be on the wolves. They have Stellan and my grandmother."

"You said you have a plan," Brigid chimes in.

I nod. "I do. Alden has a mate who is now a vampire against her will. He blames Vyvyan for the presence of vampires in Lua. If he believes his mate is gone for good, he will continue to aid his brother and his invasion to get revenge by killing Vyvyan and any other vampire he deems responsible."

Brigid sucks her teeth. "You lost me. Isn't she gone for good if she's a vampire?"

I sigh, then turn to Wilder, who looks at me as if he were miles away rather than by my side. He crosses his arms, no longer reaching for me, but his love for me lingers in his guarded expression. What I say next may send him over the edge, but I am tired of lying. I don't want to be as lost and lonely as Bennett.

"Your mom requested the Council's help to fund her research. She's been working on a cure for vampirism. Last week, Janus gave the go-ahead, and we gifted Chiara the necessary funds. I plan to infiltrate Alden's dream, convince him there's a way to save his mate and that his brother is to blame for her current condition, and then promise him the cure."

Brigid stares at me, wide-eyed, while Wilder blinks. I fidget under his scrutiny, my skin prickling with heat. He glares at me. I inhale a shaky breath, hardly able to stand it. I want to beg for forgiveness at his feet, but that isn't me. He knows me better than anyone and knows I have issues, yet he fell in love with me regardless. He pinches the bridge of his nose, asking, "Isn't it a gamble to promise Alden a cure that is still in development?"

I lift my chin, fighting my smile because he isn't running from the room, cursing my name. "Have you ever known your mom to fail at anything?"

Wilder's jaw works, but he doesn't refute me. My grin broadens.

"What about your grandmother and Stellan?" Brigid asks, gathering her long, dark hair into a thick braid.

"I'm hoping Alden will return my grandmother as part of our deal."

Brigid laughs. My resolve hardens, and so does my fist, a fact that doesn't go unnoticed by the female Blade, who smirks.

"That doesn't assure her safety if he says no," Brigid says.

"Well, it's not as if we can storm their camp and get her back. We don't even know where they're keeping her," I counter.

"I can pinpoint their location," Bennett offers quietly.

"How?" I ask.

"Scrying."

I gape at him. Sea Witches can use water to receive information or messages, and some can even use it as a form of divination to locate lost things. It's not a skill every Sea Witch possesses.

"You can do that?" I ask.

"Yes." The word is a declaration, a promise.

"It's a risk," Wilder adds as he paces in short spans. I watch him as he continues to war with himself before he says, "I think we should do it. Let's find the camp. If negotiations go to shit, at least your grandmother will have a fighting chance at survival."

I say nothing. I am determined to get my grandmother back, but I am unsure if I want to trust Bennett to help me with something so personal so soon.

Wilder gapes at me when I don't immediately answer, and he sighs, grabbing my wrist. "Can I talk to you?" he asks.

I swallow as he leans in close to whisper, "What he did is fucked up in a million different ways but, Leigh, you've given him your forgiveness. Now, can you lend him your trust?"

My gaze meets his. Wilder's lips press together, but he isn't tapping his foot or forcing my hand. He is letting it be my decision, even though he wants to work with Bennett. If, after everything, Wilder is willing to trust Bennett, then maybe I can get past the icebergs of hurt bobbing within me and work with him too. I'll deal with the consequences when Corona's fate isn't hanging in the balance.

"What materials do you need?" I ask Bennett.

Bennett rattles off the list of the needed materials, and Brigid takes notes on her phone. I grab Wilder's hand. There's so much I want to say. "I'm sorry," I murmur.

Wilder's gaze lifts heavenward as if he can't believe I am apologizing.

He deserves more, and I silently vow to do better, to be better, for him and us. I love him and must tell him before we run out of time.

But before I can, Gianna enters, followed by several others.

"What did I miss?" Gi asks.

Wilder peers down at me, a tight smile on his face, and I squeeze his hand.

CHAPTER FIFTY-SEVEN
WILDER

AS LEIGH CATCHES GIANNA, Ry, Pallas, and Marlowe up on her plan to stop the invasion, I formulate my plan to rescue her grandmother by infiltrating the wolves' camp.

With her arms crossed, Marlowe settles far away from the commotion in the center of the room against the far wall beside the closet. She assesses each person here, and I find myself doing the same to her while she is distracted.

After months of searching, having her so close confuses me. I'm unsure how to act around her anymore or whether I should include her in my plans to rescue Leigh's grandmother. Marlowe's skills would be invaluable in getting in and out of the wolves' camp undetected, but I worry about the potential consequences. If I invite her along, she might interpret it as forgiveness or belief in her claim that she's changed, even though that's not true.

When Marlowe meets my gaze, I avert my eyes. She makes me uneasy, and that's not how I want to be on the eve of an invasion.

Brigid places her hands on her hips and addresses Leigh beside me near the bed. "Alden is Lua's Enforcer. He's as mean as they come, yet you're saying you're going to get him to forsake his brother because of some girl?"

"Not just any girl, his mate," Leigh clarifies.

Brigid rolls her eyes. "I don't believe in mates."

"How do you plan on convincing him to help you?" Gianna asks, ignoring Brigid.

"Well, Ravi told me he is sleeping, and——"

"Wait, when did you talk to Ravi?" I ask as I watch Pallas help Bennett arrange his scrying materials on the floor.

Leigh sighs. "Just now. I created a psychic connection with Ravi using astral projection, like the day I visited you here." Her cheeks flush pink as we glance at the bed behind us, memories flooding back.

I see flashes of her naked body writhing against the sheets, lost in pleasure. Desire courses through me, tinged with frustration. The others watch our silent exchange, sensing the unspoken issues between us.

That night, I let Leigh distract me with sex, too caught up in the heat of the moment to push for emotional intimacy. She didn't share her fears about Alden's proposal, and now we're facing the consequences of our lack of communication. Bennett and Corvina's betrayal, the looming invasion . . . I clench my jaw, determined to break down the walls between us. No more letting physical connection eclipse vulnerability and trust. It's time to face our challenges head-on.

"What does that mean?" Marlowe asks.

"It's an out-of-body experience where my soul travels while my body remains stationary," Leigh responds.

"Are you going to astral project to Alden?" Gianna remarks.

I stiffen at the thought of her putting herself in danger, but also trust that she can handle herself.

Leigh shakes her head. "No. I am going to dreamwalk."

"Come again?" Gi says, and Leigh launches into an explanation of what that is.

I clear my throat. "Okay, so you visit Alden while he's sleeping to ensure no one walks in on your two talking. Then you offer Alden the cure and see what he says. However, we still use Bennett to locate the wolves' encampment and rescue the others while Alden is distracted. I will lead a team of myself, Marlowe, Brigid, and Isolde to extract the queen and Stellan tonight."

"Excuse me," Gianna interjects. I turn to face her as she pushes herself away from her propped position against the desk next to Ry, raising an eyebrow. "Stellan is my father," she says. Her words ring like a gunshot in the quiet room.

Bennett opens his mouth, but I silence him with a dark look. There will be time for questions later. "If anyone is going on the rescue mission, it's me."

"After everything Stellan did to deny you, Gi, you still want to go?" Leigh asks.

Brigid scoffs beside Bennett, who is lighting a bundle of sage. He will need an entire bushel to clear the negativity in this place. "You may be his kid, but you've had zero training. You'd only slow us down."

"Shut up, Brigid. That isn't up to you," Ry scolds. Brigid sticks her tongue out at him. He shakes his head. "Grow up."

Gianna meets my stare. "I refuse to stay here while you get to be the hero. Let someone else be the damsel for once."

I grimace, knowing that while Gianna is strong, Brigid is right—Gi isn't a Blade.

Leigh jumps in. "Gi has the right to be there, Wilder. If you do this, you need to take her. I want Isolde here with me, anyway."

I sigh. We shouldn't be arguing. "If I bring you along, do you promise to follow orders?"

Gi nods. "I am good at that."

My head falls. We've had countless fights this week because of Gi's refusal to listen.

"Hate to break up this merry little party, but we have a problem." Eddo raps on the door with his knuckles.

"What is it, Papa?" Brigid asks.

Eddo hands her a note with the Lua seal—two wolf heads beneath a crescent moon. Brigid eyes it, then crosses the room to give it to Leigh.

"For you," she says, her cooperation a stark contrast to her earlier stance. It's ironic seeing Brigid and Eddo here now, after they'd been so unwilling to help when I first arrived, insisting I either leave or join Stellan's fight with no middle ground.

Leigh takes the note. We all wait quietly as she opens it.

Her eyes move left to right as she reads, then she sighs and lowers the paper. "Eddo, you may not like me, but if you want to keep Corona from falling under wolf rule, you will need to gather as many Blades as possible to fight in my name. Zeus has requested a meeting at Charon Bridge. He's asked me to surrender at dawn."

Brigid's voice is tight as she responds, "What happens if you don't?"

Leigh sighs. "War." She looks at Bennett. "You need to work fast." Bennett nods. To Eddo, she says, "We need to evacuate the city, just in case."

"Understood, Your Majesty." A flicker of resolve burns in his eyes, which reminds me why I enjoyed working for him so much.

Leigh faces Gianna. "Gi, contact Hebe Hospital. Tell Doctor Dunn we need the cure, like, yesterday." Gi nods, already reaching for her phone. "Now, everyone, get out. I need to talk to Wilder alone before I go to sleep."

CHAPTER FIFTY-EIGHT
DESIREE

AS I EXIT THE BATHROOM, the frigid air from the open window gives me goose bumps. Water trickles from the short strands of my black hair, trailing down my neck before disappearing into the plush fabric of the towel wrapped around my body. The scent of soap lingers in the air, mingling with the smell of sex as I climb the steps to the lofted bedroom.

Vane sits on the edge of the bed, the tangled sheets covering his naked body. Despite the satisfaction that should come with sated desire, his brow furrows as he rests his head in his hands, his elbows pressing into his strong thighs. A pang of unease twists in my stomach.

"Did you change your mind?" I look at my packed bag on the floor. We are supposed to get ready to catch the next train out of the city, but Vane hasn't moved.

I tighten the towel around myself, suddenly feeling exposed.

Vane meets my gaze through the veil of his long lashes. With warm palms, he draws me closer by my hips. A hesitant smile tugs at the corner of his lip.

I swallow, my stomach twisting. Is he about to let me down easy? Has Vyvyan summoned him home? If he's leaving me, I won't beg him to take me with him. I am not going back to the Nest. I believe I'll be okay alone for the first time in my life, but I'd rather be with him.

"Well?" I prompt. "You don't have to say it. I know you are going back to her."

I try to pull away from Vane's grasp, but his fingers tighten. The bruises and marks left by our rough encounters have already begun to fade, but I wish I could have him tattooed on my heart. I won't forget him.

"Vyvyan?" His thumbs trace gentle circles on my skin.

I nod, not trusting myself to speak.

Vane smiles, and I frown. Is he mocking my misery? "Have you already forgotten?" he asks. I lift a brow. Vane kisses my stomach before resting his cheek against me. "I am yours. I'm not going back to Vyvyan."

I release a breath as I cup Vane's cheek, forcing him to look me in the eye. "Then what's bothering you?"

Vane presses his lips against my palm. My eyes flutter shut, and I press my thighs together, trying to stave off the growing ache. What we did in the cemetery unleashed a relentless need whenever I'm in his presence.

"Vane," I groan. For this to work, we need to be honest with each other. I won't let him distract me.

True intimacy lies in vulnerability and shared secrets.

"You're stalling," I whisper, wetness pooling between my thighs. Fuck, I am insatiable. We'll never leave Borealis, let alone this bed, if I can't control my body's response to his touch. "If we're going to be together, we must be able to talk to one another. Otherwise, I am walking out of that door and your life."

"There's nowhere you could go where I wouldn't find you." Vane inhales deeply. "My scent is mingled with yours."

I press kisses over his face and neck. He falls back onto the bed. I crawl on top of him, rubbing my heated core against his hardening length. When he reaches to touch me, I pin his arms above his head.

"Are you trying to dominate me, Desiree?" Vane asks with a wicked gleam in his eye.

"If it gets you to open up to me, then yes."

Vane tries to kiss me again, but I turn my head. He pouts. "You're being mean."

"The truth for a kiss."

Vane could overpower me in an instant, but he doesn't try. His gaze drifts from my face to my chest before he sighs. "Fine. I don't think we should leave the city yet. I just had a premonition. Lua has marched armies into Corona, camped just outside Aurora."

Hair lifts on my nape and arms. Is Wilder in danger?

Vane touches my cheek. "Leigh is going to try to negotiate peace with Alden. Alden's lover was turned into a vampire a while ago, and he blames Vyvyan for it."

My jaw slackens. Alden's true motive for coming to Borealis becomes clear—he was attempting to get close to Vyvyan. His desire to visit Little Death and explore the tunnels makes sense now.

A chilling thought crosses my mind. If he had discovered Vyvyan that night, would he have harmed her? Or would that have come after the invasion when the witches no longer stood between him and his revenge?

"Leigh needs your mom's vampire cure. She's going to trade it for peace."

A chill settles deep in my bones.

"But Mom has no cure," I whisper. Vane's brows dip. I swallow. "Earlier tonight, I went to find Mom, and when she wouldn't see me, I—" The words catch in my throat. If I tell Vane the truth, he will think less of me.

But as I meet his gaze, I see only love—love I want to believe is unconditional.

"I lost control," I admit. "I destroyed Mom's research."

Vane pulls me close. I rest my head against his chest; his slow, but steady heartbeat contrasts my racing one. "I'm sorry," he says. I stiffen. "I should have been there for you. You must've felt so alone. But I promise we will figure out how to get your mom what she needs to redo her research, even if I have to fund the project personally. I'll go to Vyvyan. I'll demand the money."

"You don't need to do that," I say. Vyvyan would never agree.

Vane holds me tighter. "I want to help."

Tears crease my eyelids. Vane has sacrificed so much of himself to help others. Vyvyan used him for centuries. His parents used him before that. I won't use him like the others. I made this mess. I'll clean it up.

"There is another way," I mutter. I take a steadying breath. "Mom's cure might not have worked, anyway. If we tell her about me, she could fashion a cure for Alden with my blood."

"You would share your secret?" Vane asks. His heart thumps faster against my ear.

"Yes."

"You are amazing," he says.

I sigh. I'm sure seeing my mom after what I did to her lab won't feel so amazing, but it is time for Mom and me to talk. We are years overdue. Though I love her, my palms grow clammy.

"You are tense." Vane's voice comes out as a seductive purr. My thighs tighten around him. "We should ease some of that tension."

I smile. "You said they're in Aurora already?" I ask. He nods. "Then there's no time." I sit up, straddling his lap.

Vane slowly tugs my towel. His heated gaze slides over my naked body, his pupils dilating. I splay my hands on his stomach. Beneath my touch, his muscles tense.

"We should go." Vane flicks his eyes to meet mine, his hardness pressing into me.

I roll my hips. "We should."

His hands slide up my waist to thumb the underside of my breasts. I lean into his feverish touch.

"Then get dressed," he commands, brushing my nipples. I rub myself against him, torturing us both. Breathy sighs escape my mouth, and he watches me in awe, his eyes now black.

The heat in my belly coils tighter. "Stop," I pant, quickening my movements. "Please. We need to go . . ."

My head falls back as euphoria builds within me, wave after punishing wave. Even with the sheet, I feel him. He's so hard and impossibly *big*. Desperate, my nails scrape his skin.

"*Heavens*, you're magnificent," Vane growls.

With each grind, the throbbing intensifies, a coil of pleasure. My clit pulses, sharp and agonizing, and tears flood my eyes. I'm so close.

Vane covers my breast with his mouth. His tongue swirls around my hardened peaks, sending electric shocks straight to my core.

I gasp his name. "Vane . . ."

And then I'm coming. My body convulses as waves of pure bliss crash over me, washing away all coherent thoughts. Vane crushes me to him until the room stops spinning.

"Okay, it's really time to go," I mutter between gulps of air.

Vane's laughter vibrates beneath me. Reluctantly, I pull away from his embrace, my legs wobble as I gather my clothes.

Vane steals one of my brother's shirts without looking away from me. His clothes are still wet from the freezing rain. "I will spend eternity watching you," he says while I yank on my jeans.

"Creeper." I roll my eyes, but I'm smiling.

Once dressed, we head toward the hospital. Several Blade vehicles line the streets, and a chilling silence lingers in the air as if the entire country is holding its breath. Whatever is happening in Aurora, the aftershocks are being felt here.

I grab Vane's hand. "Let's hurry."

CHAPTER FIFTY-NINE
LEIGH

"THANK YOU," Wilder murmurs.

I turn to him, my breath catching as our eyes lock. The intensity of his gaze makes my pulse race. His presence is comforting and intoxicating, like a cool breeze on a sweltering day, offering a momentary respite from the uncertainty surrounding us.

"For what?" I swipe my tongue across my suddenly dry lips.

The desire to kiss him is overwhelming, like a magnetic pull threatening to consume me. But there's so much we need to discuss, so many secrets I've buried deep within me these past weeks, which have festered like open wounds. My anger over Stellan's articles barely scratches the surface. It is a mere fraction of the truth that yearns to be revealed.

"For working with Bennett. I know it was a tough decision for you, but despite his hangups, we need him," Wilder says. "Who knows what will happen at dawn?"

I swallow past the lump in my throat, the weight of my guilt pressing on me. If I can't convince Alden to switch sides by giving him the cure for Tanith, Zeus will ask me to surrender. When I refuse, we will fight, and there's a high likelihood I will lose several people I love. After that, the Wolf Prince will take me prisoner. Before that happens, I owe it to Wilder to tell him how I feel. I take a deep breath and say, "It's the least I could do after I ambushed you with Marlowe."

Wilder's face tightens. I reach for his hand in a silent plea for forgiveness. I exhale when he doesn't pull away.

"Are you ready to talk to me?" Wilder asks.

I try to muster a smile, but it is a brittle, fragile thing. "I have so much to—"

The shrill ring of my phone cuts me off. I silence the number I don't recognize, but they call again.

Wilder sighs. "Answer it. It could be the Council. Maybe Janus has changed her mind."

"Hello?" I answer.

"Hello, sweetness," Vane's voice crackles through the speaker.

"Vane, I'm in the middle of something. Can I call you back?" I ask as Wilder's brow wrinkles. I shrug, having no clue why Vane wants to talk unless it's to discuss Janus and the Council. Did Janus tell them about the wolves?

"It concerns the cure," Vane says. His words are a promise and a threat.

I gasp. Chiara's search for the cure had been a closely guarded secret, not to disturb the fragile peace between our species. But with Vane's uncanny ability to uncover the truth, I should have known better than to keep it from him. He's likely angry, and the last thing I need is another enemy breathing down my neck.

"I was going to tell you—"

"Chiara's research got destroyed." I fall silent at Vane's interruption, the air in my lungs ripped away. Our leverage against the wolves, the one thing we had to bargain with, is gone.

I refuse to believe it. But why would Vane lie?

There's a rustling noise, and a feminine voice fills my ear. "Leigh, it's Desiree."

I place my hand against Wilder's chest, barely able to hear her past the ringing in my ears, but I need his heartbeat to steady mine.

If there's no cure, I have nothing to bargain with. But maybe I could still talk to him—try to make him see that Zeus is his real enemy. Tanith would still be a werewolf if it weren't for his brother. Except, who am I kidding? I've given him no reason to trust me, either.

"Don't panic. I have a plan to help," Desiree says as a car horn blares.

I suck in a deep breath. "Unless you can replicate your mom's work, I don't know—"

482

"I am the cure," she tells me. I fist Wilder's shirt. His hands steady my shoulders.

"It's a long story," Desiree says in a rush, "but drinking my blood reverses the effects of vampire venom. We are on the way to the hospital now to catch my mom before the president's mandatory shelter-in-place goes into effect. I'm sure she can package my blood for Alden to use."

I shake my head. Wait, what? Janus ordered a shelter-in-place? This country is a mess.

"I know it's a lot to take in," Desiree continues. "I had trouble accepting it myself, but I promise you, I am what I say I am . . ." Vane's muffled voice says something I can't understand, and she quickly adds, "We just got to the hospital. I'll be in touch once I know more."

"Wait, Desiree—" I protest, but the line dies.

Wilder's eyes search mine. "Desiree is with Vane?" He's not Vane's biggest fan.

"Your sister is the cure. Something about her blood turns vampires back into humans."

"Impossible," Wilder breathes.

"I believe her." It's either trust Desiree or lose it all.

He nods, unconvinced. But we cannot afford to be distracted.

Everyone is doing their part, and I need to do mine. Alden may not stay asleep much longer.

Even though there's no time, I need to say this. "I am sorry about lying to you about your mom wanting my help funding research for a cure," I blurt, even though there's no time. "I've been in a dark place after Don, and I am uncertain if I will ever fully heal, but I am trying. I should have told you about Alden's proposal, Don's letters, and about Gianna and Stellan, but I couldn't find the words. I thought I could fix everything myself by finding Stellan's mole. But I should have said something."

Wilder rolls his lips between his teeth. "I wish I could have been there more for you, Leigh." I shrug. He's here now. "But I'm not blameless either. I should have told you about how hard it was coming back here, about Eddo and Brigid, and everything. I just thought it would get easier if I dealt with it myself. You had so much going on, and I didn't want to add to your burdens. Not when I thought it would scare you away."

I palm his smooth cheek. "You could never be a burden. That day, when we were together at the palace, I said I was yours. But after everything I've done, like pardoning Marlowe." My voice trembles. "Are you still mine? Can you forgive me and love me despite my flaws?"

"I am yours. Down to my very marrow." He hugs me to him, a searing promise that brands my soul before he turns on his heel and leaves his bedroom.

"No kiss goodbye?" I challenge.

He smiles. "This isn't goodbye." Then, without a second glance, he walks out of the room.

"Send Pallas in here!"

I lie down on Wilder's bed. His scent wraps around me like an embrace. Isolde drapes a soft blanket over me while Pallas hovers nearby. "In case you get cold," she explains.

I need his Green Witch healing hands to knock me out, or else my racing mind will never let me go to sleep. Then, Pallas steps forward. He covers my eyes with his palm. The warmth of his skin seeps into mine as he channels his magic, guiding me toward the realm of dreams.

"Sleep well, Your Majesty," Pallas murmurs.

I focus on Alden, picturing his face in my mind's eye, the cadence of his voice, and a haunting melody that fills my thoughts.

With the last remnants of my energy, I forge a bridge between us, a connection that will allow me to slip into his dreams, praying that the nightmares that haunt me do not plague him, too.

CHAPTER SIXTY
WILDER

"I GOT IT!" Bennett screams as he hunches over a rippling water bowl on the floor inside Gianna's messy room at the garrison down the hall from a sleeping Leigh.

I've instructed Gianna to stop contacting my mom at the hospital. Desiree can take care of her. Instead, I need Gianna to focus on Brigid's lessons on wielding a knife to convince potential attackers that she is a formidable opponent. Ideally, she would be better off conjuring lightning to electrocute her enemies, but I'm unsure if Gianna possesses that level of power.

Bennett grins, and Marlowe mirrors his infectious excitement, her eyes light up with the thrill of impending violence. I will likely regret bringing her along on this mission, but I'd rather not leave her unsupervised. If she means what she said about changing, this is her first opportunity to prove it. However, I suspect she will bolt at the first sign of trouble, just like she did the night of the Domna Trials when she disappeared before I forfeited the competition.

"Queen Jorina and Stellan are being held in the wolves' camp on the outskirts of the city. Their tent is located at the center of the encampment. Just past the bonfire between Prince Alden and Prince Zeus's quarters," Bennett says.

I meet Marlowe's stare, and silent communication passes between us. "You got that?" I ask. She nods, her face set with grim determination.

"What's the plan?" Brigid does a press check to ensure a round is in the chamber.

All eyes turn to me. "Now that Leigh's asleep, the retrieval team will move to rescue Queen Jorina and Stellan. Bennett, you will stay here and assist Eddo and Ry with the evacuees." I focus on Marlowe. "We will drive to West Aurora, leave our car, and walk the rest of the way to the camp on foot. Then—"

"I need a gun. Mine was taken downstairs," Marlowe says, eyeing Brigid as she holsters hers.

I lift a brow. "That's because no one trusts you."

"Come on, Wilder, if I were going to shoot you, I'd have done it already," Marlowe insists.

I chew on the inside of my cheek. I'd rather take a beating of a lifetime than trust Marlowe with a gun, but then why would I bring her along at all? If she will work with us, I must believe she won't betray me.

"Fine, Brigid. Get Marlowe whatever she needs and meet us at the car."

Brigid's upper lip draws back, but she doesn't fight me. She exits the room without another word. Gianna attempts to give Marlowe a small smile before giving us a minute alone by walking over to Bennett.

"Thank you for bringing me along on this mission. I hope this means you've forgiven me," Marlowe says.

I laugh. "Not even close." I turn to leave, then say over my shoulder, "If you plan on turning your back on us when we reach the wolves, I won't give a damn about Leigh's pardon. I will hunt you down and finish you myself."

I'm in the hallway when Marlowe says, "You'll forgive me one day, Wilder."

My shoulders hike toward my ears. Maybe, but not today.

CHAPTER SIXTY-ONE
DESIREE

WE BYPASS the hospital's front entrance, opting for the loading dock where supplies are delivered. After telling me he has a way inside, Vane leads the way. As we approach our rendezvous point, a familiar figure emerges from the shadows—the black-haired healer who tried to stop me earlier crosses her arms. Her scrubs are even more wrinkled and blood-splattered now.

Our gazes meet, and I brace myself for the alarm to sound, but she remains silent.

"You owe me," she says to Vane.

I raise my brows. Do they know each other?

"You know I'll make it up to you, Lilith," Vane replies with a tone as smooth as silk. The witch smiles. Her pupils dilate before she blinks. My insides swirl with unease. I try to ignore the feeling as I pass them and climb the emergency stairs to Mom's lab.

"Don't be jealous," Vane whispers behind me. "And before you say you aren't, remember that I had to watch you go on a date with Jaxson."

A pang shoots through my chest. Jaxson should be in Glaucus by now. With the wolves' invasion looming, will the Domna trials be postponed? "You practically forced me to go on that date," I remind Vane.

"Because I wanted you to see that you had a life outside the Nest," Vane defends.

I stop walking. Now I understand his intentions—he wanted to push me toward Jaxson and away from the Nest so I could discover acceptance and belonging elsewhere. But his methods are still manipulative, even if they came from a place of care.

"We will talk later," I reply.

Vane chuckles darkly. "Your tone implies punishment."

"You are reprehensible."

Lilith clears her throat as we reach the door to Mom's floor. "Fair warning," she says. "Your mom isn't happy."

Guilt claws down my throat. I pushed everyone away—Mom, Wilder, Jaxson, even Dad. I've been selfish, focusing on my desires without considering the consequences and how they affect the people I love most. Vane's hand finds the small of my back. I lean into his touch, hesitating. Once I cross this threshold, there will be no turning back. Mom's reaction will be a burden I must bear. But the country depends on it. My loved ones depend on it.

I step inside.

The room is an anarchic mess of shattered glass and debris. The empty cage door hangs open, and the window through which I freed the bats yawns wide. Mom stands amidst the wreckage, a broom in hand, her shoulders curled.

"Mom," my voice is barely louder than the whir of the fluorescent lights still fueled by the backup generator.

Mom's shoulders reach her ears. I inch closer.

"I am sorry," I breathe.

Mom exhales, the tension draining from her posture.

I gesture to the broom in her hand. "Can I help you?"

Before she can respond, Vane takes the broom. We watch, transfixed, as Prince Vane, the leader of the vampires, *sweeps*.

"The cure was about more than you, Desiree," Mom says, sounding exhausted. I wince, remembering Vane saying something almost identical last week. "You had no right to take away the choice of others."

My gaze falls to my platform shoes. She's right. The cure will give many vampires who regret their choices, like Zev, the chance to return to their former lives. I've been so scared about how Vyvyan would react if people found out what my blood could do that I never considered how many vampires might welcome the choice. "I was angry—"

"You should have said something rather than thrown a tantrum."

My fists curl. "To say something, you would have to listen."

"What are you saying? That I am a bad mom?" she huffs, her eyes narrowing.

"You would have to be there to be a bad mom," I snap. "You haven't been there for me since I was fourteen, when your job became more important than your kids."

Mom folds her arms. Her white coat hangs from a rack near the whiteboard. "I worked to provide for *you*, Desiree. I'm sorry if—"

"I didn't want you to become the Altum Healer if it meant never seeing you! You and Dad worked hard to give us a life many Nebula dreamed of having, but at what cost? I am not saying your work isn't important, but it made me feel like *I* wasn't. My opinion never mattered growing up. I was miserable as a healer, but you and Dad didn't care so long as Wilder and I did what you wanted."

"If you hated being a healer, you should have spoken up rather than stage your death to become a vampire," Mom disputes.

The accusation stings. "I staged my death to help Dad hide the letters, to keep you and Wilder safe when you were too obsessed with your careers to notice what was happening around you. Why would I have gone to you for help when you never even noticed I was being tormented in high school? And by Juliette, no less?"

"What?" Mom asks. "*By* Juliette?"

Tears well in my eyes, hot and stinging. I blink furiously, trying to hold them back. "I didn't stop being Juliette's friend. She stopped being mine. Yet you picked her over me the other night. Do you know how much that hurt?"

To my surprise, moisture glimmers in Mom's eyes, a crack in her usually impenetrable armor. "I didn't know."

I inhale deeply. "Well, now you do, and I am not telling you this to punish you or Juliette, but because I am tired. I am so sick and tired of trying to keep things bottled up to protect everyone else's feelings. I am tired of trying to make everyone else happy. I am tired of trying to hide my feelings to spare others."

I exhale. My shoulders uncurl, and my body feels lighter than it did ten minutes ago. It feels good to get everything off my chest without fearing the repercussions.

I knew pain until I found solace in Jaxson, Vane, and my friends in the Nest. But then I lost them, too, and it has taken me this long to find my voice and come to terms with the fact that I don't need others to define my place in the world. I am enough.

"I am sorry you felt that way, Desiree." My mom's voice breaks, and so does my heart. "It's no wonder you destroyed the lab to get back at m-me."

I reach for her hand. "Mom, I'm sorry for what I did, but not all is lost." She tries to pull away, but I hold fast. "I am the cure."

Mom gasps. "What?"

"During the blackout, a daemon attacked Vyvyan and Vane. She was gravely injured, but my blood healed her. It also temporarily turned her human," I explain, and Mom listens intently to every word. "She's a vampire again now. Still, she had to wait a few days to metabolize my blood before Vane could turn her back to avoid anyone discovering what had happened."

Mom glances at Vane, who nods. "It's true."

"Then we must run some tests. Do you have anywhere you need to be? The president's lockdown will go into effect soon. We must shelter-in-place to prepare for a war with Lua." I nod, and Mom's eyes widen. "Is Wilder okay? I haven't been able to reach him in Aurora."

I shrug. "He is with Leigh, so I hope so."

Mom nods, but fear for her son's safety and the instability threatening the nation consumes her expression. But she takes a deep breath, saying, "You'll have to sleep here." She pulls away from me, turning to the whiteboard. I glance at Vane, who shrugs. We can sleep in one of the on-call rooms at sunrise. "Do you have any idea what this cure means?"

"It will mean nothing unless we find a way to synthesize it and get it to Leigh. It's the only way to stop this war." Vane is by my side. His hand finds mine.

Mom's brow lifts at our interlocked fingers. She undoubtedly wonders about Jaxson, but there's no time to explain. "Leigh needs the cure?" Mom asks instead.

I nod, my expression grim. "Prince Alden's mate was turned into a vampire. Leigh will offer him the cure in exchange for peace with Lua."

Mom's forehead pinches. "There's no reliable way to synthesize a stable cure from your blood until I've done tests, which could take weeks or longer. We also don't know how it will work with werewolves."

My smile fades. "W-what?" I hadn't considered any of that. Vane and I exchange furrowed glances. Have we already lost?

Mom scribbles on the whiteboard, the marker squeaking against the surface.

"But what if they need the cure soon, like now?" I ask.

Mom glances at me. A shadow crosses her eyes. "The only reliable way would be to take it straight from your veins. You could bring Alden's mate here, or you could—"

"Go straight to the patient," I finish.

Vane squeezes my hand, serving as an anchor in the spinning room. The thought of being at Alden's mercy, of him taking what he wants from me and then imprisoning me, turns my world on its axis.

"You don't have to do this, Desiree," Vane murmurs. "We can find another way."

But what choice do I have? The fate of my family—both witch and vampire—hangs in the balance.

"Fine," I say. "Take what you need from me for your research because there's a possibility you won't see me for a very long time."

Mom and I share a loaded stare. After a moment, Mom nods, and her doctor persona takes over. She barks orders to interns and healers, including Juliette, who glares at me from the hallway.

I smile at her. She can't hurt me anymore.

CHAPTER SIXTY-TWO
LEIGH

THE AURORA GARRISON FADES AWAY, replaced by an enchanting library I've never seen before. Intricate woodwork adorns the walls, the carvings of animals and flora so lifelike they seem poised to leap from the grain. Ancient tomes line the shelves. A fire crackles and pops in a massive hearth. As I move toward the inviting flames, I pass a window that offers a glimpse into a forest of snowy pine trees stretched out beneath an impenetrable black sky.

Alden sits before the fire in an oversized wingback chair, staring affectionately at a beautiful black wolf dozing on the floor, her glossy obsidian fur reflecting the flickering light like a miniature galaxy.

"Where are we?" I ask. I remind myself that I'm not here to trick Alden into working with me. Instead, I am banking on convincing him, despite the dream-like nature of our surroundings, that he should trust me rather than his brother. Revenge won't give Alden what he truly desires. But I will. If he doesn't sense I am dreamwalking, I will tell him. This isn't a ruse.

"The library at the Nocturn Castle," Alden replies without looking away from the wolf.

This wolf must be Tanith, his mate.

I sag into my chair with the weight of understanding. "I'm sorry," I say, but the words feel inadequate. What lengths would I go to if Wilder was taken from me? Would I burn the world for him? I can imagine it. But dedicating my life to killing others in the name of one person's loss would feel like a betrayal of my values. One life isn't worth more than thousands. "Can you tell me about Tanith?"

If I can get Alden to reflect on his love for his mate and remember the depth of their connection, I can convince him to accept the cure and leave Corona alone.

Alden laughs. The sound chimes through the library. In this setting, he is transformed—at ease.

"You caught me in a sharing mood," Alden begins, settling into his chair. "Tanith was extremely superstitious, completely obsessed with the concept of luck. She was the eldest of three siblings. Her mother and father were professors; they taught folklore and the magical integration of nature, and many of their beliefs rubbed off on her. She spent most of her life daydreaming of fairy tales."

"She must've thought she hit the jackpot when she met you, a real prince in shining armor," I tease.

Alden's smile vanishes. "I was her downfall. Her trusting nature didn't stand a chance in my family. My father and brother have always been cruel. They never understood Tanith, and it bothered her. She started withdrawing from me when she sensed they'd never accept her."

My chest aches. "What happened to her?" I ask, wanting to hear the story from his lips.

Alden shifts in his seat, the antique creaking beneath him. A shadow falls over his face.

But when I fear he'll retreat into himself, he takes a long breath and continues.

"When Tanith and I discovered we were mates several years ago, it was unexpected. Her dance troupe performed an ancient Lua folktale for my father's birthday—the story of Sirius, the first werewolf. Tanith was one of the ensemble dancers, and as soon as she started moving, my wolf instincts recognized her as mine."

A pang of envy pierces my heart. As a witch, the concept of mates is foreign to me. For wolves, it's a one-and-done deal, a profound connection they may never find again, even if a mate dies. Having her still alive but unreachable must be excruciating.

"Tanith's gentle nature softened my impenetrable core. I started to care less about my father's plans to expand our borders. But then he got sick, and I thought their plans to invade would be put to rest, and Tanith and I could focus on us, but it was too late. Zeus and my father had bullied Tanith, and she couldn't handle it. She . . . she left the palace, left me. Shortly after, vampires ambushed her on the road."

The room flickers around us, the edges blurring as if the sleeping Alden is stirring in the waking world. My breath catches. I still need him to agree to my plan.

"Wolves are not meant to become vampires," Alden goes on. "Our DNA is different. When Tanith became a vampire, she lost herself completely, becoming feral. Vyvyan is solely to blame. She would have maintained control over all her vampire offspring if she were a more competent ruler. Instead, several abandoned Corona, and Tanith suffered as a result. However, I will ensure that Vyvyan pays for her incompetence."

The small wolf stretches by the fire, and despite the heat of the flames, a chill runs down my spine. The thought of Tanith facing off against a vampire upsets my stomach. Zeus is a monster.

"Where is Tanith now?" I whisper, almost afraid to hear the answer.

Alden's shoulders sag. "Locked in a dungeon, sedated to keep her from harming herself and others."

The fire grows taller, and as I stare into the hypnotic flames, I understand Alden's pain and his thirst for revenge against the vampires. It is easier to blame an unknown entity than to believe your family could hurt you. Don and Zeus should talk.

"You know Tanith's fate is Zeus's fault, right?" I say in a soft but firm voice.

"How?" Alden asks, his voice tinged with suspicion.

"He lured her into the forest that day, knowing the vampires would get her."

Alden folds his arms. "That's not true. A mate is sacred, and Zeus would never harm her. It's a grave offense—punishable by death—to kill someone else's mate. The wronged party can challenge the offending wolf to seek justice. My brother would never betray me like that. He needs me."

"What if I had a way for you to get Tanith back?" I ask.

Alden stiffens. He trains his piercing gaze on me, and I see the wolf inside him peering out, a primal intensity burning in his blue eyes. I don't flinch away. I am here to help, not to hurt him.

"Leigh," Alden says, "I know what you are trying to do."

"I'm sorry?"

"Ravi has been my prisoner for years," he says. "He told me about dreamwalking, how to look for the signs when a Lunar Witch invades your dreams and tries to manipulate you with their words and presence, which is what you are doing now."

My muscles lock up. Calling it tension doesn't even come close. He'll never believe the truth. His story captivated me so much that I forgot to mention the dreamwalking. I knew he'd find out, but now he thinks I deliberately hid it from him.

"I'm not lying," I insist.

Alden narrows his eyes. I understand why he doesn't trust me. Lies and deception encompassed our entire relationship, with us hiding our true intentions behind a veil of diplomacy. But now, I am here to help, to offer a genuine solution to the problem that plagues us both.

"Don't bullshit a bullshitter," Alden growls.

My panic rises from my stomach to my chest.

Tanith awakens. She rests on all fours, her ears upright, and listening while her big, tawny eyes watch me distrustfully.

"Alden, please, listen to me. I have a cure for vampirism," I say.

Alden stiffens. "What?"

"There is a vampire. You met her at the club; her blood turned magical when she became a vampire. Drinking it reverses vampirism. I will offer some of it to you, but in exchange, you must go against your brother and father's orders and leave Corona untouched forever."

Alden stands abruptly, and so does Tanith. He paces before the fire with his hands behind his back. Tanith bares her fangs at me, a low growl rumbling in her throat. I stay glued to my chair, hoping to prove I am not a threat.

"How?" Alden asks. "You just conveniently have a cure *right* now?"

I flinch. Alden is no longer the vibrant prince who tricked me at the palace. Instead, he is the Lua Enforcer, ready and willing to shred me to pieces with his claws.

But I have no other choice, so I press forward. "Yes. Some vampires have special abilities. Desiree is one of them."

"Why haven't I heard about the cure before now?" Alden asks.

I take a deep breath, but my body continues trembling. "She kept it a secret from me until recently. It isn't widely known. But I'm not lying to you. Zeus is the liar. Tanith never wanted to leave you. That was the excuse he gave you to get you to comply with his invasion plans. Ravi told me the truth. He sees and hears more than he should as your prisoner. Zeus deserves your hatred, not your loyalty."

Alden smiles a half-wolf grin that makes me catalog the exits. "Ravi told you?" I nod. "Then it must be true, since Ravi is so trustworthy." I narrow my eyes, considering Ravi's words. I believe him. He has no reason to lie, especially when he's already Alden's prisoner. If he were caught being dishonest, it could put Sama in danger. "You know, I like you, Leigh. You care about the well-being of your people, but you are a terrible judge of character."

I wince, the blow landing exactly as Alden intended. Yeah, I know I have trust issues, and I am working on it. It's not like I want to put my faith in Alden, but I empathize with him, knowing nothing about Zeus other than his father's unreasonably high expectations for him to be a cunning, ruthless leader.

"Zeus will not back off easily," Alden says, his voice low and resigned.

I slide to the edge of my seat. "But the Lua army answers to you."

Alden strokes Tanith's wiry fur. "True."

"Do we have a deal?" I ask, ignoring my pounding heart. "I give you the cure, and in exchange, at dawn, you turn your army against Zeus."

"Give me that cure." He smiles. "And I'll do whatever you want."

I force myself to stay seated, though I want to jump and do a victory dance.

"For what it's worth, I am glad you were smart enough not to agree to marry me."

"Would you have done it if I had said yes?"

"I would have married you to secure your throne, regrettably consummated the relationship, made your boyfriend watch, and then killed you in front of him before locking him in a cage to live the rest of his pathetic life as my pet," he says, never losing his sadistic smile.

Yikes. I have no idea if he is serious, but a part of me believes he could be, at least about part of it. Hurt people often hurt people.

My gut churns, but I roll my eyes. "It sounds like you gave it a lot of thought."

"I could go into detail, but this conversation is over."

"Why?"

"Because your friends just entered our camp."

With a wink, Alden snaps his fingers, and the dream shatters, jolting me back to reality. I sit up in bed, my heart in my throat. Wilder's in trouble.

CHAPTER SIXTY-THREE
WILDER

WE REACH the wolf encampment in record time after leaving our car near the train station and going through the desert on foot. Navigating through the vast sea of tents, the new moon cloaks our movements. The soft white sand muffles our footsteps as we slip past the guards. Their vigilance is no match for our intimate knowledge of the terrain. The guards are focused on the distant horizon, failing to notice what's right under their noses. We move like shadows, silent and stealthy, more akin to specters than soldiers.

Ahead, the bonfire Bennett mentioned flickers, illuminating the surrounding wolves. They sit in human form, their laughter ringing through the night air. Some indulge in drink, their eyes glassy, and movements sluggish after the long journey from Lua, while others remain alert, their sharp, pointed ears attuned to any signs of intrusion.

Catching Brigid's eye, I nod, my lips in a grim line. Without a word, she understands my unspoken plan. With a silent signal, she retreats into the darkness. The night quickly swallows her as she sets off to create a distraction.

According to Bennett, the prisoner tent housing Stellan and Queen Jorina lies between the princes' grand structures. When I spot it, my fists tighten. It's small and unimposing, yet Leigh's grandmother has been confined in it for days. While Corona's leaders were distracted by internal grievances and distrust, they failed to realize the pawprints at the border belonged to an advancing army. I dread what condition we might find them in.

As we draw closer, a sense of unease prickles the back of my neck. I take a deep breath and signal Gianna and Marlowe to follow me.

We circle one of the largest tents, possibly Alden's, where Leigh should be with him now offering the cure in exchange for Corona's freedom. I pray she's successful.

In the distance, smoke billows into the night sky, carried on the desert breeze. A few wolves around the fire take notice, their heads snapping up in alarm, but it isn't until flames engulf a nearby tent, the crackling sound of burning fabric filling the air, that someone yells, "Fire!"

The wolves leap to their feet, yipping with panic, and race off to tend to the flames that Brigid has unleashed.

"Now," I whisper-yell to Gianna and Marlowe. We dart into the prisoner tent. Rough canvas brushes against my skin as I slip inside.

Darkness engulfs me, pressing in from all sides. Slowly, my eyes adjust to the pitch-black surroundings, and shapes and shadows gradually form in the gloom. In the corner, two slumbering forms catch my eye. Their bodies curled as if seeking comfort in sleep. It's Jorina and Stellan.

There are no guards, and my nerves are set on edge. Were they so arrogant not to expect an ambush, or did we fall into a trap?

Jorina and Stellan sleep with their heads against a wooden beam, their hands bound by cuffs that glint in the faint firelight filtering through the tent's entrance. The design is like the ones used at Kratos to stifle a witch's magic. Heat twists in my gut.

"Melt their restraints," I instruct Marlowe, who, to my surprise, hasn't abandoned us like I had anticipated. Despite now having what she wanted —a weapon to protect herself and a pardon from the queen—she remains by my side. There's still time for her to change her mind, though. Flames ignite in her palms.

"Don't move, Your Majesty, or I might accidentally burn you," Marlowe says.

Queen Jorina blinks awake. "Are you here to save us?" she asks, her voice hoarse.

"Yes. Now hold still."

I watch the tent's entrance with bated breath as Marlowe works behind me. To my left, Gianna's fingers twitch around her knife. The seconds tick by, each one an eternity stretched taut, until finally, there's a soft hiss of melting metal accompanied by Marlowe's whispered warning to Jorina to stay silent.

Stellan flinches as Marlowe approaches him next. He blinks his weary eyes while she works on his restraints. His gaze shifts to his daughter, and Gianna's lips curve into a half-smile that says, *Yeah, even after you abandoned me, I came for you.*

A shadow flickers over Stellan's features as he returns his attention to Marlowe, but not before I notice the tears in his eyes. He seems to understand he messed up, yet we still risked everything to rescue him. Our being here doesn't necessarily ensure our survival or freedom—that will depend on Leigh's ability to negotiate with Alden—but at the very least, it buys them some time.

When his restraints fall away, Stellan massages his wrists, chafed but not as raw as Jorina's.

"Let's collect Brigid and leave," I whisper.

I crouch to help Jorina stand, acutely aware of her cane's absence. Her clothes hang limply against her willowy, frail frame, the fabric worn and stained—a pungent odor of sweat and grime clings to her like a second skin.

"Where is Leigh?" Jorina asks.

"Safe, Your Majesty," I tell her. Gianna offers Stellan her hand. He takes it and rises, towering over her.

"You look so much like her," he notes. I assume he means Maria.

"Let's go," I say.

"Wait," a soft, accented voice calls from the shadows. "Take me with you." The words are barely louder than a whisper but carry a desperate edge.

We all pause, and Marlowe and I share a narrowed look. Neither of us noticed another presence in the room. I grip Jorina tighter as I turn toward the voice. Peering into the darkness, I find a young woman with long, matted black hair stuck to her dirty skin. Her clothes are ugly and torn, and her hands and feet are restrained.

Who the fuck is this girl?

I shift toward her.

"I sense a trap," Marlowe rushes out. But something about the girl seems familiar, as if we've met before, but I know we haven't.

"Please," the girl says. "Don't leave me with him. He's a monster."

My grip tightens on Jorina. "Who is a monster?"

The girl licks her cracked lips. "Zeus."

"We can't leave her," Gianna commands.

"If we don't, we will all end up like her," Marlowe hisses. Outside, the wolves grow louder, their voices too close for comfort.

Our window of escape is closing fast.

"Don't go without me, please! I beg you," the prisoner girl pleads.

"If we bring her with us, Zeus will be angry," Stellan says.

I scoff. Fuck Zeus. We don't cater to him.

"Who are you to Zeus?" I ask the girl.

"My name is Sama."

"She is Ravi's sister," Stellan supplies.

I flinch. If she's Ravi's sister, she's also Leigh's family.

The tent flap opens, and we all brace for action. But it's Brigid.

"Are you all trying to get caught? The time to go was five fucking minutes ago," she seethes.

I peer behind her to where there are still no guards, and the sense of dread roiling inside me expands. Something isn't right.

"Ugh, fine, but if this goes wrong, I'll say I told you so." Marlowe groans. She hurries to Sama, who recoils as if afraid Marlowe will strike her, but instead, she works on melting her restraints. At the glimpse of the old Marlowe, I smile on instinct, then stifle it. That person is gone.

"Thank you," Sama says.

"Thank me when we are miles from here."

We slip beneath the rear flap of the prisoner tent and cautiously make our way toward the exit, putting distance between ourselves and the commotion caused by the fire behind us. Our goal is to reach the car undetected. I hold my breath, not trusting myself to not make a sound.

"No, this way. Fewer wolves guard the western exit." Sama tugs Brigid's hand in the opposite direction of the car.

Another entrance comes into view, and for a moment, I believe we've made it. But the sound of howls at my back shatters that illusion. More howls and barks follow, a chilling chorus, making Jorina stiffen in my arms. I hurry after the others, but even with my help, Jorina is too slow.

"Leave me," the queen says. "I am jeopardizing your safety."

"No." Leigh would never forgive me if I left her grandmother behind. I would never forgive myself.

"There they are!" someone in the wolf army yells.

Sama's yelp pierces the air, sending a jolt of adrenaline through my veins. With a desperate tug, she yanks Brigid forward, propelling them several feet ahead of us. "It's Zeus," Sama cries out. "You need to hurry!"

Sama waves her hand in a swift, fluid motion, and tendrils of shadow, like a phantom fog, swirl around the two girls, enveloping them in a veil of darkness. The shadows dance and twist, obscuring their forms from view.

Meanwhile, the wolves' predatory gazes remain fixed on the rest of us, their eyes gleaming with a hungry intensity.

Stellan and Gianna run side by side, and I study Gi's face—the fear in my friend's eyes.

We won't all make it.

"Stellan," I croak. He looks at me, and it takes every ounce of willpower to trust him after what he did to betray us in the first place by putting his faith in the enemy, but I need his help if we want Gi and Jorina to make it out of here safely. "Take the queen."

Stellan's gaze lingers behind us. "You are the only person strong enough to carry her," I explain. He nods, then takes Leigh's grandmother from me.

"No," Gianna growls. "We all go, or none of us do."

The wolves get closer, their howls growing louder with each passing second. If they don't go now, all of us will be taken as prisoners.

"Gianna, go find Leigh. Tell her I trust she'll negotiate my release," I say. I have to. Believing in her is our only option. She will save me.

Marlowe doubles back. "If you stay, then I stay."

We hold each other's gaze, and I find myself at a loss for words. A part of me wants to tell her no, to insist that I don't need or want her company, that this sacrifice to regain my respect is nothing more than an empty gesture. But the words never come. They get caught in my throat as conflicting emotions wage war within me.

Lost in the moment, I barely register the approaching danger until it's too late. By the time I come to my senses, the wolves have already arrived, their menacing presence sending a chill down my spine. Gianna needs to leave.

"Go, now. We will distract them," I tell her.

Gianna squeezes my bicep. "Stay alive, you big idiot," she says before racing away.

Marlowe and I turn around in tandem, our hands raised in surrender. Hundreds of wolves and a tall, sinister-looking man resembling Alden with the same light eyes, but darker hair emerge from the shadows, their presence overwhelming in the clearing.

"Well, well," Zeus sings, his voice dripping with malice. "Isn't this special, Alden? Two commanders for the price of one."

Alden nods, shouldering through the crowd of wolves to stand beside Zeus. His eyes, usually so expressive, are cold and unreadable. Was Leigh able to get into his dreams? Did they talk? Is he on our side or his brother's?

"Guess it's our lucky night," he says, as if bored.

Zeus howls to the absent moon, and the sound prickles my scalp. His followers, in human and wolf form, surround us. They force Marlowe and me to our knees. Magic-reducing cuffs clamp around our wrists with a sickening finality.

As they haul us to our feet, I catch Alden's gaze, searching for any sign of the man who once claimed to seek peace, but his eyes remain shuttered, betraying nothing as his men drag us back to camp.

With each stumbling step in the sand, my mind races with a single, terrifying thought: if Alden has abandoned us, if Leigh failed to convince him, then our fate is sealed. The wolves' cruelty knows no bounds.

But even as fear claws at my heart, I cling to hope that our sacrifice will not be in vain, that our friends will make it to safety and find a way to end this war. Either way, Alden will reveal his true colors between now and morning.

CHAPTER SIXTY-FOUR
LEIGH

I PACE the Blade garrison courtyard. Each second is an eternity. With every movement in my periphery, I pray that Wilder and the others are returning from their mission. But the silence only grows.

Where the hell are they?

Alden's words from my dream replay in my mind like a haunting melody. Maybe he was playing mind games, and my friends are okay. But the disquiet in my gut refuses to subside, twisting and turning like an eel.

"Quit it," Isolde says for the umpteenth time. "They will be back any minute."

The front door flies open, and Brigid enters, holding the hand of a girl who must be Ravi's sister. She has his same round face, friendly eyes, and guarded smile.

"Sama?" I ask.

The girl flies into my arms. Her body shakes with sobs. "I'm so sorry!" she cries. "I should have stayed and helped them."

I hold her close, stroking her hair. "What happened?" I stare at the door, desperate for Wilder to walk through it and take me in his arms, to promise everything is okay.

But Brigid only walks over to the bar cart and pours herself a large drink, downing it in one gulp before pouring another. The door remains closed, Wilder nowhere to be seen.

"What happened?" I demand, suddenly unable to breathe.

Sama's sobs intensify. "We left them and—"

Gianna, Stellan, and my grandmother stumble into the garrison. My exhale is audible with relief, but my expression quickly falls when I see

Wilder is not with them. Neither is Marlowe. My ears begin to ring as Stellan sets my grandmother on her feet with care. Despite his gentleness, the sight of him ignites fury in my chest. This man was going to *sell* my country to the wolves. But I lock eyes with my grandmother, and a sob bubbles to the surface. I go to her.

Handing Sama to Pallas, I rush to my grandmother's side with tears in my eyes. "Grandmother," I say, pulling her away from Stellan.

"Leigh, something happened," Gianna announces, but I barely hear her as I gather my grandmother in my arms. Gods, I missed her.

My stomach roils. She's been Zeus's prisoner, and I had no idea. I believed she was in Glaucus this whole time, ignoring me after the news about Fynn broke, angry with me for making a mess of my time as queen, failing to unite the Council as she suggested. Instead, Zeus kidnapped her, and by her pungent smell, he abused her during her captivity. I grimace.

"If I had known, I would have come to find you," I whisper.

"Don't blame yourself. You have a country to run," my grandmother replies.

Her words cut deep, and shame eats at me like a corrosive acid. Do I have a country to run? The Council and Janus abandoned me, and part of me deserved it. I thought they were all conspiring against me, but now that I am alone, I wish I had them here to help me decide what to do about my upcoming meeting with Zeus.

"Leigh," Gianna says again, her voice insistent.

I open my eyes, expecting Wilder to be there, but my lips pinch. Still nothing. Gianna clutches her chest when I meet her stare.

"Where is he?" I ask, unwrapping myself from my grandmother's embrace.

Gianna and Stellan share a teeth-rattling look, drawing my attention to their family resemblance. They also have similar noses and mouths.

"Leigh, he chose to stay," Gianna says.

I shake my head. "Stay where?"

"With the wolves," Gianna replies. "Zeus and Alden have him and Marlowe. They are prisoners."

No. She's wrong. Alden and I are on the same side. He agreed to take the cure for Tanith.

White-hot anger pulses within me. My shadows beg for release. If he betrayed me, then there would be hell to pay.

Easy, Leigh, you don't know if Alden double-crossed you, Aradia soothes.

I exhale. Of course, he lied. He took Wilder as a prisoner to rub salt in the wound. He probably didn't believe me when I told him about the cure.

He could be playing Zeus, my father suggests.

I pause, considering the possibility. But I can only be sure of Alden's true intentions by seeing him in person. My body is numb, and every fiber of my being screams at me to rush to Wilder's side, to save him from whatever fate awaits him, remembering how Alden threatened to keep him in a cage. However, I force myself to take a deep breath.

If Alden is indeed on our side, acting rashly could jeopardize his plans and put Wilder in even greater danger. I have to trust that Alden loves Tanith enough not to give up this opportunity to save her, like I wouldn't give up on Wilder. I'll resolve this crisis come morning. It's a difficult choice, but I must focus on the bigger picture and the safety of my entire country, even if it means temporarily setting aside my desires.

Refusal claws its way up my throat. I will *not* fail.

The love of my life sacrificed himself to save my friends and family. I'll do the same for him. The words I never spoke, the confession I held back, now burn a hole in my chest. The gods won't let us both die before I tell him, just once, that I love him. I've loved him for months, silently, achingly, and now time is running out.

"We need to go get them," Isolde says to me.

"There's no time," Gianna says, glancing at the clock on the wall. Dawn will be here soon.

"Wilder could be dead come morning," Isolde insists.

I rub my swollen eyes. The decision I'm about to make will likely strain my relationship with Isolde. She will hate me for what I'm about to say, but being a leader means making tough choices that won't always be popular. It's not about making friends; it's about doing what's best for everyone. I can only hope that once this crisis is resolved and the dust settles, Isolde will understand my reasoning. Then perhaps we can still maintain our closeness.

"Everyone to the media room," I announce. "We need to talk."

"Leigh?" Pain radiates from Sol's gaze.

"Wilder knows what he's doing." He's putting his faith in me. I need to put mine in him and Alden.

Isolde takes a moment to hold my gaze before she nods, choosing to work with me rather than against me.

Each step toward the media room is akin to wading through quicksand. Pitying stares burn into my back, heavy with a sympathy and sorrow that assumes Wilder is already lost.

I bite back a sob. *They're wrong,* I want to scream. *We'll bring him home.* But the words lodge in my throat. He's a prisoner of my enemies, and the deal I made with Alden feels precariously thin, like a fragile thread dangling over an abyss. If I'm wrong about Alden, if I've misjudged him, I'll regret it for the rest of my life.

But we haven't lost yet.

CHAPTER SIXTY-FIVE
WILDER

"AGAIN."

The force of the blow snaps my head to the side. A metallic taste fills my mouth, followed by a searing heat that blossoms across my cheekbone. Pain radiates through my skull. Beside me, Marlowe grunts. Her breath comes in short, sharp gasps as a wolf in human form relentlessly pummels her, demanding information about the Council, Leigh, the vampires—anything they need to know before Zeus officially declares war on Corona come sunrise.

The wolves' frustration grows with each unanswered question. Their snarls echo in the vast darkness of the tent inside the Aurora Desert. But we remain silent. We need to hold out until Leigh meets with Zeus at dawn. Then, this nightmare will end.

A wolf guard's claws dig into my scalp as he wrenches my head back. "Do you have a death wish?" he growls. His hot, fetid breath washes over my face. I taste bile.

I bare my teeth in a bloody grin. "Do you?" I taunt, my words slurred by my swollen jaw. I memorize my torturer's face: his wide-set mouth and crooked teeth. Once free, he'll be the first one I find.

Marlowe laughs before taking another hit. Her head flies sideways, and I wince.

The guard's eyes narrow maliciously. "You know what will break you? Your little queen's surrender. Zeus promised us that he'd give her to us as a reward after Alden marries her, securing the throne for Lua." My bound hands clench into fists as he continues, "We'll break her, make her scream, and beg until she's nothing but an empty shell. And you'll get to watch—

force you to witness her degradation. You'll see the light fade from her eyes and know you can't stop it."

A fire ignites inside me so intense it threatens to consume me. I strain against my bonds until my muscles burn, but I'm helplessly stuck. I force a laugh instead, choosing defiance where physical resistance fails me. They have no idea what they're up against, no concept of the sheer power and determination that fuels Leigh's every move. They won't break her. She'll fight tooth and nail before that day comes. Still, the image he's painting is visceral enough to make my blood boil.

"Think that's funny?" the guard snarls.

"No, what's funny is your fa—"

The blow comes, swift and brutal. I grit my teeth, refusing to give him the satisfaction of a groan.

Alden rises from his seat, where he's been watching the guard beat me for the last thirty minutes, with a bored expression on his scarred face. "Enough of this. Prepare to bring them to the bridge. Let them see Leigh fail, and maybe they'll learn to cooperate."

As he drifts past me, I spit blood at his feet. *Fucking coward.*

Alden frowns, grabs me by the hair, and yanks me close, whispering, "Behave."

I glare at him as he releases me, my voice filled with venom. "She trusted you."

Alden's laughter curls my upper lip. I jerk forward, but my guard grips the back of my neck with a vice-like hold and forces me to my knees. My eyes sting from the pain.

As I kneel there, I hold on to the flickering promise of a future where Leigh and I can be together. Where our world finds peace. I envision a future where people accept our relationship despite our different backgrounds, where we can be an example of what Corona could be like if Nebula and Epsilon stop fighting long enough to learn to coexist harmoniously. Leigh would be my wife, not Alden's or anyone else's.

She drives me nuts with her secrets, but her heart is pure, and it fucking belongs to me.

I refuse to let my life end before she tells me she loves me because I know she does. It's a distant dream, threatened by each brutal blow from the wolves. Their relentless assault aims to break me, but I refuse to let go of that vision.

I cling to that dream like a lifeline, knowing that if I lose sight of it, I'll be lost forever in this sea of pain. So, I hold on. I persevere. I keep that flame alive in my heart, no matter the agony.

Ultimately, this dream is all I have left, and I won't let the wolves take it from me.

CHAPTER SIXTY-SIX
LEIGH

THE SUN RISES in the east, its warm rays offering no solace as I cross the Charon Bridge to meet Zeus. Each step upon the ancient stone feels foreboding, like crossing the Death River into Hell itself. If I become Zeus's prisoner, I'll beg for Hell itself. If I don't get Wilder back, I'll crave death. And if Alden betrayed me, absolutely *nothing* will stand in my way. Did he not believe me about Desiree? Or did I underestimate his loyalty to his brother? It's my word against Zeus's, after all.

My friends and Eddo's Blades flank me, their stances poised for battle, a silent promise that I won't face the wolves' wrath alone. The city's innocent inhabitants who didn't flee last night, including the Erinye sisters, hide behind closed doors. Ry is in position, in a building in East Aurora, ready to take down the wolves with his long-range rifle if negotiations go sideways.

Across the bridge, the wolves gather, some in human form, others as animals. Their heavy breathing mingles with the gentle lapping of the Cora River below, the only sounds in the morning silence. Even the birds refrain from their usual dawn chorus.

I lock eyes with Alden across the bridge. His expression is inscrutable, revealing nothing of his true intentions. My gaze shifts to his brother, Zeus, who is two inches shorter but no less imposing. His eyes are calculating beneath the hooded expression obscures his face. This is the man who orchestrated the vampire attack on Tanith just to secure Alden's cooperation. Saliva fills my mouth as disgust rises within me.

Such a monster doesn't deserve to sit on my throne—a throne he'd stain with the same cruelty he inflicted on his own family.

"Glorious morning, isn't it?" Zeus asks with false sincerity.

I force a smile. "You are here at the wrong time of year. I'm afraid summer has our best sunrises."

Zeus quirks a brow. "Well, it is good that you are about to surrender your throne to us so I can visit whenever I want."

I laugh. Surrendering to this pitiful excuse for a man is a joke. My fingers twitch to summon my magic, urging me to show him how unwilling I am to bend my knee. But I still have faith that Alden will ally with me.

Zeus looks behind me. "Are those useless numbers meant to intimidate me?"

I ignore him. What we lack in numbers, we make up for in tenacity. Instead, I turn to Alden. Sweat dots his brow. Maybe he isn't the emotionless killing machine he pretends to be. I study his expression, searching for a sign we are on the same side. There is none. My heart thrashes against my ribs, but as long as I stand, I can still convince him. "Alden. Don't do this."

Alden shrugs. "No hard feelings, Leigh."

"You are helping your weasel of a brother take my crown. Of course, there are hard feelings."

Zeus steps forward as if to attack me, but Alden slaps his chest. "Easy, brother. On my count, remember?"

"She called me a weasel," Zeus says through his teeth.

"You are the future king. Act like it," Alden whispers loud enough for all of us to hear.

I cross my arms over my chest. When Ravi told me what Zeus did to Tanith to control Alden, I felt sorry for him, but maybe he got it wrong. It looks like Alden controls Zeus. Perhaps I put my faith in the sibling with the most power.

I search for Ravi among the crowd behind the princes. I don't see him.

Did Alden leave him behind, or did Ravi expect me to fail? I glance back at Alden, who just stares at me without a hint of remorse. I don't have a backup plan. If he doesn't help me, Corona is doomed.

He smirks, as if he can read my mind.

"Are you ready to surrender, Leigh? Or must I use force?" Zeus asks.

"Where's Wilder?" I ask, stalling. If Alden hurt him, then I'll know he betrayed me.

Zeus's answering smile reminds me of the Harborym daemon. It's straight from Hell.

"Bring the prisoners forward!" he calls, his voice echoing off the stone bridge. A guard dressed in forest green pushes a bound and bruised Wilder and Marlowe forward.

With a cruel kick, the guard forces them to their knees. "Don't forget to kneel before your queen," the guard sneers.

I gasp. Wilder's face is battered beyond belief. Dried blood cakes his hair and stains his dark clothes. His eyes meet mine, and they hold reassurance, but also a plea for me not to panic. But panic is far from my mind. In its place, white-hot rage singes my veins.

Zeus's grin widens, relishing in their humiliation. I want to throw him into the river below, preferably with weights attached to his skinny ankles.

"That's enough, Heinrich. Fall back in line," Zeus commands. When Alden nods, the guard obeys. He melts back into the ranks, but I memorize his soulless eyes. I will make him pay in this life and the next.

"You tortured them," I say to Alden, who sighs.

"They shouldn't have broken into our camp or taken what didn't belong to them."

Zeus nods. "A monarch should never be so soft-hearted, Leigh."

"A compassionate queen isn't a weak one," I counter.

Zeus clicks his tongue as Alden groans, no longer meeting my stare. Instead, he glares at the ground.

I clench my roiling stomach.

"Face it, you lost." Triumph gleams in Zeus's eyes. "You were so busy trying to detect corruption within your Council that you never anticipated our invasion. And now, you have nothing left to do but surrender or watch as your people suffer."

Traitor. I shoot a menacing look at Alden. He let me believe we were on the same side. We were supposed to be allies, not enemies. "I told you the truth. Yet you side with Zeus? He's your enemy, not me!"

Zeus scowls at his brother before frowning at me.

"Alden told me everything," he says. My jaw drops. "He mentioned you would give him the cure to save Tanith in exchange for him turning against me."

No. "You *told* him?"

Alden meets my stare head-on. "He's my future king."

"He hurt Tanith."

"My brother is better off," Zeus says over us.

Alden doesn't so much as wince.

With a sharp glare, I shoot daggers at him. "You disgust me. Tanith is better off."

His hands turn into claws. His fingers elongate before my eyes.

"Am I making you angry?" I taunt. "Good. Be fucking angry. She would be if she saw what a coward you are. You had a chance to save her, and you didn't. I hope she hates you for it."

"Leigh, it's okay. You tried," Wilder says.

But I can't look at him. I've condemned him to death for a stupid decision to trust someone who never earned it. I knew better than to think Alden could be won over. People cling to their secrets. They don't change.

"You doomed her," I say to Alden, my voice low and cruel. The ghosts inside my head scream and kick as the wind whips my hair. "You claim that she's your mate." I laugh. "But if she were, you'd fight for her, not for this piece of shit beside you."

Zeus growls. It is a deep, menacing sound. But I don't care. He doesn't scare me. Losing my country, dooming my people—that scares me.

I give Wilder one last look, pouring all my love, my every waking thought, into that fleeting moment. I should have told him the truth in all our intimate moments, expressing how much I care about him. There is no one else for me. He sees all of me—even the ugly parts—and still chooses to find beauty in them.

My longing to kiss him one last time threatens to cripple me. If only we had more time together, we could have grown old side by side, weathering the storms of life until we were both ghosts haunting the halls of Rowan

Palace. I want a life with him, but now, our only chance to reunite might be in death.

"I love you, and I'll find you in the afterlife," I say before meeting Zeus's hateful stare, challenging him to do his worst. Beside him, Alden is now snarling in his wolf form.

Zeus raises a hand. "Wolves, prepare to—"

In one swift, razor-sharp bite, Alden tears his brother's head clean from his body. I scramble backward as the head rolls down the bridge, stopping where my feet just were. Zeus's face is frozen with the same hateful sneer he wore seconds ago.

Gianna screams somewhere behind me. I stand speechless.

What the hell just happened?

Alden emits a mournful howl, and several wolves join in lament. The haunting, anguished sound pierces my ears. Is it pain for Tanith? Or Zeus? Or both? But I am still trying to understand why he did it. He told Zeus about the cure. He taunted me for it.

"Alden?" I mutter.

Beside me now, Brigid and Isolde lower their weapons. Brigid makes a fist, signaling her father's Blades not to advance. Pallas gawks at the blood pooling from Zeus's headless neck.

Alden whimpers and trots forward through his brother's blood. He rubs his sizable canine body against my legs. "Does this mean we are on the same side?" I trail my hand across his soft, yet bloody, fur.

Alden whines and then transforms back into his human form with the sound of bones snapping. I gag. My hands rest on Alden's solid stomach. He is naked as the day he was born and speckled in blood.

"Ugh!" I push him away.

Alden catches himself before he falls, laughter rumbling in his chest. "Excuse you, I just saved your life," he retorts.

"You lied!" I screech. "You told him everything! You made me think I couldn't trust you!"

"I did," Alden replies, his tone somber. "But I had to make him think he'd beaten you to keep his guard down. I spoke to Ravi, and he told me everything. He corroborated your story."

I scream, emotions overwhelming me to the point my entire body trembles. "I was ready to fight!"

"Now, you don't have to. My brother is dead."

I pause. Holy shit. Zeus is dead.

Alden stops laughing and peers down at the fallen body. "He deserved worse."

I peer at the obnoxious prince. He didn't give up on Tanith.

"You must love her," I whisper.

"With the force of the full moon," he replies as the wolves behind him blink as if coming out of a daze. A few of them approach Alden with their hackles raised. They bare their teeth as Alden bares his back.

"Listen up!" Alden roars, his voice like a whip. "Lua will not be invading Corona today or any other day. We'll return to our land and bring my father Zeus's body. Anyone who has a problem with that or my leadership should challenge me now."

The advancing werewolves pause. My breath catches as they bow their heads to their future king.

"Smart choice," Alden says.

Unable to wait longer, I rush toward Wilder and Marlowe, dropping to my knees. I wrap my arms around Wilder's shoulders, but I question why he isn't hugging me back.

"I'm kind of tied up," he says, a hint of amusement in his voice.

"Alden!" I screech, causing him to jump. "Get these restraints off and, for the love of the gods, put on some damn clothes!"

Alden smirks. "Heinrich, release these prisoners."

The guard I vowed to kill earlier releases Marlowe first, who scampers to her feet with flames swirling around her clenched hands. The threat is clear: if Heinrich dares to touch her again, she will fry him to a crisp. He retreats, but not before bumping into Wilder.

"Now him," I command.

Heinrich removes Wilder's restraints, but isn't quick enough to get out of the way. Wilder punches him clean in the throat. Heinrich falls to his back, choking for air. Next, Wilder shifts to advance on Alden, who grins in anticipation of a fight. I step between them.

"It's over," I say. The fire in Wilder's eyes slowly fades. "Desiree saved us."

"You saved us, Leigh."

Wilder smiles as he wraps his arms around me. I do the same, holding him tight. We don't kiss; we just stand there in the center of the Charon Bridge, our hearts beating as one, until we hear a camera go off. Wilder and I pull away from each other to see Stellan taking our picture.

"This will make front-page news!" he says, a smug grin on his face.

CHAPTER SIXTY-SEVEN
DESIREE

Five Months Later

THE WEISS TRAIN Station in Glaucus looks plucked straight from the pages of a fairy tale. Intricate red gingerbread markings adorn the pristine white walls, adding a whimsical charm with the delicate patterns. The ticketing agents—dressed in old-fashioned uniforms with gleaming whistles and jaunty hats—move about with a sense of timeless efficiency.

As I stand beneath a canopy of glittering stars, the cool summer mountain air envelops me. Its crisp embrace seeping deep into my bones, filling me with a sense of wonder and anticipation.

Beside me, Vane meticulously rereads our ticket vouchers. Our mountains of luggage, mostly his rather than mine, loom nearby. As I commit our surroundings to memory, I can't help but feel a twinge of nostalgia. Vane and I have grand plans to explore the world, and who knows when I will have the chance to return to this magical place in the north? I've loved it more than I ever thought possible.

Vane's voice cuts through my thoughts. "Will you miss Lua?"

"Will you?" I counter.

We've lived ninety miles north of here with the wolves for five months. After Leigh and Alden returned to Borealis with my brother, I explained that the cure wouldn't be ready for Tanith in time. I told Alden that if he truly wanted to save his mate, he had to take both me and Vane back to his country. We were a package deal. Alden agreed, and after a quick goodbye with my brother, Vane and I left Borealis without looking back.

We might have never left the comfort of Lua if not for a letter I received from Mom three weeks ago. The cure is finally ready for mass market distribution—with approvals from Leigh, President Janus Dyer, and Vyvyan. I am expected back home for the official release party.

"I will miss the lack of sunshine," Vane says, his voice tinged with a wistful longing.

We discovered a world that defied our preconceived notions of wolves during our time with them. Instead of slumbering in caves and hibernating through the snowy months, we found sleepless cities, charming villages rivaling Glaucus's beauty, and ski resorts where wolves enjoyed winter activities beneath the ever-changing moon.

As Alden's esteemed guests, Vane and I stayed in the opulent Nocturn Castle near Tanith during her recovery. My first encounter with her, a feral vampire in chains with soulless crimson eyes, still haunts me. However, as I calmed her and fed her my blood, a remarkable transformation occurred, revealing a timid, sweet nature reminiscent of a cartoon princess.

Alden has now devoted himself entirely to Tanith. Their passion, born from years apart, was all-consuming, heedless of anyone's presence. The wedding invitation in my bag testifies to their enduring love—a ceremony hastened by the undeniable signs of Tanith's condition. Despite her attempts to hide it, my trained medical eye recognizes the symptoms of pregnancy.

"You know what else I will miss?" Vane asks mischievously. I smile, already knowing the answer.

"The food," I say.

"The fucking food!" He groans. "I don't think my taste buds will ever be the same."

Alden spoiled us rotten. We dined with him and the ailing King Simon, who barely tolerated our presence or how we ate only blood. Except, he couldn't do much since Alden was his remaining heir.

We were there for Zeus's funeral. Alden didn't cry during the sky burial. He held his face and middle finger skyward before taking Tanith's hand and turning his back on his sibling for good.

"I will also miss our adventures in the snow," Vane says in a sultry voice, evoking memories of sneaking off to secluded spots between the trees and thrilling gondola rides where I'd take Vane into my mouth.

"Those adventures don't have to end just because we are going back to Borealis," I tease.

Vane tugs me flush against him by my leather jacket. "Is that so?" His gaze hoods, dark with desire, as he watches me bite my lip.

"Maybe we could get a head start right now," I breathe against his ear. "I wonder if our train compartment is soundproof?"

He groans, nipping at my throat.

"Desiree?"

The familiar voice ties my stomach into knots. I turn to find Jaxson standing on the platform, dressed in a crisp, dark Blade uniform that accentuates his chiseled physique. He looks even more handsome than I remember, with the scent of summer and untamed wilderness clinging to him.

"Jax," I breathe, extracting myself from Vane's embrace. Jaxson nods to him, his eyes flicking between us.

"I heard you were passing through customs on your way back to Borealis," Jaxson says with a hesitant smile. "Congratulations on the cure. It's all my Anselm can talk about. He's an orderly at Psyche Psychiatric."

Heat surges inside me, a fierce, primal instinct. Mere moments ago, I was lost in Vane's passionate embrace, but now my body is readying for battle.

Who the fuck is Anselm? And why did Jax call him *his*?

"That's great," I manage to say, surprised that I mean it despite the ache in my chest. The searing jealousy recedes to a simmer. "I'm happy for you, Jax. Truly."

"Thanks, I'm happy for you, too." His gaze lifts to Vane. "How long have you two been together?"

"Five months," I admit softly.

Jaxson nods slowly. "I had a feeling there was unfinished business between you two. I guess that's what makes me a great Domna." His wry smile doesn't reach his eyes.

I want to say something to break the awkward silence, but the words stick in my throat. I love Vane, but seeing Jaxson again makes me realize I never stopped loving him, too.

Tears prick at the back of my eyes as I pull him in for a fierce hug. "I am so damn proud of you, Jax."

He clutches me tighter for a long moment before releasing me and stepping back. His eyes drink me in as if committing every detail to memory. "I missed you, sunshine. Take care of yourself, okay?"

"I will," I promise, aching with a mix of love, nostalgia, and letting go. "You do the same."

With a final nod, Jaxson squares his shoulders, and walks away, disappearing into the crowd.

Vane comes up behind me, slipping his arms around my waist. I lean into his chest. "It's okay, you know," he says softly. "You can love us both."

I twist in his arms to look up at him, searching his beautiful face for deception. There is none. "I will always love Jax. But I am desperately, completely, *eternally* in love with you. Not because you're a vampire prince or my sire, but because you're you—the man who saw me when no one else did."

Vane's eyes blaze as he holds my face, his cold rings sending sparks across my skin. "I know. And I will spend every day of forever showing you how much I love you and reminding you to love yourself."

I smile. "Let's go before my mom kills me for staying away these past few months."

The mention of killing reminds me of Vyvyan, and I'm nearly knocked off my feet by a sudden wave of insecurity. I don't know if Vane has kept in touch with her these past few months. I'm sure she knows where we are, given that our departure from Lua was no secret.

A whistle blows nearby.

"Vane," I say, "do you plan on seeing Vyvyan while we're in Borealis?"

He stiffens. "I hadn't decided," he admits, his voice measured. "She sent me a letter, asking me to return to the Nest. She said she was sorry for everything."

"She did?" I resist grabbing fistfuls of my hair.

Vyvyan apologized. That's unheard of. An apology and her signing off on the cure tells me she might have turned over a new leaf. Despite that, it doesn't change the fact she tried to kill me.

Vane sighs and traces gentle patterns along my back. "She did, and I'd be lying if I said the thought hadn't crossed my mind to see her. Vyvyan and I have a long history, and we need to discuss things, especially now that the cure is available."

I nod, trying to swallow past the lump in my throat. "I understand," I say, my voice barely audible above the train's rumble. "You don't have to go anywhere with me after the cure's release party, Vane. I mean it. It doesn't mean I love you less if you stay with her. I will be okay on my own."

He pulls me closer, his lips brushing against my forehead. "I won't go anywhere without you, Desiree. You're my everything."

I shake my head. "Some may say you are obsessed with me."

"Is that a bad thing?"

I laugh. "As a former medical professional, I'd have to say yes. As a ravenous vampire, I say no."

Another whistle sounds, drowning out Vane's laughter.

"Come on," he says, taking my hand. "We're boarding."

As we settle into our private compartment, thoughts of Vyvyan and the Nest continue to occupy my mind. Misty has been invading my dreams a lot lately. I'd love to see her again, but she also owes me an apology. She was my best friend. I listened to her and was there for her night in and night out, but when it was time for her to be there for me, she wasn't. Maybe one day, we will get back to where we were, but we have a ton to unpack before we get to that level.

Vane sits beside me, reading a newspaper, betraying his age, and I find myself mesmerized by his every movement.

"Tell me about your fondest memories during those early days with Vyvyan." I rest my head on his lap.

Vane folds the paper. "What do you want to know?"

I peer up at him through my lashes. "If it's about you, I want to know all the sordid details."

"Then, I will tell you."

CHAPTER SIXTY-EIGHT
WILDER

A FIRM KNOCK at my door interrupts the quiet of my office at the Borealis Blade Precinct.

Since our showdown with Lua in Aurora, the Council has been too preoccupied with drafting treaties to consider replacing me as the commander. I chose to stay in this position to help maintain peace between the factions, and now that the country is more stable, I find fulfillment in the work I'm doing to keep it that way. Growing up, I never envisioned myself as the commander, but now that I'm here, I can't imagine walking away from the role, not yet at least.

Soter enters. The scent of his cigarette smoke mingles with the aroma of freshly brewed coffee. His bi-colored gaze darts between Pallas, seated across from me, and myself. His eyes narrow.

Pallas spent the last five months in Aurora working with Eddo and his Blades.

"You wanted to see me," Soter states. He's not a fan of Pallas, given that Soter spent months trying to imprison him during the Nyx case last year. My Domna still possesses an inch-thick file documenting all of Pallas's alleged crimes.

Pallas smiles at him. "Hey, how's it going?"

Soter steps deeper into the room. "What is he doing back here?" he asks through gritted teeth.

I lean back in my chair. He's always wound so tight.

"Pallas works here now," I say. "He will serve as a consultant, providing insight into organized crime in Borealis and teaching us how to think like criminals to catch more of them. Eddo implemented this approach with great success in Aurora, and I plan to do the same here. You'll show him the ropes." My grin widens at Soter's flushed face.

"Excuse me?" he says, his voice low and dangerous, like the rumble of an engine.

"You heard me, Domna. You'll be Pallas's point of contact while he works with us. You will get him anything he needs."

The muscles in Soter's jaw twitch. Heat radiates off him, raising the temperature in the small office by several degrees.

"Do we have a problem?" I ask. He doesn't answer. I lean forward, the ancient wood of my desk creaking under the weight of my elbows.

Soter may not like it, but Pallas's unique perspective will be invaluable in our fight against organized crime. The supernatural underbelly of Borealis is a tangled web, and we need all the help we can get to unravel it.

"Fine," Soter grumbles.

I fight back a smile. "What was that?"

"I said, fine, I'll do it," Soter repeats, but commotion outside draws my attention. I rise from my seat to investigate. Soter follows close behind as I peek between the blinds.

Dressed in civilian clothes, Marlowe dismounts her motorcycle, which she parked in the red zone. I raise my brows. Someone tries to stop her, but she dismisses them with a wave of her gloved hand as she strolls into our building.

We went through hell together that night at the wolves' encampment, but since returning to Borealis, she's kept her distance. She hasn't stepped inside the precinct since we returned from Aurora. There are too many eyes to judge her for her past actions.

She's been hanging out around the city, making amends with the people she hurt, starting with Mom. Mom's been so busy with the cure that she still doesn't give Marlowe the time of day. She's still angry at her former friend for lying about Dad and Nyx. She's rightfully upset about not only losing her husband but also her best friend, leaving her broken in the process.

A part of me feels sorry for Mom's dismissal of Marlowe—a small, minuscule part. If she is here now, she must want something. But what?

"I thought this was the Blade Precinct," Soter remarks, glaring at Pallas. "Not a halfway house for the criminally inclined."

"Where's a criminal?"

Soter stiffens as I whirl to face Isolde. She's dressed in cut-off shorts and a cropped top, revealing a sliver of her toned midriff. Her cobalt ponytail sits high on her head, swaying with every shift of her weight. Shopping bags hang from her arms.

"What's in the bags?" I ask. Isolde's cheeks flush a delicate pink.

She sets her purchases down atop the empty chair beside Pallas, and the bags crinkle as she rummages through them. With a flourish, she pulls out a strappy orange dress. A dramatic slit runs up the side. Soter inhales a sharp breath.

"It's for the party," Isolde explains, her brown eyes sparkling. The party, thrown by the royals and the Council, will honor Mom's completion of the cure inside the first-ever Lunar Witch reentry facility before the first witches move in next week. Isolde groans, then stuffs the dress back into her bag. "You're right. I will look ridicu—"

"You will look beautiful," Soter says. Isolde gapes at him.

As I watch Isolde struggle not to smile at his compliment, a twinge of sympathy for Soter stirs within me, even as I consider the deep waters he's found himself in with her. But then I remember what an incredible douche he is and move on.

Pallas breaks the awkward silence. "What else is in the bag?"

Isolde's grin returns, genuine this time, as she pulls out a beautiful journal. The fresh leather scent fills the air as she unbuckles it and flips through the pages, the paper whispering beneath her callused fingertips as Marlowe enters my office.

Isolde frowns, still mad about Marlowe giving her the scar above her right brow when she knocked Sol out that day in Aurora to get to Leigh. "Marlowe," she says.

"Faez," Marlowe responds, but her gaze is on me.

"Give us the room," I tell my team. Isolde leaves, but Soter and Pallas glance at each other, and I remember their assignment. "Soter, show Pallas to his desk."

Soter's upper lip curls, but he doesn't fight me. He walks past Marlowe, ignoring her presence, while Pallas squeezes her shoulder in a gesture of support.

The room empties, leaving me alone with my former boss and friend. I'm eager to find out what she wants, considering she will break five months of silence to tell me.

"Looks good on you," Marlowe says once we are alone.

I fold my arms. Marlowe helped us in Aurora by telling Leigh about Stellan working with the wolves. She even stayed behind when I turned myself over to Alden and Zeus's captivity to save Queen Jorina, taking the beating of a lifetime to be with me after I thought she would run the second shit hit the fan. Our relationship may never return to what it was, but I hate her less than I did.

"What does?" I ask, my tone guarded yet curious.

She grins a flash of white teeth in the dimly lit office. "Authority."

I shake my head. "What do you want? I know you didn't come all this way to compliment me for taking your job. Or did you come here to tell me I didn't earn it, so I should give it back?"

Her brow furrows in mock concentration. "Would you?"

I lean back in my seat, assessing her. Is she challenging me?

"A pardon isn't enough to get you your job back."

Her hand cuts through the air like a dismissive blade. "That's not why I'm here, but it brings me joy to hear you defend your position. I guess the apple doesn't fall far from the tree. Seeing you sit where he sat, you remind me of him. Moran must be proud."

I wince. The phantom pain of Dad's betrayal is still fresh, though it's been almost a year since he was convicted of assassinating President Sinclair. I've visited him with Mom twice in the past five months, and we try to get along, primarily for her sake. But I don't think Dad and I will ever have a good relationship.

"What do you want, Marlowe? I was in the middle of a meeting," I say, uncrossing, and re-crossing my legs.

She gives me a pointed look. "That was work? It looked more like a social hour to me, but whatever. You're in charge."

"That's right, I am, and seeing as you no longer work here, you're trespassing. So tell me what you want, or leave." Despite my words, curiosity gnaws at me.

"That's why I am here," Marlowe begins in a softer, almost hesitant, voice. "I am leaving."

I blink. A part of me doesn't want her to go, a surprising realization that catches me off guard. "Where will you go?"

She shrugs, picking up a stapler, then an empty coffee mug from my desk that used to belong to her and setting them down, her fingers lingering on each one as if saying goodbye. "I hear Amro is nice this time of year."

"What's there?" I ask. Amro is the southernmost city in Corona. It is a vacation spot. I've never known Marlowe to relax.

She sighs. "A fresh start."

My heart lurches. Ever since I took the job as the head of the precinct, it has never felt right without Marlowe working here. I always expected to wake up one day and have her tell me she got her old job back, and I'd have no choice but to accept it because the order came from a higher authority than mine.

Somehow, her telling me she is leaving town for good hits harder than the thought of her taking back the position I currently hold—a position I convinced myself was temporary, but now I want to keep. She is the reason I am sitting in Dad's old chair. She made my childhood bearable and my return to Borealis tolerable after his arrest last summer.

Even though Borealis is no longer home to her after Chiron's imprisonment, I still thought she'd stay for me. Though I will never admit that aloud. Pallas is the only connection to her past life. Now, even he has a new job on the right side of the law.

Trying to mask my disappointment, I say, "Well, if you came to say goodbye, you could have just texted."

Marlowe narrows her eyes like a predator. "Quit being a little shit, or I won't give you your gift."

Marlowe reaches into the pocket of her riding pants and retrieves a small, black box. When she tosses it to me, I catch it, turning it over in my hand. The smooth surface cools against my skin.

"Are you proposing?" I joke.

"Open it," she encourages after I do nothing but stare.

I lift the box lid, finding a platinum pentacle pin inside. My gaze meets hers, and Marlowe folds her arms in a gesture of finality. "The commander's pin."

She grins. "Now, you can stop embarrassing yourself by wearing that pewter piece of shit the president gave you. Here." She takes the pin out of the box and gestures to my chest. "May I?"

I nod, unable to speak. Marlowe is passing the torch to me, someone she trusted as an acolyte. I never expected being the commander rather than her Domna, but I didn't foresee Marlowe being Nyx either. It's funny how things always work out, even in the bleakest days.

Marlowe's ocher eyes mist as she hovers over me. "I'm sorry for bringing up Moran earlier. You two have had a rough relationship, but someone needs to say it. I am proud of you, Wilder. I watched you grow up, protecting your sister with a fierceness and loyalty I admired. Seeing you sit in this chair because you've extended that loyalty to your country makes me smile. Caring for you and Desiree while you were kids was never a burden. I hope you know that. It was a bright spot for me. I wanted you to be my Domna; that is no secret. But now . . . I see you are exactly where you belong."

After removing my fake pin and replacing it with the real one, Marlowe adds, "There. Much better."

Thanks to the symbolism and Marlowe's confession, I gaze down at the shiny pin to mask the emotion in my eyes as my world spins.

This pin represents leadership and stability. Her giving it to me shows how much she still believes in me, even though I've made it clear I no longer believe in her. But that was to protect myself. Ever since she chose me that night, we surrendered to the wolves, and a huge part of me forgave her for what she did. She wanted to make the world a better place for the Nebula, like me, and I can't fault her for that, but she went about it the wrong way.

So much has changed since Marlowe almost suspended me after Soter accused me of being Nyx at the Harvest Festival. It turned out she was Nyx, which prompted me to get the job at the palace, where I met and fell for Leigh. I should thank her for my relationship bliss.

"Thank you."

Marlowe bobs her head in reply.

"Well, see you around, kid," she says, turning on her heel to leave.

"Wait," I rush out. She halts, peering back at me. "Is this it, or will I see you again?"

Marlowe smiles. "Are you going to miss—"

She doesn't finish. I cross the room and pull her into a hug, the scent of her leather jacket filling my nostrils with a familiar comfort. "Be safe," I tell her, and I mean it. "Stay out of trouble. My influence only travels so far."

She laughs. "Good thing you have friends in high places."

Yeah. Good thing.

CHAPTER SIXTY-NINE
LEIGH

ANOTHER GUEST'S sticky lips brush against my flushed cheek as they congratulate me, commending me for achieving what many thought impossible—opening Corona's first Lunar Witch reentry facility. Their attention quickly shifts to Chiara Dunn, who stands beside me, radiant in an off-the-shoulder forest green gown. The guest shakes her hand next, expressing awe at her remarkable feat of finding the cure for vampirism in record time.

The repurposed warehouse, now a halfway house, feels alive with celebration. As I stand in the makeshift recreational room hosting this lively part, I take a moment to reflect on our accomplishments these last few months.

A band plays energetic tunes amidst the industrial-chic decor of exposed brick and polished concrete, their melodies pulsing through the vast space. Guests mingle, engaging in lively conversations while enjoying appetizers, while others dance to the infectious rhythms. Laughter and chatter blend with the music, transforming the once-gloomy atmosphere of the former auto parts warehouse has transformed into a vibrant celebration. The energy perfectly embodies the halfway house's mission: Fostering community and joy in those transitioning back into society.

"Thank you for being here," Chiara acknowledges her admirer's praise. "I could not have done it without the Crown and Council's support and my daughter, Desiree."

I raise my brow. Where is Desi? She should stand beside her mom to bask in this momentous achievement. Her absence is notable, as is the mysterious disappearance of her date.

As I glance around for her, my reflection catches my eye in one of the freshly scrubbed windows. The crown atop my head sparkles, and I adjust it to sit straighter.

A year ago, I lived in constant fear, dreading the possibility of being killed or locked away in an asylum simply for being a Lunar Witch. However, everything changed when I found the courage to defy my family and reveal the truth about the War Letters.

The irony of the situation is not lost on me. The very people who once sought to silence me now celebrate my achievements. I've fought tooth and nail to get here, and the recognition I'm receiving feels like a hard-earned victory.

"You seem distracted," Janus whispers to me. She stands on my other side, wearing a white dress that makes her long, dark hair appear even darker, like an impenetrable void. "Isn't this what you wanted?"

I offer Janus a brief smile, acknowledging the progress we've made in our working relationship for the sake of the realm. Our relationship has improved even though she abandoned me in Aurora to deal with Zeus and Alden's invasion alone. She and the Council had prioritized protecting the capital, even at the cost of Aurora. I've admitted that their decision to vote me out was partially my fault since I kept secrets and suspected them of foul play. Janus and the others were focused on preventing the rest of the country from falling prey to the wolves. I understand their reasoning, even though their abandonment still stings.

After returning from Aurora, Janus, the Council, and I worked to repair the fragile trust between us. Forces will always try to divide us, but to avoid another invasion, we need to work together.

Ultimately, I secured peace for our nation again by placing my faith in Alden—someone I never expected to become my friend. I received his wedding invitation last week, which confirms I made the right choice by trusting him that day on the Charon Bridge. Thanks to Desiree, Alden and Tanith were reunited, and now Lua and Corona are allies once more.

"We've been standing here for hours," I whisper to Janus as I wiggle my numb toes. She smiles and lifts the long hem of her dress to reveal her practical shoes.

"Tricks of the trade, Your Majesty." She glances at my heels and compliments my gossamer silver, strapless dress. My outfit is a nod to the Nebula. Several months ago, I motioned again to disband the Labor Laws. To further solidify this, I passed a law prohibiting hospitals from branding newborns based on faction affiliation.

Both supporters and resistors have responded to my efforts to create a more unified and equal society, but I remain committed to my vision.

"Have you seen Wilder?" I ask the women on either side of me.

Chiara's motherly smile prompts me to scan the crowd for my own mother. I spot her chatting with Keris Telfour, a few other councilors, and my grandmother. My mother is a vision in ambrosia pink, adorned with multiple strings of pearls around her neck and woven into her blonde hair.

She must sense my gaze because she meets my eyes, offering a smile and a thumbs-up. A laugh bubbles out of me; the casual expression is surprising for her. Still, it's a sign that she has begun engaging with the world again after revealing the truth about her past with Don and the lies she and my father crafted to protect Fynn.

Your mother is stunning, my father's ghost whispers.

"She is," I whisper back.

The people and I have forgiven her, yet gossip columns continue to exploit her distress. They even spread false rumors that Mother secretly visits Don in prison. We did go together once, though. I remember maintaining civility with Warden Grey while Mother and Don spoke privately, seeking closure. Grey had been glaring at me; resentment still simmered beneath his professional veneer, even if it had lessened over time. Honestly, it didn't bother me much.

Warden Grey and his wife, Edith, are at the buffet, heaping food onto their plates. It's as if they are trying to fill the hole caused by Bennett's absence. He'd relinquished his Council seat just minutes after we returned from Aurora, triggering a special election. Stellan revealed that Bennett's parents' boating "accident" wasn't accidental at all. Someone had intentionally harmed them. That's when Bennett vowed to uncover the truth. I received his postcard several months ago but haven't heard from him since.

Corvina has also fled, admitting herself to Psyche Psychiatric to cope with Fynn's rejection and his subsequent death.

"I think he is on the dance floor with your cousin," Chiara says. Just then, an attendant approaches us with refreshments. Each councilor takes a drink, as does Janus, who seems preoccupied with Daphne across the room. Daphne, her hand resting protectively on her very pregnant belly, is engaged in a friendly conversation with Gianna and Stellan Navis, smiling as she speaks.

Daphne must've complimented Gianna; Stellan beams at his daughter as if she *is* the sun, and he's a planet caught in her orbit. Gi's been living with him in Aurora for the last five months, and they've been piecing together their family tree. He's the mayor there now, although his mission to create an enclave ultimately failed. I can't say Stellan and I will ever be best friends, but if Gi is happy, so am I.

I spot Wilder twirling Sama on the dance floor. Despite our distant relation, she insists I call her my cousin. Sama and Ravi, having grown up on the run, never had much family, so I agreed to the familiarity. When Alden offered them the choice between staying in Corona or returning to Lua as official residents, they chose to stay, and I invited them to move into Rowan Palace with me.

I smile as Sama giggles, watching Wilder continue to spin her. Though my feet ache, I long to join them.

"I think my sister is in love with your boyfriend," Ravi notes.

I laugh. Sama is in love with love. Just the other day, I saw her wistfully waving at the postman. "There's much to love," I reply.

Ravi takes a sip of his drink. "This is a beautiful soiree. Thank you for inviting me."

I shrug as Sama throws her head back, laughing at something Wilder said. I hand Ravi my drink. "Hold this for me," I say as he accepts my flute of sparkling wine.

"What am I supposed to do?" he asks as I walk off.

I smile as I call back, "Tell people you are grateful for them being here."

"But..."

I rush off without a second glance. I've been sharing some of my royal duties with Ravi. He's enjoyed accompanying me on public outings and has even agreed to embark on a royal tour in my place next year to see the country. He doesn't want to share the throne, citing the disastrous example of Ivah and Aradia, and I believe him. I'm trying out this new thing called trust. It's hard for me, but I'm slowly getting the hang of it.

I am proud of you, Aradia's ghost whispers. My smile widens.

As I enter the dance floor, Pallas and Isolde wave at me before they continue counting steps. Isolde—no longer part of my guard but still a friend—is a lethal Blade but a terrible dancer. However, Soter doesn't seem to care. He watches her from the edge of the dance floor, hands balled at his sides as if fighting with himself about whether to ask to cut in or not.

I have no such affliction.

"Mind if I take over?" I ask my cousin. Sama glances at Wilder before stepping aside.

Wilder's hand finds mine, his other settling possessively on my waist. A flush creeps across my cheeks as he gently pulls me closer, the space between us dissolving until our chests meet. It's far too intimate a distance, and I could not care less.

We are young and in love. Nothing else matters.

"Don't you have important people to talk to you?" he whispers.

Goose bumps prickle my skin from my shoulders to my wrists. "I *am* talking to someone important. I am talking to *you*." Wilder's smile deepens, a spark igniting in his eyes. An ache settles in my palms, a desperate urge to cup his face and lose myself in a kiss. "Come with me."

"Where are we going?" he asks as I lead him off the dance floor.

"I want some privacy, so I am giving you the grand tour."

"I like the sound of that."

Wilder and I leave the recreational room, the unspoken tension thick enough to taste, and step into the grand foyer.

"This is the check-in area for future patients and guests," I manage, biting my lip to keep the tremor from my voice as Wilder nods, feigning interest in our detailed surroundings.

He leans casually against the sleek, white check-in counter, but his gaze is anything but casual. "Where will residents sleep?" he asks, the question laced with double meaning, his voice low and husky as if confiding a secret. A slow, knowing smile spreads across my face. We both know he's not really asking about the sleeping arrangements.

"Upstairs. The apartments are quite spacious. Want to see?" I ask, the invitation hanging heavy between us, thick with the promise of something more than just a tour.

He shrugs, but the mischievous glint in his eyes betrays him. "I have some time to kill."

We stumble up the stairs leading to the future living quarters, our bodies brushing against one another, igniting sharp intakes of breath. I pause, drawing his attention to the artwork displayed on the walls. My mother handpicked each to make the hospital feel more like a home.

"My mother had this one shipped from a gallery in Glaucus," I say.

Wilder nods as if interested, but he continues to touch me, his fingers trailing along my bare arms, leaving chills in their wake. He presses a light kiss to my shoulder. We pause before another lovely landscape piece of the Aurora Desert.

"This one is my favorite," I say, my voice trembling slightly.

"Same." Wilder shifts my long hair aside to plant kisses up my neck, his tongue flicking out to taste my skin. I gasp as he reaches the sensitive spot beneath my ear. He captures my lips in a possessive kiss.

"You are distracting me," I chastise, my breath coming in short pants.

Wilder laughs, the deep sound vibrating through my body. "Sorry, I'll be good."

I shake my head. That's the last thing I want. I want out-of-control Wilder.

I lean in to kiss him again, my fingers tangling in his brown hair, pulling him closer. Our kiss deepens as he presses me against the wooden banister behind me with the red, orange, and gold landscape framing Wilder's back. It really is a beautiful piece, but not as perfect as the view in front of me. Wilder looks handsome in his black suit and tie, which he loosened when we left the ballroom. But as much as I love him in this outfit, I want him out of it.

"The rest of the tour is this way," I say, leading him by his tie.

We make it up another three steps before I push him against the wall to kiss him again, my body molding to his. His hands explore my hips before sliding higher to graze the underside of my breasts, sending jolts of electricity through my veins.

"Not here," I chastise.

We stumble toward a room with a closed door. I turn the handle and freeze; the room isn't empty. Vane and Desiree are intertwined on the bed. Desiree straddles Vane with a silk tie tied around his wrists, their lips locked in a fierce kiss. My mouth goes dry as her hand traces a slow, deliberate path down his chest. I clear my throat, and the sound feels thick and clumsy. Desi twists, her eyes widening as she sees me and her brother standing in the doorway. She flinches.

"Wilder, get out!" Desi screeches.

Vane, ever the provocateur, merely smirks. "Come for a show?"

Wilder, who didn't have a clear view at first, does a double-take. He turns green. "That's my sister, you fucking fuckwit."

I yank Wilder from the room and yell, "Carry on!"

"Is there an eyewash station in this place? Even better, is the therapist on duty yet? I need to unpack what I just saw. Otherwise, it will plague me for the rest of my life," Wilder whines.

I practically drag Wilder up the stairs, our footsteps echoing in the empty stairwell until we burst onto the rooftop. Summer heat hits us as we step outside, and the sounds of the city float up to us. Spread before us is a stunning view: the entire skyline, its lights like scattered stars against the dark night.

"They could have at least locked the door. It's like they want to get caught," Wilder continues, his voice still tinged with annoyance.

I sigh, not wanting Desi and Vane to overshadow what we were building up to. "Maybe getting caught turns them on," I purr. "Besides, you can't blame them for doing what we *are* about to do." I lean in closer, pressing my body against his. "Now, where were we?" I trail my fingers along the waistband of his pants, daring him to bring up Desi and Vane again.

His grip tightens around my waist, spinning me until my back presses against the cool brick of the building. Wilder cages me in, his body a wall of heat against mine. A delicious thrill shoots through me. I giggle, breathless, but the sound catches in my throat as his closeness ignites a deeper ache.

"You brought us to the roof." His voice is guttural against my ear, sending a tremor down my spine. I gasp, instinctually arching my neck to give him better access. "Do you want people to hear you begging for me in that flimsy dress?"

Gods. Yes.

"No one can hear us," I challenge, tilting my head back to expose my throat.

"Is that so?" he asks, his eyes darkening until black, a predatory gleam drowning out the green. He loosens his grip just enough to slide one hand lower, cupping the curve of my hip, pulling me tighter against him. "We'll see about that."

Wilder captures my lips in a kiss that robs me of breath and leaves me weak in the knees. The taste of wine on his tongue intoxicates me, a heady blend of defiance and desire. I melt into his embrace, surrendering to him. Ready to let him burn me to ash.

His kiss turns urgent, demanding, and he nips at my bottom lip, eliciting a gasp from me as rough bricks scrape against my exposed skin. I trust the celebrations won't continue without me for much longer, but right now, I only want to be here with him, lost in his touch, scent, and everything. *Him.* Everything him.

"Silver is officially my favorite color," he murmurs against my lips.

"Oh, yeah, I thought it was blue?" I manage to ask as his hand caresses my breast, his thumb brushes my nipple through the thin fabric. The other still grips my hip, holding me close, as if he fears something might separate us. But I know, with unwavering conviction, that wherever I go, he will follow. After nearly being forced apart several months ago when the Council pressured me to marry Alden, I am determined never to face a situation where I must choose between the man I love and another again.

"No, it is silver, like this dress, and your eyes."

With those words, I am completely undone by this man.

"Marry me," I breathe.

Wilder pulls back. "Now?"

"One day," I clarify. "I want to spend forever with you. I want to share all my secrets, bear your burdens, and have you like this always."

Wilder swallows hard, his expression unreadable.

Is he not ready for this? It's only been a year. Am I pushing too fast? Is it because I'm the queen?

The fabric of my skirt crinkles as his hand closes around it, bunching it higher. His fingers follow, inching upward, stealing the air from my lungs. I wet my lips, waiting for the next move.

"Ask me again," he demands in a whisper.

"Hmm," I breathe, the sound escaping as his fingers find my most sensitive spot.

He applies the perfect pressure above my panties before slipping beneath, confirming I'm drenched and ready. My eyes flutter closed, overwhelmed. His tongue demands entry, and I meet him with desperate starvation, kissing him back, only to whimper in protest as he pulls away.

"Say it again."

"Marry me."

He smiles, a wealth of promise in his expression. "I like you in silver, but I can't wait to see you wear white." He captures my lips in a slow, deep kiss while his fingers continue their relentless rhythm. He pushes me toward a place where nothing exists but the two of us, our love, and the promise of forever.

BONUS CHAPTER
DESIREE

Several Months Before Being Bitten

Play: *"A Girl Like You" by Edwyn Collins*

Fatum.

I repeat the password to Little Death as I descend the ancient stone steps deep beneath the Iron Parthenon. After the shitty day I've had, the last thing I want is to come all this way and get turned away for messing up the password. I've wanted to go to Little Death for as long as I can remember. People swear it's the perfect place to forget all your troubles. I want to be someone else for an hour and maybe find someone to kiss before turning back into a pumpkin.

The deeper I go underground, the more the moist air envelops me, thick as blood against my skin. With each step in my tall boots, the pulsing music grows louder, reaching me like inviting fingers. The massive door to the club looms ahead, and I take a deep breath. Here goes nothing.

Two gigantic bodyguards with fangs and tight black shirts glare at me, arms crossed. Their bulging biceps are the same size as my head. Do vampires work out, or are they all disgustingly fit?

"Password," they say in unison.

I clear my throat. "*Fatum.*"

One vampire hands me a lacquered red box. Inside, delicate red lace masks lie nested. Their rough texture brushes against my fingers as I pick one up and slip it over my face.

"How do I look?" I ask. One guard huffs and then slams the box shut. "That good, huh?"

When I learned tonight's password, I raced home and transformed myself. I styled my short black hair, applied careful makeup, and finally tore the tags off a daring dress I bought six months ago but haven't had time to wear. Tonight, I refuse to look in the mirror and see what I always see—the dull eyes of an overworked, heartbroken hospital intern staring back. For one night, I want to be someone else—someone desirable, someone worth wanting.

The other vampire guard opens the club door, and I step inside.

Holy shit. Mirrors and glittering lights reflect my image on every surface. I descend a few more stairs onto a crowded balcony. Pushing through throngs of bodies, I reach the balcony's edge, and my eyes widen. Little Death is gigantic. The club buzzes with excited energy. A DJ playing surprisingly good music rules over a packed dance floor. Nearby, a casino overflows as masked patrons place bets while downing drinks delivered by scantily clad servers. A few vampires indulge in a more intimate form of consumption that sends tingles through me.

No one hides here. Witches and vampires mingle openly and wantonly. I could get used to being in a place like this, where it doesn't matter if you're a Nebula or an Epsilon, a vampire or a witch; you simply exist. To me, this is paradise.

Someone vacates a seat at the bar, and I rush to take it, sliding into the chair. A drink will quell the nervous storm brewing inside me. As I wait to order, I scan the crowd for someone to talk to. I'm not Desiree here. I am someone else—someone who doesn't regret her actions, someone who doesn't let her mouth get her into trouble.

An arm snakes around my waist, pulling me into a rigid body.

I glance up at the vampire stranger and smile. He's handsome, with olive skin and black hair long enough to run my fingers through, even if his red eyes burn with enough intensity to incinerate steel. But is he handsome enough to make me forget? Jaxson's face flashes before my eyes, and I groan. Not here. Not now.

"What's your name?" the stranger asks in a deep voice, sending a shiver down my spine.

"What's the point of wearing a mask if I tell you who I am?" I reply.

The stranger's thumb glides against my ribcage. "Oh, I love a challenge," he purrs.

"Is this guy bothering you?"

I turn my attention to the other side of the bar. A petite vampire with full lips and straight cherry red hair stands with her hands on her hips, her red gaze narrowing at the vampire beside me.

His jaw hardens. "Mind your business, Misty."

Misty's lips thin. "You are my business, Ren. You're hanging out at *my* bar." She flicks her attention to me, her features softening. "Again, is this guy bothering you?"

I shake my head, not wanting to get anyone in trouble, especially myself. "No."

"Fine. Let me know if that changes," Misty says.

A cruel smirk curves Ren's lips. "You're such a bitch, Misty."

Misty rolls her eyes. Why is she so concerned about Ren?

"Wait. Can I get a double vodka soda?" I ask as she turns to the couple beside me.

Misty grins. "Celebrating or drinking to forget?"

I blink. Having someone to talk to about everything I've been juggling would be nice, but she doesn't care. She's working for tips. "Um."

"You know what, never mind. That's your business," Misty says, and I nod. "One double vodka soda coming right up." Her smile turns into a sneer as she glances at Ren before sauntering off in her vinyl red dress to pour my drink.

"Want to dance?" Ren asks.

I lean away from his touch. If Misty is wary of him, so am I. "I'm not much of a dancer."

"Want to see one of our private rooms?"

I level him with a death glare. Is this guy for real? "We just met."

Ren grins, showcasing his sharp incisors. They look more deadly than desirable. "You look lonely. I can change that." He offers me his hand.

I eye it like it's a stool sample. I came here to lose myself in someone, but not this guy. Not when his nearness makes my skin crawl. He's eyeing me like I'm candy. "I'm good."

"That's what I'd like to experience for myself."

My chest tightens. The scent of chocolate and cherries suffocates me.

"Come on. I'll rock your world."

Hard pass. I may have only had one relationship, but my instincts tell me this guy is all swagger and no substance. Besides, no means no—end of fucking discussion. "I doubt that."

"One double vodka soda." Misty places my drink on a napkin before me. Ren frowns at her, and she sticks her tongue out at him.

I reach for my drink, ready to get the hell away from creepy Ren. "Thank you. Keep the tab open." I slip off the barstool, but Ren grabs my arm. I glare at where he's touching me. I may not be a Blade, but I was raised by one.

"Where are you going, sunshine?" he asks.

My hand tightens around my drink. That was Jaxson's nickname for me. "Get your hand off me unless you want to lose it."

Ren leans close, his eyes promising retribution. "Are you threatening me?"

I hold his gaze, memorizing his features for if I need to file a Blade report later.

Loud cackling steals my attention. Misty clutches her stomach behind the bar. "Ren, you heard her. Leave. This one isn't dumb enough to fall for your tricks," she says.

"Fuck you, Misty." Ren glares at me one last time before releasing me.

My arm throbs where he held me. Prick. "Should I be worried about him coming back?" I ask Misty after Ren marches off.

Misty tuts. "He's a lazy asshole. Only goes for the weak ones."

I straighten. After everything I've endured and every cruel word thrown my way, "weak" is the last thing I am. "I see," I say, my voice igniting like fire.

"I'm Misty, by the way." She extends her hand toward me.

I take it and flinch. Her skin is ice-cold. "Desiree."

"Don't be a stranger, Desiree."

Before I can respond, Misty turns to another customer, flashing her seductive smile. I probably shouldn't have told her my real name, but something about her feels familiar and disarming, like we might have been friends in another life.

I melt into the crowd, feeling directionless but determined not to let Ren's behavior shake me. His grip on my arm will probably leave a bruise, but I've faced worse pain.

I retreat to a quiet corner, scanning the club for someone worth my time. As I drain my drink to the dregs, I let the alcohol drown my foolish thoughts about giving up and going home. I bet most people here—vampires included—are just as self-serving as Ren. Dancing is out; I don't need anyone mistaking it for an invitation for unwanted contact. Gambling isn't an option, especially when I'm saving for that loft in Asterhead. So much for escaping my troubles—I am hiding in a corner while life pulses around me.

My stomach lurches. *Outcast.* That's what Juliette called me after I got kicked out of the OR for speaking up about an attending's mistake—one that could have left our patient bleeding out on the table. The story of my life: I never receive praise for doing the right thing, and my outspokenness always frustrates others. It certainly frustrates Jaxson, my brother's best friend. Dating him worked out brilliantly—not.

I absentmindedly play with the straw in my empty cup.

Weeks have passed since the breakup, yet the wound in my chest feels as raw and fresh as ever. Meanwhile, rumors swirl about town that Jax's room at the garrison is a revolving door of lovers, while I haven't even managed a single date. Fresh tears sting my eyes, threatening to spill over.

Fuck. I need another drink.

"Why hasn't anyone plucked you, wallflower?" a smooth, masculine voice calls out.

My spine presses against the wall, and a heavy black curtain beside me conceals me from a door marked "Employees Only." I didn't hear it open. "Hello?" I call out.

"Well?" the voice asks again.

I narrow my eyes at the curtain where the voice lurks. "Maybe I'm not interested in being plucked."

"Hmm," comes the voice as intoxicating as summer wine. "You like to watch?"

I shake my head against the damask wallpaper. It's not that I enjoy watching; I just never get invited to participate. "Something like that."

"Yeah, me too."

My expression softens. A trace of sadness colors those words—unless I'm just projecting. "Is that why you're talking to me rather than enjoying the party?" I jostle the ice in my glass.

"You've seen one, you've seen them all," the stranger sighs.

One brow lifts. "You sound jaded. How can anyone be bored in a place like this?"

"I'm tired," he confesses.

"Then go to bed," I snap. With a voice like that, whoever this guy is should be with willing partners, not hiding here complaining to me. I reserve my bedside manner for work.

He laughs lightly, the sound soft like a caress. "Not until the sun comes up."

I pause. Vampire, then.

"Your heart is racing," he observes, and I claw my chest. "Are you frightened of me?"

I think of Ren, and my upchuck reflex rises. "Should I be?"

"Yes," he warns.

My feet itch to run, but I root them to the floor. We're just talking—and it's been so long since I've had a real conversation that didn't end badly. Family doesn't count. "It's hard to fear something I can't see." Emboldened, I yank back the curtain—but the space behind it stands empty. I bite my lip. Did he leave?

"I disagree. What's terrifying are the things we can't see," he whispers behind me.

I turn slowly, and my jaw drops. Before me stands the most frighteningly beautiful being I've ever seen. Crimson eyes watch me intently, soulful yet weary, never blinking. I take a tentative step back. The vampire is too tall to take in up close, towering well above Jaxson's six-foot frame. His face is the kind people pay fortunes for—strikingly handsome, sharp as glass, cold as winter. His hair is so blond that it appears white, like freshly fallen snow. My medical brain kicks in: If natural, it's likely a mutation in the KITLG gene, reducing melanin production. Or he colors it.

Looking at him is like staring directly at the sun. My gaze finds my feet, but his frosty fingers grip my chin, forcing my eyes back to his. I blink.

"Are you scared now?" he asks, his low-pitched voice making my heart race.

"No."

The vampire chuckles. "You're hurting my ego."

"Why, are you someone important?" Good grief. His lashes are impossibly long, thick, and black. Are they as soft as they look?

"Ouch." His lips twist into a wry smile.

"Well, are you?" I press as he leans closer.

"You first," the vampire counters, looming over me like a specter.

I smile, and the vampire stills as if caught off guard. Is it because I lack fangs? "I am no one." I peer toward the exit.

"I find that hard to believe."

With a sigh, I place my empty drink beside my feet, careful not to kick it over. I fold my arms like a shield across my chest. "Believe it. You've chosen to converse with the least interesting person here."

"No, Ren takes that title, not you," he says. I laugh at the amusement in his tone.

Wait. Has this vampire been watching me? I'm unsure if I should be flattered or uneasy. As the daughter of the Blade Commander, maybe I should be more aware of my surroundings. Dad would be so disappointed. "Why did you single me out?"

"You are hard not to notice," he replies, and my toes curl in my boots. An ancient, otherworldly aura surrounds him. Just how long has he been alive? And why do I care so much?

The vampire smiles, a knowing glint in his eyes. "The pulse in your neck keeps jumping the longer you stare at me."

"Your pupils dilated. I think you like that," I counter.

"I do."

I gulp. "So you're the one with the fear kink, not me."

"I believe the correct term is schadenfreude," he whispers close to my face.

"So you admit you take pleasure in other people's misfortunes?"

The vampire shrugs. "Depends on the person."

"You're sick, you know that?" I retort, but my words lack bite.

"Are you shaming me? I thought healers were more open-minded." He grins.

My lips part. "How did you . . ."

He leans in so close that his breath fans my inflamed cheek. "Desiree is such a pretty name."

I jerk away from him. The vampire laughs, but I recognize the sound for what it is—a warning, like the bright colors of a venomous snake. "H-how do you know my name?" I demand, my voice trembling.

He taps my temple, and I flinch. "It's all here in your head. Your name is Desiree Dunn. You work as an intern at Hebe Hospital. You are a Nebula, a Green Witch, and a fraternal twin."

My feet falter backward. Vampires with magic aren't unheard of, but only one possesses mind-reading abilities . . . "What's your name?"

The vampire frowns.

"Tell me," I repeat. I need to hear him say it if he's who I think he is.

He performs a flawless bow. "Vane Bathory. At your service, madame."

You've got to be fucking kidding me. I'm speaking to a goddamn prince? Articles featuring his name litter the Hebe cafeteria. I should go before I make a fool of myself any further. My head is a messed-up place, and he has an all-access pass.

Vane straightens. "Not impressed?"

"Is that what you want? For me to fawn all over you?" I say, no longer meeting his stare, contemplating how fast I can run in these shoes.

"You sound annoyed." He cocks his head.

"I don't like people toying with me." It happens too regularly, and I'm sick of it.

Vane inhales deeply. "How was I toying with you?"

A low growl inches up my throat. Fuck this.

I turn to leave, but Vane calls, "I-I am sorry." Unlike Ren, he doesn't use force to stop me, but the sincerity in his tone makes me pause.

"Why are you sorry?" I glance over my shoulder at him.

"You are upset; it is my fault," he insists.

I choke down laughter. Vane is a century-old vampire, and he is apologizing to me. Me—a witch who is otherwise a blip on his radar. I cover my smile with my hand.

"What is it?" he asks. "What's funny?"

"No one has ever apologized to me for something *they* did."

Vane scowls, and my laughter dissipates like smoke. Even when displeased, he is more attractive than ever. I want to study him. We don't know much about vampires, but Vane, besides the red eyes and cold, cold skin, appears primarily human. How?

"Then you are spending time with the wrong people," he says.

My posture sags. All I do is surround myself with people who want me to fail.

"Take it off," he demands.

My breath catches. "Take what off?"

"The mask," he clarifies, unblinking.

Sirens go off inside my head. We wear masks here for a reason—to hide, to become someone else. The second I show him my face, admitting I am who he says I am, the illusion I created by coming here tonight will break like bones. "You want me to take off my mask?" It occurs to me that he isn't wearing one.

"I want to see you without it."

He watches me struggle with his request before I bark, "Why?"

"Humor me," he says, a hint of a challenge in his voice.

I close my eyes and inhale deeply. We are alone in a dark corner, and no one is paying us any attention. If I refuse him, there's no telling what he'll do. I remove the mask with shaky hands.

"Happy?" I ask through my teeth. For some reason, removing the mask feels more revealing than if I were naked before him.

"Very," he replies. I lift my eyes to his.

He's smiling as if I were the sun and he's spent his entire life in the dark. My heart drums in my chest, drowning out the music.

"Why did you come here tonight, Desiree?" Vane asks. His gaze roves over my face, tracing every acute angle of my expression.

I shrug, not wanting to delve into details about Jaxson. Wait. It worked. I forgot all about Jax for five blissful minutes, and I have this beautiful stranger to thank for it. "Why does anyone?"

He remains silent, waiting for me to answer—his demeanor statue-like.

"Don't you have compulsion powers? You could always force me to tell you." Maybe that would be easier. That way, I won't regret my words later.

"Where's the fun in that?" he teases.

I groan. How the hell did I capture this predator's attention?

"Come." Vane offers me his hand, ancient gold rings adorning his fingers.

I stare at them. "Where?"

"Tell me you are scared," he taunts, inhaling deeply. "I love the taste of terror."

The hairs on my nape lift. Yes, I am scared, but I am also curious.

I tentatively slip my hand into his. He tugs me closer until my chest presses against him. His heart beats faster than mine. With his opposite hand, he cups my cheek, his thumb grazing my red-stained bottom lip. "My favorite color."

My knees wobble. "Cliché."

Vane's laugh echoes through the semidarkness. I should be freaked out, run home and pretend this night never happened. But I came here seeking transformation, hoping to become someone different. Here's my chance.

I grab the soft material of his dress shirt, fisting it in my palm. His gaze zeroes in on my lips. I rise on my tiptoes.

Vane doesn't move. "Are you sure?"

"Shh," I say, and press my lips to his. His lips are softer than I imagined and firm against mine. Is he not going to push me away?

I open my eyes with a sigh. Raw, animalistic need contorts Vane's face, and I freeze. My lips part to apologize, but his mouth crashes against mine, his tongue claiming me in a kiss so deep I can barely breathe. Yet the lack of air only intensifies the ache building low in my belly. He could steal every last breath from my body, and I'd die happy.

Vane stops kissing me, and I whimper. "Come with me."

Keeping my eyes closed, I reply, "Where?"

"To my private quarters."

Opening my eyes, I shake my head. "I'm not sleeping with you."

"That's fine, but I'm not letting you out of my sight, either." He leans in, his eyes ablaze with urgency, and kisses me again, as if he's starving for another taste. I lose myself in the moment, kissing him like I've never kissed anyone before. It's possessive and claiming, wild and unrestrained. In that electric connection, I discover a part of myself I never knew existed, surrendering entirely to the intoxicating pull between us.

Things could be different with him. Perhaps I could be different, too.

Moments later, Vane opens a shrouded door, revealing a long, empty, rocky corridor lit by ancient bronze torches. He offers me his hand again. After a deep breath, I take it, stepping into Vane's world, ready for whatever comes next.

BO✛∏US CHAPTER

Want the bonus NSFW chapter for Leigh and Wilder?

**Scan the QR code below to download
the eBook edition of *Take Root*:**

ACKN⊕WLEDGMENTS

Once again, I am writing the acknowledgment section for my second published book, and I wouldn't be here without your support. Thank you for reading my stories and for your unwavering encouragement!

Emily, I am grateful for the time you spent reading and rereading my pages, helping me refine the story and the characters' journeys. Your guidance and love for my characters have been instrumental in shaping me into the writer I am today. Without you, *Raise Hell* and *Take Root* would be vastly different stories, if they existed at all.

Kaila, your friendship is a true gift. Thank you for alpha-reading *Take Root* and recognizing its potential from its earliest stages. Witnessing your editing skills firsthand has been a delight, and I am thrilled that you have grown to love Vane as much as I do.

My husband, Ian, thank you for your patience and understanding when I was so immersed in this story that I would forget to buy groceries. At least the dogs never went hungry, even if we did!

To my sister, Anika, my constant cheerleader: Thank you for reminding me that our family members will read the sex scenes, making me feel awkward. I appreciate the mental image you've provided (lol).

Erin, my PA, I am grateful for how you make me feel like a big fish in a small pond, even when I am just a small fish in a vast ocean. Your presence is a shining light in my world.

To my street team, thank you for tirelessly promoting my books at every opportunity. Your dedication and enthusiasm mean more to me than you could ever know.

Jolie, my bestie since third grade, I don't know what I would do without you. Not only have you been by my side through all of life's ups and downs over the years, but I also needed your eagle eye and attention to detail in those crucial final rounds of proofreading. Thank you for catching my missing punctuation marks and typos and being among the first to read the completed draft.

To Laura, my weapons specialist, who ensures my characters don't reload their revolvers 17 times in one scene or put silencers on shotguns.

To my small writing group, Kathryn, Vanessa, Wren, Alice, and Genna: I am so glad we have each other to remind us to keep going when the hard days almost win. Your support and encouragement are my lifeline. Also, thanks for never judging my character art addiction.

Finally, to my readers, I hope you loved *Take Root* as much as, if not more than, *Raise Hell*. This book was a challenge to write, but your constant encouragement kept me going and shaped it into the story it is today. I am full of love and appreciation for each one of you.

ABOUT THE AUTHOR

Brit K.S. has always been a voracious reader of many books — but all her favorites have kissing in them. Growing up in Laguna Beach, CA, she wrote stories, plays, and truly awful poetry that didn't improve with age. At college, the boy next door stole her heart, and in 2021, they tied the knot in England with a ceremony that was equal parts Elfhame and Starfall. Brit currently spends her time in Atlanta, GA, with her husband, their two fur babies, and many, many cups of iced coffee.